Stories from the Shahnameh of Ferdowsi

Volume II

FATHERS

❧ AND ❧

SONS

Stories from the Shahnameh of Ferdowsi

Volume II

TRANSLATED FROM THE PERSIAN BY
Dick Davis

Mage Publishers
Washington, DC
2000

THIS IS A MOHAMMAD AND NAJMIEH BATMANGLIJ BOOK
PUBLISHED BY MAGE

A COMPLETE LIST OF ILLUSTRATIONS, CREDITS AND
ACKNOWLEDGMENTS CAN BE FOUND STARTING ON PAGE 295

LIBRARY OF CONGRESS CATALOGING-IN-PUBLICATION DATA
Fîrdawsi.
[Shâhnamah. English. Selections]
Fathers and sons/translated from the Persian by Dick Davis.
p. cm.--(Stories from the Shahnameh of Ferdowsi; v. 2)
ISBN 0-934211-53-1 (alk.paper)
I. Davis, Dick, 1945-. II. Title. III. Series:
Fîrdawsi. Shâhnamah. English. Selections; v.2.
PK6456.A13D38 2000
891'.5511--dc21
00-034867

Printed in Korea

FIRST EDITION
CLOTH BOUND
ISBN 0-934211-53-1

MAGE BOOKS ARE AVAILABLE THROUGH BOOKSTORES
OR DIRECTLY FROM THE PUBLISHER.
VISIT MAGE ON THE WEB AT http://www.mage.com
OR CALL 1-800-962-0922 OR 202-342-1642
TO ORDER BOOKS OR TO RECEIVE OUR CURRENT CATALOG.

❧ CONTENTS ❧

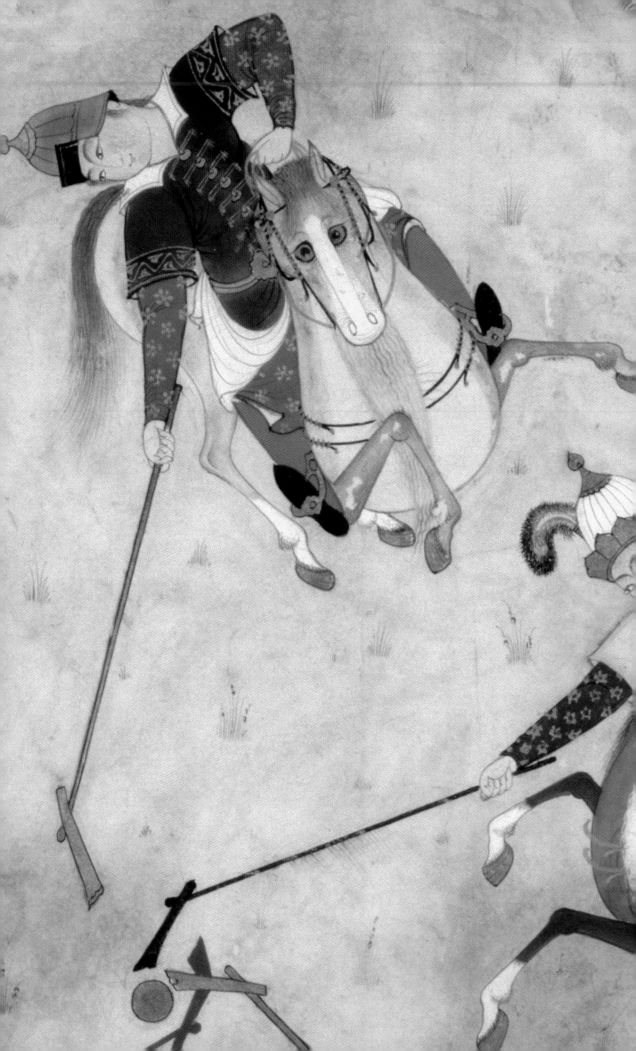

⊰ INTRODUCTION ⊱

The Lion and the Throne, the first volume in our collection of stories from the *Shahnameh* of Ferdowsi, ends with the gripping tale of Sohrab, in which a father inadvertently kills his son on the battlefield. The second volume, *Fathers and Sons*, is largely taken up with stories that develop in different ways the theme of father-son conflict introduced so dramatically by the Sohrab tale.

The Lion and the Throne dealt with the earliest myths and legends of ancient Iran. Beginning with the reign of the first kings, and the establishment of civilization, it then recounts the story of Zahhak and his rebellion against Jamshid (it is in this tale that the theme of father-son conflict is first introduced, in Zahhak's murder of his father Merdas). Zahhak's evil reign is ended by the rebellion of the blacksmith Kaveh, whose victory enables Feraydun to become king. Feraydun's reign is marred by his decision to divide up his realm between his three sons, and the murder of the youngest son, Iraj, by the two older brothers. Iraj's grandson, Manuchehr, avenges his father's death by killing the brothers, and as one of them—Tur— had been given Central Asia to rule (called Turan after him), this moment marks the beginning of the generations long conflict between Iran and Turan which is the basis of so many of the legendary tales of the *Shahnameh*.

It is during Manuchehr's reign that we first hear of the family of Nariman, whose descendant Sam is both the ruler of Sistan, and the loyal champion of Manuchehr. Sam's son Zal is born an albino and, taking this as a bad omen, Sam has the boy exposed on a mountain side. He is rescued by the magical Simorgh who rears him: when Zal is an adolescent Sam hears of his son and the two are reunited. But the conflict between Zal and his father is not over yet: Zal falls in love with Rudabeh, princess of Kabol and a descendant of Zahhak. Sam is horrified that a son of his should marry someone of Zahhak's lineage, but the lovers' wishes finally prevail, and from their union is born the greatest of Persia's legendary heroes, Rostam.

Rostam is both a kingmaker (when the Persian king Nozar is killed by the Turanian king, Afrasyab, Rostam goes off in search of a new king, Qobad, whom he brings back to Iran to be crowned) and, as his father had been before him, a champion of the kings he serves. But the king who succeeds Qobad, Kavus, is a particularly impulsive and difficult monarch, and Rostam has numerous conflicts with him. The most dramatic of these culminates in Rostam's killing his own son, Sohrab, on the battlefield.

In his retelling of the legends of pre-Islamic Iran, Ferdowsi's extraordinary skill as a narrative poet enables him to keep many strands of thematic interest going at once. On the most superficial level the poem functions as a chronicle, recording the succession of kings, dynasties, and wars that made up the account of Iran's ancient history as it had come down to the poet. In this volume we take this narrative through its later legendary phases, beginning with characters (like Seyavash and Rostam) whose origins must be sought in prehistoric myth, and ending with a character, Sasan, who—while still clearly belonging to legend in the details of his story as they are presented in Ferdowsi's poem—bears the name of an actual historical figure, and whose fanciful tale is meant to account for the rise of a real dynasty, that of the Sasanians, who ruled Iran from the mid-third century CE until the Arab conquest of the seventh century. It is in this volume, too, that Rostam, the greatest of the legendary figures of the poem, dies. After his death the Shahnameh gradually divests itself of the mythic qualities of its earlier sections, and becomes a quasi-history, still filled with legendary events and personages, but also displaying an increasingly close relationship to the historical record.

As well as the development of this bare chronicle, involving the transition from legend to history, the tales in Fathers and Sons continue a theme that was prominent in the stories included in The Lion and the Throne, that of conflict between a king and his champion or chief warrior. As a number of scholars have pointed out this is a fundamental motif in the epic traditions of many cultures, particularly cultures that have a strong Indo-European heritage. The Iliad opens with exactly such a conflict; many of the stories associated with the legendary British King, Arthur, are based on similar struggles, as are numerous European medieval verse romances. What distinguishes the Shahnameh from other epics, with which it shares this basic preoccupation, is the earnestly ethical treatment that is given to the theme. It's always hard when reading a poem based on folk or collectively known material to determine what exactly a particular poet's contribution is, but Ferdowsi does seem to take the ethics of the situations he describes much more seriously than other authors who use the same stories, and the Shahnameh's strongly ethical bias seems to be his own. In elaborating this concern Ferdowsi tends to present what is basically the same situation (a king does or demands something which his champion considers to be unethical or otherwise undesirable) and then offers different solutions or outcomes to the problem. The champion may reluctantly acquiesce, or he may refuse to have anything to do with the matter, or he may try to dissuade his king, or even actively oppose him, or he may vacillate between some or all of these reactions. It is as if Ferdowsi is constantly probing at the problem, but is unable to come up with a one-answer-fits-all solution, so that each individual case must be lived through and experienced according to its particular circumstances. What remains fairly constant (and there is only one king treated in *Fathers and Sons* of whom this is not true) is that the king is virtually always in the wrong in these arguments, and that we, the poem's audience, are more or less unequivocally invited to be on the side of the champion rather than his monarch.

This conflict between monarch and champion, which perhaps indicates a more fundamental struggle between the interests of the governors and the interests of those whom they govern, runs throughout the whole poem; it is there in the legendary stories dealing with Rostam's family and it is still there at the poem's end in the anecdotes taken from Sasanian history. But in the close of the legendary section of the poem, the section with which this volume deals, this concern is paralleled by another conflict with which it is often intertwined, that between a father and his son. The two great stories that frame this volume, that of Seyavash and that of Esfandyar, are prime examples of the way in which these two themes are interwoven. And as in the political realm, where the champion is seen as morally superior to his monarch, so in the familial space presented in the *Shahnameh*, the son is always seen as morally preferable to his father. This tension becomes particularly noticeable in the story of Esfandyar (arguably the climactic tale of the entire *Shahnameh*), as the necessity of obedience to monarch and father has become religiously locked in to the society's ethos by the advent of Zoroastrianism which, as it is presented in the *Shahnameh* at least, insisted on the absolute obedience of a son to his father, and of a subject to his king.

Kay Khosrow, the one king in this volume who does not appear as ethically compromised, is clearly offered as the paradigmatically ideal monarch. Rostam has a difficult and exasperating time with the Persian king who precedes Khosrow (Kavus) and he experiences equally fraught relations with the two kings that succeed him (Lohrasp and Goshtasp), but he enjoys a wholly amicable relationship with Khosrow. Khosrow is in fact the poem's great exception as a legendary monarch, in that his reign is untainted by failure or disaster. A reason for this is to be found in the nature of his family, a theme which parallels that of the world of politics. He never knows his father (who dies before he is born) and he has no sons. He thus is able to escape the perpetual round of father-son conflict and recrimination to which other kings seem condemned. His removal from the ties of family gives him a distance from worldly affairs that enables him to fulfill the functions of the perfect monarch. So great is this distance that when he must choose between his apparent duty to Iran and his concern for his own ethical integrity, he has no hesitation in choosing to put his own ethical state first, to the consternation of his subjects, as we see in the wonderfully haunting story of his abdication and disappearance.

Not all the stories in this volume have such weighty concerns. The most famous story here is probably that of Bizhan and Manizheh, a beautifully touching and exciting romance that deals, in *Romeo and Juliet* fashion, with love between the children of sworn enemies. It's true that here too there is father and son conflict, most obviously between Giv and his son Bizhan. But Ferdowsi introduces a new twist by making the conflict in Turan not a father-son conflict, but a father-daughter one, between Afrasyab and Manizheh. But neither the Giv-Bizhan argument nor the Afrasyab-Manizheh quarrel occupy the foreground of our attention, which is filled with the love and sufferings of the young hero and heroine. Another tale given here which has only a tangential relationship with the father-son theme is that of Forud, one of the most affecting and powerful narratives of the poem's legendary section (and strangely enough, perhaps because of its relative simplicity, it is one of the least well known). And for good measure a story is included that typifies Rostam's wily prowess against malevolent magic, in the story of the Akvan Div. This is a tale that is very basic in its original conception (by means of a clever trick a good hero defeats a bad demon) but which Ferdowsi lifts into the realm of ethical literature by his parting admonition that the audience interpret the story allegorically and not literally.

The *Shahnameh* is immensely long (the standard edition runs to nine volumes), and to have translated every word of every story of the sections covered here would have been a monumental task. In making my selections, if I had to glide over something it seemed best to leave aside the kind of material which the *Shahnameh* shares with epics the world over (accounts of battles and derring-do); instead, I have concentrated on those episodes which are particularly distinctive, which show the material in its most idiosyncratically Persian light, and which I believe display the poet's genius to the best advantage. The omitted passages have been presented in summarized form, so that the reader has a sense of the ongoing momentum of the narrative as it continues between specific tales.

A Note on the Illustrations

Most of the illustrations in this volume are taken from the miniatures in the great *Shahnameh* made in the 1520's and 30's for the Safavid monarch, Shah Tahmasp. As a young prince Shah Tahmasp grew up in Herat, where he showed an early interest in miniature painting, both as a practitioner (some specimens attributed to the young prince exist) and patron. The prevailing aesthetic of the Herati court was one of aristocratic charm and elegance, and the paintings produced there continued and refined the Timurid style, emphasizing clarity, grace, and a feeling of simultaneous sumptuousness and emotional restraint. When the young Tahmasp moved to Tabriz in 1522 he and his entourage of artists encountered a quite different style, one that was impulsively imaginative and exuberant, that valued dynamism and splendor rather than refinement, emotional intensity rather than restraint. The miniatures produced for the great *Shahnameh* that bears Tahmasp's name (also called the Houghton *Shahnameh*, from its last owner before its leaves were dispersed) are a remarkable synthesis of these two styles, both elegant and exuberant, graceful and filled with emotional intensity. So famous has this manuscript become that its paintings are often seen as one of the great peaks of Persian art, a standard by which all other miniatures (particularly those illustrating a *Shahnameh*) are to be measured. But other schools and other aesthetic ideals continued to flourish in Iran, as a number of the miniatures reproduced here demonstrate. The miniatures from the manuscript prepared for the Timurid prince Mohammad Juki, now in the collection of the Royal Asiatic Society of London (dated to 1444, and thus preceding the Tahmasp *Shahnameh* by some seventy years), are fine examples of the extreme sensitivity and delicacy of the Herat school. In the late sixteenth century, Shiraz became a particularly important venue for the production of miniatures from outside the court milieu, and the paintings produced there often have an earthy directness very different from the styles of either Herat or Tabriz. Other provincial styles also developed, and the exodus of some of the most famous Persian painters to India in the middle of the sixteenth century contributed to the development of a distinctively Indo-Persian school of painting which is also represented here.

Persian miniatures are renowned for the vivid variety of brilliant colors they juxtapose with one another. Sometimes, though, the paintings as they appear to us now differ from the artists' wishes, because a few of the colors they used have changed in hue over time. This is particularly true of silver, which blackens after a while. And there is one strange detail that recurs in the *Shahnameh* of Tahmasp, which seems to have nothing to do with the deterioration of a pigment: wherever it appears, the face of Kay Kavus has been, apparently deliberately, blacked out at some later stage in the manuscript's existence. Why this should have been done is a mystery: Kavus is a very unsatisfactory king, and it may be that some royal personage was recording his irritation with Kavus's bad example. Or perhaps a partisan of Rostam, who is shabbily treated by Kavus, felt enraged enough to deface the manuscript in this way.

For Western readers used to Western canons of art, the aesthetics of Persian miniatures can at first sight be a little hard to grasp. The insistent realism of so much Western art is not what is being striven for, and to look for it is to be disappointed. Persian painters (like Persian poets) tend to represent the world as one might desire it to be rather than as it is, as idealized

rather than as flawed. Even the battle scenes can appear balletic rather than terrifying in their exuberance, and calmer scenes are almost always a beautifully patterned interplay of subtle forms and brilliant colors rather than a brutally direct representation of actuality. Although specific faces can register emotion, and details can have a wonderful incidental (often humorous) force, in general the emotional power of the paintings comes from their overall patterned effect, whether it be one of serenity, severity, or dynamic activity.

One question of realism that has troubled some viewers is that the figures in the paintings don't "look like Iranians." And indeed they do tend to look more like people from central or eastern Asia, rather than the middle eastern stereotypes. The most important reason for this is that, although we know that Persian painting existed before the Mongol invasions of the thirteenth century, it was only after these invasions that paintings in books began to be produced on a wide scale in Iran. Mongol canons of art were derived from Chinese canons, and so they liked the paintings they commissioned to look like Chinese paintings. Pre-Safavid Persian painting is deeply indebted to Chinese models, in its representations of clouds, drapery, and landscape—and, naturally enough, of the human form. Further, it was natural for Mongol patrons to want the kings and heroes in their paintings to look as they did; this too would contribute to a privileging of central or far eastern facial types. And even though the Iranian Mongol dynasties eventually became quite independent of the Mongol homeland, these artistic standards were renewed in the Timurid period by extensive contacts between eastern Iran and China. Another factor is the inherent formalism of artistic canons: many people in north eastern Iran do in fact look extremely like the figures in Timurid miniatures, but even if they didn't the fact that "eastern" features had become the standard way of representing a beautiful face in a miniature would have ensured that the type would survive as an ideal well into the period in which it no longer corresponded to the reality found in the world in which the painters lived.

A Note on the Text

The stories have been translated directly from Ferdowsi's text as it has been published in a number of eminent scholarly editions. For most stories I have used predominantly the edition of the *Shahnameh* edited by Khaleghi-Motlagh (New York, 1988–1997), which is as yet incomplete. For the stories of the death of Kavus, the abdication of Kay Khosrow, the death of Rostam, and the Reign of Bahman I have used volumes v and vi of the text of the Moscow Edition, edited by Berthels (Moscow, 1966-1971). For the story of Rostam and Esfandyar I have used the text edited by Azizollah Jowaini (*Nabard-e andisheh-ha dar hemaseh-ye Rostam o Esfandyar*, Tehran, 1995). Texts of the *Shahnameh* differ from one another, often considerably: usually these variants are of more interest to scholars than to the general reader, but occasionally they can make someone familiar with the poem from a spurious source feel that something has gone wrong somewhere. A couple of very noticeable examples of this occur in the present volume. For example, Seyavash's queen was generally thought to be called Farangis: it is now clear that this was a misreading for Farigis, which is the correct form. More startling than this, is that in most manuscripts of his tale Seyavash marries twice, the first time with Piran's daughter Jarireh, and the second time with Afrasyab's daughter Farigis (or Farangis). But it is clear from Khaleghi-Motlagh's edition that the marriage to Jarireh was a later interpolation, inserted to account for the maternity of Forud, who is Seyavash's son but not by Farigis. The marriage to Jarireh has therefore been omitted from the present translation. Although these are the most obvious instances of the ways in which the present translation occasionally, in the light of recent scholarship on Ferdowsi's text, differs from the more commonly known versions of some stories, there are a number of other smaller discrepancies, which are here for the same reason.

I'd like to close this brief introduction with a note on the form of the present translation. The form adopted here is what scholars call a prosimetrum, a mixture of verse and prose. At its best such an arrangement can have an operatic drive and opulence, with the verse moments serving as arias of vivid intensity punctuating the overall narrative flow of the stories. Its use here is inspired by the ancient and popular Persian tradition of *naqqali*. The *Shahnameh* as it has existed in the popular imagination in Iran, has been passed on by skilled performers, called *naqqals*, who recite the *Shahnameh* in exactly this fashion, giving the bulk of the narrative in prose, but highlighting particularly telling, emotional, or dramatic moments by the use of verse. It is hoped that this translation too will reach a wide and varied audience (as opposed to a largely scholarly one), and it is therefore appropriate that it appear in a form that parallels the *Shahnameh*'s popular transmission within the folk culture of Iran itself.

Dick Davis

ᲠᲘ THE LEGEND OF SEYAVASH ᲚᲘ

A Turkish Princess Is Discovered

One day at cockcrow Tus, Giv, and a number of other knights rode out from their king's court; taking along cheetahs and hawks, they set off for the plain of Daghui to hunt for wild asses. After they'd brought down a great quantity of game, enough for forty days, they saw that the land before them was black with Turkish tents. In the distance, close to the border between the Persian and Turkish peoples, a thicket was visible, and Tus and Giv, followed by a few others, rode over to it. To their astonishment, they discovered a beautiful young woman hiding there, and Tus said to her, "How is it a girl as radiant as the moon is in this thicket?" She answered, "Last night my father beat me; he came back drunk from a feast and, as soon as he saw me, he drew a dagger and began shouting that he would cut my head off, and so I fled from our home."

The knights asked her about her family, and she explained that she was related to Garsivaz who traced his lineage back to Feraydun. Then they asked how it was that she was on foot. She said that her horse had collapsed in exhaustion, that the quantity of gold and jewels she'd brought with her, together with her crown, had been stolen from her by bandits on a nearby hill, and that one of them had beaten her with the scabbard of his sword. She added, "When my father realizes what's happened, he'll send horsemen out to find me, and my mother too is sure to hurry here to stop me going any further."

The knights could not help but be interested in her, and Tus said quite shamelessly, "I found this Turkish girl, I rode on ahead of the rest of the group, she's mine." Giv responded, "My lord, didn't you and I arrive here together, without the others? It's not fitting for a knight to get so argumentative about a slave girl." Their words became so heated that they were ready to cut the girl's head off, but to resolve the matter one of the company suggested they take her to the Persian king's court, and that both should agree to whatever the king decided.

And so they set out for the court, but when Kavus saw the girl he laughed and bit his lip and said to the pair of them, "I see the hardships of the journey were well worth it, and we can spend a day telling stories about how our heroes went hunting with cheetahs and snared the sun. She's a delicate young doe, and prey like that's reserved for the very best." He turned then to the girl and said, "What family are you from, because your face is like an angel's?" She answered, "My mother's nobly born, and my father's descended from Feraydun; my grandfather is Garsivaz, and his tent is always at the center of our encampment." Kavus said, "And you wanted to throw to the winds such a fine lineage, not to speak of your lovely face and hair? No, you must sit on a golden throne in my harem and I'll make you the first of all my women." She answered, "My lord, when I saw you, of all heroes I chose you for my own."

> *Enthroned within his harem now—arrayed*
> *With rubies, turquoise, lapis, gold brocade—*
> *She was herself an unpierced, precious gem,*
> *A princess worthy of a diadem.*

The Birth of Seyavash

When spring with all its glorious colors came, Kavus was told that his encounter with this radiant beauty had resulted in the birth of a splendid son. The loveliness of the boy's face and hair was rumored throughout the world; the king, his father, named him Seyavash and had his horoscope cast. But the horoscope was not auspicious; taking refuge in the will of God, Kavus was saddened to see that the stars did not augur well for the boy's future.

Shortly afterwards Rostam came to the court and addressed the sovereign: "It's I who should undertake the education of this lion cub; no courtier of yours is more suited to the task; in all the world you won't find a better nurse for him than I shall be." The king pondered the suggestion for a while and, seeing that his heart had no objection to it, he handed into Rostam's arms his pride and joy, the noble infant warrior. Rostam took the boy to Zavolestan and there constructed a dwelling for him in an orchard. He taught him how to ride and all the skills appropriate for a horseman; how to manage bridle and stirrups, the use of bow and lariat; how to preside at banquets where the wine goes round; how to hunt with hawks and cheetahs; what justice and injustice are; all that pertains to the crown and throne; what wise speech is; what warfare is and how to lead his troops. He passed on to him all the arts a prince must know, toiling to teach the boy, and his labors bore good fruit. Seyavash became a prince without a peer in all the world.

Time passed and now the youth was hunting lions with his lariat. He turned to Rostam and said, "I need to see my king; you've taken great pains in teaching me the ways of princes, and now my father must see the skills that Rostam's taught me." Rostam gathered presents for him—horses, slaves, gold, silver, seal-rings, crowns, thrones, cloth, carpets—and whatever his own treasury could not supply he sent for from elsewhere. He had Seyavash splendidly equipped, since the army would be observing him, and to keep the boy's spirits up, he accompanied him part of the way. His people decked the road in splendor, mixing gold and ambergris and sprinkling the mixture on him as he passed. Every house and street was decorated and the world was filled with joy, gold coins were scattered beneath the horses' hooves, their manes were smeared with saffron, wine, and musk; in all Iran there was not one sad soul.

Seyavash was welcomed at the court with great pomp and ceremony; festivities were held and Kavus lavished gifts on his son, reserving only the royal crown, saying that the boy was as yet too young for such an honor. But after eight years had passed he made him lord of Kavarestan, the land beyond the Oxus, and the royal mandate was inscribed on silk according to ancient royal custom.

Sudabeh's Love for Seyavash

Now when the king's wife, Sudabeh, saw Seyavash, she grew strangely pensive and her heart beat faster; she began to waste away like ice before fire, worn thin as a silken thread. She sent someone to him saying, "If you were to appear in the royal harem one day it would cause no alarm or surprise." Seyavash replied:

> "I don't like harems and I won't agree
> To plots and intrigues, so don't bother me."

At dawn the following day Sudabeh hurried to the king and said, "Great lord, whose like the sun and moon have never seen, whose son's a matchless paragon, dispatch this youth to your harem where his sisters and your women can set eyes on him; we'll do him homage and give him presents, and the tree of loyalty will bear sweet fruit." Kavus replied, "Your words are wise, your love is equal to a hundred mothers' love." He called Seyavash to him and said, "Blood ties and love will not stay hidden long; you've sisters in my harem, and Sudabeh loves you like a mother. God has created you in such a way that everyone who sees you loves you, and those who are your kin should not have to be content with glimpsing you from a distance. Pay a visit to my womenfolk, stay with them for a while and let them honor you." But when Seyavash heard the king's words, he stared at him in astonishment:

He strove to keep his heart unstained and clean
And pondered what it was the king might mean:
Perhaps Kavus felt some uncertainty
And meant to test his faith, or honesty.
He knew the king was sly and eloquent,
Watchful and warily intelligent.
He thought, "And if I go there, Sudabeh
Will corner me and pester me to stay."
He said, "Send me to men of proven sense,
To councilors of deep experience,
To those who'll teach me how to fight, who know
How I should wield a sword, or shoot a bow,
Who know how kings hold court, how courtiers dine,
The rules that govern music, feasts, and wine:
What will I gather from your women's quarters?
Since when has wisdom lived with wives and daughters?
But if these are your orders, I will do
Whatever seems appropriate to you."

The king replied, "Rejoice, my son, and may wisdom always guide you; I've heard few speeches so eloquent and it does a man good to hear you talk like this. But don't be so suspicious; be cheerful, drive away such gloomy thoughts. Now, your loving sisters and Sudabeh, who loves you like a mother, are all waiting for you in the harem." Seyavash said, "I shall come at dawn and do as you command."

There was a man, whose heart was cleansed of all evil, called Hirbad, and he had charge of the king's harem. To this wise man Kavus said, "When the sun unsheathes its sword, pay attention to what Seyavash tells you." Then he told Sudabeh to prepare jewels and musk to scatter before his son. When the sun rose above the mountains, Seyavash came to his father and made his obeisance before him; Kavus talked to the boy for a while then summoned Hirbad and gave him his orders. He said to Seyavash, "Go with him, and prepare your heart for new delights."

The two went off together lightheartedly enough, but when Hirbad drew back the curtain from the harem's entrance, Seyavash felt a presentiment of evil. The womenfolk came forward with music to welcome him; he saw bowls of musk, gold coins, and saffron on every side, and as he entered gold, rubies, and emeralds were scattered before his feet. He trod on Chinese brocade worked with pearls and saw facing him a golden throne studded with turquoise and draped in gorgeous cloth; there sat the moon-faced Sudabeh, a paradise of tints and scents, splendid as Canopus, a tall crown set on the thick black curls that fell clustering to her feet. Beside her stood a slave, her head humbly bowed, her mistress's gold-worked slippers in her hands.

As soon as she saw Seyavash enter, Sudabeh descended from the throne; She walked coquettishly forward, bowed before him, and then held him in a lengthy embrace. Slowly she kissed his eyes and face, gazing as if she could never grow weary of him. She murmured, "Throughout the day and for three watches of the night I thank God a hundred times for your existence. No one has ever had a son like you, no king has ever had a prince like you." Seyavash knew what all this kindness meant, and that such friendship was improper; he hurried over to his sisters, who greeted him respectfully and sat him on a golden throne. After spending some time with them he returned to the king's audience hall, and the harem buzzed with chatter: "That's what I call a real prince, so noble and so cultivated ...," "He seems an angel, not a man at all ...," "And his soul just radiates wisdom ...."

Seyavash went to his father and said, "I have seen your harem; all the splendor of the world is yours, and you can have no quarrel with God. In treasure and power and glory you surpass Jamshid, Feraydun, and Hushang." The king was overjoyed at his words and had the castle decorated like a spring garden; father and son passed the time with wine and music, giving no thought to the workings of Fate. At nightfall Kavus made his way to the harem and questioned Sudabeh: "No secrets from me now, tell me what you thought of Seyavash, of his behavior, of how he looks, of his conversation. Did you like him? D'you think he's wise? Is he better from report or when you see him face to face?" Sudabeh replied, "The sun and moon have never seen your equal, and who in all the world is like your son? This is not something to be secretive about! Now, if you agree, I'll marry him to one of his own kin; I have daughters from you and one of them would surely bear him a noble son." Kavus replied, "This is my desire exactly; the greatness of our name depends on it."

When Seyavash came to his father the following morning Kavus cleared the court and said: "I have one, secret, unfulfilled request of God: that my name should live through a son of yours, and just as I was rejuvenated by your birth, so you will know delight in seeing him. Astrologers have said you will father a great son, to keep our name alive in the world. Now, choose some noble girl as your consort; look in King Pashin's harem, or there is King Arash's clan; look about for someone suitable." Seyavash said, "I am the king's slave, obedient to his wishes; but Sudabeh shouldn't hear of this, she won't like it. And I'm having no more to do with her harem." The king laughed at Seyavash's words; he thought all was firm ground and had no notion of swampy water lurking beneath the straw. "You worry about choosing a wife," he said, "and don't give Sudabeh a thought. She speaks well of you and only wants what's best for you." Seyavash showed pleasure at his father's words and bowed before the throne, but inwardly he still brooded over Sudabeh's intentions.

Sudabeh Tries Again

The next day Sudabeh sent Hirbad to Seyavash, saying, "Tell him to put himself to the trouble of honoring us with his noble presence." Seyavash came to the harem and saw her seated on her throne, her crown set on her bejeweled hair, her beautiful womenfolk standing by, as if the palace were a paradise. She descended from her throne and sat him there, then stood before him submissively, her arms folded across her chest, like a serving girl. She motioned to the young women, lovely as uncut jewels, and said, "Look on this place, and on these gold-crowned virgin girls whose characters are compounded of coyness and modesty. If one of them pleases you, tell me: go forward and examine her face and stature." Seyavash glanced at the girls, but they were all too shy to return his gaze. One by one they passed before his throne, each silently reckoning her chances of being chosen. When the last had gone by, Sudabeh said, "How long will you stay silent? Won't you tell me which one you like? Your face is like an angel's, and anyone who glimpses you in the distance wishes you were hers. Look carefully at these girls, and choose whichever's suitable for you." But Seyavash sat there silent, thinking that it would be wrong to choose a wife from among his enemies; the story of what the king of Hamaveran had done to Kavus came to his mind, and the fact that Sudabeh was this man's daughter and, like him, was full of wiles and hatred for the Persian people. As he opened his mouth to answer, Sudabeh removed her veil and said:

> "The moon's of no account beside the sun,
> And now you see the sun. Come now, choose one
> Of these young virgins, and I'll have her stand
> Before you as your servant to command.
> But first, swear me an oath you'll never try
> To wriggle out of: King Kavus will die,
> And when that happens I will turn to you:
> Value me then as he was wont to do.
> I stand here now, your servant girl, I give
> My flesh to you, the soul by which I live;

Take anything you want from me, I swear
I won't attempt to slip free from your snare."
She clutched his head and ripped her dress, as though
All fear and shame had left her long ago.
But Seyavash's cheeks blushed rosy red,
Tears filled his eyes, and to himself he said,
"May God who rules the planets succor me
And save me from this witch's sorcery.
If I speak coldly to her she'll devise
Some spell to make the king believe her lies.
My best course is to flatter her; to calm
Her heart with glozing chat and gentle charm."

And so he said to Sudabeh: "Who in all the world is your equal, who is fit for you except the king? Your daughter is enough for me, no better bride for me exists. Suggest this to the king and see what he replies. I swear I'll look at no one else until she's grown as tall as I am. As for this liking you've conceived for my face, well, God has made me as you see me; but keep this as our secret, tell no one, and I too will keep the matter dark. You are the first of all our womenfolk, and I think of you as my mother." Then he left, with sorrow in his heart.

When Kavus arrived in the harem, Sudabeh told him of Seyavash's visit, saying that he had seen all the young women there but only her own daughter had pleased him. Overjoyed, the king had the treasury doors flung open and a great treasure prepared, while Sudabeh watched in wonder. She was determined to bend Seyavash to her will by any means possible, or, if she could not, to destroy his reputation.

Once more she sat upon her throne arrayed in all her splendor and summoned Seyavash. She said, "The king has prepared treasures for you, crowns and thrones such as no man has ever seen, immeasurable quantities of goods, enough to weigh down two hundred elephants. And he's going to give you my daughter as a bride. But look at me now; what excuse can you have to reject my love, why do you turn away from my body and beauty? I have been your slave ever since I set eyes on you, weeping and longing for you; pain darkens all my days, I feel the sun itself is dimmed. Come, in secret, just once, make me happy again, give me back my youth for a moment. I'll reward you with far more than the king has offered— bracelets, crowns, thrones. But if you refuse me and hold your heart back from my desires, I'll destroy you with the king and make him look on you with loathing."

Seyavash replied, "God forbid I should lose my head for the sake of my heart, or ever be so disloyal to my father as to forget all manliness and

wisdom. You are the king's consort, the sun of his palace; such a sin is unworthy of you." Then Sudabeh sprang from her throne and stretched out her claws at him, crying, "I told you all the secrets of my heart and now you want to ruin me, to make me a laughingstock?" She tore her clothes, clawed at her cheeks, and screamed so loudly the sound was heard in the streets. A tumult of wailing went up from the palace and its gardens, and hearing it, Kavus sprang from his throne and hurried to the harem. When he saw Sudabeh's scratched face and the palace abuzz with rumors, he asked everyone what had happened, never suspecting that his hard-hearted wife was the cause of all this. Sudabeh stood wailing and weeping in front of him, tearing at her hair, and said, "Seyavash came to my throne room and clasped me tightly in his arms, saying he had never wanted anyone but me; he flung my crown aside and tore my clothes from my breasts."

Kavus questioned her closely, and in his heart he said, "If she is telling the truth, and is not simply trying to stir up trouble, the only possible solution is for Seyavash to be executed. The wise say that, in cases like this, honor demands blood." He cleared the harem of everyone but Sudabeh and Seyavash, and then, turning first to Seyavash, calmly said, "You must hide nothing from me. You didn't do this evil, I did, and now I must bear the consequences of my own foolish talk; why ever did I order you to go to the harem? Now I must suffer while you tell me what happened. Keep your eye on the truth now, and tell me exactly what occurred."

Seyavash told him the story and of how wild with passion Sudabeh had been, but Sudabeh broke in, "This is not true, he wanted no one in the harem except me. I reminded him of all the king had given him, of our daughter and all the treasure that was to be his, and I said I'd add more in gifts to the bride; but he said he wanted only me, and that without me girls and treasure were nothing to him. He flung his arms about me, his embrace was unyielding as a rock, and when I wouldn't do what he wanted, he yanked at my hair and scratched my face. I'm pregnant with a child of yours, my lord, and I suffered so much I thought I would lose our baby there and then; the world turned dark before my eyes."

Kavus said to himself, "I can't trust what either of them says; this is not something to be decided quickly, crises and worry cloud a man's judgment. I have to search out carefully which of the two of them is guilty and deserves to be punished." To this end he sniffed at Seyavash's hands and at his arms and body. Next he turned to Sudabeh, and on her he smelt the scents of wine, musk, and rosewater. There was no trace of such scents on Seyavash; there was no evidence that he had touched her. Kavus grew grim, despising Sudabeh in his heart, and to himself he said, "She should be hacked to pieces with a sword." But then he thought of Hamaveran and of the outcry that would arise if Sudabeh were harmed, and also he remembered how when he had been in captivity there, alone and friendless, she had ministered to him day and night; the memory of this tormented him and he said nothing. Thirdly, she was a loving woman and he felt she should be forgiven for her faults. And fourthly, he had young children by her, and he could not bear the thought of their grief if anything should happen to their mother. But Seyavash was innocent, and the king recognized his righteousness. He said to him, "Well, think no more of all this; follow the ways of wisdom and knowledge. Mention this matter to no one; we mustn't give gossip any kind of encouragement."

Sudabeh's Plot Against Seyavash

When Sudabeh realized that Kavus despised her, she began to plot against Seyavash, nourishing the tree of vengeance with her wiles. One of her intimates was a witch who was enduring a difficult pregnancy, and Sudabeh gave her gold, persuading her to take a drug that would abort the twins she carried. Sudabeh said she would tell Kavus the babies were hers, and that she had miscarried because of Seyavash's evil behavior. The woman agreed; when night fell she swallowed the drug, and two ugly devil's spawn were still-born from her. Sudabeh hid her and then lay groaning on her bed as if in labor. Her maidservants came running and saw the two dead devil's spawn on a golden salver, while Sudabeh screamed and tore at her clothes. Kavus woke trembling at the noise and was told what had happened to his wife. He hardly drew breath for the rest of the night and at dawn he hurried to the harem, where he saw Sudabeh stretched out, her quarters in an uproar, and the two dead babies lying pathetically on the golden salver. Her eyes awash with tears, Sudabeh said, "See the work of this paragon of yours, and like a fool you believed his lies!"

Kavus was sick at heart; he knew this was something he could not ignore and he brooded on how to resolve the situation. He had astrologers summoned; he told them of Sudabeh's history and of the war with Hamaveran, then showed them the dead babies, and asked their opinion. The men set to work with their astrolabes and charts and after a week declared that poison did not turn to wine by being placed in a goblet, and that these two babies were not Sudabeh's or the king's, but the spawn of an evil race. For a week Kavus kept his own council, but then Sudabeh appealed to him again saying, "I was the king's companion in adversity, and my heart's so wrung with grief for my murdered babies I hardly live from one moment to the next." But Kavus turned on her and said, "Be quiet, woman, enough of these sickening lies of yours." Then he ordered the palace guards to search high and low throughout the city for the babies' mother; they found her nearby and dragged her before the king. For days he questioned her kindly and made her promises, then he had her tied up and tortured, but she refused to confess. Finally he gave orders that she was to be threatened with execution and that, if she still stayed silent, she be sawn in two; but her only reply was that she was innocent and did not know what to say.

When Kavus was told of her response he went to Sudabeh and informed her of what the astrologers had said, but Sudabeh's reply was that they only said this because they were afraid of Seyavash. She added that, even if he felt no grief for their dead children, she had no other recourse than him and was content to leave the resolution of this quarrel to the world to come. She wept more water than the sun draws up from the Nile, and Kavus wept with her.

He dismissed her and summoned his priests and explained the situation. They advised that he try one of the two by fire, for the heavens would ensure that the innocent would not be harmed. He had Sudabeh and Seyavash called and said that in his heart he could trust neither of them unless fire demonstrated which of the two was guilty. Sudabeh's answer was that she had demonstrated Seyavash's guilt by producing the two miscarried babies, and that he should undergo the trial as he had acted evilly and sought to destroy her. Kavus turned to his young son and asked him his opinion. Seyavash replied that hell itself was less hateful than her words, and that if there were a mountain of fire, he would pass through it to prove his innocence. Torn between his love for Sudabeh and his regard for his son, Kavus decided to go ahead with the trial. He had a hundred caravans of

camels and another hundred of red-haired dromedaries bring wood, and servants piled it into two huge hills, between which was a narrow pathway such as four horsemen might with difficulty pass through. While the populace watched from a distance,

> Kavus had priests pour thick pitch on the pyre;
> Two hundred men dashed out to set the fire
> And such black clouds of smoke rose up you'd say
> Dark night usurped the brilliance of the day.
> But then quick tongues of flame shot out and soon
> The plain glowed brighter than the sky at noon,
> Heat scorched the burning ground, and everywhere
> The noise of lamentation filled the air;
> They wept to see the prince, who came alone
> On a black horse before his father's throne;
> His helmet was of gold, his clothes were white
> And camphor-strewn, according to the rite
> That's used in preparation of a shroud.
> Dismounting from his horse, he stood, then bowed.
> Gently his father spoke, and in his face
> The prince saw conscious shame and deep disgrace.
> But Seyavash said, "Do not grieve, my lord,
> The heavens willed all this, and rest assured
> The fire will have no strength to injure me;
> My innocence ensures my victory."

When Sudabeh heard the tumult she came out on the roof of her palace and saw the fire; muttering to herself in rage, she longed for evil to befall the prince. The whole world's eyes were fixed on Kavus; men cursed him, their hearts filled with indignation. Then Seyavash wheeled, urging his horse impetuously into the fire; tongues of flame enveloped him and both his horse and helmet disappeared. Tears were in all eyes, the whole plain waited, wondering if he would re-emerge, and when they glimpsed him a shout went up, "The young prince has escaped the fire!" He was unscathed, as if he'd ridden through water and emerged bone dry, for when God wills it, he renders fire and water equally harmless. Seeing Seyavash, all the plain and city gave a great cry of gratitude, and the army's cavalry galloped forward scattering gold coins in his path; nobles and commoners alike rejoiced, passing on the news to one another that God had justified the innocent. But Sudabeh wept and tore at her hair and scored her cheeks with her nails.

جوازدست سودابه آواشینند برآمد بابویان وآتش

همی خواست کورا بداندبروی همی کشت خوبان پراز کفن

Seyavash appeared before his father and there was no trace of fire or smoke or dust or dirt on him; Kavus dismounted, as did all the army, and the king clasped his son in his arms, asking his pardon for the evil that had been done. Seyavash gave thanks to God that he had escaped the flames and that his enemy's designs had been destroyed. The king heaped praise on him and the two walked in state to the palace, where a royal crown was placed on the prince's head and for three days the court gave itself up to wine and music.

But on the fourth day Kavus sat enthroned in majesty, his ox-headed mace in his hand, and peremptorily summoned Sudabeh. He went over what she had claimed, then said, "Your shameless behavior has tormented my heart for long enough; you played foul tricks against my son, thrusting him into the fire; you used magic against him, and no apology will avail you now. Leave this place and prepare yourself for the gallows; you do not deserve to live and hanging is the only fit punishment for what you have done." She answered, "If my head's to be severed from my body, I am ready, give your orders. But I want you to harbor no resentment against me in your heart, so let Seyavash tell the truth—it was Zal's magic that saved him." But the king burst out, "Still at your tricks? It's a wonder you're not hunch-backed with the weight of your impertinence!" And then he turned to the court crying, "What punishment is suitable for the crimes she has commit-ted in secret?" All answered, "The just punishment is that she suffer death for the evil she has done." Kavus said to the executioner, "Take her and hang her in the public way, and show no mercy." When all abandoned Sud-abeh in this fashion, the women of the court broke into loud lamentation, and Kavus turned pale, his heart wrung by their cries.

Seyavash said to the king, "Torment yourself no more about this matter; forgive her for my sake. Now, surely, she'll accept good guidance and reform her ways." And to himself he said, "If Sudabeh's destroyed, the king will regret it eventually, and when that happens he'll blame me for her death." Kavus, who had been looking for some excuse not to kill Sudabeh, replied, "For your sake I forgive her." Seyavash kissed his father's throne and then rose and left the court; the women of the harem flocked about Sudabeh, bowing before her one by one.

And after some time had passed the king's heart once again inclined to Sudabeh, and his love was such that he could not tear his eyes from her face. Once again her evil nature reasserted itself and she began to weave her secret spells, plotting against Seyavash. And, listening to her, Kavus once again began to turn against his son; but, for the moment, he concealed his suspicions.

Kavus Learns of a New Attack on Iran

News came to the lovesick Kavus that Afrasyab and a hundred thousand Turkish cavalry were menacing his borders. Reluctant to give up his life of ease and pleasure, he summoned a council and addressed them thus: "God did not make this Afrasyab of earth, air, fire, and water, as he did other men. How often has he sworn peace with us, but as soon as he can gather an army together, he forgets all his oaths and promises. There's no one but myself who can confront him and turn his day to darkest night; if I don't eclipse his glory he'll attack Iran and lay waste our territories as swiftly as an arrow flies from the bowstring." His advisors said, "Your army is sufficient without your presence; why waste wealth recklessly? Twice already your rashness has delivered the kingdom into your enemies' hands. Choose some warrior worthy of war to carry out this task for you." He answered, "But I see no one here who can confront Afrasyab; no, it's my boat that must be launched for this undertaking. Now leave me, and let me prepare my heart for what's to come."

Hearing this, Seyavash grew pensive, and thoughts crowded his mind like a dense thicket. To himself he said, "I should fight this war, and I must persuade Kavus to give command of our armies to me. In this way God will free me both from Sudabeh and my father's suspicions; and besides, if I can overcome such a force, I shall win fame for myself." He strode forward, his sword belt buckled on, and said, "I am capable of fighting with the king of Turan, and I shall humble his heroes' heads in the dust."

His father agreed to his request and made much of him, loading him with new honors and giving him treasure with which to equip the army. Then Kavus summoned Rostam and said to him, "No mammoth has your strength, and you showed your unparalleled wisdom and discretion when you raised Seyavash. Now he's come to me, his sword belt buckled on, talking as if he were a young lion. He wants to lead the expedition against Afrasyab; you're to accompany him, and see you never take your eyes off him. If you are watchful, I can sleep easily, but if you relax your vigilance, then I must bestir myself. The world rests safely because of your sword, and the moon in its sphere is yours to command." Rostam said:

> "I am your slave, obedient to you,
> Whatever you command me I shall do;
> My refuge is prince Seyavash, and where
> His crown is, heaven too, for me, is there."
> Heartened by Rostam's words Kavus replied,
> "May wisdom be your spirit's constant guide!"

Preceded by the din of fifes and kettledrums, the proud commander Tus appeared at court and the king flung open his treasury doors to equip the assembled warriors. Helmets, maces, sword belts, armor, lances, and shields were distributed, and the king sent the key to the treasury where uncut cloth and other wealth was stored to Seyavash, saying that he was to administer it as he saw fit. He chose twelve thousand cavalry, men from Pars, Kuch, Baluch, Gilan, and the plain of Saruch, and twelve thousand infantry; for leaders he chose men like Bahram and Zangeh, Shavran's son, and he also selected five priests to hold aloft the Kaviani banner.

Seyavash gave orders that they assemble on the plain outside the palace, and so crowded did the area become, it seemed there wasn't room for one more horseshoe; before the host the Kaviani banner floated like a glittering moon. Kavus came out, quickly inspected the troops, and addressed them:

> "May fortune favor you! May all who fight
> Against you be deprived of sense and sight;
> As you set out, may health and luck be yours,
> May you return as happy conquerors."

War drums were strapped on the elephants' backs; Seyavash gave the order to mount and advance. His eyes awash with tears, Kavus accompanied them for the first day's journey. Finally father and son embraced, each weeping like a cloud in springtime, and each felt within his heart that he would not see the other again. Kavus turned back to his court, and Seyavash led his warlike army on toward Zavolestan, where Zal, Rostam's father, awaited them. There a month passed with wine and music; Seyavash spent his time with Rostam, or with Rostam's brother Zavareh, or seated cheerfully with Zal, or hunting wild game through the reed beds.

But after a month Seyavash and Rostam led the army forward, leaving Zal and his hospitality behind. Men flocked to their banner from India and Kabol, and as they neared Herat, troops poured in from every side. The heavens still smiled on them as they approached Talqun and Marvrud, and so they went forward toward Balkh, injuring no one, not so much as by an unkind word.

On the enemy's side, swift as the wind, Garsivaz and Barman led their army forward; the leaders of the vanguard, Barman and Sepahram, heard that a new prince, mighty as a mammoth, was leading an army forth from Iran. Quick as a skiff that cleaves the waves, they dispatched a messenger to Afrasyab, telling him of Seyavash and his great army and that warriors like Rostam, death's harbinger, accompanied him. They pleaded with him to come at once, with fresh troops, for the wind was in the sails of their venture and the ship plunged forward.

But Seyavash confronted them before any answer could arrive, and Garsivaz, hemmed in by Iran's troops, had no choice but to give battle; he decided to make a stand before the gates of Balkh. Two great battles were fought on separate days, and then Seyavash staged a successful infantry attack against the city's gates. As the Persians poured into the city, Sepahram led the Turanian retreat back across the Oxus to Afrasyab.

Seyavash Writes a Letter to His Father

As soon as Seyavash and his army had entered Balkh, he ordered that a fitting letter, inscribed on silk, with ink compounded of musk, spices, and rose water, be written to the king. He began by thanking God from whom all victories proceed, who rules the sun and the revolving moon, who exalts kings' crowns and thrones, who raises to glory and strikes down in sorrow whomsoever he wishes, and whose ways are beyond all human why or wherefore. Having invoked God's blessings on his father, he continued: "By the grace and *farr* of the world's king, I came to Balkh in high spirits and favored by fortune. We fought for three days and on the fourth, victory was ours; Sepahram has retreated to Termez, and Barman fled like an arrow shot from a bow. My troops occupy the countryside as far as the Oxus and the world submits to my glory. Now, if the king so orders me, I shall lead our army further and continue the war."

When this letter reached the Persian king he felt that his crown and throne had been elevated to the heavens, and he prayed to God that this young sapling of his should grow and bear ripe fruit. In his happiness he had an answer written as splendid as spring, as cheerful as paradise: "I pray to God who rules the sun and moon and maintains the world that he keep your heart happy and free from sorrow and disaster, and that victory, glory, and the crown accompany you forever. Impatient for battles of your own, armed with fortune, skill, and righteousness, you led off your army, although your lips still smelled of mother's milk. May your body ever keep its skill and your heart always attain to its desires. But now that you have the upper hand, you should hold back somewhat. Make good use of the time you've gained; see that the army doesn't scatter, fortify your camp:

> "This Turk you're dealing with is sly and base,
> Malevolent, and of an evil race;
> He's powerful, imagining that soon
> He'll lift his head above the shining moon.
> Be in no hurry now for war; hold back,
> Let Afrasyab advance, let him attack;
> When once he's crossed the Oxus he will see
> Carnage destroy his dreams of victory."

He set his seal to the letter and called for a messenger, ordering him to make all haste to Seyavash. When Seyavash saw his father's missive, he kissed the ground and banished all thoughts of sorrow from his heart; he laughed and touched the letter to his head, took note of its contents, and in his heart felt only loyalty to its commands.

But, for his part, the lion-warrior Garsivaz fled like wind-blown dust to the king of Turan, where bitterly and plainly he told him how Seyavash, aided by Rostam and an infinite army of famous fighters, had attacked Balkh. He said, "To each one of us there were fifty of them, armed with ox-headed maces, and their bowmen surged forward like a fire. The eagle does not fly as they flew. For three days and nights they fought, until our leaders and horses were exhausted, but when one of their side grew tired, he retired from the battle and rested, then returned with renewed vigor." But Afrasyab leapt up like flame and screamed, "What's all this babble about sleep and rest?" He glared at him as if he'd hack him in two, then yelled in fury and drove him from his presence. He gave orders that a thousand of his henchmen be summoned for festivities and that the plains of Soghdia shine with Chinese splendor.

Afrasyab's Dream

Afrasyab passed the day with them in pleasure, but as the sun sank from sight, he hurried to his bed and tossed and turned there in the bedclothes. When one watch of the night had passed he trembled and cried out in his sleep, like a man delirious with fever. His servants ran to him in an uproar, and when Garsivaz heard that the light of the throne was dimmed, he hurried to the king's bedchamber and saw him lying there sprawled in the dirt. He took him in his arms and said, "Come, tell your brother what has happened." Afrasyab answered, "Don't ask me, don't say anything to me now; hold me tightly in your arms for a moment and let me gather my wits." After a while he came back to himself and saw his chamber filled with lamenting retainers. Torches were brought and, shaking like a wind-blown tree, he was helped to his bed. Again Garsivaz questioned him: "Open your lips, tell us this wonder."

The great Afrasyab answered him thus: "May no one ever see such a dream again; I've never heard that any man, young or old, has passed such a night. In my dream I saw a plain filled with snakes, the world was choked with dust, and eagles thronged the sky. The ground was dry and parched, as though the heavens had never blessed it with rain. My pavilion was pitched to one side, and our warriors stood around it. A dust storm sprang up and toppled my banner, and then on every side streams of blood began to flow; they swept away my tent, and my army that numbered over a thousand was mere lopped heads and sprawled bodies. Like a mighty wind, an army attacked from Iran; what lances they brandished, what bows! Every horseman had a head spitted on his lance and another head at his saddle; clothed in black, their lances couched, a hundred thousand of them charged my throne. They flung me from my seat and bound my arms behind me; I stared desperately around but saw none of my own people there. A haughty warrior dragged me before Kavus, and there on a shining throne sat a young man of no more than fourteen. When he saw me bound before him, he roared like a thunder cloud and hacked me in two with his sword. I screamed with the pain, and my screams awoke me."

Garsivaz said, "The king's dream can only mean what his friends would want for him: you will attain to your heart's desire and those who wish you ill will be destroyed. We need a wise, experienced dream interpreter; we should call our priests and astrologers to the court."

Wondering why they'd been summoned, a group appeared at court. Afrasyab had them enter, seated the most distinguished in the front, and chatted a little with each man. Then he said, "My wise, pure-hearted councilors, if I hear a word about this dream of mine from anyone in the world, I shall not leave a single head here on its body." Then, to allay their fears, he distributed a great deal of gold and silver among them and described his dream to them. When the chief priest had heard the dream he was afraid and asked pardon of the king, saying, "Who among us could interpret this dream, unless the king promises to deal justly with us when we give him our opinion?" The king promised they would come to no harm, and an eloquent spokesman for the group began: "I will reveal the inner meaning of the king's dream. A young prince accompanied by experienced councilors will lead a mighty and vigilant army here from Iran; the boy's father has had his horoscope cast and it predicts that our country will be destroyed. If the king fights with Seyavash, the face of the world will turn crimson as brocade with the blood that's shed; the Persians will not leave one Turk alive, and the king will regret giving battle. And if the young prince should be killed by the king, Turan will be left with no king to lead it, this land will be convulsed by a war of vengeance for Seyavash. Then you will recall these truths, when our land is ruined and depopulated; and, even if the king became a bird, he could not outsoar the turning heavens that look on us at times with fury, at times with favor."

When he heard this Afrasyab was alarmed and put all thoughts of war from his head; he told Garsivaz at length of the destruction that had been prophesied if he fought with Seyavash. He concluded, "Instead of looking for world dominion, I've no choice but to sue for peace. I'll send him gold, silver, crowns, thrones, and countless jewels, and I'll withdraw from the territories they ceded before. Then perhaps this disaster can be averted and my tears will damp this fire down. If I can seel Fate's eyes with gold, then the heavens may look favorably on me again. But we can only read what Fate has written; justice is whatever the heavens will for us."

At sunrise the country's nobles came to court, wearing their diadems of office and with loyalty in their hearts. Having gathered together his wisest and most experienced men, Afrasyab addressed them:

"In all my life, Fate's given me no more
Than battles, conflict, and unending war.
How many from this noble company
Have been destroyed in war because of me;
How many gardens are now overgrown,
How many cities sacked and overthrown,
How many orchards fought through; far and wide
My troops have scarred and scoured the countryside.
And when the king's unjust, goodness must flee,
Hiding itself in stealth and secrecy;
The wild ass suffers an untimely birth,
Streams fail and dry throughout the earth,
The hawk's squabs grow up blind, beasts' teats turn dry,
The musk-deer makes no musk to know him by;
Righteousness flees from crookedness in fear,
On all sides dearth and misery appear.
But tired now of the evil ways I trod,
I long to trace the virtuous paths of God;
In place of sorrow, pain, and enmity,
I'll nourish knowledge, justice, amity;
Through me the world will be at rest; no more
Will death surprise us, and untimely war.
Iran and wide Turan are mine by right,
How many kings pay tribute to my might!
If you agree hostilities should cease,
I'll write to Rostam now, proposing peace;
To Seyavash I'll send rich tokens of
My hopes for harmony and mutual love."

One by one his councilors agreed to peace and reconciliation, saying that he was their king and they his slaves. When they had left, Afrasyab turned to Garsivaz and said, "Make ready for the road, don't waste words; choose two hundred warriors and prepare gifts for Seyavash: Arab horses with golden saddles, Indian swords with silver scabbards, a gem-encrusted crown, a hundred camel-loads of carpets, two hundred slave girls and as many boys. Tell him we've no quarrel with him, that we make no claim on Iran. Say, 'We accept that Soghdia, the land as far as the Oxus, is ours; thus it has been since the time of Salm and Tur, when all the world was turned upside down and the innocent Iraj was slain. I pray that God will grant us peace and happiness, that your good fortune will bring peace to the world, and that war and evil will disappear. You are a king yourself; speak to the king of Iran, see if you can soften his warlike ways.' Flatter Rostam, take him slaves and horses with golden bridles, load him with gifts so that our plan is successful, but, as he's not a king, don't present him with a golden throne."

When Garsivaz had gathered the gifts together, they made a splendid show. He hurried to the Oxus and sent a nobleman ahead to Balkh to announce his coming. As soon as Seyavash heard of Garsivaz's approach, he consulted with Rostam as to what should be done.

Garsivaz arrived and Seyavash commanded that he be admitted to the court; seeing him, he stood, smiled, and asked his pardon. Garsivaz paused at a distance and kissed the ground; shame was apparent in his face, and his heart was filled with fear. Seyavash motioned him to a place near the throne and asked after Afrasyab. Garsivaz sat and took stock of the prince's splendor and then addressed Rostam, "When Afrasyab heard of your coming, he sent me here with a trifling present for Seyavash." He signaled that the gifts be paraded before Seyavash; the road from the city gates to the court was thronged with the slaves and valuables he'd brought, and no one could reckon their value. Seyavash was well pleased with what he saw and he listened to Afrasyab's proposals. The wary Garsivaz kissed the ground, made his obeisance, and left the court.

Rostam said, "We should entertain him for a week before we give an answer. We must think carefully and consult with others." A house was fitted up for Garsivaz and stewards sent to look after him, while Seyavash and Rostam turned the proposal over at length. Rostam was suspicious of the speed with which Garsivaz had come and, as was prudent, had scouts posted to keep an eye on the approaches. Seyavash questioned him, then said, "We have to get to the bottom of why they are seeking peace; what's the best antidote for a poison like him? Who are his closest kin? If he were to send a hundred of his warrior relatives here as hostages, that would show us his real objectives. God forbid he's holding back simply out of fear, and that under this show of good intentions he's actually beating his war drums. Once we've arranged all this we should send someone to my father Kavus to persuade him to give up his dream of vengeance." Rostam agreed, "You're right; this is the only way to conclude the treaty."

At dawn the next day Garsivaz appeared at court, belted and crowned as was appropriate; he kissed the ground before Seyavash and greeted the prince. Seyavash said, "I have been weighing your words and deeds care-

fully; the two of us agree that we should wash all thoughts of vengeance from our hearts. Take this answer to Afrasyab: 'If you are plotting an attack on us, know that he who sees the ends of evil should refrain from evil and that a heart adorned with wisdom is a priceless treasure. If there is no poison hiding in this draught you offer, if malevolence has no place in your heart, then let Rostam choose a hundred of your kin, whose names will be given to you; you will send these men to me as guarantors of your good faith. Further, you will evacuate those Iranian towns you occupy, withdraw to Turan, and cease to plan for war. There should be only righteousness between us; I for my part will not prepare for war, and I shall send a letter to King Kavus advising him to recall our armies.'"

Garsivaz dispatched a horseman, saying, "Gallop to Afrasyab and don't pause for sleep on the way; tell him that I've accomplished all he wished for, but that Seyavash demands hostages before he'll renounce this war." When the message was delivered, Afrasyab writhed inwardly, uncertain what he should do. He communed with himself: "If I'm to be deprived of a hundred of my own kindred, my court's power will be broken, there'll be no one left here who has my well-being at heart; but if I refuse him these hostages, he'll think all I've said is a lie. I shall have to send them if he won't agree to any other terms." He counted off a hundred of his kinsmen, according to the list drawn up by Rostam, presented them with gifts and robes of state, and sent them to the Persian prince.

Then he gave orders that the drums and trumpets be sounded; the royal pavilion was dismantled and his army evacuated Bokhara, Soghd, Samarkand, Chaj, and Sepanjab, moving toward Gang without excuses or delay. When Rostam learned of their withdrawal he ceased to worry; he hurried to Seyavash, told him what he'd heard, and said, "Since things have turned out well, Garsivaz should be allowed to return." Orders were given that a robe of honor be prepared and that weapons, a crown, and a belt, together with an Arab horse with a golden bridle and an Indian sword in a silver scabbard, be brought. When Garsivaz saw the prince's gifts, he seemed as astonished as a man might be who saw the moon descend to the earth. He left full of praises for the prince, and his feet seemed to skim the ground in gratitude.

Seyavash sat on his ivory throne, the crown suspended above him. He searched his mind for someone eloquent, who could give words persuasive force; he needed some nobleman from the army who would get on well with Kavus. Rostam said to him, "Who is going to dare open his mouth about such a subject? Kavus is as he always was, his anger is always there, neither less nor more. All I can suggest is that I go to him; I'd split the earth open if you ordered me to, and I think only good can come of my mission." Seyavash was overjoyed at his words and gave up all thoughts of looking for another messenger.

Seyavash Writes a Letter to Kavus

The prince and Rostam sat down together and talked at length. Seyavash summoned a scribe, and a letter was written on silk. He began by praising God who had given him victory and glory, whose orders none can evade, the Lord of wealth and dearth, Creator of the sun and the moon, Bestower of the crown and throne, who knows all good and evil. The letter continued: "I reached Balkh rejoicing in my fate, and when Afrasyab heard of my coming the clear water in his goblet turned to pitch. He knew that difficulties hemmed him in, that his world was darkened and his luck at an end. His brother came offering me wealth and beautiful slaves, begging the king of the world for peace, and resigning authority to him. He promised to keep to his own territories, to leave Iran's soil, and to harbor in his heart no thoughts of war. He sent a hundred of his relatives to me as guarantors of his word. Rostam comes to you asking that you pardon him, since he is worthy of our kindness." Rostam set off for the king with a contingent of men, his banner fluttering overhead.

For his part Garsivaz returned to the king of Turan and told him of Seyavash, saying, "As a prince he has no equal for handsomeness or nobility of action, for intelligence or kindness or dignity or eloquence; he's brave, speaks well, is a good horseman, and he and wisdom are like old companions." The king laughed and said, "Policy beats warfare, then, my brother! I was disturbed by that nightmare I had, which is why I looked for some way out of this. Well, I've accomplished what I wanted with gold and treasure."

Meanwhile Rostam reached the king of Iran's court. As he entered, Kavus descended from the throne and embraced him, asking after his son and their battles and wanting to known why Rostam had returned. Rostam began by praising Seyavash, then handed over the letter. While the secretary was reading it to him Kavus's face grew black as pitch and he turned on Rostam: "He's young, I know, and has seen nothing of the world's evil, but you, who have no equal in the world, whom all great warriors long to match themselves against, haven't you seen Afrasyab's wickedness, and how he has deprived me of rest and sleep? I should have gone, I longed to fight with him, but they told me not to, saying I should let the young prince manage things. And where God's punishment was called for, you let yourselves be beguiled by wealth he's looted from the innocent and by a hundred misbegotten Turks, bastards whose fathers no one can name. What does he care about such hostages? They're water under the bridge to him. But if you've taken leave of your senses, I'm not tired of warfare yet: I'll send someone resourceful to Seyavash, tell him to burn Afrasyab's presents and to send the hostages in shackles here, where I'll hack their heads off. And as for you, you must lead your army into enemy territory where, like wolves, they're to plunder all they find until Afrasyab comes out to fight you."

Rostam replied, "My lord, don't upset yourself about this, but listen to me for a moment. The world is now subservient to you, and you yourself advised the prince not to advance across the Oxus, but to wait for Afrasyab to attack. And so we waited, but he sued for peace. It's not right to attack someone who's looking for peace and reconciliation. And the righteous will not look kindly on someone who breaks his oath. Seyavash fought like a fearless leopard, and what else was he fighting for but the crown and throne, wealth and security, and our homeland Iran? He has gained all these, and there is no point in wildly looking for war now; don't darken your bright heart with such muddied notions. If Afrasyab reneges on his promises, then we can fight; we're not tired of battle, and that will be the time for swords and warfare. Don't ask your son to break his oath; lies do not become the crown. I tell you plainly, Seyavash will not go back on his word and he would be horrified to know what you're planning."

Then Kavus started up, glaring at Rostam in fury, and said, "So everything comes out now, does it? So it was you who put these thoughts in his head, you who tore the desire for vengeance from his heart? You only looked for your own ease and comfort in all this, not for the glory of our crown and throne. You stay here; Tus is the one to strap war drums on his elephants and complete this business. I'll send a messenger to Balkh, and the message he takes will be a bitter one. If Seyavash can't agree to my commands, then he's to resign command of the army to Tus and return here with his companions, and I'll deal with him as he deserves."

Rostam was enraged and replied, "The heavens themselves don't lord it over me; if you think Tus a better warrior than Rostam, you'll learn soon enough how rare men like Rostam are." And he stormed from the king's presence with hatred in his heart, his face flushed with anger. Kavus immediately summoned Tus and ordered him to set out. Tus had drums and trumpets sounded to muster the army for the journey.

Kay Kavus's Answer to Seyavash

Kavus summoned a scribe and had him sit beside him. He dictated a letter full of belligerent, angry words. Having praised the God of war and peace, Lord of the planets Mars and Saturn and of the moon, Creator of good and evil and of kingly glory, he went on: "Young man, rejoicing in your strength and fortune, may the crown and throne be yours forever. If you have neglected my commands, it's because the sleep of youth has beguiled you. You've heard what this enemy did to Iran when he beat us in battle. Now is no time for you to fall for his wiles; if you don't want fortune to forsake you, don't push your young head into his trap. Send these hostages you've secured here, to my court; it's no surprise if he's deceived you, he's done it to me often enough, persuading me by his glozing words to call off my attacks. I said nothing about a truce, and you've disobeyed my orders, enjoying yourself with pretty girls instead of getting on with the war. And as for Rostam, he can't get enough of gifts and riches. But it's conquest by the sword that you should depend on, it's conquered land that gives a king glory. When Tus arrives he'll sort out your affairs. You're immediately to load the hostages with chains and mount them on donkeys. Fate won't look kindly on this truce of yours; when the news spreads in Iran, it'll cause an uproar. Get on with your task of vengeance; attack by night and make a second Oxus of their blood. Then Afrasyab won't stay sleeping long; he'll advance to give battle. But if you feel sorry for that devil incarnate, if you don't want to break your word to him and have no stomach for war, then hand the army over to Tus and get yourself back here."

When Seyavash received the message and saw its graceless language, he called over the courier, who told him how Rostam had been received, and about Tus and Kavus's rage. Seyavash was saddened to hear of the treatment meted out to Rostam, and he fell to brooding on his father's actions, on the day of battle, and on the Turkish hostages. He said:

"A hundred noble knights, all innocent,
Of royal lineage: and if they're sent
To King Kavus he'll neither ask nor care
About their lives, but hang them then and there.

And what excuse can I then bring before God? The world hems me in with evil: if I make war on the king of Turan, God and my own men will condemn me; and if I hand over the army to Tus and return to Kavus, evil will come to me from him, too. I see evil to the left and to the right, and evil ahead of me. Sudabeh has brought me nothing but evil, and I don't know what else God has in store for me."

He summoned two noblemen from the army, Bahram and Zangeh, cleared his tent of everyone else, and sat them down. He told them what had happened to Rostam and went on, "Countless evils surround me; the king's kind heart was like a leafy tree bestowing shade and fruit, but everything was turned to poison when Sudabeh deceived him. His harem became my prison, and my life's laughter turned to misery; the fruit of her lust was the fire I passed through. I chose war as a means of escape from her clutches. And when we came to Balkh and defeated the enemy, they retreated from our land and sent us presents and hostages. Our priests advised us to turn aside from war, as we had secured all we had fought for and there was no point in shedding more blood. I will not order further fighting, since I fear to break my oath. Disobedience to God is contemptible, and if I turn from righteousness, I shall forfeit both this world and the world to come; I shall be as Ahriman would wish. And, if I fight, who knows to which side Fate will give the victory? Would that my mother had never borne me, or that in being born I had died; my fate is like a massive tree whose fruit is poison and whose leaves are sorrow. I have sworn a binding oath before God and if I break it disaster will erupt on every side. The whole world knows I have made peace with the king of Turan; everyone will revile me, and I shall deserve it. And how can God look kindly on me if I turn again to vengeance, cut myself off from the ways of faith, and flout the laws of earth and heaven? I shall leave this place and seek out somewhere where my name will be hidden from Kavus; but may all be as God wills. Zangeh, I ask you to undertake a heavy responsibility; go quickly to Afrasyab's court and return to him the hostages and presents he has given us. Tell him what has happened." And to Bahram he said, "I leave our armies, elephants, and war drums, together with this frontier area, under your command. Wait till Tus comes and then hand everything over to him; count out to him all the treasure, every crown and throne, item by item."

Bahram's heart was wrung with sympathy for his commander's pain; violently he wept and cursed the country of Hamaveran. The two noblemen sat grief-stricken, then Bahram said, "This is not the way forward; without your father there is no place for you in all the world. Write the king another letter, ask for Rostam back. If he tells you to fight, fight. Best not to bandy words with him; there's no shame in apologizing to your father. We'll wage war as he commands us to; don't brood on this, flattery will bring him round. The crown and throne, the army and court, all will be useless without you. The king's brain is like a brazier filled with coals, and all his plans and wars are mere folly."

But Seyavash could not accept their advice, since the heavens secretly willed another fate for him. He answered them: "The king's command transcends the sun and moon for me, but neither commoner nor noble, neither lion nor mammoth, can oppose God; a man who disobeys God's commands abandons himself to bewilderment. I can neither plunge these two countries into warfare again nor go back to the king with his orders neglected and there face his wrath and disappointment. If you are alarmed at my orders, ignore them; I shall be my own messenger and leave this encampment."

Hearing this, the warrior's hearts failed within them; as if seared by fire they wept at the prospect of separation from their commander, fearing what fate held in store for him. Zangeh replied, "We are your slaves, sworn to serve you, faithful unto death." Seyavash said, "Go to Turan's commander and tell him what has happened to me; say that this truce has meant sweetness for him, but only pain and poison for me. Say that I will not break the oath I swore to him, and that if this means I am to be exiled from the throne, then God is my refuge, the earth will be my throne and the heavens my crown. Tell him I cannot go back to my father. Ask him to allow me free passage through his territories, to wherever God wills I should wander. I shall seek out some distant country where my name will remain hidden from Kavus, where I shall not have to hear his reproaches and can rest awhile from his fury."

Zangeh's Mission to Afrasyab

Taking a hundred warriors as escort, Zangeh reached the Turkish king's capital. As he approached, Afrasyab rose from the throne, embraced him, and made much of him. When the two were seated Zangeh handed over a letter and repeated all he had been told. Afrasyab's heart was wrung by what he read and heard, and his head whirled with confused notions. He had Zangeh billeted according to his rank and then summoned Piran. Clearing the court, he shared with him Kavus's childish talk, which showed his evil character and his plans for war. As Afrasyab spoke his face clouded with anxiety; worry and sympathy for Seyavash filled his heart. "What," he asked, "is the remedy for all this? What would it be best for us to do?"

Piran replied, "May you live forever, my lord. In all matters you are wiser than I am, and more able to carry out what must be done. But this is my opinion: whoever has the opportunity to help this prince, either secretly or openly, either by giving him wealth or taking pains on his behalf, should do so. I've heard that in stature, sense, dignity, chivalry, and all that's fitting for a prince, there's no nobleman in all the world who is his equal. But seeing is better than hearing, and we have seen how nobly he acted over the hundred hostages he held, opposing his father on their behalf. He's cast aside hopes of the crown and throne and is turning to you for help. It would not be wise or right, my lord, to let him simply pass through our territories; our noblemen would blame you for this and you would sadden the prince. And then consider, Kavus is old, he cannot reign for much longer; Seyavash is young, he possesses the royal *farr*, and he will soon inherit the throne. If my lord acts wisely in this matter he will write to Seyavash welcoming him as a father would. Give him a place in this country, offer him respect and kindness; marry one of your daughters to him, treat him with honor and dignity. If he stays here with you, it will bring peace to your land, and if he returns to his father Fate will look kindly on you. Iran's king will be grateful to you and the world's noblemen will praise you. If Fate brings Seyavash here, our two countries will rest from warfare, as the world's creator would wish."

When Turan's commander had heard Piran out and looked at the facts, he brooded for a while, weighing what should be done. Then he said, "Your advice pleases me; no one in the world has your experience and wisdom. But there's a proverb that seems apposite here:

> *Bring up a little lion cub, and you*
> *Will be rewarded when his teeth show through;*
> *Forgetting all the kindness he's been shown*
> *He'll maul his master when his claws have grown."*

But Piran said, "May the king look at this matter wisely: will a man display his father's bad qualities when he has opposed those very qualities? Don't you see that Kavus's days are numbered, and that this being so, he must die soon? Then with no trouble at all Seyavash will inherit his country and its treasures and glory; our country and his, and their crowns and thrones, will then be yours. And is this not the height of good fortune?"

Afrasyab's Answer to Seyavash

Hearing this, Afrasyab took a wise decision and called in an experienced scribe. He began his letter with praise of the world's creator and continued: "May this God bless the prince, lord of the mace and sword and helmet, who is righteous and who fears God, in whose soul there is no injustice or crookedness. I have received Zangeh's message, and my heart is grieved at your king's treatment of you. But what else does a fortunate man seek for in the world than a crown and throne? And these you have; all of Turan will do your bidding, and I feel the need of your kindness. You'll be my son and

I will be like a father to you, a father who seeks to serve his son. Kavus has never shown you the kindness I will; I'll open my treasury to you, assign you a throne, and keep you as my own child so that you will be a remembrance of me in the world when I am gone. If I let you pass through my kingdom, commoners and nobles alike will condemn me, and you will find the going hard beyond my borders, unless you have supernatural powers. You'll see no land there and will have to cross the Sea of China. But God has made this unnecessary for you; stay here and live at ease; my army, territories, and wealth are at your disposal. And you won't have to search for excuses to leave: when you and your father are reconciled, I'll load you with presents and willingly send you on your way to Iran. You won't be at odds with your father for long; he is old and will soon grow tired of his differences with you. Once a man reaches sixty-five the fire of anger begins to fail in him. Iran and all its wealth will be yours. I have accepted God's command that I succor you, and no harm will come to you from me."

Afrasyab sealed the letter and, having given Zangeh gifts of gold and silver, a splendid cloak, and a horse with a gold-worked saddle, he sent him on his way to Seyavash. Zangeh reported to his prince what he had seen and heard, and Seyavash rejoiced at this, but at the same time his heart was filled with sorrow and anxiety that he had to make a friend of his enemy, since when did cooling breezes ever blow from a raging fire? He wrote to his father, saying, "Despite my youth I have always acted wisely, and the king's anger against me grieves my heart. His harem was the cause of my first sorrow, making me traverse a mountain of fire, and in my trial the wild deer wept for me. To escape such shame I set out for war, riding confidently against its monstrous claws. Two countries rejoiced at the peace I fashioned, but the king's heart hardened against me like steel. Nothing I did pleased him, and since he is sick of the sight of me, I shall not stay in his presence. May happiness always inhabit his heart, while sorrow drives me to the dragon's maw. I do not know what will become of this, or what secrets of good and ill the heavens hold in store for me."

Next he gave orders to Bahram: "Keep your fame bright in the world; I hand over to you my crown and royal pavilion, the wealth I've levied, and the throne, our banners, cavalry, elephants, and war drums. When the commander Tus arrives, hand them over to him just as you've received them." He selected three hundred horsemen for his own use, together with a quantity of coins, jewels, and armor. Then he summoned his officers and addressed them: "Piran, sent by Afrasyab, has already crossed to our side of the Oxus. He bears a secret message for me, and I shall go out to welcome him. You must remain here; you are to regard Bahram as your leader and to obey his orders." The warriors kissed the ground before Seyavash.

Seyavash Travels from Iran to Turkestan

As the sun set, and the air grew dark and the world forbidding, Seyavash led his men toward the Oxus, his face obscured by tears. At Termez the streets and roofs were decorated to welcome him, so that spring with all its tints and scents seemed to have come, and each of the towns they passed through seemed like a bride arrayed in splendor. At Qajqar he dismounted and rested for a while. When news of his approach arrived, Piran chose a thousand knights and rode out to welcome him, taking as a gift four richly caparisoned white elephants and a hundred horses with gold-worked saddles. As soon as Seyavash saw his banners and heard the elephants' trumpeting he hurried toward him. The two embraced and Seyavash said, "Why have you troubled yourself by travelling like this? My only hope has been to see you alive and well." Piran kissed his head and feet and his handsome face and gave thanks to God, saying, "O Lord of what is hidden and what is plain, if I had seen such a man in a dream it would have restored my youth to me." To Seyavash he said, "I praise God that I see you before me as clearly as the daylight. Afrasyab will be like a father to you, and all on our side of the Oxus are as your slaves. I have over a thousand henchmen who are yours to command, and if you can accept an old man's service, I stand ready to obey you."

> The two rode forward then, their cheerful chat
> Wandering at random over this and that;
> The towns they passed were filled with music's sound,
> And scattered musk and gold obscured the ground.
> But seeing this, the prince's eyes grew dim,
> Old, melancholy memories troubled him;
> His heart recalled great Rostam's land, Zabol,
> The grandeur and the beauty of Kabol—
> Then all Iran beset him, place by place,
> He blushed for shame and turned away his face;
> But wise Piran saw all his misery
> And bit his lip in pain and sympathy.

They rested a while and, gazing in wonder at him, Piran said, "You seem like one of the ancient kings. You've three qualities which together make you unique: first, that you're of the seed of Kay Qobad; another, that you speak so honestly and eloquently; and third, that your countenance radiates grace." Seyavash replied, "You are renowned throughout the world for your good faith and kindness, for your hatred of evil and Ahriman; swear to me now and I know you will not break your word. If my presence here is good, I should not weep; but if it is not good, then tell me, show me the way to

another country." Piran said, "Don't dwell on the fact that you've left Iran; trust to Afrasyab's kindness and be in no hurry to leave us. His reputation is bad in the world, but this is undeserved; he's a God-fearing man. He's wise and cautious in his councils and is not given to making hasty, harmful decisions. I'm related to him, and I'm both his champion and adviser. In this land over a hundred thousand horsemen are mine to command; twelve thousand are from my own tribe and, if I wish, will wait on me day and night. I've weapons, territory, flocks of sheep, and much more in reserve; I can live independently of everyone. All that I have I place at your disposal if you will agree to live here. I've accepted you as a trust from God, and I shall let no harm come to you; though no one knows what Fate holds in store for him." Seyavash was comforted by these words; his spirits revived and they sat to their wine, Piran as a father, Seyavash as his son.

Cheerful and laughing, they pressed on to Gang, a beautiful site where the Turkish monarch held court. Afrasyab came rushing out on foot to greet them, and as soon as he saw the king approaching, Seyavash dismounted and ran forward. They embraced, kissing each other's eyes and head, and Afrasyab said, "The world's evil sleeps. From now on neither revolt nor war will break out; the leopard and the lamb will share one watering place. Brave Tur set the world in a turmoil, but now our countries are tired of war. They have fought for too long, blind to the ways of peace; through you we shall rest from battles and the longing for blood-revenge. The land of Turan is your slave, the hearts of all here are full of love for you. All I have, my body and my soul, are yours. May you live healthily and happily here; all our treasures are yours. I will treat you with a father's love and always smile upon you."

Seyavash replied, "May your lineage never forfeit its good fortune." Then Afrasyab took Seyavash's hand, led him to the throne, and sat down. He gazed at Seyavash's face and said, "I know of nothing like this in all the earth. In the world men are not like this, with such a face, such stature, such royal *farr*." And turning to Piran he said, "Kavus is old and sadly wanting in wisdom if he can give up such a noble and accomplished son."

Afrasyab had one of his palaces set aside for his guest; it was spread with gold-worked carpets, and a golden throne with legs fashioned like the heads of buffalo was placed there. The walls were hung with Chinese brocade, and a multitude of servants was assigned to it. Seyavash entered, and its arch seemed to touch the heavens; he sat on the throne lost in thought until a servant called him to dine with the king. The meal passed in pleasantries, and then the courtiers sat to their wine while musicians played in the background. Afrasyab pledged his heart to Seyavash and swore he'd know no rest without him. They drank till darkness fell; by the time everyone was tipsy Seyavash had forgotten about Iran, and in this drunken state

he returned to his own quarters. Afrasyab said to his son Shideh, "Take some of our nobles at dawn to Seyavash, as he's waking up, and have them present him with gifts—slaves, fine horses, gold-worked boots—and have the army take him cash and jewels. Do this in a dignified, becoming way." The king himself sent many more gifts, and so a week passed by.

Seyavash Displays His Skills before Afrasyab

One evening the king said to Seyavash, "Let's get up at dawn tomorrow and enjoy ourselves at polo; I've heard that when you play, your mallet's invincible." Seyavash agreed and the next morning they made their way laughing and joking to the field, where the king suggested they divide up their companions, with Seyavash heading one team and he the other. But Seyavash said, "I can't be your rival, choose some other opponent and let me ride on your side, if you think I'm good enough." Afrasyab was pleased by this and thought everyone else's remarks mere chaff in the wind by comparison. Nevertheless he insisted, "By the head and soul of Kavus, you're to play against me; and see you do well, so that no one says I've made a bad choice for an opponent." Seyavash replied, "I and all the warriors here, and the game itself, are yours to command." For himself the king selected Golbad, Garsivaz, Jahan, Pulad, Piran, Nastihan, and Human, who was known for being able to scoop the ball from water. To Seyavash's side he sent some of his own henchmen, including Ruin and the famous Shideh, Andariman, who was a great horseman, and Ukhast, who was like a lion in battle. But Seyavash said, "Which of these men is going to try for the ball? They all belong to the king, and I'll be the only one playing on my side. If you'll allow me, I'll choose some of my own men." The king agreed and Seyavash selected seven Iranians who were worthy of the honor.

At the field's edge drums thundered out, cymbals clashed, and trumpets blared. The ground seemed to shake with the din, and dust rose into the sky as the horsemen took the field. The king struck the ball up toward the clouds; Seyavash urged his horse forward and before it touched the ground he smote the ball so hard that it disappeared from sight. Afrasyab ordered another ball to be tapped toward Seyavash; the prince lifted it to his lips and the sound of trumpets and drums rang out. Then he mounted a fresh horse, tossed the ball into the air, and hit it such a blow with his mallet that it seemed to rise to the moon's sphere, as if the sky had swallowed it. The king laughed out loud, and his nobles were startled enough to exclaim, "We've never seen a horseman with such skills." Afrasyab said, "This is how a man who has God's *farr* is!"

A royal pavilion had been erected at the field's edge and there Seyavash sat with the king, who gazed happily at his princely guest. Then he called to

the warriors, "The field, mallets, and balls are yours!" The two sides fell to, and dust rose up, obscuring the sun. The Turks strove hard to get possession, but without success; Seyavash was alarmed by the Persians' behavior and called out in Pahlavi, "This is a playing field, not a battlefield for you to be raging and struggling like this; give way, and let them have the ball for once." The Persians let their reins go slack and stopped encouraging their horses. The Turks struck the ball and rushed forward like fire. When Afrasyab heard the Turks' shout of triumph he realized what that sentence in Pahlavi had meant. He said to Seyavash, "I've been told that you have no equal as a bowman." Seyavash drew his Kayanid bow from its casing and Afrasyab asked to look at it and have one of his men test it. He praised it highly and handed it to Garsivaz, ordering him to string it. Garsivaz struggled to notch the string, but to his chagrin was unable to. Seyavash took the bow from him, knelt, bent back the shaft and strung it. The king laughed and said, "Now that's the kind of bow a man needs; when I was young I had one just like that, but times have changed. There's not another man in Iran or Turan who could manage this bow in battle, but Seyavash with his great chest and shoulders wouldn't have any other."

A target was set up at the end of the lists; without saying a word to anyone Seyavash mounted his horse, yelled his war cry, and galloped forward; one arrow struck the center of the target and, as the warriors watched, he notched another (made of poplar wood, with four feathers) to the string and in the same charge again transfixed the target. Gripping the reins in his right hand he wheeled around and once again sent an arrow home. Then he slipped the bow over his arm, rode back to the king, and dismounted before him. The king stood and called down blessings on him, and the two made their way happily back to the palace.

They sat to food and wine, accompanied by courtiers worthy of the honor, and after a few draughts had been downed and the company was growing merry they toasted Seyavash. While they were still feasting Afrasyab conferred a splendid robe on Seyavash, a horse with all its trappings, a sword and diadem, clothes and a quantity of uncut cloth the like of which no one had ever seen, silks, purses stuffed with coins, turquoises, male and female slaves, and a goblet filled with rubies. He ordered that all this be counted out and then conveyed to Seyavash's palace. He commanded his kinsmen to think of themselves as a flock of which Seyavash was the shepherd. Then he turned to the prince and said, "We must go hunting together; we'll enjoy ourselves, and the hunt will put sad thoughts out of our minds." Seyavash said, "Whenever and wherever you wish."

And so one day, accompanied by a group of Turkish and Persian warriors, they started out with cheetahs and hawks for the hunt. Seyavash spied a wild ass on the plain and left the group behind as he set off like the wind in pursuit. His reins grew light, his stirrups heavy, as he galloped forward over the rough terrain. He caught up with the ass and slashed it in two with his sword; the two halves were absolutely equal in weight (as if his hands were a balance and the ass weighed silver) and when the king's companions saw this they exclaimed, "Here is a swordsman worthy of the name!" But to one another they murmured, "An evil has come to us from Iran. Our leader is put to shame by him; we should oppose the king in this." Seyavash rode on through gullies, over mountains and across the plain, bringing down prey with arrows, sword, and lance, piling up carcasses everywhere, until the group was sated with hunting and made its way cheerfully back to the king's palace.

Whether in good spirits or gloomy, the king wished to be with no one but Seyavash; he took pleasure in his company alone, no longer admitting Garsivaz and Jahan into his confidence. Day and night he spent with Seyavash, and it was Seyavash who was always able to bring a smile to his lips. In this way, with all its mingled joy and grief, a year went by.

Piran's Advice to Seyavash and to Afrasyab

Seyavash and Piran were sitting one day, chatting of this and that, when Piran said, "You're like a man who's only passing through this country; what will remain of Afrasyab's kindness to you when you die?

> You're now the close companion of our king,
> As loved by him as pleasure is in spring,
> And you're Kavus's son—your glory here
> Has raised you to the moon's auspicious sphere,
> And this is where you ought to lead your life.
> But you've no brothers here, no kin, no wife,
> You're like a solitary flower beside
> An empty field; you need to choose a bride.
> Forget Iran, its sorrows and its wars;
> When once Kavus has died, Iran is yours.
> Here in the royal castle's women's quarters
> The king has three incomparable daughters,
> And Garsivaz's household boasts of three
> Descended from a noble ancestry,
> And I myself have four girls, each of whom
> Will be your slave if you will be her groom.
> But best would be if you can marry one
> Of Afrasyab's girls; you will be his son.
> The finest of them's Farigis, whose grace
> Knows no competitor in any place;
> She's tall and slender as a cypress tree,
> Her hair's a musky crown; you'll never see
> A woman more accomplished or more wise.
> If you should wish to gain this noble prize
> I'll be your messenger and go-between
> To ask the king if she can be your queen."

Seyavash gazed at Piran and said, "What God wills cannot stay unfulfilled; if this is heaven's course, then I cannot oppose it. If I'm not to reach Iran again, or see Kavus's face again, or that of the great Rostam who brought me up, or Bahram's or Zangeh's, or the faces of any of our warriors, then I must choose a home here in Turan. Be as a father to me and arrange this marriage, but keep it secret for now." Having said this, he sighed repeatedly, and his eyelashes glistened with tears. Piran replied, "A wise man doesn't fight with Fate; if you once had friends in Iran, you've entrusted them to God and left them behind. Your home is here now."

Piran bustled off to the court and waited for a while near the throne until Afrasyab said, "Why are you standing here? What's on your mind? My army and wealth are at your disposal, and if I've some prisoner whose release will be dangerous for me, I'll set him free if you should ask. Now, what do you want from me?"

The wise councilor answered, "May you live for ever; I've all the wealth and power I need. I bring a secret message from Seyavash. He says to you, 'I am grateful for the fatherly welcome you have given me here; now I need you to arrange a marriage for me. You have a daughter called Farigis, and I should be honored if I were considered worthy of her.'" Afrasyab grew pensive and replied, "I've gone through this before and you didn't agree with me. A man who nourishes a lion cub will regret it once the lion's grown. And astrologers have predicted that the union of these two will produce a prince who will conquer the world and destroy Turan; the first crown he will seize will be mine:

Why should I plant a tree whose bitter root
Will only serve to nourish poisoned fruit?

A child that comes from Kavus and Afrasyab will mingle fire and flood; how can I know whether he will look kindly on Turan? And if he favors Iran, then it will be as if I've purposefully taken poison. A man doesn't deliberately pick a snake up by the tail. As long as he's here I'll treat him like a brother, but that's all."

Piran said, "Any child of Seyavash will be wise and good-natured. Pay no attention to what astrologers say; arrange matters for Seyavash. A prince of our two peoples will be lord of both Iran and Turan, and both countries will be at peace after long warfare. There can be no more splendid lineage than that of Feraydun and Kay Qobad. And, if heaven has another fate in store for us, thinking will not change it. This is a splendid chance, the answer to all you have desired."

The king replied, "I hope your advice turns out well. I accept your suggestion; see that the matter is carried out appropriately." Piran bowed, left the court, and hurried to Seyavash. He went over what the king had said, and that night the two washed all sorrows from their hearts with wine.

Seyavash Becomes Related to Afrasyab

When the sun raised its golden shield into the sky, Piran said to Seyavash, "Bestir yourself, you're to be the princess's guest, and I'm ready to do whatever you order me to in this affair." Seyavash was uneasy in his heart and shamefacedly said to Piran, "Do whatever you think's appropriate; you know I've nothing to hide from you." Piran bustled off to his house and had his wife Golshahr choose a splendid wedding gift: uncut cloth, gold woven Chinese brocade, trays of emeralds, beakers of turquoise filled with musk and sweet-smelling wood, two princely crowns, two torques, a necklace, two earrings, sixty camel-loads of carpets, three sets of clothes with designs worked in red gold and jewels, thirty camel-loads of silver and gold, a golden throne and four chairs of state, three pairs of slippers worked in emeralds, three hundred slaves with gold caps, a hundred more bearing gold beakers. All this, together with ten thousand dinars, was taken to Farigis by Golshahr and her sisters. She kissed the ground before the princess and said, "The sun is to be joined with the planet Venus; tonight you must go to the prince and shine in his palace like the full moon."

And so Farigis, resplendent as the full moon, came to the young prince. The festivities lasted a week; no one, not even the birds of the air or the fish in the sea, slept during that time; from end to end, the earth was like a garden filled with happiness and music-making. Afrasyab loaded his son-in-law with gifts and gave him a charter written on silk, making him lord of the lands that stretched to the Sea of China, and in confirmation of his sovereignty he sent a golden throne and crown to Seyavash's palace.

A year went by, and then one day a messenger from Afrasyab arrived at Seyavash's palace. The king said, "It would be right for you to separate yourself from me somewhat. I've given you the land that stretches toward China; make a tour of your territories and choose some city that delights your heart. Make that your happy home, and never swerve from righteousness."

Seyavash was pleased at this advice; he had fifes and kettledrums sounded, the baggage train fitted out, and litters prepared for Farigis and the women of her entourage. As he led out his army Piran accompanied him with his own troops, and the two made their way toward Piran's homeland, Khotan. There the prince stayed as Piran's guest for a month, feasting and hunting. When the month was over the din of drums rang out at cockcrow and, with the army led by Piran, Seyavash entered the appanage he had been granted by Afrasyab.

When it was known they had arrived, the local chieftains gave them a splendid welcome, filling the land with the sound of harps, lutes, and flutes.

> They reached a fertile and well-watered place,
> Possessed of every strength and natural grace:
> The setting's natural limit was the sea,
> A highway marked the inland boundary,
> To one side mountains reared above the plain,
> A place of hunting grounds, and wild terrain;
> The streams, the groves of trees, made weary men
> Feel that their ancient hearts were young again.

Seyavash said to Piran, "I shall build here, in this happy place: I'll raise a splendid city filled with palaces and porticoes. My capital will be worthy of the crown and throne and will soar as high as the moon's sphere." Piran replied, "My lord, do as you see fit. I will contribute everything necessary; knowing you, I have no more need for wealth or land." Seyavash said, "All my treasure and goods are from you; I see you striving everywhere on my behalf. I'll build a city here such that everyone who sees it will be amazed." But the astrologers reported that the site was inauspicious, and when Seyavash heard this the reins slackened in his hands and tears fell from his eyes. Piran asked, "My prince, why should this grieve you so much?"

And Seyavash said, "As the heavens roll
They cast my spirit down and sear my soul.
The wealth with which my treasury is filled,
The goods I've sought, the palaces I build,
Will pass into my enemy's fell hand.
Before long, death will take me from this land.
And why should I rejoice when I foresee
That others will sit here in place of me?
I'm not long for this world, and soon, God knows,
I'll need no palaces or porticoes;
My throne will then be Afrasyab's, and he
Though innocent connives to murder me.
And so the ever-turning skies bestow
Now joy, now sorrow, on the world below."

Piran said, "O my lord, why do you bewilder your soul in this way? Afrasyab has cleansed all evil from his heart and renounced all thoughts of vengeance; and while the soul stays in my body I will stay faithful to you. I won't let even the wind so much as disturb your hair." Seyavash said, "Your reputation is unsullied, and I see only goodness come from you. You know all my secrets; I bring you tidings from God himself, for I am privy to the secrets of the turning heavens. I will tell you what must be, so that later when you see how the world turns you will not wonder at my fate. Listen then: not many days will pass before I shall be slain, although I am innocent of sin; another will inherit my throne and palace. You are true to your word, but the heavens will otherwise. Slander and an evil fortune will bring evil on my innocent body. Iran and Turan will rise against one another and life will be overwhelmed by vengeance. From end to end our lands will suffer, swords will usurp the time; innumerable red, yellow, black, and purple banners will throng the skies of Iran and Turan; endless the pillage and slaughter, the theft of accumulated treasure; countless the countries whose streams will turn brackish, their soil trampled beneath war horses' hooves. Then the lord of Turan will regret what he has said and done; but when smoke rises from his pillaged cities, regret will be useless. My spilt blood will set Iran and Turan to wailing, and all the world will be in turmoil. Thus He who holds the world has written, and it is by his command that what has been sown is reaped. Come, let us rejoice and feast while we may; the world passes; why tie your heart to it, since neither our efforts nor the wealth we delight in will remain?"

Hearing him, Piran's heart was stricken with grief, and to himself he said, "If what he says is true, I am the cause of this evil. It was I who expended so much effort to bring him to Turan, I then who sowed the seeds of this war of vengeance. I took the king's words as so much wind when he said as much to me." But he consoled himself, "Who knows the

secrets of the heavens? He remembers Iran, Kavus, and the days of his greatness, and it is this that's disturbed him." As they rode forward all their talk was of the mysteries of fate, but when they dismounted they put the subject aside and called for wine and musicians. For a week they feasted, telling tales of the ancient kings; on the eighth day a letter came from Afrasyab ordering Piran to lead his troops on a tour of inspection, collecting tribute as he went. First he was to travel to the Sea of China, then to the border with India and the Indian Ocean, and from there to Khazar in Turkestan.

The shout to assemble went up from the doorway of Piran's tent; to the din of drums troops amassed to receive their orders, and then the columns set out on the itinerary the king had commanded.

Afrasyab's Letter to Seyavash

One night, at about the time men sleep, a messenger from Afrasyab came hurrying to Seyavash. The letter he bore was filled with kindness: "Since you left I am never happy. I have identified a place here in Turan where you could live; however cheerfully and splendidly you pass the time where you are, return to my kingdom and confound those who are envious of your good fortune."

Seyavash gathered his troops and set off to the appointed place, as the king had commanded him. With him came a hundred camel-loads of dirhems, forty of dinars, and a thousand red-haired Bactrian camels made up the baggage train. Ten thousand swordsmen guarded the litters carrying the women of his court, and the thirty camel-loads of precious goods—rubies, turquoise, torques, crowns and earrings, sweet smelling woods, musk and ambergris, brocade and silk, as well as goods from Egypt, China, and Persia. He came to the chosen place, named Khorram-e Bahar (The Joy of Spring), and there constructed a city of palaces, porticoes, public squares, orchards and gardens; the place was like a paradise, and in the desert wastes he made roses, hyacinths, and tulips grow. On his palace walls he had frescoes painted showing royal battles and banquets. One was of King Kavus with his crown, torque, and royal mace; Rostam stood next to his throne, and with him were Zal, Gudarz, and the rest of Kavus's entourage. On the opposite wall Afrasyab was painted, together with his warriors and the chieftains Piran and Garsivaz. At each corner of the city was a dome that reached to the clouds; and there, their heads among the stars, musicians would sit and sing. The city was called Seyavashgerd, and the world rejoiced in its existence.

On his return journey from India and China, Piran came to visit Seyavash. He was curious to see what the prince had done with the site and hurried forward, together with a crowd of well-wishers worthy of the honor. The prince and his troops came out to greet him; seeing him in the distance Piran dismounted, as did Seyavash, and the two embraced. They walked together through the city, where so recently there had been only a wilderness of thorns, and Piran praised Seyavash and the magnificent buildings and orchards he saw laid out on every side. He said, "If you were not endowed with knowledge and the royal *farr*, how could you ever have founded such a place? May it last as your memorial until the end of the world, and may you and your descendants live here as victorious kings until then."

When he had seen a portion of the city he reached Seyavash's palace and turned toward Farigis's quarters. The princess scattered coins before him in welcome, asked about the hardships of his journey, and seated him on a throne, while her servants stood in waiting for his orders. He praised all he saw, and then they turned to feasting, wine, and music. They spent a week in this way, at times lighthearted and cheerful, and at times quite drunk. On the eighth day Piran handed over gifts he had brought from his travels: rubies and other princely gems, coins and jewel-studded crowns, silks, horses with saddles of leopard skin and gold-worked bridles; to Farigis he gave a diadem and earrings, a necklace, and a gem-encrusted torque.

After leaving Seyavashgerd Piran returned to his own land of Khotan. Entering his women's quarters he said to his wife, Golshahr, "Whoever has not set eyes on paradise should travel where I have been, to see the angel Sorush enthroned in splendor. Go for a while, and refresh your soul with the sight of Seyavash's city." Then, quick as a skiff that cleaves the waves, he traveled on to Afrasyab. He listed the countries he had visited and the tribute he had levied, then mentioned Seyavash, saying all he had seen and answering the king's questions: "Heaven's glories do not equal that city, nor is the sun more splendid than Seyavash. I saw a city unparalleled in all of Persia and China: wisdom and that prince's soul have combined to make a paradise of gardens, public places, and flowing streams. From a distance Farigis's palace glitters like a vast jewel. Men revile the world, but you have no cause for complaint now. If Sorush himself were to descend from the blue heavens he would not be possessed of such magnificence, glory, and wisdom as is your son-in-law. And our two countries rest from war, returning to life like a man who has lain unconscious and revives again."

The king was happy to hear these words, believing that the tree of his good fortune had borne fruit. He told Garsivaz what he had heard, and said, "Visit Seyavashgerd and see what kind of a place it is. Seyavash has given his heart to Turan and forgotten Iran; he's renounced its crown and throne and said farewell to King Kavus, Gudarz, and Bahram. In the thorn-brakes here he has created a city; he has built Farigis tall palaces and treats her with honor and respect. When you see him, speak kindly to him and act with suitable deference, whether out hunting, seated at court with his Persian

جو یک بهره زان شهر خرم بُد
بایوان و باغ سیاوش رسید

entourage, or drinking and feasting. Take him abundant presents—whatever you can lay your hands on in your treasury—and give Farigis presents, too, and congratulate her on her good fortune. If your host welcomes you with smiles, stay in his pleasant city for two weeks."

Garsivaz Visits Seyavash

Garsivaz chose a thousand Turanian knights and set off in high spirits for Seyavashgerd. Hearing of his approach Seyavash and a detachment of troops hurried out to meet him; the two embraced and Seyavash enquired after the king's health. He welcomed Garsivaz to the palace and had his escort billeted appropriately. On the next day Garsivaz brought Seyavash the king's letter together with a robe of state; when Seyavash saw the robe the king had bestowed on him, his spirits opened like a flower in springtime. He and his nobles took Garsivaz about the city, and when they had surveyed it, building by building, they returned to the palace. There they saw Farigis wearing a diadem studded with turquoise, seated on her ivory throne, and surrounded by maidservants. She descended and welcomed Garsivaz, asking after the king and her hometown. Garsivaz seethed with resentment, but his outward behavior was punctilious and respectful. In his heart he said, "Let another year pass and Seyavash will have no time for anyone: he has sovereignty here, a crown and power, wealth, land, and an army." But though inwardly he writhed in anguish and his face turned pale, he hid what was in his heart, saying to Seyavash, "Your efforts have been rewarded; may you live for many years enjoying your good fortune." Two golden thrones were placed in the palace, and there Garsivaz and Seyavash sat, while musicians played heart-bewitching music on harps and lutes.

At sunrise on the next day Seyavash and Garsivaz went out to an open space to play polo. Garsivaz threw down the ball and Seyavash struck it so hard that it disappeared as though the heavens had swallowed it, while his opponent's mallet struck only dust that spurted up from the plain. Thrones were set at the edge of the field for the two heroes, who watched as their men displayed their prowess with javelins. Garsivaz suggested that Seyavash himself show his martial valor before the Turks, and he assented.

Seyavash Displays His Skill to Garsivaz

The prince exchanged his throne for his saddle. Five suits of mail, each heavy enough to tire a man, were bound together and set up at the field's end, while all the army watched. Seyavash owned a spear that had belonged to his father, who had used it in the war against Mazanderan; this he grasped and then like a maddened elephant he charged, plunging the spear into the suits of mail, shattering their fastenings and scattering them at will.

Garsivaz's men collected the broken remnants from the field. Then the prince had four Gilani shields—two made of wood and two of iron—bound together as a target. He called for his bow, and thrust six poplar wood arrows in his belt; three more he kept in his fist, and one he notched to the bowstring. Then he galloped toward the target and loosed the first arrow: it pierced all four shields, as did all ten of his arrows one after another, while young and old roared their approval.

Garsivaz said, "My prince, in all Iran and Turan you have no equal. But let's you and I engage in a wrestling match, grasping each other's belts and straining to throw one another, here, in front of our troops. I'm the foremost warrior of the Turks, and you won't see many horses to rival mine; there's no one else here who's fit to oppose you. If I can throw you from your saddle to the ground, you'll have to accept that I am the better warrior and have the better mount, and if you succeed in throwing me, I'll never show my face on a battlefield again." Seyavash replied, "Don't say such things: you are a great lord and a great warrior, your horse is superior to mine, and I reverence your helmet. Choose some other Turk to face me." Garsivaz said, "It will only be a friendly contest, for a moment, with no malice or hard feelings involved." But Seyavash replied, "It would not be right; where I fight is no place for you. When two men oppose one another, they may smile but their hearts are filled with fury. You're the king's brother and your horse's hooves tread down the moon. I'll do whatever you order me to, but I can't consent to this. Choose some lion warrior from among your companions, set him on a fine, fleet horse, and if you're still intent on having me fight, you'll see his head in the dust." Garsivaz laughed, and turning to his Turks called out, "Which of you wants to humble the greatest of warriors, and so be renowned throughout the world?" No one responded, till Gorui spoke up, "If no one else will oppose him, I'm his match." Seyavash frowned at this, but Garsivaz said, "My lord, he has no equal in our army." Seyavash said, "If I'm not going to fight with you, combat with anyone else is contemptible. But choose two, and I'll fight against both together." A Turk called Damur joined Gorui, and Seyavash faced them, while they circled him. Then he lunged forward and grabbed Gorui by the belt, dragging him from his saddle to the ground, all without having to use his lariat. Next he wheeled toward Damur and seized him by the neck, lifting him lightly from his horse, so that all the onlookers were astonished. As if he were carrying a mere ant rather than a warrior, he rode over to Garsivaz, dismounted, released Damur, and sat down laughing on his throne. Garsivaz was secretly enraged by what he had seen and his face flushed. The two returned to the palace and spent a week feasting according to Persian custom, drinking wine and listening to singers, flutes, and lutes.

On the eighth day Garsivaz and his entourage made preparations to leave. Seyavash wrote a friendly letter to Afrasyab and loaded Garsivaz with presents.

At first the journey home was filled with praise
Of Seyavash and all his princely ways,
But Garsivaz said, "When this Persian came,
The only gift he brought for us was shame.
Our king has welcomed him—to our disgrace,
Humiliation stares us in the face.
Great Gorui and brave Damur, two men
Whose like Turan won't quickly see again,
Were forced by this high-handed Persian knight
To look like fools who don't know how to fight.
And this won't be the end of it; I fear
The consequences of his presence here."

And so he talked until they reached Afrasyab's court, muddying the streams of goodwill toward Seyavash. When they arrived, Afrasyab questioned him eagerly, and after he had read Seyavash's letter he laughed aloud, in the best of spirits. Malignant Garsivaz saw the king's gladdened face, and as evening came he left the court, his heart a mass of pain and hatred.

All night he writhed in anguish, and when night's black cloak was torn aside he made his way to Afrasyab again. The court was cleared of strangers and the two sat together. Garsivaz began, "Your majesty, Seyavash is not the man he was; he receives messengers from King Kavus and also from Rum and China; he drinks Kavus's health and a mighty army has gathered around him. Soon he will be a threat to you. If evil had not darkened Tur's heart, he would not have slain Iraj, but since that time our two countries have been like fire and water, each heartsick at the other; and you are crazy enough to want them to unite? You might as well attempt to trap the wind. If I had hidden this evil from you, the world would have condemned me."

The king's heart was hurt by this report, and he began to brood on Fate and its sorrows. He said, "Affection sprung from our common blood guides you to speak like this. Let me weigh the matter for three days; if wisdom agrees with your assessment, I'll say what remedy to adopt."

On the fourth day Garsivaz appeared at court, his sword belt tight about his waist, his diadem of office on his head; Afrasyab summoned him and went over the matter of Seyavash. He said, "How you remind me of our father, Pashang! And who else have I in the world besides you? It's you I must tell my secrets to, and you must plumb them thoroughly and give me your advice. That dream I had, which upset me for a while and confused me, prevented me from fighting against Seyavash. But no harm's come to me from him; since he's bid farewell to the throne of Iran and wisely woven his fate with mine, he has never once disobeyed my orders. And I've treated him well; I gave him a country to rule over, and wealth, and I've

made no mention of our grievances against him. I've made a blood alliance with him; I gave him my daughter, the light of my eyes, and I've renounced all thoughts of vengeance against Iran. If, after all this, I were to suspect him, the world would rebuke me; I haven't the least excuse to move against him. If I were to harm him our nobles would condemn me, I'd be a byword for bad faith everywhere. And if I harmed an innocent man could God who rules the sun and moon approve of this? I can see no other solution than to summon him to my court and then send him back to his father: if it's sovereignty he wants, he can take his quarrel elsewhere."

Garsivaz said, "My lord, you can't treat this matter so lightly. If he goes back to Iran now, our whole country will be destroyed. Whenever you welcome a stranger into your family he becomes privy to all its secrets; if you try and distance yourself from him now, who knows what insanity may come from this? He'll be your enemy, and you'll be rubbing salt into open wounds. As has been well said, the man who brings a leopard up sees only trouble as his reward."

His words seemed true to Afrasyab, who regretted what he had done and foresaw only disaster. He replied, "I see no good in this affair, neither in its beginning nor in its end. We must look for what the heavens reveal; in every situation delay is better than haste. Wait until the sun has shone on this for a while, until we get some sense of God's will, and who it is that heaven's light looks favorably upon. If I summon him to court, I'll be able to sound his secrets, and if I bring disloyalty to light, then I shall have to harden my heart against him; no one can blame me then, since evil deserves punishment and there's an end to the matter."

But Garsivaz, intent on vengeance, said, "You are wise and honest, my lord, but consider: if Seyavash, with all his power and royal *farr*, with his God-given might, with that mace and sword of his, should come here, to your court, then the sun and moon will be darkened for you. Seyavash is not the man you saw; his crown outsoars the heavens. And you would not recognize Farigis, who seems beyond all earthly needs. Your army would go over to him, and you'd be left like a shepherd with no flock. If the army sees a prince as handsome, generous, and wise as he is, it's not going to be content with you as its sovereign. And you can't simply keep him in his own city, grateful to you for what you've done for him and still willing to serve you. No one has ever seen a lion and an elephant mate, or fire above while water flows below.

> *If someone wraps a lion cub in silk,*
> *A little whelp, who's not yet tasted milk,*
> *It keeps its nature still, and, once it's grown,*
> *Fights off an elephant's attack alone."*

Then Afrasyab became despondent and beset by care; old memories of ancient wrongs and thoughts of vengeance filled his heart.

From then on Garsivaz visited him continually, filling the king's heart with calumny, until one day Afrasyab cleared the court and said to him, "Go and visit him; don't stay long, but give him this message from me: 'Don't you have any desire to quit your round of pleasures and see someone else? Come here with Farigis for a while; I need to set eyes on your face again and enjoy your wise company. There is good hunting in our mountains, and wine and milk in our emerald goblets. We can spend time pleasantly together, and when you wish to return to your own city, you'll be seen off with music and festivities. Why is it forbidden for you to drink with me?'"

Garsivaz Visits Seyavash for the Second Time

His heart filled with malevolence, his head with deceit, Garsivaz hurried off on his mission. When he was close to Seyavashgerd he selected a smooth-talking soldier and said to him, "Go to Seyavash and say to him from me, 'My

noble and ambitious lord, I beg you by the soul of Turan's king, and by the soul and crown of King Kavus, not to trouble yourself to come out of your city to greet me. Your fame, *farr*, lineage, crown, and throne raise you above such concerns, and the winds themselves stand ready to serve you.'"

The envoy arrived and kissed the ground before Seyavash, who was saddened by Garsivaz's message; he withdrew and pondered for a while over what it might mean, saying to himself, "There is some secret hidden here." When Garsivaz reached the court Seyavash went out on foot to meet him, questioning him about his journey, the king, and affairs of state. Garsivaz handed over Afrasyab's letter, which delighted Seyavash, who exclaimed, "I'd outface swords and adamantine walls for his sake; I'm ready to travel to his court; you and I shall link our reins and ride together. But first we must feast and drink in these golden gardens, for the fleeting world is a place of sorrow and grief, and woe to him who does not seize pleasure where he can."

Garsivaz said in his heart, "If I return to the king with him, his chivalry and wisdom will trample my plans underfoot; my words will count for nothing, and my council will be seen as a lie. I must make some scheme to lead him astray." For a while he stood in silence, staring at Seyavash's face. Then tears flowed from his eyes, and seeing this, Seyavash asked in sympathy, "My brother, what is it? Is it a sorrow you can't talk about? If your tears are because you're upset with Turan's king, I'll ride with you now and fight against him until I know why he's humiliating you; and if some formidable enemy has appeared in your life, I'm ready to help you in any way I can. Or if Afrasyab is at odds with you because someone has been slandering you and so replaced you in his favor, tell me about it so that I can help look for a remedy."

Garsivaz replied, "No, there's nothing like this between me and the king, and I've no enemies my wealth and martial skill can't deal with. Thoughts of our lineage welled up in my heart, and I remembered true tales from the past. How evil first came from Tur, who lost God's *farr*; you've heard of how he schemed against the humble Iraj and so began the endless vendetta of our peoples, and how from then until the time of Afrasyab, Iran has been like fire and Turan like water, never mingling in one place, always rejecting wisdom and good council. And Turan's king is worse than Tur; his ox had not been skinned yet, who knows what he'll do? You don't know how evil his nature is, but if you watch and wait, you'll see. Think first of how with his own hand he stabbed Aghriras. The two were brothers, of the same mother and father, and yet he killed Aghriras, who had committed no crime. And there have been many other innocent nobles whom he has destroyed. My concern is that you remain vigilant and safe; since you came here, no one's been harmed by you, you've always striven for justice and decency, and the world has been made more splendid by your knowledge. But Ahriman has filled the king's heart with resentment against you. I don't know what God wills in all of this. But you know that I'm your friend whatever good or evil should appear; I don't want you to think later on that I knew of this and didn't warn you."

Seyavash replied, "Don't trouble yourself about this. God is with me, and the king has given no sign that he wishes to destroy me. If he were angry with me, he wouldn't have distinguished me by giving me a country to rule over, together with his own daughter, wealth, and troops. I'll return with you to his court and make his darkened moon splendid again. Wherever truth shines out, lies lose their luster. I shall show Afrasyab my heart, brighter than the sun in the heavens. Be cheerful, and give up these dark suspicions."

Garsivaz said, "My kind lord, don't imagine he is as you once saw him. For all your knowledge and stature, you can't distinguish pretence from goodness, and I fear bad luck will come of this. He has tricked you, blinded you with glory. You were foolish to rejoice when he made you his son-in-law; he lured you away from your own people and gave a great feast and made you his familiar, so that the world began to gossip about it. You're not a wiser man than Aghriras, and you're no closer to him than he was; before their horrified troops Afrasyab cleaved his brother's waist in two with a dagger. Take this as a lesson, and put no trust in the fact that you're related to him. There, I have told you what's in my heart. You abandoned your father in Iran and made a place for yourself here in Turan; you trusted our king's talk and became his friend in sorrow. But this tree you planted has bitter roots and its fruit is poison." His heart was filled with treachery, but he sighed as he spoke and his eyelashes were wet with tears.

Seyavash stared at him in bewilderment, and tears streamed from his eyes; he remembered the prophecies of his evil destiny, that the heavens would deprive him of love, that he would not live long but die while still a young man. His heart was wrung and his face turned pale, his soul was saddened and sighs escaped his lips. He said, "However I look at this, I cannot see that I deserve punishment. No one has heard that I have done or said anything wrong. If I have made free with his wealth, I've also striven on his behalf, and whatever evil comes to me I shall not swerve aside from his commands. I'll accompany you, without my troops, and we'll see what has turned the king against me."

Garsivaz replied, "Ambitious lord, it would be better for you not to come. A man should not step heedlessly into fire or trust himself to ocean waves. You'd be rushing into danger and lulling your good luck to sleep. I will act for you in this and throw cold water on the fire. Write an answer setting out the good and evil of the situation; if I see that he has no thoughts of vengeance and that the days of your glory are renewed, I'll send a messenger here on horseback, lightening the darkness of your days. I trust in God, who knows what is open and what is hidden, that the king will return to righteous ways, leaving aside crookedness and evil. And if I see that his mind is still dark, I'll send a messenger immediately, and you should wait no longer but leave at once: it's not far from here to the borders, a hundred and twenty parasangs to China, and three hundred and forty to Iran. In the former everyone looks favorably on you; in the latter your father longs to see you and the whole country is yours to command. Don't delay, but write to both countries and be prepared to fly to either."

> No longer vigilant, no longer wise,
> Prince Seyavash believed his specious lies.
> He said to him, "I put my trust in you,
> I acquiesce in all you say and do;
> Go, plead my cause before the king, and seek
> For righteousness and justice when you speak."

Seyavash Writes to Afrasyab

He summoned a scribe and dictated his letter. After invoking God and praising wisdom, he addressed Afrasyab: "O wise beneficent king, may you live forever. You summon me and I am grateful; but you have summoned Farigis, too, and she has been ill for some time. She hardly touches her food and has not the strength to walk. She keeps to her bed, and I sit beside her pillow. My heart is filled with anxiety, seeing her hovering between this world and the next. When her illness eases she will be ready to serve you; but my worry for her well-being is the reason I cannot visit you now." He had the letter sealed and handed it to Garsivaz, who asked for three of his fastest horses and rode day and night back to Afrasyab's palace.

On the fourth day he reached the court, and when the king saw him exhausted from the journey he asked him why he had hurried back so quickly. Garsivaz replied, "When evil threatens there's no time for delay. Seyavash treated everyone with contempt; he didn't come out to meet me, he wouldn't listen to what I said, he didn't read your letter, he kept me standing before his throne. Letters were constantly coming to him from Iran, but the gates of his city were closed against me, and troops flocked to him from Rum and China. If you don't deal with him soon, your fist will close on wind and nothing more; he'll make war on us and seize both Iran and Turan. And once he leads his men to Iran who will dare attack him? I've told you what I've seen, now suffer in the crisis you created."

When Afrasyab heard him, ancient wrongs revived in his mind. In his anger he said nothing to Garsivaz, but fire roared in his heart and his head seemed filled with wind. He ordered fifes, cymbals, trumpets, and Indian chimes to be sounded and led his army out from Gang: once more he planted the tree of vengeance.

While the deceitful Garsivaz was straining in the stirrups on his journey home, Seyavash made his way to the inner apartments of his palace. His face was pale and his body trembled. When Farigis saw him she said, "My lion lord, what's made you lose your color like this?" He answered, "My love, I have no honor left here in Turan; if Garsivaz speaks truly, my life has come full circle."

> Queen Farigis clutched wildly at her hair
> And clawed her rosy cheeks in her despair,
> Blood clogged her musky curls, tears stained her face,
> Distractedly she cried, "Leave, leave this place,
> But where in all the world will welcome you?
> Now, quickly, tell me what you plan to do;
> Your father's rage excludes Iran, you say,
> China would shame you, Rum's too far away—
> Your only refuge in the world is He
> Who rules the sun and moon eternally.
> May years of pain destroy the scoundrel who
> Corrupted the king's heart and slandered you."

And Seyavash said, "Garsivaz will be arriving at Afrasyab's court about now."

Seyavash's Dream

On the fourth night Seyavash slept in Farigis's arms; he began to tremble and started up from sleep, roaring like a maddened elephant. Beside him his wife said, "My prince, what is it?" Then she called for tapers, and for sandalwood and ambergris to be burned before him. Again she asked, "My king, what did you see in your dream?"

Seyavash said, "Tell no one what I've dreamed. My love, my silver cypress tree, I saw an endless river, and on the further shore a mountain of fire, and men with lances crowded the bank. The fire began to overwhelm my city, Seyavashgerd. On one side there was water, on the other fire, and between them was Afrasyab mounted on an elephant. He saw me and frowned, and blew on the fire to make it flare up." Farigis said, "This can only have a good meaning; sleep now for the rest of the night."

But Seyavash rose and called his troops to the palace courtyard. His dagger in his hand, he began to prepare for battle and sent out scouts to watch the road from Gang. When two watches of the night had passed, one of the scouts galloped back from the plain, saying, "Afrasyab and a great horde of soldiers have appeared in the distance; they are hurrying this way." And then a courier brought a message from Garsivaz: "Save yourself; nothing I said had any effect and the fire sends out clouds of threatening smoke. Decide what you must do and where you should lead your army." Still Seyavash did not suspect his behavior, believing all that he told him. Farigis said, "My wise king, don't think of me, put no trust in Turan but saddle a swift horse and flee. You must stay alive; save your own head and give no thought to anyone else."

Seyavash replied, "My dream was true, and the glory of my life darkens; my time on earth draws to its close and only bitterness remains. But this is the heavens' way, bestowing now pleasure and now sorrow; if my palace reached to the stars, still the world's poison would have to be tasted; and if I lived for one thousand two hundred years, still my resting place would be the dark earth. You are five months pregnant, and if the fruit maturing in your womb should grow to ripeness, you'll be delivered of a splendid prince. Name him Kay Khosrow, and may he be a consolation for your sorrows. Soon, by Afrasyab's command, my luck will sink to sleep; though I am innocent they will cut my head off, and my crown will be soaked in my vitals' blood. I'll have no coffin, shroud, or grave, no mourners to lament my death; I shall lie like a stranger in the dirt, my head severed from my body by a sword blow. The king's bodyguards will drag you naked through the streets, and Piran will come to beg you from your father. He'll take you in your wretchedness to his castle; a warrior will come from Iran and lead you and your son secretly across the Oxus. Your son will be placed on the throne, and from the fish in the sea to the birds of the air all creation will serve him. A huge army will come from Iran intent on vengeance; the world will be filled with tumult. Armies will clash in the war of my revenge, the earth will groan from end to end in torment, and Kay Khosrow will throw the world into confusion." This was his farewell to Farigis: "Dearest wife, I must leave; harden your heart, and bid farewell to ease and luxury." She scored her cheeks and tore out her hair, her heart filled with grief for her husband, her eyes with tears. The two clung to one another in their grief, then, weeping and heartsick, Seyavash left her apartments.

He went to the stables where his Arab horses were kept and found black Behzad, who on the battlefield outran the wind. Lifting off his halter Seyavash wept, took Behzad's head in his arms, and whispered in his ear, "Let no one near you until Kay Khosrow returns; he will replace your bridle. Then you must bid farewell to this stable and bear him out to war and vengeance." He hamstrung all the other horses, wild as a fire that burns through reeds; then he and his warriors set out for Iran, their faces blinded by tears.

Afrasyab and Seyavash Meet

But after they had traveled half a parasang they were confronted by the army of Turan. Seeing them in their armor, with their swords at the ready, Seyavash buckled on his breastplate and said to himself, "Garsivaz spoke the undeniable truth." Each side eyed the other's ranks; before this neither had felt any enmity for the other. Turan's cavalry held back out of fear of Seyavash. The Iranians drew up in battle order and prepared for bloodshed: all of them were ready to fight alongside Seyavash; neither delay nor reproaches would be of any use now. They said, "If we're killed we won't go down to the dust alone; they'll see what battle with Persians means and not consider us contemptible." Seyavash said, "There is no sense to this; this battle has neither head nor tail to it. We'll shame ourselves, and my gift to my father-in-law is to make war on him. But if the heavens decree that I shall be destroyed by evil, I have no strength or desire to oppose God's will. As the wise have said, there is no point in striving against an evil fate." Then he called out to Afrasyab, "Great and glorious king, why have you come with your army ready for war; why do you wish to kill me, though I am innocent? You will stir up the armies of our two countries, and fill the land with curses."

Garsivaz replied, "You senseless fool, when has such talk ever been worth anything? If you're so innocent, why have you come before the king armed? A show of bows and shields is no way to welcome a monarch."

The sun rose as Garsivaz spoke, and Afrasyab ordered his men to draw their swords and roar their war cry as if Judgment Day had come. He said, "Grasp your weapons, and make this plain a sea of blood to float a ship on."

There were a thousand Persian warriors there, all good fighting men, but they were surrounded on all sides and slaughtered. Seyavash was wounded by arrows and lances and fell from his black horse; as he lay in the dust Gorui wrenched his hands behind his back and bound them tight as a stone. They set a yoke on his shoulders and dragged him on foot, hemmed in by soldiers, his face bleeding, toward Seyavashgerd; the prince had never seen such a day as this.

Afrasyab said, "Take him off the road, to a stony place where no plants grow, and cut off his head. Let his blood sink in the hot soil there; fear nothing, and be quick about it." But the army cried out as with one voice, "Great king, what is his sin? Why would you kill someone for whom the very crown and throne will weep? In the days of prosperity do not plant a tree whose fruit will be poison."

Piran's clear-sighted younger brother, Pilsom, was there. He said to Afrasyab, "The fruit of this tree will be pain and sorrow; the wise say that one who acts circumspectly has little to regret, that reason soothes anger, that haste is the work of Ahriman, bringing guilt to the soul and pain to the body. There's no sense in cutting off a subject's head precipitately. Keep him in chains until time teaches you the best course; act when wisdom's wind has touched your heart. A wise king does not sever a head that's worn a crown. And, if you kill this innocent, his father Kavus and Rostam, who brought him up, will seek revenge. Men like Gudarz, Gorgin, Farhad, and Tus will bind war drums on their elephants; the mammoth-bodied Giv, who despises all enemies, and Kavus's son Fariborz, a lion who never tires of battle, will ready themselves for a war of vengeance. The plains will be thronged with warriors; neither I nor any like me in this company will be a match for them. But Piran will be here at dawn; wait and hear his advice."

Garsivaz said,

> "Pay no attention to a young man's prattle:
> Vultures feed on their warriors killed in battle;
> If you're afraid of vengeance, this will be
> Sufficient cause for Persia's enmity.
> You've done enough harm—must you once again
> Listen to raw advice from foolish men?
> If this prince calls, from Rum's and China's borders
> Swordsmen and troops will flock to hear his orders.
> You've wounded the snake's head—now you're afraid,
> And want to wrap its body in brocade?
> Well, spare him if you wish, but I won't be
> A part of it, you've seen the last of me;
> In some dark cave I'll hide myself away
> And live in fear until my dying day."

Then Damur and Gorui came forward, plausibly twisting their words: "Don't worry about spilling Seyavash's blood, delay is wrong when there's work to do. Take Garsivaz's good advice and destroy your enemy. You set the trap and caught him, don't hesitate now. You have the leader of the Persians in your grip, now break the hearts of those who oppose you. You've destroyed his army already, how do you think the Persian king is going to look on you? If you had done nothing against him from the beginning, this could have been overlooked; but now it's better if he disappear from the world entirely."

The king replied, "I've seen no sin in him, but the astrologers say that hardship will come because of him. But if I spill his blood, a whirlwind of vengeance will arise from Iran. I have brought evil on Turan, and sorrow and pain on myself. To free him is worse than killing him, and killing him is grief and agony to me. But neither wise nor evil men know what the heavens will bring."

Farigis heard this talk and came before the king, her cheeks bloodied, her hair smeared with dust, wailing and trembling with pain and fear. She said, "Great king, why will you make a widow of me? Why have you given your heart to lies? In your glory you cannot see the misery before you. Don't cut off an innocent prince's head; the ruler of the sun and moon will not approve of this. Seyavash abandoned Iran and, with all the world to choose from, made his obeisances to you; he renounced his crown and throne and father's goodwill for your sake. And he became your ally and support; what more do you want from him? Who has deceived you? And I am innocent, do not mistreat me, for the world is fleeting, casting one into a pit of misery and raising another to glory; but both descend to the dark earth finally. Do not listen to malignant Garsivaz's lies and so make yourself an emblem of evil throughout the world. You've heard what the Arab tyrant Zahhak suffered at Feraydun's hands, and what the great king Manuchehr did to the malevolent Salm and Tur. In Kavus's court live men like Rostam, who is contemptuous of Turan and at whose name the world trembles, Gudarz of whom lions are terrified, Bahram, and Zangeh, the son of Shavran. You are planting a tree whose leaves will bring blood and whose fruit is vengeance. The world's glory will darken and curse Afrasyab; you are ruining yourself, and you will have long years in which to remember my words. You're not out hunting now, bringing down some wild ass or deer; you're destroying a prince, and the throne and crown will curse you. Do not cast the land of Turan to the winds, or make this an evil day that you'll regret."

Having said this she gazed at Seyavash's face, wailing and clawing her cheeks. The king pitied her but seeled up the eyes of wisdom and said, "Leave, get back to the palace; what do you know of what I mean to do?" They took Farigis and locked her in a dark room deep in the palace.

Seyavash Is Killed

Garsivaz looked at Gorui, who turned his face aside, and stepped before Seyavash, abandoning all chivalry and shame. He grasped the prince by the hair and began to drag him away; Seyavash cried out, "Great God, who rules our earthly state and destiny, bring forth a bough from me that will be like a shining sun to my people, who will seek revenge for my death and renew my ways in my own land." Pilsom followed him, his eyes awash with tears, his heart filled with sorrow. Seyavash said to him, "Farewell; may Fortune weave her threads with yours forever; convey my greetings to Piran. Tell him the world has changed, that I had other hopes of Piran when I was like a willow tree bending before the wind of his advice. He told me that when my luck turned he would be at my side with a hundred thousand infantry and cavalry, that he would be like a pasture for my foraging. But now that I'm haled before Garsivaz, on foot, despised and wretched, I see no one here to befriend me or to weep for me."

Garsivaz and Gorui dragged him away from the army and the city to a waste place on the plain. Gorui took the dagger from Garsivaz, and when they had reached the appointed place they threw the prince's mammoth body to the ground. Knowing neither fear nor shame, they held a gold dish at his throat to catch the blood and severed the head of that silver cypress tree. The prince's head sank into endless sleep, never to awake. Gorui took the dish to the place that Afrasyab had ordered, and emptied it. A wind rose up, and darkness obscured the sun and moon; people could not see one another's faces, and all cursed Gorui.

> *I turn to right and left, in all the earth*
> *I see no signs of justice, sense, or worth:*
> *A man does evil deeds, and all his days*
> *Are filled with luck and universal praise;*
> *Another's good in all he does—he dies*
> *A wretched, broken man whom all despise.*

Seyavash's palace resounded with lamentation; his slaves cut off their hair, and Farigis too cut her musky tresses and bound them about her waist and clawed at her cheeks' roses. Loudly she cursed Afrasyab, and when he heard her cries he ordered Garsivaz to drag her into the streets, and there to strip her and have her beaten, so that she would miscarry the seed of Iran, saying, "I want nothing to grow from Seyavash's root, neither a tree nor a bough nor a leaf; I want no scion from him worthy of a crown or throne."

One by one the nobles of his entourage condemned him, saying that no one had ever heard of a king or minister who had given such an order. Pilsom came weeping and heartsick to Lahak and Farshidvard and said, "Hell is better than Afrasyab's realm, and this land will know no rest or peace now; we should go to Piran and seek help for these tormented women."

They saddled three fine horses and hurried to Piran's castle, where they arrived covered in sweat and dust. They told him that Seyavash had been dragged on foot, bound, and with a yoke placed about his neck; that he had been forced to the ground by Gorui with his face twisted up like a sheep's while a basin was held to catch his blood; that his head had been severed and that his body lay like a silver cypress felled in a meadow. They said that a heathen shepherd of the deserts would not slit a man's throat in such a way, that all the land mourned for Seyavash, and that tears stood in all eyes like dew.

Piran fell from his throne in a faint, and when he came to he tore at his hair and clothes and heaped dust on his head. Pilsom said to him, "Hurry, pain is heaped upon pain: Farigis will be killed, guards have dragged her by her hair to the court; don't turn your back on her distress."

Piran had ten good horses brought from his stables and in two days and nights the group arrived at Afrasyab's court. They saw the gates thronged with warders and executioners, and Farigis dragged forward, as if insensible, by guards with drawn swords in their hands. The court was in a tumult, weeping and lamenting and condemning Afrasyab, saying that he would have Farigis hacked in two, that this horrific crime would utterly destroy his sovereignty and that no one would ever call him king again. Piran rode forward like the wind, and everyone with any sense rejoiced. Farigis saw him through her bloody tears and said, "See what evil you have brought upon me, you have thrown me living into the fire." Piran dismounted and tore at his clothes in grief; he told the guards crowded about the gates to delay carrying out their orders.

Then, weeping and heartsore, he rushed before Afrasyab and said, "Great king, live prosperously and wisely: what evil has darkened your benevolence, what demon has gained power over you, destroying all shame before God in your soul? By killing the sinless Seyavash, you've thrown your own honor and glory in the dust. When this news reaches Iran the court will go into mourning, and their nobles will lead a great army here intent on vengeance. The world was at peace and God's ways prevailed, and now some demon has burst from hell and deceived the king's heart: curses on the devil who perverted your heart! For long years you'll regret this, living in pain and sorrow. And now that you've dealt with Seyavash, you turn against your own child? But Farigis has no desire for glory or sovereignty; don't make yourself a byword for cruelty by killing your pregnant daughter; you will be cursed throughout the world for as long as you live, and when you die hell will be your home. If the king would brighten my soul he will send her to my castle; and if you fear her child, wait until it is born; I'll bring it to you, and then do to it whatever evil you wish."

Afrasyab replied, "Do as you say; you have made me unwilling to shed her blood." Heartened by this, Piran went to the gates, paid off the guards, and took Farigis away from the court and its lamentations. He brought her to Khotan and, when they arrived, entrusted her to Golshahr, his wife, saying, "Hide this lovely woman away; look after her well." Days passed, and Farigis, whose glory lit the world, grew heavier.

The Birth of Kay Khosrow

On a dark, moonless night, when birds and beasts were sleeping, the lord Piran saw in a dream a candle lit from the sun. Seyavash stood by the candle, a sword in his hand, crying out in a loud voice, "This is no time for rest; rise from sleep, learn how the world moves onward; a new day dawns and new customs come; tonight is the birthnight of Kay Khosrow."

Piran trembled in his sleep and woke; he roused Golshahr and said, "Go to Farigis; I dreamed of Seyavash, more splendid than the sun, who said to me, 'How long will you sleep? Rise, and run to the feast of Kay Khosrow, who will rule the world.'"

When Golshahr reached Farigis she saw that the princess had already borne her son. She ran back lightheartedly, shouting the news to all the world, and said to Piran, "He's like the sun and

moon together; come and see the little marvel, see what God has created in
his goodness; you'll say he's ready for a crown, or for a helmet and battle."
As soon as Piran saw the prince he laughed and scattered coins for him; his
great stature seemed more fitting for a one-year-old child than a newborn
baby. Gazing at the child, Piran wept for Seyavash and cursed Afrasyab. To
his nobles he said, "If I am killed for this, I'll say it: I shall not let Afrasyab
get his clutches on this child, even if he throws me to wild beasts."

At the time the sun unsheathes its sword, as Afrasyab was waking up,
Piran came hurrying in; after the room was cleared, he approached and
said, "Sun king, world conqueror, wise and versed in magic arts, another
subject was added to your rule last night. He seems a capable, intelligent
child and is as fair to look on as the moon. If Tur could live again he'd long
to see him, for he resembles Feraydun in majesty and glory. No picture in a
palace is as magnificent as this prince; in him the royal splendor is
renewed. Now distance evil thoughts from your mind, mercy will become
both your crown and your heart."

> God cleansed all hatred from the monarch's mind;
> He knew that Seyavash had been maligned;
> He sighed for him, tortured with pain and guilt,
> Mourning his malice and the blood he'd spilt.

He said, "I've heard enough about this newcomer; everyone talks about
him. The land is full of disturbances because of him, and I remember what I
was told; that from the mingled line of Tur and Kay Qobad a great king
would be born, the world will turn to him, and all the cities of Turan will
pay him homage. But let what must come, come; there's nothing to be
gained by worry and grief. Don't keep him among your courtiers; send him
off to the shepherds, and see that he doesn't know who he is or why he is
there." He said whatever came into his head, thinking that this ancient
world was young and malleable.

Piran left the court in high spirits, giving thanks to God and praising the
king. He traveled home deep in thought. Once there he summoned shepherds
from the mountains and said, "Keep this boy as dearly as your own souls,
keep him safe from wind and dust, see that he wants for nothing and never
suffers." He gave the shepherds many gifts, and sent a wet nurse with them.

By the time the boy was seven years old his lineage began to show. He
fashioned a bow from a branch and strung it with gut; then he made a
featherless arrow and went off to the plains to hunt. When he was ten he
was a fierce fighter and confronted bears, wild boar, and wolves. Soon, still
using the same rough bow he'd made, he progressed to leopards and lions.
By now he would take no orders from the shepherd who looked after him,
and so his guardian descended from the mountains and went whining to

Piran. He said, "I've come to complain to your lordship about our young hero; at first he hunted deer and didn't look for lions or leopards. But now it makes no difference to him whether he's after a lion or a deer. God forbid any harm should come to him; I'm yours to command my lord." Piran laughed, and said, "Lineage and skill won't stay hidden long!"

He rode to where the young lion was living and ordered him to step forward. Seeing the boy's noble stature, he dismounted and kissed his hand. Then he gazed at him, taking in the signs of kingly glory in his face; his eyes brimmed with tears and love filled his heart. He folded the boy in his arms and held him there for a long time, brooding in his heart on the boy's fate. He said, "O Khosrow, follower of the pure faith, may the face of the earth be bright for you." Khosrow replied, "My lord, everyone speaks well of your kindness, and I see you're not ashamed to embrace a shepherd's son." Piran's heart was wrung at these words; he blushed and said, "My boy, you call to mind our ancient heroes; the world is yours by right and you're deprived of it. No shepherd is kin to you, and I could tell you much more about this." He called for a horse and royal clothes for the young man, and, as the two rode together back to Piran's castle, Piran grieved in his heart for Seyavash. He kept the boy by him and brought him up; but though he delighted in his company, he feared for him because of Afrasyab, and his anxiety gave him no rest. And so the heavens turned for a few years more, and Afrasyab's heart grew milder. One night a messenger arrived summoning Piran to the king's presence. When he arrived Afrasyab said to him, "Every night my heart is filled with thoughts of evil and sorrow. I think of that child of Seyavash and it's as if he has darkened all my days. How can it be right for a shepherd to bring up a descendant of Feraydun? If it's fated that evil will come to me from him, my precautions won't change God's will. If he can forget about the past, let him live happily, and I will, too; and if he shows any signs of evil, then he'll lose his head, as his father did."

Piran replied, "My lord, you need no councilor to advise you. What does a little child who's ignorant of the world know about the past? Don't trouble yourself about this matter any more. What's that saying, 'The teacher's stronger than the father, and a mother's love counts most of all'? Now, for my sake, swear me an oath, as solemn as those sworn by the ancient kings, that you won't harm the boy." Afrasyab's granite heart softened at Piran's words, and he swore a solemn royal oath:

> "By day's bright splendor, by the dark blue night,
> By God who made the earth and heaven's light,
> Who made earth's beasts and human souls, I say
> I shall not harm this child in any way."

Piran kissed the ground and said, "Just king, without peer or equal on the earth and in the heavens, may wisdom always guide you, may time and space be as the dust beneath your feet."

Piran Takes Kay Khosrow to Afrasyab

Piran hurried back to Kay Khosrow, and his cheeks glowed with happiness. He said to Khosrow, "Drive wisdom from your heart; if he talks about battles answer with banquets, appear before him like a fool, talk as an idiot talks. If you can keep clear of sense, you'll get through today safely." Then he placed the Kayanid crown on his head and buckled the Kayanid belt about his waist. He had him mounted on a high stepping horse, and the two came to Afrasyab's court while crowds gathered to gaze with tears in their eyes, and heralds called before them, "Clear the way, a new prince approaches."

When they reached the court the grandfather's face was wet with tears of shame; then he stared at his grandson, saying words of friendship but revolving evil in his mind. He gazed for a while at the youth's stature and splendor, and as he looked his face turned pale. Watching him, Piran began to tremble and despaired of Khosrow's life. The king's face seem closed and forbidding, but then kindness entered his heart.

He said, "Young man, you are new to the court; tell me what you know about the shepherd's life. What do you do with your sheep, how do you lead them to their pasture?"

Khosrow answered, "There's no hunting; I've no bow or bowstring or arrows."

Then Afrasyab asked him about his teachers, and the good and evil fortune he had seen.

Khosrow answered, "Where there's a leopard, the hearts of sharp-clawed men burst with fear."

Thirdly he asked him about his mother and father, about Iran, and about his food and where he slept.

Khosrow answered, "A fierce dog can't bring down a ravening lion."

The king laughed at his replies and turned to Piran saying, "His mind's awry; I ask him about the head and his answer's all about feet. No good or evil is going to come from him; men intent on revenge don't behave like this. Go, hand him over to his mother, and set someone trustworthy to look after them. Let them go to Seyavashgerd. Keep bad councilors away from him, but give him whatever he needs in the way of money, horses, slaves, and so forth."

Hurrying a little, Piran hustled Kay Khosrow from Afrasyab's presence; they reached home safely with Piran well pleased by what had happened

and convinced that the evil eye was seeled. He said, "God's justice has bestowed a new tree on the world, and now it gives its fruit." He opened wide the doors of his ancient treasury and equipped the prince with all he needed—silks, swords, jewels, horses, armor, crowns, belts, thrones, purses of coins, carpets, and cloth and everything else he might require.

Then he sent Farigis and Kay Khosrow to Seyavashgerd, which had become a wilderness of thorns; even the beasts of the field came to pay homage to them, and men gathered from every quarter and bowed before them, saying, "From the noble tree's uprooted stock a new shoot has sprung. May the evil eye be far from our universal lord, may Seyavash's soul be filled with light." The ground of the ruined city revived and the weeds turned to tall cypresses. From the place where Seyavash's blood had been spilt a green tree sprang up; on its leaves the prince's face could be seen, and its scent was like the scent of musk. It flourished in the winter's cold as freshly as in spring, and it became the place where those who mourned for Seyavash gathered together.

> This crone will see her infant suck and play,
> And while he sucks she'll snatch her breast away;
> Such is the world to which our hearts are bound
> Before we're hurried pell-mell underground.
> If Fortune raises one above the skies
> Fortune will cast him down before he dies;
> Turn from this world's inconstant vanity
> And put your trust in God's eternity.

When Rostam learned of Seyavash's death he dragged Sudabeh from Kavus's harem and killed her for her part in the young prince's downfall. He then attacked Turan and laid much of it to waste in a war of vengeance. Afrasyab however escaped and lived to fight another day.

The Persian hero Giv was sent to Turan to find and bring Kay Khosrow, and his mother Farigis, to Iran. After their hazardous journey, crossing the river Jayhun to the Iranian side, Kay Khosrow was acclaimed by the Persian court as Kavus's heir. Only Tus demurred, as he believed that both he and Fariborz had a better right to the throne than Khosrow.

Khosrow became the ruler of Iran, and his grandfather Kavus retreated into the background. Khosrow immediately began preparations for a lengthy campaign to subjugate Turan and bring Afrasyab to justice for his murder of Seyavash. The malcontent Tus was made commander of the Persian army, and sent on a preliminary expedition against Turan.

درفش کرفته بربست اندرو

ببشد یالب آب کلزریون

✣ FORUD, THE SON OF SEYAVASH ✣

When a great warrior embarks on war he should not trust his army to an enemy; only tears which no doctor can cure will come of this. Someone who is from a noble family but who cannot achieve any kind of greatness is made savage by his failure. It is unwise for a king to trust any man who remains subject to others and unfulfilled in this way. If the heavens deny him his desires, his loyalty to the king is always suspect; there is no goodness in him, and ambition always gnaws at his heart. When you hear this tale through, you will know the nature of such a man.

Tus Leads His Army to Turan

The sun had reached its zenith, bringing Aries beneath its sway, and the world was filled with a light like white wine. From Tus's encampment the din of drums and the squeal of trumpets rang out; the land resounded with war cries and the neighing of horses, and the air was dark with the dust of armies gathering. The sun and moon were obscured, and everywhere the clatter of armor and the trumpeting of elephants could be heard.

Red, yellow, blue, and purple banners thronged the sky, and in the center was the banner of Kaveh, surrounded by horsemen from the clan of Gudarz. A tucket sounded, and Kay Khosrow appeared at the entrance to his tent, crowned and carrying his mace. Wearing golden boots as a sign of office, Tus went forward with the banner of Kaveh. He was followed by chieftains descended from Nozar, each wearing a torque and a diadem; one by one they paraded before Khosrow.

The king addressed them: "Tus leads this army; he bears the Kaviani banner, and you must be ready to obey his orders. Following royal custom, he should harm no one on the march; let no chill wind touch farmers, craftsmen, or any other civilian. Fight only with opposing warriors; harm no one who offers you no harm, for the world is fleeting and we are not here long.

Under no circumstances should you pass through Kalat; if you do so your enterprise will fail. May the soul of Seyavash be as the sun; may his place in the other world be one of hope. He had a son, by a daughter of Piran; the boy closely resembled his father. He and I were born at the same time, and he was like me when we were young, open and cheerful in his manner. He lives now in Kalat with his mother, ruling the area in royal splendor. He knows none of our Persian chieftains by name; you must not ride that way. He has a fine army, besides which the road through his territory lies over a difficult mountain pass. He himself is a brave warrior and horseman, of noble lineage and with a champion's strength. Take the way through the desert; there is no point in passing through a lion's territory."

Tus replied, "May Fortune always favor your desires; I shall travel as you have commanded, since your commands bring only success."

Quickly Tus led off his troops and Kay Khosrow retired to take council with Rostam and his nobles and priests. They spoke of Afrasyab, of Kay Khosrow's anxieties, and of his father's suffering.

The army progressed, stage by stage, until they came to a place where the road divided. In one direction lay a waterless desert, and in the other Kalat and the road to Jaram. The elephants with their war drums in the van of the march paused until Tus arrived; the men waited to see whether he would obey orders or take the road the army itself would have preferred. When he reached them Tus talked with his officers about the hot, waterless way; he said to Gudarz, "Even if the dust of this desert were of amber and its sands of musk we would still have a weary journey ahead of us, and we will need water and rest. Therefore it's better that we make for Kalat and Jaram, and we can rest at Mayam for a while. On both sides of the road the area is cultivated and there's flowing water; why should we put ourselves to the trouble of slogging through the desert? I've been through Jaram once before, when the army was led by Gazhdaham, and it's not a difficult journey, except there's a bit of going up and down hillsides. It's best we go this way then, and not count off the desert parasangs."

Forud Learns of the Approach of the Persian Army

Forud was told that the face of the sun was dimmed by an approaching army's dust, and that the earth seethed like a rushing river with horses and elephants. "Your brother," they said, "is bringing an army up from Iran, seeking revenge for the murder of his father." Forud was an inexperienced youth; when he heard this his heart was filled with anxiety, and his soul darkened. He went out to inspect the surrounding mountainside and had the gates to his castle fastened behind him. He gave orders that no herds or flocks of sheep were to be left on the plains or mountain pastures, that all of them were to be brought within the perimeter wall. When he had supervised the

سوار و پیاده بزین کمر | سنع تیغ دار و همه نیزه ور | زبانگ پتره میان و کو | همی گرس اندر سوا شتر

سپهدار و شمشیر زن هنی نامر | همی رفت کرد در کارزار | بماند خیره تخوار و فرو | ازان لشکر شکرو شادی

چنین گفت کانون درفش مهلا | بگوی و مدار ایچ کو نهان | چنین گفت کان سپهکر درفش | سوران و آن تنهای غث

پس پشت طوس سپهبد بود | که در جنگ برخاسله بدو | درفشی پس پشت او دیگر است | جو خورشید تابان بدو

برادر پدر سست با فرو کام | سپهبد فریبرز کاوس نام | پس شما سپهکر درفش زرگ | دلیران بسیار و کرد

ورا نام رستهم کرد به خون | که لرزان کند پل اسپ خون | پش کو رپیکر درفش دراز | یکبرد اندر سر لشکری

flocks being brought up the mountainside he returned to the castle and secured the gates. From Jaram the din of distant drums resounded, and toward Mayam dust obscured the sky.

Forud's mother was Jarireh, who still grieved in her heart for Seyavash. Forud came to her and said,

> *"Dear mother, from Iran an army comes*
> *Led by great Tus, with elephants and drums;*
> *What's your advice? What tactics should we try?*
> *If they attack us how should we reply?"*

His mother said, "My son, you're always so eager to fight, but God forbid such a day should dawn for you. Your brother Kay Khosrow is now the new king of Iran; he knows very well who you are, and that you and he had the same father. Piran gave me to your father from the first, and if he hadn't done so Seyavash would never have taken a Turkish wife. You are of noble, royal descent on both sides. If your brother is seeking revenge in order to vindicate the spirit of Seyavash, you should join him and prepare yourself for war. Put on your Rumi armor and ride out to battle, your heart filled with rage, your head ringing with war cries. Go in the van of your brother's army; as he is the new king, so you will be the new champion seeking revenge. It is fitting for even leopards and sea monsters to grieve at Seyavash's death, and for the birds of the air and the fish of the sea to curse Afrasyab; no heroic prince like Seyavash will ever appear again in the world, neither as regards glory or civility or dignity or justice. You are this great man's son, you're every inch a king and you should ready yourself to exact revenge, to show whose blood runs in your veins. Observe this approaching army and find out who is leading it. Call your warriors about you and prepare gifts—wine, fine robes, noble horses, tables of food, swords, helmets, barding, armor, Indian daggers. In all the world, your brother is a sufficient treasure to you; may you lead his army on this war of revenge, you as the new champion, he as the new king."

Forud said to his mother: "Which Persian should I speak to? On the day of battle, which of them can I depend on? I know none of them by name, and none of them have sent any messages to me."

Jarireh replied, "My prince, when you see their army's dust in the distance, search the ranks for Bahram and Zangeh, the son of Shavran. Have them show you proof of who they are, for you and I need have no secrets from them. Don't be separated from these two; they were your father's lieutenants when he was a prince. May you and your good name live forever; may Seyavash's soul abide in glory. Now, keep what I tell you in mind; go out with Tochvar and with no other soldiers. When you ask who is who in their army, Tochvar will be able to tell you."

Forud said, "Mother, you're like a lion, and it's your councils that give our tribe its splendor."

A lookout ran in from the walls and cried,
"The Persian army fills our mountainside,
The plain and passes are all thronged with men,
You'd say we'll never see the sun again;
The way up to our castle's like a sea
Of banners, elephants, and cavalry."

Tochvar and Forud galloped out of the castle gates, but the young man's luck was dimmed by dust, and when the heavens turn aside, neither rage nor kindness suffice.

Forud said to Tochvar, "Don't keep from me anything I ask you; when we see the Persian chieftains with their banners and maces of office, and golden boots, tell me the names of everyone you know." They made their way to a high point from which they could look down on the groups of Persians below. There were so many golden helmets and golden shields, golden maces and golden belts, that a man would say there was no gold left in any mine on earth and that a cloud had passed overhead and rained down jewels. There were cavalry and infantry, swordsmen and lance bearers, and their drums thundered with such a noise that the vultures of the air cowered away in fear; thirty thousand warriors, armed and ready for combat,

crowded the mountainside. Forud and Tochvar stared in astonishment at the mass of men and their gear.

Forud said, "Now, tell me the chieftains' banners, and don't hide anything from me." Tochvar replied, "The banner with the device of an elephant belongs to Tus, and those horsemen with glittering swords who crowd around it are his bodyguard. The banner behind him, with the device of a shining sun, belongs to your father's brother, Fariborz. Behind him, the huge banner that's surrounded by such a mass of warriors, the one with a shining moon, belongs to young Gostaham, Gazhdaham's son, whose valor makes elephants tremble in terror. The one beyond that, with the device of a wild ass, stands before the brave warrior Zangeh, the son of Shavran. The banner studded with stars, with a red ground and a black silk fringe, belongs to Bizhan who in battle stains the sky with blood. The banner with the dark, lion-terrifying tiger belongs to Shidush, a huge mountain of a man. The one behind that, with a buffalo, with all the lance bearers crowded around it, belongs to Farhad, who seems blessed by heaven in all he does. The banner with the wild boar on it belongs to Gorazeh, and the one bearing the device of a wolf belongs to the chieftain Giv."

Tus Sees Forud and Tochvar on the Mountainside

When the Iranians caught sight of Forud and Tochvar high on the mountain, Tus was furious and ordered the elephants with their war drums to halt. He said, "This will alarm our soldiers; a nimble horseman must ride up to the summit and see who those two warriors are, and what they're doing up there. If they're our men they'll be whipped with two hundred lashes, and if they're Turks they're to be caught and brought here. If they're killed in the encounter then their bodies are to be dragged in the dust; we should do this without fear of any consequences. If they're spies sent in secret to count our number, let them be hacked in two where they are, and their bodies tossed from the mountainside."

Bahram, of the tribe of Gudarz, volunteered, saying, "I'll ride up to the summit and do as you command." He urged his horse out of the army's ranks; determinedly, he made his way up the mountain. Forud turned to Tochvar and said, "Who's this approaching us with such contempt? He's in such a hurry he seems quite unconcerned by us; he's riding a fine dun horse and has a lariat looped at his saddle." His councilor answered, "He's not someone to be handled roughly; I don't know who he is, but I think he's one of Gudarz's men. When Khosrow returned to Iran from Turan, one of the king of Turan's helmets went missing; I think he's wearing it, and his armor seems royal, too. He's surely one of Gudarz's clan, but let's ask him."

Bahram approached the top, and roared aloud
As if he were a threatening thundercloud,
"Who are you on the mountain's summit there?
Our trumpets blare, our drums' din fills the air,
And can't you see our army's countless hoard
Led by great Tus, our leader and our lord?"

Forud replied, "You've been offered no scorn, don't speak scornfully to us. Talk civilly, as a knight should, and keep your cold, contemptuous words unsaid. You're not a lion and I'm not a wild ass; this is no way to behave with me. You're no greater than I am, neither as a warrior, nor as a man, nor in brute strength. You've a head, feet, a heart, a brain, sense, a loud voice, and eyes and ears; look, I have all those, too, so don't threaten me. I'm going to question you, and if you answer me as befits a knight, I shall be pleased."

Bahram replied, "Say on, then, you in the sky up there while I'm down here on the ground!"

Forud said, "Who is leading this army off to war?"

Bahram answered, "Tus leads us, with the Kaviani banner and his war drums; he's accompanied by chieftains like Gudarz, Giv, Shidush, Farhad, Gorgin, Gostaham, Zangeh, and Gorazeh."

Forud said, "Why haven't you mentioned Bahram? The list is incomplete without him. Of all the clan of Gudarz, he's the one that I want to hear about, but you say nothing about him."

Bahram replied, "Well, my lion-warrior, and what have you to do with Bahram?"

Forud said, "This is what I heard from my mother. She said, 'When the army approaches you, welcome them and ask for Bahram, and also for another warrior called Zangeh, the son of Shavran; these two were brought up with your father, they shared the same wet nurse, and you should try not to miss them.'"

Bahram replied, "May fortune favor you; are you the fruit of that royal tree? Young prince, are you Forud? If so, long may your shining soul flourish!"

He said, "Yes, I'm Forud, a sapling from that toppled cypress."

Bahram said, "Show me your body, uncover the mark of Seyavash." Forud showed him his upper arm, on which there was a dark mole, like a dash of amber on a rose petal, such that no painter could reproduce it, even with a pair of Chinese compasses. Bahram knew then that the person before him was descended from Qobad and of the seed of Seyavash. He dismounted and made his obeisance to Forud and then ran up the mountain toward him. Forud too dismounted and sat on a rock and said to Bahram, "Great leader, lion in battle, seeing you alive and well, I could not be happier if my eyes beheld my father here; I came to this summit to find out which chieftains were with the Persian army and who was leading it. I shall hold as splendid a feast as my means allow, in order to delight your commander. I shall distribute horses, swords, maces, and all manner of other goods, and then I shall set out with you to Turan, intent on vengeance. I am the right man to prosecute this war; in the saddle I am like a mounted fire, burning all before me. Tell your commander to come up the mountain so that he and I can spend a week together laying plans, and on the eighth day, when the war drums ring out and Tus is seated in the saddle, I shall in bitterness of heart, and with a fury that no man has ever equaled, prepare myself to avenge my father's death."

Bahram replied, "My young, noble, chivalrous prince, I shall tell Tus all that you have told me, and I shall kiss his hand asking him to respect your wishes; but our leader is not a wise man and he has little time for advice. He has skill and wealth and is of the blood royal, but he has scant respect for the king. He's always quarreling with Giv, Gudarz, and the king about Fariborz and the succession, and he constantly says, 'I am of the seed of Nozar, I am worthy to be king of the world.' He's likely to ignore my words, or to be infuriated by them and attack me. He's a willful, unpredictable man. Apart from myself, don't let anyone else who comes in search of you catch sight of your helmet; if someone else comes, don't greet him. And then Tus dislikes me in his heart, because he wishes that he and Fariborz were rulers. He said to me, 'See who's on that mountain, don't ask him why he's there but let your mace and dagger speak for you. Why should anyone be on that mountain today?' If he takes your message calmly, I will bring you the good news and lead you to the army; if anyone else comes, do not trust him. Not more than one warrior should ride up to you at a time, this is our leader's way; if anyone approaches consider him well, and if need be, retreat to your castle and bar the doors."

From his belt Forud drew a mace; its handle was of gold and encrusted with turquoise. He said to Bahram: "Take this as a remembrance from me and keep it whatever happens; if Tus welcomes me, all will be well and there will be many other presents—horses, saddles, crowns and royal jewels."

When Bahram returned to Tus he said, "May wisdom fill your faultless soul: the man we saw was Forud, the son of King Seyavash, who was slain despite his innocence. He showed me the birth sign of those descended from Kavus and Kay Qobad."

But evil Tus replied, "These men you see,
These drums and trumpets, all belong to me;
My orders when I sent you there were clear:
'Don't say a word to him, but bring him here.'
So he's a prince, is he? And who am I,
According to this castle in the sky?
What have I seen from your Gudarz's clan?
Nothing but brazen traitors, to a man.
A lion doesn't guard that mountainside;
One useless horseman made you run and hide."

Rivniz Fights with Forud

Tus turned to his troops: "Great fighters, destroyers of our enemies, I want an ambitious warrior who'll face this Turk in combat, who'll sever his head with a dagger and bring it here to me." Rivniz, Tus's son-in-law, responded to the call; this battle would be his last.

Bahram said to him, "Champion, fear the Lord of the sun and moon and don't rush into something that will dishonor you. If a knight rides out against that prince, he won't escape with his life." Tus was angered by Bahram's words and he ordered a few warriors to ride up toward the summit of the mountain. But as they were leaving Bahram called out to them, "Don't think this will be an easy

task. It's Kay Khosrow himself who's on that mountain, and a hair of his is worth more than any hero. If anyone here never saw Seyavash's face, then let him ride up the mountainside to see it now." When they heard this the warriors returned to camp.

But Tus's son-in-law, whom the heavens watched with scorn, took the way from Jaram toward Mount Seped, his heart filled with a furious longing for combat.

When Forud caught sight of him, he readied his bow, and said to Tochvar, "Tus has treated my overtures of peace with contempt. The knight riding up toward us is not Bahram, and anxiety fills my heart. Watch him, and tell me whether you recognize him; and why is he clothed from head to foot in iron armor?" Tochvar replied, "This is Rivniz, the one brother among forty sisters, all as lovely as the spring. He's deceitful, untrustworthy, a flatterer; but he's also young and brave and Tus's son-in-law."

Forud said, "This is no time to be praising him, when he's about to fight me. As soon as he gets closer I'll send him back to his sisters' skirts. If he feels the wind of my arrows and lives, no longer count me as a man. Now, should I shoot at his horse or at him; you're experienced at this, what do you advise?" Tochvar said, "Shoot at the rider, and let Tus grieve for him. Tus knows that in the goodness of your heart you offered him peace, but he's foolishly decided to make war on you, and in so doing he shames your brother."

When Rivniz was a bowshot away, Forud drew back his Indian bow and loosed an arrow of poplar wood, which pierced the knight's helmet, pinning it to his skull. He fell, and his horse turned, dragging Rivniz's head in the dust. Tus was watching from the heights in Mayam, and when he saw this the mountainside blurred and darkened before his eyes. But as the wise say, an evil nature is repaid in kind, not once but many times.

Tus's Son, Zarasp, Fights with Forud

Then Tus said to Zarasp, "Make your heart bright as fire, put on knight's armor, exert yourself and avenge our fallen champion; if you do not, I see no one who will." Zarasp prepared for combat and placed his helmet on his head; his heart was filled with a longing for revenge, and his head whirled with impatience.

The lion warrior said to Tochvar, "Another rider is coming. Look and see if you recognize him; is he a prince, or one of the common soldiers?" Tochvar replied, "The time has come to fight in earnest; this is Tus's son, Zarasp, who won't turn his horse aside from a raging elephant. He is married to one of Rivniz's sisters and has come to avenge his brother-in-law. As soon as he can make out your helmet, loose an arrow against him, so that this crazy commander Tus will realize we're not to be despised."

Forud urged his horse forward and as he did so loosed an arrow toward Zarasp: it pierced the armor at his waist and entered his body. Blood flowed from the wound, and his soul departed; he fell, and his horse turned and galloped back to camp. A great cry went up from the Persian army, and Tus wept with rage and grief; in haste he pulled on his armor, lamenting for the two dead warriors and shaking like a leaf. Like a mountain he sat in the saddle, as if he were astride some great elephant, then grasped the reins and set off toward Forud, his heart filled with a longing for revenge, his head whirling with grief and pain.

Tus Fights with Forud

Tochvar cried out to Forud, "A moving mountain approaches our mountain: it's Tus, their commander, who's come to fight against you in combat. You should not pit yourself against an experienced monster like this; get into the castle and bar the gates, and then we'll see what Fate decrees. Now you've killed his son and son-in-law you can't expect a friendly welcome from him."

Forud was young and flared up against Tochvar saying, "When battles are to be fought—whether it's against Tus or a raging elephant or a ravening lion or a sea monster or a tiger—a man gives himself to combat heart and soul; he doesn't start smothering the fire with mud."

Tochvar, in his experience, said, "Princes do not despise good advice. Even if you were made of iron and could rip a granite mountain up by its roots, you're still one solitary knight. If thirty thousand Persian warriors come up this mountain to fight against you, not only your castle but the very stones of this mountain will be razed and not a jot will survive. And the expedition to avenge your father's death will suffer a setback that will never be reversed." But he did not say what should have been said long before and, following the advice of this worthless councilor, Forud gained only war and death.

The prince tugged at the reins, turning his horse toward the castle, and notched another arrow to his bow. Within Forud's castle walls were eighty female attendants; they were watching from the battlements, and when they saw the young hero turn back, their spirits sank.

Tochvar addressed Forud: "If you're determined to oppose Tus it's better you don't destroy him; kill his horse beneath him, because a Persian prince won't fight on foot even if hard-pressed. And then one arrow might not finish him; his henchmen are certain to follow him up the mountain. You have never faced his fury, and you can't deal with both him and them." Forud heard him and drew back his bow; the arrow struck Tus's horse, which lowered its head and fell lifeless to the ground. Enraged, Tus made his way on foot back down the mountain, his shield slung around his neck, his body caked in grime. Forud yelled taunts after him, "What happened to the great champion then, who runs away on foot from a single horseman? What kind of a show does that make in front of his army?" The women on the battlements laughed, and Jaram re-echoed with their scornful cry,

> "The old man ran from the young hero's bow,
> Straight down the mountain, quick as he could go."

When Tus reached the base of the hillside, warriors clustered about him saying, "You've come back safe and sound and this is no time for tears." But Giv turned aside, ashamed to see his leader return on foot. He said, "This young man has gone too far; if he's a prince, and wears the earrings of his office, how can he treat our great army so contemptuously? We're not here to agree to whatever he wants to propose. Even if Tus was hasty and over-bearing, this Forud is making a mockery of our mission. We came here to sacrifice our lives in a war of vengeance for Seyavash; we should not forget this. Forud has destroyed Zarasp, a great knight descended from Nozar, and he left Rivniz's body weltering in its own blood. What further humiliations are we waiting for? Even if he were Jamshid's son and had Qobad's brain, he's still embarked on the course of an ignorant fool."

Giv Fights with Forud

As he spoke he fastened on his armor; he mounted his horse, which was like a mighty dragon, and set off toward Jaram. When Forud saw him, a cold sigh escaped his lips and he said, "This army has no sense of its luck, good or bad; one after another they come, each braver than the last, shining like the sun in Gemini. But this is not a wise course, and a head without wisdom is like a body without a soul. If they aren't victorious, I fear for their war of vengeance, unless Khosrow comes to Turan, and then he and I shall stand shoulder to shoulder in this war for our father and crush our enemies like dirt in a fist. Now, tell me, who is this haughty warrior, over whose weapons they'll have to weep?"

Tochvar looked down the mountainside and, unaware of the effect of his words, was like one who sows thorns in a meadow. He said, "This man is a

terrible dragon whose breath can bring birds down from the sky. He has destroyed three armies from Turan, orphaned innumerable children, crossed mountains, rivers, and deserts, deprived countless fathers of their sons, and placed his foot on the neck of slain lions. It was he who took your brother to Iran, getting him across the Oxus when no boat could be found. His name is Giv, and he's a mammoth of a man, a raging flood in battle. No arrow will pass through his breastplate: he wears Seyavash's armor when he fights and fears neither lances nor poplar wood arrows. Shoot your arrow at his horse and see if you can wound that. Then he'll have to dismount and go on foot back to camp as Tus did, his shield slung about his neck."

Forud drew back his bow and the arrow flew, piercing the horse's chest. Giv toppled from his collapsing mount and began to make his way back down the mountain. A laugh of derision went up from the battlements, and Giv seethed with chagrin beneath their taunts. The Persian warriors went to him saying, "Thanks be to God it was your horse that was wounded, and not you."

But his son Bizhan, who was a headstrong youth, railed against him: "My father's a conqueror of lions, he's outfaced raging elephants, so why did a single horseman make you turn tail like this? You always used to be in the thick of the fighting, and now because your horse is wounded you run off like a drunkard!" Giv said, "When my horse was wounded I'd no choice but to quit the field," and then angrily reproached Bizhan for his presumptuous remarks. Bizhan turned his back on him; Giv exploded in rage and struck at him with his horsewhip, shouting as he did so, "Haven't you been told you should think before picking a quarrel? You've neither sense nor brains nor wisdom, my curses on whoever brought you up!"

Bizhan's heart was filled with bitter fury, and he swore a solemn oath before God that he would not take saddle from horse until either he had avenged Zarasp or died in the attempt. He went to Gostaham, his heart filled with grief, his mind with rage, and said, "Lend me a horse that can ride up that mountain; I'm going to put my armor on and show just who is a man and who isn't. A Turk has installed himself on that summit in full view of the army. If we leave here there will be a lot of hard riding to do, and I've only two horses that can carry a man in full armor; if one of them's killed here, I'll never find his equal either for speed, strength, or endurance."

Gostaham replied, "This is not sensible; you should not go rushing into disaster. Think of Zarasp, Rivniz, our matchless leader Tus, your father who brings down lions—all of them seen off by this Turk; no one can defeat that granite mountain and enter the castle unless he has a vulture's or a Homa's wings."

Bizhan said, "Don't break my heart; I'll tear myself limb from limb if I don't do this. I've sworn by the moon, by God who holds the world, and by our sovereign's crown that I'll not come down from that mountain until I have avenged Zarasp or am slain like him."

Gostaham replied, "This is not the road you should be taking; wisdom knows nothing of such fury."

Bizhan burst out, "Then I shall go on foot to avenge Zarasp, keep your horses!"

And Gostaham said, "I would not have one hair of your beard harmed. I've a hundred thousand horses, their tails braided with royal jewels; choose one and have him saddled, and if he's killed, so be it."

He owned a splendid horse, swift as a wolf, lean-bellied, tall and eager for combat. Bizhan, filled with youth's ambition, had him armored with barding. But when he thought of Forud's prowess, Giv's heart was thrown into anxiety. He called Gostaham to him, and they talked about youth's impetuous fire; he sent back with him Seyavash's armor and royal helmet. Gostaham gave them to Bizhan who put them on as quickly as he could and set off in high spirits, accoutered as a mighty warrior, up Mount Seped.

Bizhan Fights with Forud

The young prince turned to Tochvar: "Another of their men is coming. Look there, and tell me the name of this young chieftain for whom they'll soon have to weep and wail."

Tochvar replied, "Iran has no warrior like him; he's Giv's only son, and his father loves him more than his wealth and his own soul. He's a brave champion, victorious as a lion. Again, shoot at the horse; you must not break the Persian king's heart by killing this lad. And anyway, he too is wearing the armor that Giv wore, and it's proof against arrows and lances. He's likely to fight on foot and you won't be his equal then; look at that sword he bears, glittering like diamonds."

Forud loosed an arrow at Bizhan's horse, which fell as if lifeless; Bizhan disentangled himself from his falling mount and began to climb up to the summit, his drawn sword in his hand.

> He shouted to Forud, "Courageous knight,
> Wait where you are and see how lions fight;
> Know that this unhorsed warrior won't turn back
> But sword in hand I'll climb your mountain track;
> Wait for me, face me man to man, and then
> See if you ever want to fight again!"

When he saw that Bizhan was not withdrawing, Forud shot an arrow at him, but Bizhan lifted his shield and harmlessly deflected it. He reached the summit and readied his sword; Forud retreated, and the battlements behind him rang with shouts. Bizhan ran after him, and with his sword hacked at the barding of Forud's horse; he pierced it, and the horse fell in the dust. Forud scuttled into the gatehouse of his castle and the sentinels immediately barred the gates behind him. Those on the battlements hurled rocks down at Bizhan, knowing that no time should be lost. Bizhan yelled back, "You were mounted and ran away from a man on foot. Aren't you ashamed of yourself? Where are your courage and fame now, Forud?"

When Bizhan got back to Tus he boasted, "My lord, that knight could humiliate a whole plain full of soldiers; you shouldn't be surprised if the hail of his arrows turned a granite mountain to water, there's no greater fighter anywhere." Tus's response was to swear an oath of vengeance, saying, "I'll raze his castle and see the dust of its ruins obscure the sun; I'll fight a battle of revenge for Zarasp and destroy that malignant Turk; I'll make the stones of his castle glisten like coral with his blood."

Jarireh's Dream

When the shining sun disappeared and dark night spread its army across the sky, a thousand horsemen entered the castle of Kalat as reinforcements. The gates were fastened behind them, and the night was filled with the sound of armaments and the bells of their horses' gear.

Jarireh, Forud's mother, slept at her son's feet, and the darkness was filled with pain and sorrow for her. She dreamed of a great fire that raged in their castle, and then spread until the whole mountain was a mass of flame which consumed the castle and all the women in it. She started up from sleep, her soul in anguish, and went on the battlements to gaze out on the world. She saw all the mountain filled with the glitter of spears and armor, and ran weeping to Forud, saying "Wake up, my son, the stars have turned against us; all the mountainside is thronged with our enemies, and their spears and armor threaten our gates!"

> The young prince said, "Dear mother, do not cry.
> If Fate has willed that I am soon to die
> You weeping will not make my death delay;
> Each man must leave on his allotted day.
> My father too was young when he was killed,
> Now I must bow to what the heavens have willed.
> As he was put to death by Gorui
> So this Bizhan intends to murder me.
> But I will fight; if I'm to die, I'll slaughter
> All who attack, and I'll not beg for quarter."

He distributed helmets and armor to his men; then he placed a helmet on his own head, tightened the belt about his Rumi armor, and grasped his royal bow.

Forud Fights with the Persians and Is Killed

When the shining sun rose into the sky's vault, the war cries of chieftains rang out on all sides, mingling with the clatter of heavy maces and the din of drums, bugles, fifes, and Indian chimes. Forud led the Turkish troops out from the castle, and the top of the mountain was so clogged with dust, arrows, and maces that it seemed like a sea of pitch. The ground had disappeared, there was hardly room to fight, and the rocks and precipitous mountain slopes alarmed the horses.

Battle was joined and, as the sun journeyed across the sky, Forud's army steadily lost ground. On the heights and in the gullies the Turks were killed; Fortune was against the young man, although he himself still fought like a lion and the Persians watched him in wonder. But when he saw that all his companions had been killed, and that he could not fight on alone, he tugged at the reins, turned, and fled up the mountain to his castle. Roham and Bizhan lay in ambush for him, and as he approached Bizhan appeared on horseback in front of him and bore down on him. As soon as he saw Bizhan's helmet Forud readied his mace, but as he did so Roham rode out of the ambush behind him, yelling his war cry, an Indian sword in his grasp. He struck a mighty blow that caught Forud on the shoulder, severing his arm, and rendering him unfit for battle. Forud groaned with the pain and urged his horse forward; he reached the castle gates, which were slammed to and bolted behind him.

Jarireh ran to him and took him in her arms, and she and their attendants bore him to an ivory couch. At the hour of his death he was still too
young to have worn the crown. His mother and the women cut off their
musky tresses, and Forud struggled for life while wailing surrounded his
couch and anguish filled the castle. Barely opening his lips, Forud said, "It's
right for you to mourn; the Persians will come now intent on plunder, they
will enslave you and raze my castle and its ramparts to the ground. Those of
you who pity me, whose faces burn for my sorrow, go to the battlements
now and cast yourselves down from them, so that not one of you remains
for Bizhan to boast of. He it is who has taken my life from me, who has
destroyed me in the days of my youth." After he had said this, his cheeks
turned sallow, and in pain and grief his soul departed.

The womenfolk fled to the battlements and all of them threw themselves down on the rocks beneath. Jarireh set fire to the castle and fed it
with their treasures. Then she went to the stable and with a sword slashed
the remaining horses' bellies and lacerated their legs, and the horses' blood
spattered her face. Lastly she made her way back to where Forud lay. She
drew a dagger from the folds of his clothes and ripped open her belly with
it; she placed her face against her son's and died.

The Persians had torn up the gateposts and poured into the castle, intent
on plunder. But when Bahram came on Forud and Jarireh his heart broke
with grief. Weeping, he turned to the Persian troops and said, "This man has
died even more wretchedly and terribly than his father did. Seyavash was
not killed by a mere squire, and his mother did not die beside him; neither
was his castle burned like a reedbed nor his chattels and treasures
destroyed. Fear God, my friends, and the turning of the heavens, whose arm
is long in apprehending evil-doers and who is merciless to sinners. Have
you no shame before Kay Khosrow, who spoke so gently and at such length
to Tus, who sent you here to avenge the death of Seyavash and who gave
you such wise council? When he learns of his brother's spilled blood, you
will lose all favor with him. And what good can be expected from men like
Roham and that hothead Bizhan?"

Meanwhile Tus and his entourage of Persian chieftains, including Gudarz
and Giv, made their way up the mountainside to Kalat, their war drums
sounding as they came. Entering the room where Forud and his mother lay
dead, they saw Bahram seated beside the bodies, weeping and lamenting,
and Zangeh to one side, a group of warriors clustered about him. Forud lay
on the ivory couch like a toppled teak tree, his face fair as the full moon,
and it was as though Seyavash himself lay there, asleep in his armor. Gudarz
and Giv and the other warriors wept to see him, and Tus too wept bloody
tears, both for his son and for Forud. Gudarz, Giv, and the others there
turned on him and said, "A commander should not act hastily, and rage ruins

all he does. Through rage and haste you have thrown this young prince, with all his splendor and nobility, to the winds; and the same passions destroyed both Rivniz and Zarasp, who counted Nozar among their ancestors. Without wisdom, ability and rage together are like a sword eaten away by rust."

Tus ordered that a royal tomb be built on the mountain top. Within it, on a golden couch, they placed the prince's body dressed in cloth of gold and with a golden belt. His head was embalmed with camphor and his body with rosewater and musk. The tomb was sealed, and the army moved on; so passed this lionhearted prince.

After Forud's death, Tus led the Persian army deep into Turan, and Afrasyab's counselor, Piran, was put in charge of Turan's defenses. Success had made the Persians careless, and Piran was able to inflict a severe defeat on them by ambushing them at night.

Kay Khosrow eventually heard of Tus's insubordination in attacking Forud, and of his army's defeat at the hands of Piran. He angrily recalled Tus and appointed Fariborz as commander in his place. But the Persians suffered defeat again, and the remnants of their broken army fled back toward Iran. Turan allied itself with other Asian peoples and nations, including China, in the hope of finally defeating Iran. Rostam began to intervene in the conflict and the tide of battle turned in Iran's favor: Afrasyab and his allies were routed, although Afrasyab managed to escape again, and the border areas between Iran and Turan were once more under Persian control. At this point Rostam, who could now move about Turan more or less at will, encountered a notorious demon, the Akvan Div.

همه لشکر کش زیر و زبر ... پدر
کهی شاد مایین دمد کار دو ... کرد

پدر بی سپر
چنین آمد این که

یکی شهر فرمود آنجا فراخ
پر از باغ و ایوان و میدان و کاخ

بدانجا که آن روشنی بر دمید
از و تیرگی شد ناپدید

ᔐ THE AKVAN DIV ᔓ

Listen to this tale, told by an old Persian. Here is what he said:

One day Kay Khosrow rose at dawn and went to a flower garden to hold court. He had spent the first hour of the day there, surrounded by his chieftains—Gudarz, Rostam, Gostaham, Barzin, Garshasp (who was descended from Jamshid), Giv, Roham, Gorgin, and Kharrad—when a herder of horses came in from the plains with a request for help.

"A wild ass has appeared in my herd," he said. "He's like a demon—a div—who has slipped his bonds, or you could say he's like a savage male lion. He's constantly breaking the necks of my horses. He's colored just like the sun, as if he'd been dipped in liquid gold, except for a musk-black stripe that runs from his mane to his tale. He's as tall as a fine bay stallion, with big round haunches and sturdy legs."

Khosrow knew very well that this was no wild ass, since a wild ass is never stronger than a horse. He turned to Rostam and said, "I want you to deal with this problem; go and fight with this animal, but be careful, for it may be Ahriman who is always looking for ways to harm us." Rostam replied:

> "Your Fortune favors any warrior who
> Fearlessly serves your royal throne and you:
> No dragon, div, or lion can evade
> My fury and my sword's avenging blade."

He mounted his great horse Rakhsh and, lariat in hand, left the king and his courtiers to their pastoral pleasures. When he arrived at the plain where the herdsman kept his horses, the wild ass was nowhere to be seen. For three days he searched among the horses, and then on the fourth he caught sight of him galloping across the plain like the north wind. He was an animal that shone like gold, but beneath his hide all was ugliness and sin. Rostam urged his horse forward, but as he closed on the wild ass he changed his mind. He said to himself, "I shouldn't kill this beast with my dagger; I ought to noose it with my lariat and take it still alive to the king." Rostam whirled his lariat, intending to snare it by the neck, but as soon as the ass saw the lariat, he suddenly disappeared from before the hero's eyes. Rostam realized that he was not dealing with a wild ass, and that it would be cunning he would have to call on, not strength. He said, "This can only be the Akvan Div, and somehow he must be made to feel the wind of my sword's descent. I've heard from a knowledgeable man that this is the area he haunts, but it's strange that he should take on the shape of a wild ass. I must find some trick by which my sword can stain that golden hide with blood."

Then once again the beast appeared on the plain, and Rostam urged his horse forward. He notched an arrow to his bow, and as he rode like the wind, the arrow flew ahead like fire. But at the moment he drew back his royal bow, the ass once again disappeared. For three days and nights Rostam rode about the plain, until he began to feel the need for water and bread, and he was so exhausted that his head sank down and knocked against the pommel of his saddle. Looking around, he caught sight of a stream as inviting as rosewater; he dismounted and watered Rakhsh, and as he did so he felt his eyes closing in sleep. He loosened the girth and removed the poplar wood saddle from Rakhsh's back and set it down as a pillow beside the stream. He spread out his saddle cloth and lay down to sleep on it, while Rakhsh cropped the grass nearby.

When the Akvan Div saw Rostam asleep in the distance, he transformed himself into a wind rushing over the plain. As soon as he reached the sleeping hero he dug out the soil all round him, and then lifted him up toward the heavens on a great crag of excavated earth. Rostam woke and was alarmed; his wise head whirled in confusion, and as he wriggled this way and that the Akvan Div called out to him:

> "Hey, Rostam, mammoth hero, make a wish!
> Am I to throw you to the ocean fish,
> Or hurl you on some arid mountainside?
> Well, which is it to be, then? You decide."

Rostam realized that in this div's hands all wishes would be turned upside down. He thought, "If he throws me down on a mountain, my body and bones will be smashed. It'll be much better if he throws me in the sea, intending the fishes' bellies to be my winding sheet."

پشه نهاد بیریان

و دیو بدکو آشفته بود

و پی درخشان کاه بام

جای درّاج و قمری نوان

ستایش گرفت آفریننده را | رمانند و از بدتن بنده را | برآسود و بگشاد کرد دمی

کمند و سلاحش خو بفکنم | زره را بپوشید شیر دژم | بدانجای آمد کجا خفت

بدر رخش رخشان درآمد غار | جهانجوی شد تند با روزگار | برآشفت و برداشت...

پاده همیرفت جویان شکار | بپش اندر آمد یکی مرغزار | همه پشه و آبهای...

Rostam replied, "The Chinese sages teach,
'Whoever dies in water will not reach
The heavens, or see Sorush; his fate will be
To haunt this lower earth eternally.'
Throw me upon some mountain top, and there
I'll terrify a lion in its lair."

When the Akvan Div heard Rostam's request, he roared and bore him toward the sea.

"I'm going to hurl you somewhere," he replied,
"Beyond both worlds, where you can't run or hide."

Then he flung him deep into the ocean's depths; but as he descended through the air toward the water, Rostam drew his sword and with this he kept off the sharks and sea monsters that made for him. With his left arm and leg he swam, and with the right he warded off attacks. He struck out immediately, as befits a man used to fighting and hardships, and after a short time, by going steadily in one direction, he caught sight of dry land.

Once he had reached the shore and given thanks to God who had delivered him from evil, he rested and took off his wet tiger skin, spreading it beside a stream until it was dry. He threw away his soaked bow and armor and set off, leaving the sea behind him. He found the stream by which he had slept and where he had been confronted by the evil-natured div.

But his splendid horse Rakhsh was nowhere to be seen in the pastures there, and Rostam railed against fate. Angrily he picked up the saddle and bridle and set off through the night in search of him. As dawn broke he came on a wide meadow filled with clumps of trees and flowing streams. There were partridges everywhere, and he could hear the cooing of turtle-doves; then he found Afrasyab's herdsman, asleep among the trees. Rakhsh was there, charging and neighing among the herd's mares, and Rostam whirled his lariat and snared him by the head.

He rubbed Rakhsh down, saddled him, slipped the bridle over his head, and mounted. Then calling down God's blessing on his sword he set about rounding up the horses. Their thundering hooves woke the bewildered herdsman, who called to his companions for help; grasping lariats and bows, they came galloping to see who the thief was who had dared come to their meadow and challenge so many of them. When Rostam saw them he drew his sword, roared like a lion, "I am Rostam, the son of Zal," and fell upon them. When he had slaughtered two-thirds of them, the herdsman turned and fled; Rostam followed in hot pursuit, an arrow notched to his bow.

It happened that at this time Afrasyab was coming to this very meadow, in a hurry to inspect his horses. He arrived with his entourage and with wine and entertainers, intending to relax for a while in the place where the herdsman watered the herd every year.

But as he drew near the spot there was no sign of either the herdsman or his horses. Then he heard a confused noise coming from the plain, and in the distance he saw the horses galloping and jostling one another, and Rakhsh was visible through the dust sent up by their hooves. Soon the herdsman appeared and told him the whole astonishing story of how he had seen Rostam not only drive off the whole herd single-handed, but also kill many of the herdsman's companions besides.

It became a matter of urgent discussion among the Turks that Rostam had appeared there alone. They said, "This has gone beyond a joke; we must arm ourselves and respond. Or have we become so weak and contemptible that one man can come and kill whoever he wishes? We can't allow a solitary horseman to turn up and drive off our whole herd of horses."

Afrasyab Goes in Pursuit of Rostam

Afrasyab set off with four elephants and a detachment of soldiers in pursuit of Rostam. When they were close enough, Rostam unslung his bow from his shoulder and came riding toward them; he rained arrows down on them as thickly as the clouds rain down dew and then set about them with his steel sword. Having killed sixty of them, he exchanged the sword for his mace, and dispatched forty more. Afrasyab turned tail and fled. Rostam captured the four white elephants, and the Turanian soldiers despaired of life as he pursued them for two parasangs, raining down blows of his mace against their helmets and armor like a spring hail storm. Then he turned back and added the elephants to his plunder.

He returned to the stream in triumph, and once again met with the Akvan Div, who said,

> "Don't you get tired of fighting constantly?
> You fought the savage monsters of the sea,
> Got back to land and, once you'd reached our plain,
> It seems you couldn't wait to fight again!"

When Rostam heard him he roared like a warrior lion; he unhitched his lariat from his saddle and flung it toward the div, who was caught about the waist. Rostam twisted in the saddle and raised his mace, then brought it down with a blow like a blacksmith at his forge. The blow landed on the div's head and his skull and brains were smashed by its force. Rostam dismounted

دگر باره اکوان برو باز خورد | نشستی بدو گفت سیر از هنر | برستی ز رای و چنگ نهنگ | بهشت آمدی ای زبیجان لنگ
تهمتن چو بشنید گفتار دیو | برآورد چون شیر جنگی غریو | ز فتراک کبش کشان کمند | بند سخت و آمد میان بر
بپیچید بر زین و کرد زگران | برآهخت چون پیک آهنگران | بزد بر سر دیو چون پیل مست | سر و مغز او کشت ز ان هم کر

and with his glittering dagger severed the div's head. Then he gave thanks to God who had given him victory on the day of vengeance.

You should realize that the div represents evil people, those who are ungrateful to God. When a man leaves the ways of humanity consider him as a div, not as a person. If you don't appreciate this tale, it may be that you have not seen its real meaning.

Once Rostam had cut off the div's head, he remounted Rakhsh and, driving the herd of horses before him, together with whatever else he had looted from the Turks, he set off toward Khosrow's court. News reached the king that Rostam was returning in glory; he had set off to noose a wild ass, and now he had defeated a div and captured elephants besides. The king and

his court went out to meet him, the courtiers wearing their crowns of office; the procession included elephants, trumpets, and the imperial banner. When Rostam saw the banner and realized that the king was coming to greet him, he dismounted and kissed the ground; the army shouted its approval and the drums and trumpets sounded. The nobles dismounted and only Khosrow remained in the saddle; he ordered Rostam to remount Rakhsh and the procession made its way cheerfully back to Khosrow's camp.

Rostam distributed the horses to the Iranian army, keeping none back for himself, as he considered only Rakhsh suitable to be his own mount. The elephants he gave to Kay Khosrow, as worthy of a lionlike king. The court spent a week rejoicing with wine and music and entertainers, and when Rostam was in his cups he told the king about the Akvan Div, saying, "I never saw such a majestic wild ass, of such a splendid color; but when my sword cut its hide, it was an enemy I saw, not a friend. It had a head like an elephant's, long hair, and a mouth full of boar's tusks; its two eyes were white and its lips black; its body didn't bear looking at. No animal is like him, and he'd turned that whole plain into a sea of blood; when I cut his head off with my dagger, blood spurted into the air like rain."

Kay Khosrow was astonished; he set down his wine cup and thanked God for creating such a hero, the equal of whom the world had never seen.

Two weeks passed with feasting, pleasure, and telling stories, and when the third began Rostam decided to return home in triumph. He said, "I long to see Zal, my father, and I can't hide this wish any longer. I shall make a quick journey home and return to court, and then we can plan our campaign. Capturing a few horses is too trivial to count as vengeance for the blood of Seyavash."

Kay Khosrow opened the doors of his treasury. He had a goblet filled with pearls brought, and five royal robes worked with gold, as well as Rumi slaves with golden belts, girls with gold torques about their necks, carpets and an ivory throne, brocade and coins and a crown studded with turquoise. All these he sent to Rostam saying, "Take them as a present for your journey. But stay today; tomorrow we can think about your leaving." Rostam stayed that day, drinking with the king, but when night came he was determined to leave. The king accompanied him two parasangs of the way, and then the two embraced and bade farewell to one another. Kay Khosrow took the way back to his court, and the world was filled with his justice and goodness, while Rostam continued on the journey to Zabol.

A night as black as coal bedaubed with pitch,
A night of ebony, a night on which
Mars, Mercury, and Saturn would not rise.
Even the moon seemed fearful of the skies:
Her face was three-fourths dimmed, and all the night
Looked gray and dusty in her pallid light.
On plain and mountainside dark henchmen laid
Night's raven carpet, shade on blacker shade;
The heavens seemed rusted iron, as if each star
Were blotted out by tenebrous, thick tar;
Dark Ahriman appeared on every side
Like a huge snake whose jaws gape open wide.
The garden and the stream by which I lay
Became a sea of pitch; it seemed that day
Would never come, the skies no longer turned,
The weakened sun no longer moved or burned.
Fear gripped the world and utter silence fell,
Stilling the clamor of the watchman's bell,
Silencing all the myriad cries and calls
Of everything that flies or walks or crawls.
I started up, bewildered, terrified;
My fear awoke the woman at my side.
I called for her to bring me torches, light;
She fetched bright candles to dispel the night
And laid a little feast on which to dine,
Red pomegranates, citrons, quinces, wine,
Together with a polished goblet fit
For kings or emperors to drink from it.
"But why do you need candles now?" she said.
"Has sleep refused to visit your soft bed?
Drink up your wine and—as you do so—I
Will tell a story from the days gone by,
A story full of love and trickery,
Whose hero lived for war and chivalry."
"Sweet moon," I said, "my cypress, my delight,
Tell me this tale to wile away the night."
"First listen well," she said, "and when you've heard
The story through, record it word for word."

The Story Begins

When Kay Khosrow decided on revenge for his father's death, he put the world's affairs on a new footing; the crown of Turan began to lose its luster, and the Persian throne gained in glory. The heavens smiled on Iran and its people; the world was renewed again, as in its early days, and Khosrow washed his face in the waters of loyalty and good faith, although no wise man will put his trust in this world where all things flow away like water.

One day Khosrow was sitting with his warrior chieftains at an entertainment. His throne was draped with brocade and he wore a jeweled crown; in his hand was a cup encrusted with rubies and filled with wine, and the heart-ravishing sound of harps echoed in his ears. Their wine cups filled with wine like rubies from the Yemen and white roses set out before each one, his loyal nobles surrounded him: Kavus's son Fariborz, Gostaham, Gudarz, Farhad, Giv, Gorgin, Shapur, Nozar's son Tus, Roham, and Bizhan. Serving girls stood before Khosrow, their hair like musk, their skin like jasmine; all the court was alive with color, perfumes, and beauty, and the king's chancellor presided over the feast.

A doorman entered and went over to the chancellor; he said that a delegation from the Ermani tribe, who inhabit the border region between Iran and Turan, were outside asking to see the king. They had traveled a long way and were demanding justice. The chancellor relayed their request to the king who granted them audience; they were brought in according to court protocol, their arms crossed over their chests, and when they had kissed the ground they presented their petition to the throne. In deep distress they said, "Great king, may you live victorious and forever. We have traveled a weary way from our country, Erman, which lies between Iran and Turan, and we bring you a sorrowful message. You are the scourge of evil in seven countries, the prop of the helpless, and long may you flourish! Our country borders Turan, from which great disasters have come to us. Within our marches, toward Iran, is a forest, parts of which we have cultivated. It's full of fruit trees and we also pasture our flocks there; in short, we depend on this area and we appeal to the king to help us. Innumerable wild boar have overrun this forest; their tusks are like an elephant's, they're of mountainous size, and they are destroying the land of Erman, killing our animals, trampling our crops, smashing with their tusks trees that have been there for longer than anyone can remember. Granite is not as tough as their tusks, and we fear that our good fortune is at an end."

When the king had heard them out he pitied their plight and he turned to his chieftains:

> "Who is ambitious for success and fame?
> Which warrior here is worthy of the name?

> *Who'll chop these wild pigs' heads off with his sword?*
> *I won't be miserly with my reward!"*

Then he ordered his treasurer to bring in a golden tray heaped high with jewels jumbled pell-mell together; near this was set a quantity of brocade, and ten horses branded with Kavus's mark and caparisoned with golden bridles were led in. Once again he turned to his nobles and said,

> *"Who here will do the bidding of the throne,*
> *And with his efforts make my wealth his own?"*

No one answered, except Bizhan, son of the great warrior Giv: he stood and said, "Long may your realm and clan flourish, and the world submit to your authority. I will undertake this mission, my body and soul are yours to command."

Giv glanced up and it was clear that he was worried by his son's remark. He made his obeisance to the king, then turned to Bizhan: "This is mere young man's talk. What makes you so sure of your strength? A youth might be knowledgeable and of good family but he won't manage anything without experience. He has to see the world first, both good and bad, and he has to taste life's bitterness. Don't go wandering off where you've never been before, and don't make such a fool of yourself in front of the king!"

Bizhan was a quick-witted young man whose star was rising; he was infuriated by his father's talk and he turned directly to the king: "Don't think I'm not capable of this; believe me, I have the strength of a young man and the wisdom of a graybeard: I'll cut these wild pigs' heads off or I am not Bizhan, the son of Giv, destroyer of armies." Khosrow responded, "You are full of talents, and may you always be our shield against evil; any king who has a subject like you would be a fool to fear his enemies." Then he turned to Gorgin, Milad's son, and said, "Bizhan is young and ignorant of the way: be his guide and companion to where the river marks the boundary of our domain."

Bizhan tightened his belt, placed his helmet on his head, and prepared to leave. He took Gorgin as a companion to turn to if anything should go wrong, and the two set off with hawks and cheetahs intending to hunt as they proceeded on their long journey.

Like an elephant foaming at the mouth, Bizhan gave chase to wild asses and gazelles, slicing off their heads; his cheetahs brought down mouflon, ripping their bellies open, the rest of the flock scattering in terror. With his bow Bizhan was like another Tahmures, the binder of demons, and his hawks' talons made such havoc among the pheasants that their blood spotted the jasmine plants by the wayside. Indeed, Bizhan and Gorgin went forward as if the plain were their private hunting park.

They reached the forest of wild boar; the animals were milling about with no knowledge that Bizhan had saddled his horse to deal with them, and the young warrior was enraged by their number and effrontery. He said to Gorgin, "Let's go in together, or, if you'd rather, you wait over by the lakeside there, while I attack them with my arrows. When you hear them squealing among the trees, have your mace ready for any that escape me."

But Gorgin said, "This is not what we agreed to before the king: you took all the jewels and gold and silver, and you agreed to do the fighting; all you could expect from me was that I show you the way here." Bizhan frowned in astonishment at this response; nevertheless, he entered the forest like a lion and set about shooting arrows at the herd of boar. His war cry was like a spring cloud's thunder, and the trees' leaves came pattering down like rain. He went after the herd like an enraged elephant, a glittering dagger in his hand; they turned to charge him, tearing up the ground with their tusks, sparking fire where their tusks struck rock, as if they would burn the world. One sprang at Bizhan like a devil, ripping open his armor, then withdrew and rubbed its tusks against a tree, as if it were an armorer honing a sword on stone. But when it renewed its attack, the young warrior plunged his dagger into its belly, splitting its mammoth body in two. Then the remaining boar scattered like foxes, their bodies wounded, their hearts sick of combat. Bizhan lopped off the heads of those he'd killed with his dagger and fixed them to his saddlestraps. He intended to take the tusks back to the king and to display the severed heads to the court as a demonstration of his prowess; their combined weight would have exhausted a buffalo.

Resentful and scheming, Gorgin emerged from where he had been lurking; he was so filled with chagrin that the forest appeared like pitch to him. He congratulated Bizhan and made a show of rejoicing at his success, afraid of the shame that might come to him from this business. Ahriman twisted his heart; forgetful of God, for the sake of his own reputation, he began to plot against Bizhan and spread a snare before him.

He said, "My congratulations; you've a warrior's heart and a wise man's soul; God and your good fortune have given you victory here. There's something I wanted to tell you: I've been in these parts a few times before, with Rostam, Giv, and Gostaham. Tus was here, too, and Gazhdaham. What splendid deeds we did on this wide plain then; how famous we became, and how dearly Khosrow loved us! But the heavens have moved on since then. About two days' journey from here, toward Turan, there's a place where people gather to hold festivals; you'll see a wide pasture, all green and gold, a sight to rejoice any free man's heart. The landscape is filled with copses of trees, flowers, flowing streams; it's a place worthy of a hero. The ground's as soft as silk, the air's scented like musk, the streams seem to flow with rosewater; jasmine tendrils bow down to the ground with the weight of their flowers, and the roses there are incomparably beautiful; pheasants strut among the rosebushes, and nightingales sing from the cypress branches.

"In a few days from now the whole area will be like a paradise, the meadows and mountain slopes dotted with groups of angelic young women, all led by Manizheh, the daughter of Afrasyab. She and her attendants will be staying there; the Turkish girls are cypress-slender, smelling of musk, with faces like rose petals, languorous eyes, lips that taste of wine and rosewater. If we hurried we could be there in a day, and we could seize a few of these delectable girls and take them back in triumph to Khosrow."

When Bizhan heard this his young blood was roused; he agreed to the venture, partly from a thirst for fame, but partly too for the pleasure it promised. The two set off on the long journey, one urged on by desire, the other by malice. They traveled for a day between two forested areas, and then spent two cheerful days hunting in the Ermani grasslands. Gorgin knew that Manizheh was not far off, and that the whole plain was as bright as a pheasant's eye with her entourage, and so he repeated to Bizhan what he had said about the festival held there.

Bizhan said, "I'll go on ahead; I'll spy out the festival from a distance, to see how the Turanians manage these things. Then I'll ride back here and we can decide what to do. I'll be able to think better once I've seen them." Then he turned to his steward and said, "Bring me my golden diadem that looks so splendid at banquets, and the torque and earrings Kay Khosrow gave me, and the armbands covered in jewels that I have from my father." He also asked for a jeweled belt, then wrapped himself in a splendid Rumi cloak and fixed an eagle's feather to his diadem. His horse Shabrang was saddled and he set off for the festival, his ambitious heart filled with curiosity.

When he came in sight of the festivities, he stretched out beneath a cypress tree, to stay out of the sun. He was close to the princess's tent, and he felt his heart fill with longing. The whole plain echoed with the sound of music and singing, as if welcoming his soul. The princess peered from her tent and saw the stretched-out warrior, his cheeks as bright as Canopus in the skies above Yemen, or like jasmine petals encircled by dark violets, an imperial diadem on his head, a brocade cloak covering his body. Within her tent the princess felt the force of love, and she made no attempt to veil herself from the stranger. She said to her nurse,

"Go quickly over there; find out for me
Who's lying underneath that cypress tree:
I think it's Seyavash, or else he seems
More like the angels that we see in dreams.
Ask him, 'What brings you here? Won't you at least

Join in our festival and share our feast?
Are you Prince Seyavash, then? Or are you
An angel's child? Because whichever's true,
You've lit in me a fire that makes me fear
The world will end and Judgment Day is near.
I've come here every year to celebrate
The spring's arrival on this happy date,
But never saw a stranger here before:
Now I've seen you, and I shall see no more.'"

When the nurse reached Bizhan, she bowed to him and spoke as Manizheh had instructed her. Bizhan blushed like a rose, then said confidently enough, "Messenger of your beautiful mistress, I am not Seyavash, nor am I born of an angel; I'm from Iran, from the land of the free. I am Bizhan, Giv's son, and I traveled here from Iran to fight against wild boar. I cut their heads off and left them lying in the dirt; I'm going to take their tusks back to my king. When I heard about this festival, I put off returning to my father: I thought my good fortune might show me the face of Afrasyab's daughter in my dreams. And now I see this plain decked out like a Chinese temple with splendor and wealth. If you treat me well I'll give you a golden diadem, earrings, and a belt; take me to your beautiful mistress, and incline her heart favorably toward me."

The nurse returned to Manizheh and whispered in her ear, describing his face, his stature, and how God had made him. Straightaway Manizheh sent her back, with the message, "If you come over to me and brighten my dismal soul, you will find you have gained what you dreamed of." When Bizhan heard this, the time for talk was over; full of hope and curiosity, he walked from the tree's shade to the princess's tent.

He entered the tent, tall as a cypress; Manizheh embraced him and removed his gold-worked belt. She asked him about his journey, and which warriors had accompanied him on his expedition. "And why," she said, "should such a handsome and noble person be tiring himself out with a mace?" She washed his feet in rosewater and musk and had an elaborate meal set before the two of them; wine was brought and the tent was cleared of everyone except Manizheh's musicians, who stood before them with lutes and harps. The ground was spread with brocade sewn with gold coins and embroidered like a peacock, and the tent was filled with the scents of ambergris and musk. Old wine in crystal goblets overcame the warrior's defenses; for three days and nights the two were happy in each other's company, till finally drink and sleep defeated Bizhan.

The time for departure came, and Manizheh felt she could not bear to be separated from Bizhan; seeing his sad face she called her serving girls and had them prepare a soporific drug which they mingled with his drink.

They fitted up a traveling litter, so that one side was for pleasure, the other for sleep; the sandalwood of the sleeping area was drenched in camphor and rosewater, and there they set the unconscious warrior. As they approached the town Manizheh covered him with a cloth; stealthily, at night, Bizhan was conveyed into the castle, and she mentioned her secret to no one.

After his long sleep Bizhan awoke to find his beloved in his arms; he was in Afrasyab's palace, and Manizheh's face was beside him on the pillow. He started up in alarm and cried out to God for protection against Ahriman: "How can I ever escape from this place? Listen to my sufferings, take revenge for me on Gorgin; he it was who led me into this, who deceived me with a thousand tricks."

But Manizheh said, "Live happily, my love, and reckon as wind what has not yet happened. All kinds of fate come to men, sometimes feasting, sometimes fighting." They prepared to eat, not knowing whether a gallows awaited them or a marriage ceremony. Manizheh called for musicians; each of the young women was dressed in Chinese brocade and, to the sound of their lutes, Bizhan and Manizheh passed the day in pleasure.

Afrasyab Learns of Bizhan's Presence

A few days passed in this way, and then gossip caused disaster's tree to tremble. A rumor reached the court chamberlain, and he secretly investigated the matter, tracing the reports back to their source. He inquired as to where the interloper was from and why he had come to Turan; when he found out, he feared for his own life and made all haste to save himself. He saw no choice but to tell the king and ran to him with the news: "Your daughter has taken a lover from Iran." Outraged by Manizheh's behavior, the king shook like a willow tree in a storm, called on God to aid him, and sent for his councilor Qara Khan. "Give me," he said, "good advice as to what to do with this shameless woman."

Qara Khan replied, "First enquire more closely into the accusation. If the matter turns out to be as you say, then I have nothing to add. But hearing about something is not the same as seeing it." Afrasyab turned to Garsivaz and said, "How much we've endured at the hands of Iran and will endure in the future! And now Fate has added a faithless daughter to my troubles from that country. Go with loyal horsemen and watch the gates and roofs; tie up any stranger you find within the palace and bring him here."

His men surrounded the inner palace, occupied the roofs, and kept a watch on the exits while Garsivaz approached the main door. He found it secured from the inside, and sounds of feasting and revelry could be clearly heard. Garsivaz tore the door from its hinges and leaped into the chamber beyond; immediately, he made his way to the room where Bizhan was.

When he saw Bizhan, his blood boiled with rage; three hundred serving girls and musicians were there, singing to lutes and serving wine. Bizhan sprang up in fear, his one thought being how he could fight without his armor or his horse Shabrang. He was alone and his father Giv could not help him now; God was his only recourse.

He had always kept a glittering dagger inside one boot, and this he now drew as he leaped toward the door, saying:

> "I am Bizhan, Giv's warlike son; I claim
> An ancient Persian family's noble name.
> No one skins me, unless he's sick of life
> And wants his head slashed open with this knife;
> And if the earth resounds with Judgment Day,
> No man will ever see me run away.
> If you insist on war, prepare for war—
> I'll soak my fists in your Turanian gore
> And hack your heads off. But if you agree
> To intercede before your king for me,
> I'll tell him why I'm here. You are a knight,
> Be chivalrous and we won't need to fight."

Garsivaz saw what Bizhan was about, but he also saw the sharp dagger in his hand and knew that he meant it when he said he would soak his fists in their blood. He swore a solemn oath that he would do as Bizhan suggested, and with his promises he managed to cajole the dagger from Bizhan's hand. He then talked him into allowing himself to be bound in fetters; they trussed him up like a caught cheetah.

> When Fortune turns her face away from you,
> What can your manly skills or virtues do?

And so Bizhan was haled before Afrasyab, bareheaded, and with his hands bound. He greeted the king and said, "If you want the truth from me, here it is: I had no desire to come to this court and no one is to blame for my being here. I came from Iran to destroy a herd of wild boar and found myself near your borders. I sent my people to search for a lost hawk, while I sheltered from the sun under a cypress tree and fell asleep there. A denizen of fairyland came and spread her wings over me and gathered me up, while I was still sleeping, to her bosom. She separated me from my horse and took me along the path where your daughter and her escort of soldiers were. The plain was filled with horsemen, and various litters and palanquins passed me by. In the distance an Indian parasol appeared, surrounded by Turanian cavalry, and as it came closer I saw that the parasol covered a splendid litter in which lay a beautiful young woman; a crown was on the pillow beside her. The being that held me repeated the name 'Ahriman' a few times and then like a mighty wind swooped down among the horsemen; suddenly she set me in the litter and whispered a spell over the woman there so that she remained asleep until we entered the castle. I wept to see her, but I've committed no sin, and Manizheh has suffered no stain or taint of guilt in all this. I think the being who did this to me must have been a fairy of ill omen."

But Afrasyab said, "Bad luck's caught up with you, and none too soon. You came from Iran with your bow, looking for a fight and hoping to make a name for yourself; now you stand in front of me defenseless as a woman and with your hands tied, prattling about dreams as if you were drunk. You think you can deceive me with your lies?"

Bizhan replied, "You majesty, listen to what I have to say for a moment, and realize its truth: a boar can fight anywhere with its tusks, as a lion can with its claws; warriors need a sword, a mace, a bow in order to fight against their enemies. You can't have on the one side a man naked and with his hands tied, and on the other a man armored in mail; no matter how brave it might be, how can a lion fight without its claws? If the king wishes me to show my prowess before his men, let him have a horse and a heavy mace brought here. Then he can set a thousand of his horsemen against me, and if I leave one of them alive, never call me a man again."

When he heard this, Afrasyab glared at Bizhan in fury and turned to Garsivaz. "You see how he's still plotting against me; the evil he's done already's not enough for him, he asks to be allowed to kill my men in combat! Take him bound as he is and get rid of him; have a gallows erected before my castle gates so that everyone who passes by will see him. String him up and never mention him to me again, so that the Persians will know not to come snooping around here any more."

As they dragged Bizhan to the door he wept in bitterness of heart, and said, "If God has written on my forehead that I am to die in an evil time, I fear neither death nor the gallows. I fear the warriors of Iran; I fear that my enemies among them will call me a coward because I was strung up unwounded; I fear that my noble ancestors will reproach me, and that my soul will linger here, having shamed my father."

The Arrival of Piran

God pitied his youth and confounded his enemies' plans. While the pit for the gallows was being dug, Piran appeared in the distance; as he approached he saw a gallows being erected with a noose swinging from it and called out, "Who is to be hanged here? And is the king's gateway a fitting place to raise a gibbet?"

Garsivaz answered, "This is for Bizhan, the king's enemy, who comes from Iran."

Piran urged his horse forward and came up to Bizhan; he saw he was in great distress, naked, dry-mouthed, and pale, with his hands tied tightly behind his back. He said, "How did you come to be here? Did you come to Turan looking for bloodshed?" Bizhan told him his tale of bad luck, and Piran wept to hear it. He ordered the soldiers to pause before hanging him, to wait until he had talked with the king and pointed out to him where his best interests lay.

He entered the court humbly, his arms folded across his chest, bowed before Afrasyab, and waited. The king realized he had some petition to make and laughed, saying:

> "Out with it then! Tell me, what's your request?
> Noblest of all my chieftains, and the best,
> If you want gold or jewels or wealth from me,
> If you want troops, or arms, or sovereignty,
> You know my goods are yours, as payment for
> Your peerless services in peace and war."

Loyal Piran kissed the ground, stood, and said, "May your auspicious reign never end; the world's kings praise you and your splendor is like the sun's. Whatever I have—be it people, wealth, or authority—is from you; my request is not for myself, since no subject of yours wants for anything. I have given the king advice on many matters many times before this, but my advice was not followed. I told you not to kill Kavus's son, Seyavash, who was of royal lineage and who was tireless on your behalf, as this would make Rostam and Tus your enemies, bringing them from Iran on their war elephants, tearing apart the bonds that unite us. And have you not seen the damage the Persians have done to our country, trampling two-thirds of it underfoot, making our lives bitter as brackish water? And Zal's sword is still not sheathed; his son Rostam is still lopping off heads with it and staining the sun with blood. Now that there's the chance of peace, you're looking to stir up new troubles, foolishly sniffing at the poisoned blossoms of hatred. If you spill Bizhan's blood, once again the dust of vengeance will rise up from Turan. The king is wise and I am his subject, but open your heart's eyes to the truth. Think how the king of Iran has profited from our enmity, and yet you're trying to provoke it further, to make disaster's tree bear fruit again. We cannot survive a second war against them; no one knows Giv, and that monster Rostam, or iron-fisted Gudarz better than you do."

Piran threw cold water on the raging fire, but Afrasyab replied, "And you don't know what Bizhan has done to me, embarrassing me before all Turan and Iran. Can't you see the humiliation that shameless daughter of mine has brought to my white hairs, destroying my women's reputation in the world? My whole country and army will make fun of my disgrace for ever. If he escapes from me with his life, everyone will reproach me; I'll spend the rest of my days weeping, disgraced, and despised."

Piran repeatedly called down heaven's blessing on the king and said, "My noble lord, favored by fortune, all is as you say, and it's your reputation that's at stake. But consider my suggestion carefully: chain him in heavy chains, such that he'd rather die on the gallows than suffer the pain they bring. This will teach the Persians a lesson, and they won't be in such a hurry to plot against us in the future. Any man who languishes in your dungeons is not going to be reckoned a useful warrior."

The king followed his advice and said to Garsivaz, "Prepare a dark pit and heavy chains: bind his arms tightly, shackle him hand and foot, and hang him head down within the pit so that he sees neither sun nor moon. Take elephants, and have them drag here the huge rock that the Akvan Div wrenched from the ocean depths; cover the pit's entrance with it, and let Bizhan suffer there till he loses his mind. Then go with your cavalry to that shameless hussy Manizheh's palace and destroy it; strip her of her crown and status and say to her, 'Wretched woman, you deserve neither crown nor throne; you have shamed the king before his ancestors and dragged their noble name in the dust.' Then hale her to the pit and say to her,

> 'See in this pit now, naked and alone,
> The man you set beside you on your throne;
> You were the springtime of his life; now be
> His friend and jailer in adversity.'"

Garsivaz strode from the king's presence to carry out his evil orders. Bizhan was dragged from beneath the gallows to a deep pit, loaded from head to foot with heavy chains, and lowered head down into its darkness. A stone was placed over the opening, and from there Garsivaz led his men to Manizheh's quarters; her wealth was plundered, and the crown torn from her head. Barefoot, clad only in her shift, her hair loose, her face smeared with blood and tears, Manizheh was dragged stumbling to the pit's edge. There Garsivaz said to her, "Here is your lord and household; you're to be this prisoner's jailer forever."

For a day and a night Manizheh wandered moaning about the wilderness. As dawn approached she came back to the pit's edge and scrabbled away the dirt beneath the stone till she could force her hand into the darkness. When the sun rose above the mountain tops she began to go from door to door, begging for bread. At the end of the day she brought the scraps she had collected and pushed them through the opening she'd made, offering them to Bizhan. And so, in grief and wretchedness, she passed her days.

Gorgin Returns to Iran without Bizhan

After a week, Gorgin saw that Bizhan had not returned and he began to search for him everywhere, his face bathed in tears of shame. He regretted what he had done and wondered how he could have betrayed his companion like this. He hurried in the direction Bizhan had taken and went through the groves of trees looking for him, but he saw no one and heard not even so much as a bird's song. He scoured the meadows calling for his friend, and finally caught sight of Bizhan's horse in the distance. The reins were loose, the saddle had slipped down, and the horse's lower lip hung pendulous, as if the animal were consumed with rage. Gorgin gave Bizhan up for lost, certain that he would never return to Iran: either he had been strung up on a gallows or was languishing chained in a pit, but it was clear that Afrasyab had harmed him in some way. Gorgin flung down his lariat and turned aside his face in shame; he was sorry for what he had done and longed to see his friend. He led Bizhan's horse back to their camp and rested there for a day; then he set out for Iran, travelling day and night without stopping to sleep.

When the king learned that Gorgin was returning without Bizhan, he told Giv to ask Gorgin what had become of his son. Giv ran weeping into the street, his heart filled with anxiety, crying out, "Bizhan has not come back, and why should he stay with the Ermani?" He ordered that a horse he had used in crises before be saddled; inwardly raging like a leopard, he rode out to meet Gorgin, intending to ask him where Bizhan was, and what had happened. To himself he said, "This Gorgin has secretly and suddenly tricked him; if I find it's true that he's coming back without Bizhan, I'll cut his head off there and then."

Gorgin saw Giv approaching. He dismounted and ran forward, then groveled in the dust before him, his head bared and his cheeks scored by his nails. He said, "My lord, you are the king's elect, the leader of his armies, why have you come out to meet me, your eyes flowing with tears? I return sick at heart, and seeing you, my wretchedness increases; I look at you and my face is bathed in shame's hot tears. But don't fear for him; no harm has come to him, and I can give you proof of this."

When Giv heard the warrior's words and saw his son's dusty, desolate horse led by Gorgin, he fell from his own mount as if unconscious. His head sank into the dust; moaning, he tore at his clothes and hair and beard, and cried out, "God of the heavens, who has placed intelligence and love in my heart, now that I have lost my son it is right that the bonds of life dissolve in me; take me to where the blessed spirits live, you who know better than I do the extent of my heart's sorrow. In all the world he was all I had, as a companion and as a help in times of trouble; now that ill fortune has taken him from me, I am left here to grieve alone."

Again he turned to Gorgin. "Tell me what happened, from the beginning. Did Fate suddenly snatch him away, or did he leave you of his own accord? What disaster overtook him? Tell me what snare the heavens laid for him, what devil confronted him and destroyed him in the uplands there. Where did you find his abandoned horse? Where did you lose sight of Bizhan?"

Gorgin replied, "Calm yourself, and listen to my words carefully. Know, then, my lord—and may your presence always lend splendor to our court— what happened, and how it happened, while we were fighting the wild boar. We traveled from here to confront the herd and when we reached the borders of Erman we saw a once-wooded region that had been leveled as flat as the palm of a hand; all the trees had been torn down, and the whole area was full of boars' lairs. We seized our spears and went to work, yelling to drive the boar into the open and fighting like lions; the day ended and we still weren't tired of our task. Like charging elephants we drove them before us, and we hacked out their tusks with chisels. Then we set off on the return journey to Iran, rejoicing and hunting as we came. Suddenly a wild ass appeared, more beautiful than any ever seen before; its coat was like that of Gudarz's horse, it had Farhad's horse's muzzle, feet like the Simorgh's, but with steel hooves, and its head, ears, and tail were like those of Bizhan's horse, Shabrang. Its mane was like a lion's, and it was as swift as the wind; you'd think it had been sired by Rakhsh. It made for Bizhan like a towering elephant, and he noosed it with his lariat, but it charged off into the distance, dragging Bizhan out of sight. Their struggle sent a cloud of dust into the air and both the wild ass and his captor disappeared from view. I searched everywhere, until my mount was exhausted, but I found no trace of Bizhan: all I could discover was his horse, trailing its saddle in the dust. I stayed there for a long time calling Bizhan's name, but finally I gave up and decided that the wild ass must have been the White Demon. My heart burned with anxiety, wondering how his struggle with the Demon had turned out."

When Giv heard this speech he knew that something terrible had happened; he saw that Gorgin was talking at random, his eyes downcast, his fearful face the color of straw, his trembling voice indicative of his guilty heart. Giv thought that his son was lost to him, and he saw that Gorgin was lying; Ahriman plucked at his heart, and he longed to take revenge for his son's disappearance, no matter how shameful such a course might seem. But then he reflected that this would clarify nothing. "What good will it do me to kill him now?" he thought. "It will only make Ahriman glad and profit Bizhan nothing at all. I must look for another way forward. I'll tell Gorgin's tale to the king and see if that will clear matters up; I can easily take my revenge later, as he has no defense against my spear if I choose to use it."

Giv roared at Gorgin, "You devil's spawn, you've taken the sun and moon from my life, you've stolen away the king's chosen champion, you're forcing me to travel the world in search of relief for my sorrow—how can you sleep or rest enmeshed in such lies and deceit? But I shall go before the king, and after that I shall be revenged on you with my dagger."

And so he went to the king, and after greeting him respectfully and wishing him long life and good fortune, he said,

> "In all the world I had but one delight—
> My son, for whom I fretted day and night,
> For whose pure soul I wept paternal tears;
> To lose him was the worst of all my fears.
> And now Gorgin returns alone and tries
> To hide his guilty soul with specious lies;
> He brings bad news of my beloved son
> And has no sign of him to show but one—
> A riderless, led horse. Your majesty,
> Look closely at this matter and you'll see
> That my demand for vengeance here is just;
> Gorgin has brought my head down to the dust."

The king was moved by Giv's grief; he turned pale and grew sick at heart thinking of Bizhan. He asked Giv, "What did Gorgin say about where Bizhan is?" Giv told him Gorgin's tale, and Khosrow answered, "Think no more of this, mourn no longer; Bizhan is alive and you should live in hopes of seeing your lost son again. I have agreed with my priests that I and my troops shall soon set out for Turan to fight in the war of vengeance for Seyavash: I and my elephants will overcome that country, and Bizhan will be there by my side, fighting like a devil on our behalf. Grieve no more; I am as eager as you are to see him again." Giv left his presence, his heart filled with pain and grief, his cheeks sallow, his eyes wet with tears.

When Gorgin arrived at Khosrow's court he found it empty; the courtiers had left with Giv to comfort him. Gorgin went forward, shamefaced and apprehensive, kissed the ground before Khosrow, and greeted him. He placed the boars' tusks, glittering like diamonds, before the king, and said, "May the king be victorious in all things, may all his days be springtime, and may the heads of all his enemies be cut off as I cut off these boars' heads!"

Khosrow looked at the tusks and questioned Gorgin about the expedition, asking how he had been separated from Bizhan and what disaster had befallen him. At first Gorgin was speechless, but then he began to tell his lying tale, trembling from fear of the king. But before he could finish, Khosrow, realizing that his confusion indicated his guilt, started up and pushed him away from the throne, reviling him: "Haven't you heard the old saying that even a lion who arouses the vengeance of Gudarz's clan will perish miserably? If you weren't such a wretch, and so certain to come to a bad end, I'd have your head twisted off like a chicken's!"

Khosrow gave orders that blacksmiths fashion heavy shackles for him, and that his feet be fettered, so that he could reflect on the evil he'd done. To Giv, Khosrow said, "Calm yourself, we must begin the search for Bizhan. I shall send out a thousand horsemen to see if they can find news of him, and if we hear nothing at first, do not despair. Wait until spring brings in the new year, and the sun renews the world; then when the flowers reappear and the earth turns green again, and the breezes are laden with scent, I shall pray to Hormoz. I shall have the world-revealing cup that shows the seven climes brought to me, and I shall invoke God's blessings on our noble ancestors. Then I will tell you where Bizhan is, since the cup will answer my prayers."

Giv's heart was reassured, and he thanked the king and wished him long life and prosperity.

As soon as Giv had left the king's presence, he sent out horsemen in every direction to see if they could find some trace of his son. They covered all Iran and Turan but found nothing, so that when the spring came and the world was renewed the king turned to the world-revealing cup.

Hopeful for news of his son, Giv entered the court, and when Khosrow saw him bent over and withered away with worry, he put on the Rumi cloak he wore to pray. He cried out to God, calling down blessings on the sun as it inaugurated the new year, and asked for strength and help to defeat the power of Ahriman. Then he returned in solemn procession to his palace, replaced the crown on his head, and took the cup in his hands. He stared into it and saw the world's seven climes, the turnings of the heavens, all that happened there, and how and why things came to pass. He saw from the sign of Pisces to that of Aries, he saw Saturn, Mars, the sun, Leo, Venus, Mercury above, and the moon below. The royal magician saw all that was to be seen. Searching for some sign of Bizhan, his gaze traversed the seven climes until he reached the land of the Gorgsaran, and there he saw him, bound with chains in a pit, longing for death; beside him princess Manizheh stood, ready to serve him. The king turned toward Giv and his smile lit up the council chamber. "Rejoice, Bizhan is alive, rid yourself of your anxiety. He is imprisoned, but this is small cause for grief, because he is alive and a noble woman is attending him. He suffers terrible pains, and it hurts me to see him like this, weeping, despairing of help from his family, trembling like a willow tree. But who can go to his rescue, who is loyal enough to undertake this expedition, to save him from his sorrows? Only Rostam, who can pluck monsters from the sea's depths, is fit for this task. Go to Zavolestan and travel day and night without rest; take my letter but breathe not a word of it to anyone as you go."

Khosrow's Letter to Rostam

A scribe was called in and the king dictated a friendly letter to Rostam:

> *"Great Rostam, noblest of our warriors,*
> *Whose deeds remind us of our ancestors,*
> *Leopards submit to you, sea-monsters roar*
> *In terror when you walk upon the shore,*
> *Persia's stout heart, prop of our sovereignty,*
> *Prompt with your help in all adversity:*
> *The demons of Mazanderan were slain*
> *By you, your mace destroyed their evil reign.*
> *How many kings, how many enemies*
> *You've conquered, and how many provinces!*
> *To pluck from darkness any mortal who*
> *In peril or affliction turns to you,*
> *The Lord has given you a mammoth's might*
> *And lionhearted courage when you fight.*
> *Gudarz and Giv in their despair now ask*
> *For your assistance in a worthy task;*
> *You know how close this clan remains to me,*
> *Never have they endured such agony.*
> *Giv has a single son, and all his joy,*
> *His hopes of life, are centered on this boy;*
> *To me he's been a loyal courtier who*
> *Will do whatever I command him to.*
> *Now, when you read this letter, don't delay,*
> *Return with Giv, hear what he has to say;*
> *In council we'll decide what must be done*
> *To save this noble warrior's captive son.*
> *I'll provide men and treasure, you're to free*
> *Bizhan from his Turanian misery."*

Khosrow sealed the letter; Giv took it, made his obeisance to the king, and went home to prepare for the journey. He rode with his clansmen, quick as a hunted animal, covering two days' travel in each day, crossing the desert and heading for the River Hirmand. When he reached Gurabad a lookout saw him and shouted that a warrior and his entourage were approaching the riverbank; the leader carried a Kaboli sword in his fist, and they were followed by a banner flapping in the wind. Rostam's father, Zal, heard the lookout's cry and rode out to meet them, so that they would have no reason to act hostilely toward him. As he saw Giv coming, his face downcast and preoccupied, he said to himself, "Something has happened to the king, there's no other reason for Giv to come here." When he met up with them he asked after the king, and how the war with Turan was faring. Giv greeted him respectfully from Khosrow, and then unburdened his heart, telling him the tale of his lost son. He asked for Rostam, and Zal answered, "He's out hunting wild asses: when the sun goes down he'll be back." Giv said, "I'll go and find him, I have a letter from Khosrow I have to give him." But Zal answered, "Stay here, he'll be here soon; come to my house and spend the day feasting with me."

But as Giv entered the outer court Rostam was seen returning from the hunt. Giv went out to greet him and dismounted before him. Hope flared up in his heart and the color came back to his face, although his eyes were still filled with tears. When Rostam saw the anxiety in his expression and the marks of tears on his face, he said to himself, "Some disaster has happened to Iran and to the king." He dismounted and embraced Giv, asking after Khosrow, and then for news of Gudarz, Tus, Gazhdaham, and various other warriors at the Persian court such as Shapur, Farhad, Bizhan, Roham, and Gorgin. When Giv heard the name "Bizhan," a cry escaped from his lips and he said to Rostam, "My lord, all kings honor you, and I am happy to see you and to hear you speak so kindly; those you ask after are well, and they send their greetings to you. But you don't know the terrible calamity that has stricken me in my old age; the evil eye has lighted on Gudarz's clan and destroyed all our good fortune. I had one son in all the world; he was both my boy and my confidant, my councilor. He has disappeared from the face of the earth; no one in my clan has suffered such a calamity. I've ridden day and night searching the world for Bizhan. But now, at the turning of the year, our king has prayed to God and seen in the world-revealing cup that he is in Turan, loaded down with chains; seeing this, Khosrow sent me here to you. I stand before you, my heart filled with hope, my cheeks sallow with grief, my eyes blinded by tears: I look to you as my one recourse in all the world, as you are ready to help everyone in their time of need."

He wept and sighed, and as he handed over Khosrow's letter he told Rostam of the business with Gorgin. Rostam too wept as he read the letter, and loathing for Afrasyab welled up in him. He cried out for Bizhan and said, "Think no more of this; Rostam will not remove the saddle from Rakhsh's back until he has taken Bizhan's hand in his and destroyed the chains and prison that hold him. By God's power and the king's good fortune, I shall bring your prince back from Turan."

They went to Rostam's castle, where Rostam went through Khosrow's letter and said to Giv, "I understand what's to be done, and I shall carry out the king's commands. I know what services you've rendered, to me and to the court, and though I rejoice to see you here, my heart grieves for Bizhan. But you should not despair; I shall act as the king orders me and do my best to rescue your son, even if God should separate my soul from my body in the attempt. I'm ready to sacrifice my soul, my men, and my wealth on Bizhan's behalf. With God's help and our victorious king's good fortune, I'll free him from his chains and the dark pit where he languishes and return him to the Persian court. But now, you must be my guest for three days, and we shall drink together and take our ease; there is no thine or mine between you and me. We'll feast here and tell tales of the heroes and kings of old, and on the fourth day we'll set out for Khosrow's court."

Impulsively Giv stepped forward and kissed the hero's hand, chest, and feet. He praised Rostam and wished him eternal strength and wisdom. When Rostam saw that Giv was reassured he said to his steward, "Set out a feast, call our councilors and chieftains." After the banquet, Zavareh, Faramarz, Zal, and Giv sat in a bejeweled hall where musicians and wine servers entertained them; their hands were stained with ruby wine, the goblets glittered, and the harps resounded. And so three days and nights passed in pleasure and happiness; on the fourth they prepared to set out. Rostam ordered the baggage train to be made ready, laid his ancestors' mace in the saddle, and mounted Rakhsh. Rakhsh pricked up his ears, Rostam's head seemed to overtop the sun, and he and Giv, together with a hundred selected Zavoli horsemen, set out impatiently on their journey to Iran.

As Rostam approached the Persian heartland, the pinnacles of Khosrow's castle could be seen in the distance and a welcoming wind came down to him from the heavens. Giv said, "I shall ride on ahead and announce your coming."

Giv reached the court and made his obeisance to Khosrow, who asked him about his journey and where Rostam was. Giv replied, "Great king, your good fortune makes all things turn out well; Rostam did not refuse your orders. When I gave him your letter he reverently placed it against his eyes, and he has come here as befits a loyal subject, his reins twisted with mine. I rode on ahead to announce his coming to you."

Khosrow's answer was, "And where is this prop of our nobility, this paragon of loyalty now?" He ordered Gudarz, Tus, and Farhad, together with two companies from the army, to go out and greet the approaching hero. The din of drums rang out and the welcoming party was drawn up; the world was darkened by their dust, and in the gloom their lances glittered and their banners fluttered. When they reached Rostam they dismounted and bowed before him, and he too descended from his horse and asked each one for news of the king. Then everyone remounted and the group made its way to the royal palace.

Rostam Addresses Kay Khosrow

When Rostam entered the audience hall he ran forward, invoking the blessings of Hormoz upon the king. He then called on the angel Bahman to protect his crown, the angel Ordibehesht to protect his person, the angel Shahrivar to give him victory, the angel Sepandarmez to watch over him, the angel Khordad to bring prosperity to his lands, and the angel Mordad to watch over his flocks.

Khosrow stood, motioned Rostam to sit beside him, and said, "You are the champion of the world's kings; what men conceal you know, and what you do not conceal is still unknown to them. The Keyanids have chosen you before all others; you are the support of their army, the guardian of Iran, the refuge of their troops. I rejoice to see you here, valiant and vigilant as ever. Now, are Zavareh, Faramarz, and Zal well? What news can you give me of them?" Rostam knelt and kissed the throne and replied, "Victorious king, all three are well and prosperous, thanks to your good fortune. Blessed are those whom the king remembers!"

Khosrow ordered his chamberlain to summon Gudarz, Tus, and other courtiers of the first rank. The steward had the royal gardens prepared; a golden crown and throne were placed beneath a tree whose blossoms were beginning to fall, royal brocades were spread on the grass, and the flower gardens glowed like lamps at night. Near where the king sat a tree was placed so that its shade covered him; its trunk was of silver, its branches of gold encrusted with rubies and other precious stones; its leaves and buds were made of emeralds and agates that hung like precious earrings. Golden oranges and quinces grew from the branches; they were hollow inside and filled with musk macerated in wine, and their surfaces were pierced like a flute's, so that the scent diffused through the air, delighting the king. The wine servers who stood before the guests had bejeweled crowns, and their cloaks were of brocade shot with gold; they wore torques and earrings, and the bodices of their clothes were worked with gems. The faces of the servants who burned sandalwood before the king and played on harps glowed like rich brocade. All hearts rejoiced to be there; the wine went round and even before it took effect the guests' faces shone like pomegranate blossoms.

Khosrow sat Rostam in the place of honor beneath the tree and said to him, "My noble friend, you are Iran's shield against all evil, protecting us as the Simorgh spreads out her wings. You have always been ready to serve Iran and her kings, and with your mace and the might of your royal *farr* you destroyed the demons of Mazanderan. You know how Gudarz's clan has served in good fortune and bad, always ready to do my bidding and to guide me toward the truth, and Giv especially has been my bulwark against all evils. Such a sorrow has never come to this clan before, for what sorrow is greater than the loss of a child? If you do not agree to help us now no other lion-warrior will; think what must be done to save Bizhan, who languishes a captive in Turan. Whatever horses or arms or men or treasure you need, take them, and give the matter no more thought!"

Rostam kissed the ground, rose quickly, and said,

> "Your majesty, you're like the radiant sun
> Bestowing light and life on everyone:
> May greed and anger never touch your reign
> And may your enemies live wracked with pain.
> Monarch with whom no monarch can compete,
> All other kings are dust beneath your feet,
> Neither the sun nor moon has ever known
> A king like you to occupy the throne.
> My mother bore me so that you could live
> Sure of the service that you knew I'd give;
> I've heard the king's command and I agree
> To go wherever he might order me.
> The heavens can rain down fire but I won't leave
> This mission that I undertake for Giv
> Until success is mine—and I won't ask
> For chiefs or troops to help me in this task."

Gudarz, Giv, Fariborz, Farhad, and Shapur, together with the other assembled chieftains, called down the world Creator's blessings on Rostam, and the company sat to their wine, as happy and radiant as the springtime.

Gorgin Sends a Letter to Rostam

When Gorgin heard of Rostam's presence at the court, he realized that here was the key to his deliverance. He sent him a message: "O sword of fortune, scabbard of loyalty, banner of greatness, treasury of faith, gateway of generosity, imprisoner of disaster, if it does not pain you to hear from me, let me tell you of my sorrows. The hunchbacked heavens have doused the torch of my heart and left me in darkness; what was fated to happen to me has happened. If the king will forgive me my sins and restore me my good name, I'm ready to throw myself into fire before him, I'll do anything to rid myself of this disaster that has come to me in my old age. If you will ask for me from the king, I will follow you with all the energy of a wild mountain sheep. I shall go to Bizhan and grovel before him, in hopes of getting back my good reputation."

When Gorgin's message reached Rostam, he sighed, troubled by Gorgin's sorrow and by his foolish request. He sent the messenger back and told him to say to Gorgin, "You fearless fool, haven't you heard of what the leopard said to the sea monster: 'When passion overcomes wisdom, no one can escape its clutches; but the wise man who overcomes passion will be renowned as a lion'? You talk like a cunning old fox, but you didn't see the trap set for you. How can I possibly mention your name before Khosrow for the sake of such a foolish request? But you're so wretched that I'll ask Khosrow to forgive your sin and brighten your life's darkened moon. If God wills that Bizhan be freed from his chains, you'll be set free, too, and no one will take any further revenge on you. But if the heavens will otherwise, you must despair of life. I shall go on this mission, armed with God's strength and the king's command, but if I don't return successfully, prepare yourself for Gudarz and Giv to wreak vengeance on you for their child's death."

Two days and nights passed and Rostam made no mention of the matter; on the third day, when Khosrow was seated on his ivory throne, the hero came to him. He began to talk about Gorgin's miseries, but the king cut him off: "You're my general, and you're asking me to break the oath I swore by my throne and crown, by the lord of the sun and moon, that Gorgin would see nothing from me but suffering until Bizhan was freed from his chains. Ask me for anything else, for thrones, seal-rings, swords or crowns!"

Rostam replied, "My noble lord, if he did wrong, he repents of it and is ready to sacrifice his life in a good cause; but if the king will not forgive him, his name and reputation are lost forever. Anyone who strays from wisdom's path sooner or later regrets the evil that he does. It would be right for you to remember his former deeds, how he was always there in every crisis, and how he fought steadfastly for your ancestors. If the king

can grant me this man, it may be that fortune will smile on him again."
Khosrow allowed his request, and Gorgin was released from the dark pit
where he had been chained.

Then the king asked Rostam how he intended to go about his task, what
he would need in the way of troops and treasure, and who he wanted to
accompany him. He added, "I fear Afrasyab will kill Bizhan in a fit of impatience. He has a demon's nature and he's impulsive; he might well suddenly
destroy our warrior." Rostam replied, "I shall prepare for this task in secret;
the key to these chains is deceit, and we must not act too hastily. We must
tug back on the reins, and this is no time for maces, swords, or spears. I'll
need a quantity of jewels, gold, and silver; we'll go with high hopes, and
when we're there, fear will make us cautious. We'll go as merchants, and
this will give us a good excuse to linger in Turan for a while. I'll need carpets and clothes, and things to give as presents."

Khosrow gave orders that his ancient treasuries be opened; the king's
treasurer brought brocades and jewels, and Rostam came and selected
whatever he needed. He had a hundred camel-loads of gold coins made up,
together with a hundred mule-loads of silver, and he had the court chamberlain choose a thousand lion hearted warriors. Seven noblemen—Gorgin,
Zangeh, Gostaham, Gorazeh, Farhad, Roham, and Ashkash—were to go
with him as his companions and as guardians of the wealth. When these
men were summoned, Zangeh asked, "Where is Khosrow, and what's happened that he has called for us like this?"

Rostam and the Seven Persian Heroes Enter Turkestan

At dawn the chamberlain appeared at the castle gates, and the seven heroes
stood before the chosen troops, fully armed and ready to sacrifice their
souls if need be. At cock crow, as the sky whitened, war drums were fastened on the elephants and Rostam, tall as a cypress tree, appeared in the
gateway, mace in hand, his lariat hitched to his saddle. He called down
God's blessings on his country, and the group set off.

They neared the border with Turan, and he called the army's leaders to
him. He said, "You are to stay here, alert and on guard; you are not to leave
this place unless God divides my body from my soul; be prepared for war,
however, have your claws ready for blood."

The army stayed on the Persian side of the border while Rostam and his
nobles pressed on to Turan. But first they disguised themselves as merchants, removing their silver sword belts and dressing in woolen garments.
They entered Turan as a richly laden caravan, accompanied by seven horses,
one of which was Rakhsh; there were a hundred camel-loads of jewels, and a
hundred mule-loads of soldier's tunics and armor. The bells on the animals

and the clatter of their progress made a noise like the trumpets of Tahmures; the whole plain was filled with their din until they reached the town where Piran lived. Piran was away hunting; when Rostam saw him returning, he had a goblet filled with jewels and covered with a fine brocade cloth and two horses with jeweled bridles and draped with brocade led forward. Servants took the gifts to Piran's palace, and Rostam accompanied them. He greeted Piran respectfully, as one whose virtues were known both in Iran and Turan. By God's grace Piran did not recognize Rostam; he said to him, "Where are you from, who are you, and why have you come here in such a hurry?" Rostam replied, "I am your servant, sir; God's led me to your town to refresh myself and rest. I've come the long and weary way from Iran to Turan as a merchant; I buy and sell all sorts of things. I've traveled here assured of your kindness, and hope has now conquered my heart's fears. If you will take me under your wing's protection, I shall stay here to sell jewels and buy horses. Your justice will ensure that no one harms me, and your benevolence will rain down blessings upon me." Then he set before Piran the goblet filled with jewels and had the splendid Arab horses, that had no trace of wind-blown dust on their immaculate coats, led forward. Invoking God's benediction, he handed the presents over, and the bargain was made.

When Piran saw the jewels glittering in the goblet he welcomed Rostam warmly and sat him on a turquoise throne, saying, "Be happy here, be sure you'll be safe in my city; I'll give you quarters near to my palace and you need have no fears for your goods, no one will give you any trouble. Bring everything you have of value here and then look for customers. Make my son's house your personal headquarters, and think of yourself as one of my family." Rostam replied, "My lord, I brought this caravan from Iran for you, and all that I have in it is yours. Wherever I stay will be suitable for me, but with my victorious lord's permission, I'll stay with the caravan; there are all kinds of people traveling with me, and I don't want any of my jewels to disappear." Piran said, "Go and choose any place you desire; I'll send guides to help you."

Rostam chose a house for his party to stay in, and a warehouse for his goods. News spread that a caravan had come to Piran's castle from Iran and customers began to arrive from all quarters, particularly when it became known that there were jewels for sale. Buyers for brocade, carpets, and gems converged on the castle, and Rostam and his companions decked out their warehouse so that it shone like the sun itself.

Manizheh Comes to Rostam

Manizheh heard about the caravan from Iran and hurried to Piran's city. Unveiled and weeping, Afrasyab's daughter came before Rostam; wiping her tears from her face with her sleeve, she said,

> "I wish you life and long prosperity,
> May God protect you from adversity!
> May heaven prosper all you say and do,
> May evil glances never injure you.
> Whatever purposes you hope to gain
> May all your efforts never bring you pain,
> May wisdom be your guide, may fortune bless
> Iran with prosperous days and happiness.
> What news have you? What tidings can you bring
> Of Persia's champions, or of their king?
> Haven't they heard Bizhan is here, don't they
> Desire to help their friend in any way?
> Will he be left by Giv, by all his kin,
> To perish in the pit he suffers in?
> Fetters weigh down his legs, his arms and hands
> Are fixed to stakes by heavy iron bands
> He hangs in chains, blood stains his clothes, I weep
> To hear his groans, and never rest or sleep."

Rostam was afraid when he heard her, and he burst out as if in rage, pushing her toward the street: "Get away from me, I don't know any kings, I know nothing about Giv or that family, your words mean nothing to me!"

Manizheh stared at Rostam and sobbed pitifully. She said, "You're a great and wise man and your cold words don't suit you. Say nothing if you wish, but don't drive me from you, for my sufferings have worn away my life. Is this the way Persians treat people? Do they deny news to the poor and wretched?"

Rostam said, "What's the matter with you, woman? Has Ahriman told you the world's coming to an end? You disrupted my trade, and that's why I was angry with you. Don't let what I said upset you; I was worried about selling my goods. As for the king, I don't live in the city where he does, and I know nothing about Giv or his clan; I've never been to the area where they live."

Quickly, he had whatever food was available set in front of the poor woman, and then he questioned her as to what had made her unhappy, why she was so interested in the Persian king and nobility, and why she kept her eye on the road from Iran the whole time.

Manizheh said, "And why should you want to know about my sorrows and misfortunes? I left the pit with my heart filled with anguish and ran to you thinking you were a free and noble man, and you yelled at me like a warrior attacking an enemy. Have you no fear of God in you? I am Manizheh, Afrasyab's daughter; once the sun never saw me unveiled, but now my face is sallow with grief, my eyes are filled with bloody tears, and I wander from house to house seeking charity. I beg for bread; this is the fate God has visited upon me. Has any life ever been more wretched than mine? May God have mercy on me. And poor Bizhan in that pit never sees the sun or moon, but hangs in chains and fetters, begging God for death. His pain adds to my pain, and I have wept so much that my eyes can weep no more. But if you go to Iran again and hear news of Gudarz, or if you see Giv at Kay Khosrow's court or the hero Rostam, tell them that Bizhan lies here in deep distress and that if they delay it will be too late. If they wish to see him alive, they should hurry, for he is crushed between the stone above him and the iron that binds him."

Rostam wept tears of sympathy and said to her, "Dear lovely child, why don't you have the nobles of your country intercede for you with your father? Surely he would forgive you and feel remorse for what's happened?" Then he ordered his cooks to bring Manizheh all kinds of food, and especially he told them to prepare a roasted chicken folded round with soft bread; when they brought this, Rostam dexterously slipped a ring into it and gave it to Manizheh, saying, "Take this to the pit, and look after the poor prisoner who languishes there."

Manizheh hurried back to the pit, with the food wrapped in a cloth and clutched against her breast. She passed it down to Bizhan just as she'd received it. Bizhan peered at it in astonishment and called out to her, "Dearest Manizheh, you've suffered so much on my behalf. Where did you get this food you're in such a hurry to give me?" She said, "From a Persian merchant who's come with a caravan of goods to Turan; he seems like someone who's passed through many trials, a noble and splendid man. He has a great many jewels with him and has set up shop in a big warehouse in front of Piran's castle. He gave me the food wrapped in a cloth and told me to bring it to you, and said that I could return for more later."

Hopeful and apprehensive, Bizhan began to open the bread, and as he did so he came on the hidden ring. He peered at the stone set in it and made out a name, then he laughed in triumph and astonishment. It was a turquoise seal, with the word "Rostam" engraved on it with a steel point, as fine as a hair. Bizhan saw that the tree of loyalty had born fruit; he knew that the key that would release him from his suffering was at hand. He laughed long and loud and when Manizheh heard him laughing, chained in the darkness as he was, she was alarmed and feared that he had gone mad.

She called down to him, "How can you laugh when you can't tell night from day? What do you know that I don't? Tell me. Has good fortune suddenly shown you her face?"

Bizhan replied, "I'm hopeful that fate will finally free me from this pit. If you can swear to keep faith with me, I'll tell you the whole tale from beginning to end, but only if you'll swear yourself to secrecy, because a man can sew up a woman's mouth to prevent idle talk and she'll still find some way to free her tongue."

Manizheh wept and wailed, "How wretched my fate is! Alas for the days of my youth, for my broken heart and my weeping eyes. I've given Bizhan my body, my soul, and my wealth, and now he cannot trust me. My treasury and my jeweled crown were plundered, my father cast me out, unveiled and humiliated, before his court, and now that Bizhan sees hope he leaves me in despair. The world is dark to me, my eyes see nothing, Bizhan hides his thoughts from me, and only God knows all things."

Bizhan replied, "What you say is true. You lost everything for my sake. I should not have said what I said. My kindest friend, my dearest wife, you have to guide me now, the agony I've suffered has turned my brains. Know then that the man selling jewels, whose cook gave you the food you brought, has come to Turan looking for me; that's the only reason he's here selling jewels. God has taken pity on me and I shall see the broad earth once again. This jeweler will save me from my long agony, and you from your grief and beggary on my behalf. Go to him once again and say to him in secret, "Great hero of the worlds' kings, tender-hearted and resourceful, tell me if you are Rakhsh's lord."

Manizheh hurried to Rostam like the wind and spoke as Bizhan had instructed her. When Rostam saw her come running like this and heard what she said, he knew that Bizhan had entrusted her with their secret. His heart melted and he said, "May God never withdraw his kindness from you, my lovely child. Tell him, 'Yes, I am Rakhsh's lord, sent by God to save you. I have traveled the long road from Zavol to Iran and from Iran to Turan for your sake.' Tell him, but let no one else know of this; in the darkest night listen for the least sound. Spend the next day gathering firewood in the forest, and when night comes, light a huge bonfire."

Overjoyed at his words and freed from all sorrow, Manizheh hurried back to the pit where Bizhan lay bound. She said, "I gave the great lord your message, and he confirmed that he was the man you said he was. He told me to wipe away my tears and to say to you that he had come here like a leopard to find you, and now that he had done so you would soon enough see his sword's work. He will tear up the ground and throw the stone that covers you to the stars. He told me that when the sun releases its grip on the world and night comes I'm to build a huge fire so that the stone and the pit's whereabouts shine like the daytime, and he will be able to use the glow as a guide to us."

Bizhan said, "Light the fire that will deliver us both from darkness," and he prayed to God, saying, "Pure, splendid, and just, release me from all sorrows and strike down my enemies with your arrows; give me justice, for you know the pains and grief I have suffered; allow me to see my native country again and to smash against this stone my evil star." Then he addressed Manizheh:

"And you, who've suffered long and patiently,
Who've given heart and soul and wealth for me,
Who thought that, undergone for me, distress
Was but another name for happiness,
Who cast aside your kin, your noble name,
Your parents, crown and land, to share my shame:
If in my youth I find I'm free again,
Delivered from this dragon and this pain,
I'll bow before you like a man whose days
Are passed before his God in prayer and praise;
Prompt as a slave who waits before his lord,
I'll find for you a glorious reward."

Manizheh set about gathering firewood, going from branch to branch like a bird, her eyes fixed on the sun to mark when it would drop behind the mountains. And when she saw the sun disappear and night draw its skirts over the mountain slopes, at that moment when the world finds peace and all that is visible fades from sight because night's army has veiled sunlight in darkness, Manizheh quickly lit the flames. Night's pitch-black eyes were seeled; Manizheh's heart pounded like a brass drum as she listened for the iron hooves of Rakhsh.

For his part, Rostam put on his armor and prayed to the God of the sun and moon, saying "May the eyes of the evil be blinded, give me strength to complete this business of Bizhan." He ordered his warriors to prepare for battle; poplar wood saddles were placed on their mounts, and they made ready to fight.

They set out toward the distant glow, and traveled expeditiously. When they reached the great stone of the Akvan Div and the pit of sorrow and grief, Rostam said to his seven companions, "You'll have to dismount and find some way to remove that stone from the mouth of the pit." But no matter how hard the warriors struggled, they could not shift the stone; when Rostam saw how they sweated to no avail, he too dismounted and hitched up his skirts about his waist. Praying to God for strength, he set his hands to the stone and lifted it; with a lion's power he flung it into the forest, and the ground shuddered as the stone landed.

He peered into the pit and, sighing in sympathy, addressed Bizhan: "How did such a misfortune happen to you? Your portion from the world was to have been one of delight, how is it that the goblet you took from her hands was filled with poison?" Bizhan answered from the darkness, "Your journey must have been long and hard; when I heard your war cry, all the world's poison turned to sweetness for me. You see how I have lived, with iron as my earth and a stone as my sky; I've suffered so much pain and grief that I gave up all hope of the world."

Rostam replied, "The shining Keeper of the World has had mercy on your soul, and now I have one request to ask of you: that you grant me Gorgin's life, and that you drive from your heart all thoughts of hatred for him." Bizhan said, "What do you know of my experiences with this companion of mine; my lionhearted friend, what do you know of how Gorgin treated me? If I ever set eyes on him again my vengeance will be like God's last judgment."

Rostam said, "If you persist in this hatred and refuse to listen to what I have to say, I shall leave you chained here in this pit; I shall mount Rakhsh and return whence I came." When he heard Rostam's words, a cry of grief rose up from the pit, and Bizhan said, "I am the most wretched of our clan's heroes. The evil that came to me was from Gorgin, and now I must suffer this, too: but I accept, and drive all thoughts of hatred for him from my heart."

Rostam lowered his lariat into the pit and brought Bizhan out of its depths, wasted away with pain and suffering, his legs still shackled, his head uncovered, his hair and nails grown long, all his body caked with blood where the chains had eaten into the flesh. Rostam gave a great cry when he saw him weighed down with iron and set about breaking the fetters and shackles. They made their way home, with Bizhan on one side of Rostam and the woman who had succored him on the other; the two young people recounted their sufferings to the hero, who had Bizhan's head washed and fresh clothes brought for him. Then Gorgin came forward and sank to the ground, striking his face against the dust; he asked pardon for his evil acts

and for the foolish things he had said. Bizhan's heart forgave him, and he forgot all thoughts of punishment.

The camels were loaded with their goods, Rostam put on his armor once more, and the Persian warriors mounted, with drawn swords and maces at the ready. Ashkash, who was a wary fighter, always on the lookout for whatever might harm the army, led off the baggage train. Rostam said to Bizhan, "You and Manizheh should go with Ashkash. Afrasyab will be so enraged we can't rest tonight; I'm going to play a trick on him within his own walls, and his whole country will laugh at him tomorrow." But Bizhan's answer was, "If I'm the one who's being avenged, I should be at the head of this expedition."

Rostam and Bizhan Attack

Rostam and the seven warriors left the baggage train in Ashkash's capable hands and set out. Letting their reins hang slack on their saddles and drawing their swords, they arrived at Afrasyab's palace at the time when men turn to drunkenness, rest, and sleep. They attacked and confusion reigned: swords glittered, arrows poured down, heads fell severed from bodies, mouths were clogged with dust. Rostam stood in the portico of Afrasyab's palace and yelled, "So you sleep well, do you, you and your valiant warriors? You slept in state while Bizhan was in the pit, but did you dream of an iron wall confronting you? I am Rostam, the son of Zal; now is no time for sleep in soft beds. I have smashed your chains and removed the stone you set as Bizhan's keeper; he is free of his fetters, and rightly so, since this was no way to treat a son-in-law! Were Seyavash's sufferings, and the war that came from them, not enough for you? You had no right to seek Bizhan's life, but I see your heart's stupefied and your mind's asleep." And Bizhan cried out, "Misbegotten, evil-minded Turk, think how you dealt with me when you were on your throne and I stood chained before you; then, when I was bound motionless as a stone, you were savage as a leopard, but now I walk freely on the face of the earth, and the ferocious lion slinks off."

Afrasyab struggled with his clothes and called out, "Are all my warriors asleep? Any man who wants jewels and a crown, block these enemies' advance!" Cries and a confused noise of combat resounded on all sides, and blood streamed beneath Afrasyab's door; every Turanian warrior who ventured forward was killed, and finally Afrasyab fled from his palace. Rostam entered the building and distributed among his men its cloth and carpets, the noble horses with their poplar wood saddles covered with leopard skins and jewels, and the king's womenfolk, who took the Persian heroes by the hand.

They left the palace and packed up their plunder, having no intention of staying any longer in Turan. Because of the baggage they carried and to avoid a bitter outcome to their expedition, they urged the horses forward as fast as they could. Rostam became so exhausted by their haste that even the weight of his helmet was a trouble to him, and his companions and their horses were so weak they had hardly a pulse left in their arteries. Rostam sent a messenger to the forces he had left when he crossed into Turan, saying "Draw your swords from their scabbards; I am certain that the earth will soon be black with an army's hooves. Afrasyab will muster an army of vengeance, and follow us here; their lances will darken the sunlight."

At last the returning group reached the waiting army; they made themselves ready for battle, their lances sharpened, their reins at the ready. A lookout saw horsemen approaching from Turan and Rostam went to Manizheh in her tent and said, "If the wine has been spilt, its scent still lingers: if our pleasures are past, the memory of them is still ours. But this is the way of the world, giving us now sweetness and pleasure, now bitterness and pain."

Rostam's Battle with Afrasyab

As soon as the sun rose above the mountain tops Turan's warriors had begun to prepare for their onslaught. The town was filled with a deafening clamor: horsemen mustered in their ranks before Afrasyab's palace, Turan's nobles bowed their heads to the ground before him, and all were eager to exact vengeance from Iran. They felt that the time had passed for words; a remedy had to be found, since what Bizhan had done had disgraced their king forever. "The Iranians do not call us men," they said. "They say we are women dressed as warriors."

Like a leopard, Afrasyab strode forward and gave the signal for war: he ordered Piran to have the war drums strapped on their elephants, saying, "These Persians will make fun of us no more." Brass trumpets, bugles, and Indian chimes rang out before the palace. Turan was in an uproar as the army set out for the Persian border, and the whole earth seemed like a moving ocean.

A lookout saw the earth heaving like the sea and ran to Rostam: "Prepare to fight, the world has turned black from the dust flung up by their horsemen." But Rostam replied, "There's no cause for fear; dust is what they'll come to if they fight with us." Leaving the baggage with Manizheh, he donned his armor and came out to inspect his troops, roaring like a lion, "What use is a fox when it's caught in a lion's claws?" Then he addressed his men:

> *"The day of battle's come: my noble lords,*
> *Where are your iron-piercing spears, your swords?*
> *Now is the time to show your bravery*
> *And turn our vengeance into victory."*

The trumpets blared and Rostam mounted Rakhsh. He led his men down from the mountainside as the enemy were passing through a defile to the plains. The two sides ranged themselves behind walls of iron-clad warriors. On the Persian side, Ashkash and Gostaham and their horsemen made up the right flank, the left was commanded by Farhad and Zangeh, while Rostam himself and Bizhan were in the center. Behind them towered Mount Bisitun, and before them was a wall of swords. When Afrasyab saw that the enemy forces were led by Rostam, he put on his armor uneasily and ordered his men to hold back. He had them form defensive ranks; the air darkened and the ground disappeared. He entrusted his left flank to Piran, and the right to Human; the center was held by Garsivaz and Shideh, while he himself kept an eye on all parts of the line.

Like a massive mountain, Rostam rode up and down between the armies and called out

> *"You miserable, wretched Turk—you shame*
> *Your throne, your warriors, and your noble name.*
> *Your heart's not in this fight: how many men*
> *You've mustered in your army's ranks, but when*
> *The battle's joined at last and I attack,*
> *I'll see no more than your retreating back.*
> *And did my father never say to you*
> *The ancient proverbs that are always true?*

'A herd of milling asses cannot fight
Against a single lion's savage might;
All heaven's stars will never equal one
In glory and in radiance—the sun;
Words won't give courage to a fox, no laws
Can make an ass develop lion's claws.'
Don't be a fool, and if you want to save
Your sovereignty, don't act as if you're brave;
If you attack this time, in all this plain
You won't escape alive from me again!"

When the Turkish king heard these words he trembled, heaved a bitter sigh, and cried out in fury, "Warriors of Turan! Is this a battlefield, or a banqueting hall?"

When they heard their commander's voice a great shout went up from the Turanian ranks; dust rose into the sky obscuring the sun, war drums were fastened on elephants, horns and trumpets sounded, and the line of armored warriors made a solid iron wall. The plain and mountain slopes re-echoed with cries from men on both sides, in the dusty air the glitter of swords flashed as if the world's end had come, and blows from steel maces rained down on armor and helmets like hail. Rostam's banner, with its dragon device, seemed to eclipse the sun; wherever he rode, severed heads fell to the ground. With his ox-headed mace he was like a maddened dromedary that has slipped its tether, and from the center of the army he scattered his enemies like a wolf.

On the right flank Ashkash pressed on like the wind, eager for combat with Garsivaz; on the left Gorgin, Farhad, and Roham pushed back the Turkish warriors; and in the center Bizhan went triumphantly forward as if the battle were a celebratory feast. Warriors' heads fell like leaves from a tree, and the battlefield became a river of blood in which the Turkish banners lay overturned and abandoned.

When Afrasyab saw the day was lost and that his brave warriors had been slain, he threw away his Indian sword and mounted a fresh horse: he separated himself from the Turkish army and rode toward Turan, having achieved nothing by his attempt to ambush the Persians. Rostam sped after him, raining arrows and blows on the intervening Turks; like a fire-breathing dragon he followed him for two parasangs, but finally returned to camp, where a thousand Turkish prisoners were waiting. There he distributed to the army the wealth his men had captured, loaded up the elephant train with baggage, and set out in triumph to Kay Khosrow.

Rostam Returns with Bizhan from Turan to Iran

When news reached the king that the lion was returning victorious, that Bizhan had been released from the prison where he'd been held, that the army of Turan had been smashed and all their hopes had come to naught, he prayed to God for joy, striking his face and forehead against the dust.

Gudarz and Giv hurried to Khosrow. The noise of the approaching army's war drums and trumpets could be heard; then the ground in front of the king's palace was darkened by horses' hooves, the clamor of trumpets and horns resounded throughout the city, the banners of Gudarz and Giv were raised, chained leopards and lions were led out on one side and on the other were mounted warriors. In this fashion, as the king had commanded, the army went out to greet the returning victors.

When Rostam emerged from the approaching group, Gudarz and Giv dismounted, and all the Persian nobility followed suit. Rostam too dismounted and greeted those who had come to welcome him. Gudarz and Giv addressed him, "Great commander, may God hold you forever in his keeping, may the sun and moon turn as you would wish, may the heavens never tire of you; you have made us your slaves, for through you we have found our lost son; it is you who has delivered us from pain and sorrow, and all Persians long to serve you."

The nobles remounted and processed toward the king. When they were close to the city, Khosrow came out and welcomed Rostam as the guardian of all his heroes. Rostam saw that the king himself was coming to greet him and he dismounted once more, saying he was humbled that the king had put himself to this trouble. Khosrow embraced him and said, "You are a root stock of manliness and a mine of virtues; your deeds shine like the sun, for their goodness is seen everywhere." Quickly Rostam took Bizhan by the hand and handed him over to his father and his king. Then he brought the thousand Turanian prisoners bound before the king, and Khosrow called down heaven's blessings on him, praising Zal, who had such a son, and Zavol, that had nurtured such a hero.

Next the king addressed Giv: "The hidden purposes of God have looked kindly on you: through Rostam He has restored your son to you." Giv replied, "May you live happily and forever, and may Rostam's luck remain ever fresh and green, and may Zal rejoice in his son."

Khosrow gave a great feast for his nobles, after which the company went to a splendid hall where they were plied with wine and entertained by richly dressed musicians whose cheeks blushed like rich brocade, and who accompanied their songs with the bewitching sound of harps. There were golden trays heaped with musk, and to the front of the hall was an artificial pool filled with rosewater; in his glory, the king seemed like a cypress topped by the full moon, and when the nobles left his palace every one of them was drunk.

At dawn Rostam returned to the court, prompt to serve his prince and with not a care in his heart; he asked for permission to return home, and Khosrow discussed this with him for a while. He ordered his chamberlain to bring in a suit of clothes sewn with jewels, a cloak and crown, a goblet filled with royal gems, a hundred saddled horses, a hundred laden mules, a hundred servant girls, a hundred serving youths—all these he gave to Rostam, who kissed the ground in thanks. The hero then placed the crown on his head, girt himself in the cloak and belt, made his farewells to the king, and took the road to Sistan. And his noble companions, who had seen so much sorrow and joy and suffering at his side, were also given presents, and they too left the king's palace in good spirits.

When the king had said farewell to his champions, he settled contentedly on his throne and summoned Bizhan. He asked him about the pains and sorrows he had endured, the narrow pit where he'd languished, and the woman who had ministered to him. Bizhan talked at length, and as the king listened he was moved to pity, both for him and for the torments Afrasyab's poor daughter had endured. He had a hundred sets of clothes of cloth of gold worked with jewels brought in, as well as a crown, ten purses of gold coins, slaves, carpets, and all manner of goods and said to Bizhan, "Take these to your grieving Turkish friend: speak gently to her, see you don't make her sufferings worse, think what she has gone through for your sake!

"Live your life in happiness with her now, and consider the turnings of Fate, who lifts one to the high heavens so that he knows nothing of grief or pain, and then throws him weeping beneath the dust. It is fearful, terrible, to think on this. And while one is brought up with luxury and caresses, and is thrown bewildered and despairing into a dark pit, another is lifted from the pit and raised to a throne where a jeweled crown is placed on his head. The world has no shame in doing this; it is prompt to hand out both pleasure and pain and has no need of us and our doings. Such is the way of the world that guides us to both good and evil. Now you should never need for wealth, and I wish you a heart free from all sorrow."

T he war between Iran and Turan continued, but Turan's forces were inexorably driven back and defeated by Khosrow's army. In one encounter Piran was killed (by Gudarz) and his death was lamented by both Kay Khosrow and Rostam who remembered him as a noble, conciliatory counselor who had protected fugitive Persians in Turan, and tried when possible to make peace between the two peoples.

Piran died stoically, accepting his fate, but when Afrasyab was finally captured and brought before Kay Khosrow he pleaded for his life and was ignominiously executed.

Still alive, but living in retirement and far from the center of events, Kay Kavus felt that, with the death of his lifelong enemy, his life's last mission had been accomplished.

⇜ THE OCCULTATION OF KAY KHOSROW ⇝

Once Kavus felt that his land was safe, he opened his heart to God and said: "O thou who art the guide to every blessing and who art higher than all fate, through you I found *farr*, glory, good fortune, greatness, my crown and my throne. You have given no-one else the treasure and fame that you gave to me; I asked you for a warrior who would avenge the blood of Seyavash, and I saw my farsighted grandson, ambitious, glorious and wise, a man who outshines all former kings. But now I have lived for a hundred and fifty years and my hair that was as black as musk has turned as white as camphor. My body that was as straight and elegant as a cypress is bent like a bow, and if my days are to come to an end I shall not see death as a misfortune."

A short while later he died; all that remained of him in the world was his name. The lord Kay Khosrow came from his palace and sat himself down on the black earth: dressed in black and dark blue, devoid of all glory, the Persian nobles walked before him on foot. They mourned their king for two weeks, and built him a palatial tomb, ten lariat-lengths high. His body was treated with a salve compounded of camphor and musk, and then wrapped in robes of silk and brocade. Attendants placed him on an ivory dais, and anointed his head with camphor and musk. Kay Khosrow left the chamber, and the door to the king's resting place was sealed. No one ever saw Kavus again: he rested from war and revenge forever.

> Such is the passing world that you must leave,
> All men must die, and it is vain to grieve.
> No learning will suffice against Death's hand,
> Whose might no arms or helmet can withstand;
> And—king or prophet—in the end you must
> Descend to dirt, and slumber in the dust.
> Pursue desire, consider life a game
> And, if you can, look out for luck and fame—
> But know the world's your enemy; your head
> Will lie in dust, the grave will be your bed.

The king mourned his grandfather for forty days, shunning the crown and throne and pleasure. Then he sat himself on the ivory throne and placed on his own head the heart-delighting crown. The army assembled and the nobility came before him in their golden diadems: they acclaimed him as king and scattered jewels over his crown. The victorious champion was enthroned, and from end to end the world rejoiced.

Kay Khosrow Becomes Sated with Kingship

Sixty years passed, and all the world was under the king's command. The king's great soul began to brood on his power and on the passing of time. He said, "I have cleansed all inhabited lands of malevolent souls, from India to China to Byzantium, from the east to the west; mountains and waste-lands and deserts and fertile plains—all are under my command. The world has no fear now of evil beings, and I have lived for many days. Although it was revenge I sought, God granted me all that I wished. My soul must not become filled with hubris, with foul thoughts and the ways of Ahriman. I shall then be as evil as Zahhak, or like Jamshid who suffered the same fate as Tur and Salm. On the one side I'm descended from Kavus, and on the other from that wicked wizard Tur: my ancestors are Kavus and Afrasyab, who even when he slept dreamt only of crookedness and trickery. One day I shall become ungrateful to God, terror will touch my soul's radiance, the divine *farr* will leave me and I shall swerve toward crookedness and evil; I shall go forward into darkness until my head and crown are tumbled in the dust. I shall leave an evil name behind me, and my fate before God will be evil. My flesh will decay and my bones will lie scattered on the ground; virtue will fail, ingratitude will take its place, and in the other world my soul will dwell in darkness. When another has taken my crown and throne, and trampled on my fortune, all that will remain of me will be an evil name; the rose that grew from my age-old struggles will be a briar, no more.

"Now that I have sought vengeance, adorned the world with splendor, killed those who rose against God and whom it was necessary to kill, there is not a place on earth which does not recognize my authority: however wealthy or strong they may be, the great of the earth are my servants. I am grateful to God that he has given me this *farr*, and that the heavens' revolutions have looked favorably on me. It is best that I turn now toward God, that I seek him while I can still do so honorably, as one who has prayed to him privately: he will take my soul to the abode of the blessed, for this crown and throne will perish. No one will ever have more fame or happiness or greatness or peace of mind than I have enjoyed: I have reached life's bourn, I have seen the world's secrets, its good and evil, what is plain and what is hidden, and I have seen that whether a man tills the soil or reigns as a king he must finally pass through death."

The king ordered his chamberlain to send away anyone who might come seeking him, and to do this politely, with sweet words, avoiding all harshness.

He shut the doors to his court, loosened his clothes, and began to lament his state. He washed his head and body preparatory to praying: with the torch of wisdom he sought out a path toward God. Then he strode to the place where he prayed, and spoke to the Judge of all secrets:

> "O higher than all souls, of unmatched worth,
> Who makes fire spurt forth from the darkened earth,
> Look on me now, vouchsafe me wisdom here
> To know the truth, to know what I should fear.
> I'll pray to you incessantly and strive
> To do good deeds whilst I remain alive—
> Absolve me of the evil I have done,
> Let me not trespass against anyone.
> Drive sin out from my soul and keep me free
> From demons and their cunning sorcery:
> Let me control desire that won control
> Over Zahhak's, Kavus's, Jamshid's soul.
> If devils hide the road to what is right
> Evil will triumph when I come to fight—
> Save me from demons' wiles, let me avoid
> The snares by which my soul will be destroyed:
> Lead me, protect me, be my constant guide
> To where the just eternally abide."

The Persians Plead with Kay Khosrow

Day and night he stood in prayer; his body was in the palace but his soul was in another place. After a week his strength began to fail; he found he could stand no longer and on the eighth day he returned to his throne. The champions of the Persian army were bewildered by their king's behavior, each of them ascribing it to a different cause.

The king took his place on the throne, and the chamberlain drew back the curtain that separated him from his courtiers. The commanders entered, their arms crossed in humility over their chests; among them were Tus, Gudarz, brave Giv, Gorgin, Bizhan, and the lion-like Roham. When they saw the king they prostrated themselves before him and said: "O brave and just king, possessor of the world, noblest of the noble: no king like you has ever assumed the throne. All champions serve you, and we live only because you keep watch over us. You have laid all your enemies low, and there is no one left in the world for you to fear. We have no notion why the king's thoughts should be darkened at a time like this; now is the time for you to rejoice in your good fortune, not to grieve your life away in anxiety. Whether we have done something to upset the king, or whether it is another matter that is no fault of ours, may he tell us what troubles him, so that we can reassure him and bring fire back to his cheeks. And if some secret enemy disturbs his peace may the king inform us who it is: each king who has worn the crown has seen the value of his wealth and might in this, that he could cut off his enemies' heads, or sacrifice his own head when he put on a warrior's helmet and rode out to war. Tell us what you are hiding, and we will find a remedy for it."

The great king answered: "Set your minds at rest my champions: the world contains no enemy that troubles me, and my wealth is all intact; nothing the army has done has offended me, and none of you is guilty of sin. When I rode out in vengeance for my father's death I spread justice and righteousness throughout the world; there is no portion of the black earth that has not known my seal's imprint. Sheathe your swords, and grasp the winecup; drink, rejoice, and replace the noise of bowstrings with the sounds of flutes and harps. For a week now I've prayed before God: I have a hidden desire which I long for God to grant me. When he answers my prayer this will be a blessing for me and I shall tell you openly what it is. Meanwhile you too should pray to God on my behalf, for it is he who gives us strength for good and evil. Pray to him for guidance, then give yourselves to wine and cheerfulness, forgetful of all sorrow. Know that this unstable world makes no distinction between a king and his subject, that it snatches away both the old and the young, and that from it both justice and tyranny come to us."

Sadly and anxiously the nobles left his presence, and the king ordered his chamberlain to admit no one to him. That night he returned to the place of prayer and opened his lips to the Lord of Justice:

"O higher than the highest, show to me
The ways of righteousness and purity:
Guide me to heaven, let me leave behind
This fleeting habitation of mankind,
And let my heart shun sin, so that I might
Pass to the realms of everlasting light."

Giv Travels to Zabol

After a week had passed and Khosrow had still not reappeared, a confused murmuring could be heard: the nobles gathered together and there was much discussion of the ways of great kings, both those who were god-fearing and those who had lived as tyrants. Finally Gudarz, Giv's father, turned to his son and said, "Fortune has favored you and you've always given your support to the crown and throne; you've undergone many troubles for Iran's sake, putting your loyalty before your family and homeland. Now a crisis is before us, and we should not take it lightly: you must travel to Zabol and tell Zal and Rostam that the king has turned away from God and has lost his way. He has barred his court's door to the nobility, and takes council with demons. We've tried to reason with him, and our words were meant well, but though he heard us out he gave us no answer: we can see that his heart is confused, and his head is full of wind. We're afraid that he'll go astray as Kavus did, and that demons will lead him into evil paths. Tell Rostam and Zal that they are heroes, that they are the wisest and most capable of men: have them assemble the astrologers and sages of Zabol and bring them here to Iran. Since Khosrow has hidden his face from us, the kingdom is full of rumors: we have tried every remedy and now all our hopes rest on Zal and his son."

Giv chose a number of warriors as his retinue and set off for Sistan. There he told Rostam and Zal what he had seen and heard: Zal was saddened by his words and said, "Truly, grief has become our companion." Then he ordered Rostam to call together the astrologers and priests of Sistan and Kabol, so that they could accompany them on the journey to Iran. Sages of all kinds gathered at Zal's court, and the group set out.

The king prayed for seven days and on the eighth, at daybreak, he returned to his throne and had the chamberlain draw back the curtain from the outer door. The chieftains and priests streamed into the audience hall, and Khosrow received them graciously as befits a king, motioning them to

their places. But they stood before him, their hands crossed in reverence over their chests, and none sat in the place where he had been assigned. They said, "Immortal soul, just lord of all the world, might and the royal *farr* belong to you, and from the sun to the fish beneath the earth is yours. Your clear soul knows all beings: speak wisely to us. We stand before you as your slaves and champions: tell us what we have done that you forbid us access to you. Days have passed like this, and our hearts are filled with foreboding. Tell your secret to us, the guardians of your distant frontiers; if your sorrow is from the sea we shall dry it up, and spread it with a mantle of powdered musk; if it is from a mountain we shall level it and with our daggers spit your enemies' hearts; if wealth will cure your sorrow there will be no lack of cash. We are all guardians of your glory, and we weep in sympathy for your sorrows."

The world's lord answered: "I am not without need of my champions; but my heart has no anxiety about my might or men or wealth, and no country's produced an enemy for me to worry about. My heart has conceived a desire which I'll not relinquish: in the dark night and the bright day I have hopes of its fulfillment. When I achieve it I will tell you what my secret prayers have been. Go now, victorious and happy, and rid your minds of evil thoughts." All his nobility paid him homage, but their minds were clouded with sorrow. When they had left, the king ordered that the curtain be lowered; and he who had won so many victories sat weeping by the door, with despair in his heart.

Kay Khosrow Sees the Angel Sorush in a Dream

Again the world's lord stood in prayer, asking for guidance:

> *"Lord of the heavens, Lord of unmatched might,*
> *Of goodness, justice, and celestial light,*
> *What shall my kingdom profit me if you*
> *Remain unsatisfied with all I do?*
> *But, good or evil, may my deeds suffice*
> *To win for me a place in paradise."*

He prayed before God, wailing and groaning in his anguish, and after five weeks of prayer, one night, as the moon rose, he fell asleep. He slept, but his bright soul became wisdom's companion and did not sleep. In his dream he saw the angel Sorush whisper in his ear, "O king, good fortune and benevolent stars have guided you, and you have seen enough of torques and crowns and thrones. If you would leave this world you have found what you are seeking; you will find a home beside the Source of Righteousness, there is no need for you to sojourn in this darkness any longer. Give your treasures to those who are deserving; relinquish this fleeting world to another. When you enrich the poor, and your own people, you will be made stronger. You will not remain here long now; choose a king in whom all creatures, down to the smallest ant, can place their trust. And when you've given away the world, you cannot rest: you must prepare for your departure."

When the exhausted king woke he saw that the place where he had been praying was awash with water: he wept and placed his face against the ground, giving thanks to God. He said, "If I can soon move onward, God has given me all I desire." He dressed himself in clothes that had never been worn before and ascended his throne: there he sat, but wearing neither his torque, nor the royal jewels, nor his crown.

Zal and Rostam Reach Iran

At the week's end Rostam and Zal arrived in Iran full of apprehension as to what was afoot. Hearing of their approach a group of heavy-hearted Iranian nobles led by Tus and Gudarz hurried out to greet them. They said: "The devil Eblis has led our king astray. What is his court but his army? And yet for days and nights now no one has seen him except during the brief moments when the court doors are opened to us. My lords, Khosrow has changed from that cheerful and glorious monarch you knew; his cypress stature is bent, and the roses of his cheeks have turned pale as a quince. I don't know what evil eye has struck him, and why he withers like a shriveled petal, unless it is that the Persians' luck is clouded and misfortune strikes him from an evil star."

Brave Zal said to them: "It may be that the king is sated with power; all seems well and then difficulties arise, pleasure and pain both come to us. Do not grieve over this, grief will only weaken your grip on life: we shall talk with him, our advice will make the stars favorable again."

The group traveled to the court, where immediately the curtain was drawn back and they entered in good spirits. Zal, Rostam, Tus, Gudarz, Gorgin, Bizhan, Gastahom, and a great many other nobles and their retainers crowded into the audience chamber. When Khosrow heard Rostam's voice from beyond the curtain, and saw Zal's face, he was puzzled and leapt up from the throne; he extended his hand to them and asked them why they had come. Then he questioned the sages of Zabol and its environs, and motioned them to seats in his court: the Iranian nobles too were assigned places according to their rank.

Zal greeted the king and wished him long life, listing the great monarchs of the past and saying that he had seen none who equaled Khosrow in stature and possession of the Divine *farr*, in chivalry, victory, and benevolence: he hoped that the king would reign forever, continuing to bestow justice on the world and enjoying the fruits of conquest, for there was no noble who was not as dirt beneath the king's feet, no poison for which the king's mere name was not a remedy. Then he continued: "We have heard unwelcome news, and hearing it we hurried to your court: we have consulted astrologers with their Indian charts, seeking to know the heaven's secrets and why it has exiled Iran from its benevolence. A messenger came saying that the victorious king has ordered that the curtain that guards his court not be drawn back, and that the king hides his face from his people. Sympathy for the Persians has made me fly here like an eagle, like a skiff over water, so that I might ask the world's lord what secret anxiety is troubling him. Three things cure all ills, and make the throne wholly secure. These three are wealth, effort, and chivalrous men: without these no battles can be fought. And the fourth is that we praise God, praying before him day and night, for it is he who helps his slaves, and saves them from harm. We shall give great wealth to the poor, in hopes that God will clarify your soul, and that wisdom will course through your brain again."

Kay Khosrow's Answer to Zal

When Khosrow had heard Zal out he gave him a wise answer. He said: "Old man, your words and thoughts are always welcome; from the time of Manuchehr until now you have advised the court well. And your mammoth-bodied son Rostam has been a prop to the Kayanid kings, the cynosure of the court: it was he who brought up Seyavash and taught him virtue. When an army caught sight of his massive mace, his helmet and mighty stature, many would flee without fighting, abandoning their bows and arrows on the battlefield. He guided my ancestors in their wars of vengeance. If I list all your exploits I will be talking for a hundred generations, and if my words seem flattery they will, if examined truly, be seen to underestimate you. But as to your question about why I have not granted audience; the world has become contemptible to me, and for five weeks now I have stood in prayer before God, the Just Guide, asking that he absolve me of past sins and illuminate the darkened moon of my life; asking

that he take me from this fleeting world and that I suffer here no longer. I have been close to abandoning the ways of righteousness, to twisting my head aside as other kings before me have done; now that I have achieved all I sought I must prepare to leave this world, and good news has reached me. Last night at dawn I slept and an angel came to me from God, saying 'Rise, the time for your departure has come, your sleepless sorrow is over.' My reign, and all my concern for the army, crown, and throne, are drawing to an end."

Zal Advises Kay Khosrow

The courtiers listened to him in bewilderment, and sorrow filled their hearts. But Zal was angered, and heaved a cold sigh. He said to the assembled Persians: "This is not right, wisdom has no place in his mind. I have never seen a king who talked in this way, and since he has spoken his mind so must we. When he says such things we are under no obligation to agree with him. It's as if a demon has been advising him; he's abandoned the path of God. Feraydun and the god-fearing Hushang never grasped at such straws: I shall tell him the truth even if it means I shall suffer for it." The Persians answered him: "No Kayanid has ever talked like this: we are all behind you in what you tell the king."

Zal stood and addressed Kay Khosrow: "Just king, listen to the words of an old and experienced man, and if my advice seems crooked to you make me no answer. Speech in support of what is right is bitter, and this bitterness closes the door against injury and loss. You should not be offended by the true words that I say here, in this company. Your mother bore you in Turan, and you grew up there; you're the grandson on one side of Afrasyab, who practiced black magic even in his sleep. Your other grandfather was that malevolent king Kavus whose dissembling face hid a heart filled with trickery and cunning. He ruled from the east to the west but he wanted to fly up to the heavens and count the stars there. I advised him at length not to try this, and my words were bitter: he heard my advice but it did him no good and I left him with a heart full of sorrow and pain. He rose into the air and tumbled to earth; God granted him his life but he felt no gratitude, his head was filled with dust, his mind with terror. You led a hundred thousand armed warriors to battle on the Chorasmian plain, and before the armies you fought on foot with Pashang. If he had conquered you, Iran would have been open to Afrasyab's forces, but God delivered him into your hands. You were able to kill whoever men feared, whoever gave no thought to God's law. I told you to cease your wars then, that the time for forgiveness and rejoicing had arrived. But now worse times than ever have come to Iran, and men's hearts are filled with a more terrible fear; you've abandoned God's ways, and strayed into an evil path. You'll get no profit from this, and it will not please God. My king, if this is what you want no one will support you; you'll regret these words, think of what you're doing and don't follow demons' orders. If you persist in this devilish plan God will cut you off from his *farr*; you will live a life of pain and sin and no one will call you king again. If you ignore my advice you are following Ahriman; pain will be yours, and you will lose good fortune, the homage due to a king, and the throne itself. May wisdom guide your soul, may your mind remain pure and steadfast!"

Zal fell silent and the whole company spoke in his support, saying: "We agree with all that this old man has said: the doorway to truth should not be concealed!"

Kay Khosrow's Answer to Zal

When Khosrow had heard him out he said nothing for a while, and remained lost in thought. Then he spoke quietly, weighing his words. "You have seen the world's ways Zal, and you have lived long years chivalrously and well. If I spoke coldly to you here before this assembly, God would not approve of such an evil act. Also, Rostam would be upset, and when he is upset Iran suffers; his efforts on Iran's behalf far outweigh the wealth he has received as a reward. The heavens made him my shield, the scourge of evildoers, leaving them time for neither sleep nor food. I shall answer you mildly, my words won't break your heart." Then in a voice that all could hear he said, "My victorious lords, I have heard everything that Zal has said before this assembly. I swear by God himself that I am far from obeying demons: it is to God that my soul inclines, for I see him as the cure to my suffering. In clarity of heart I have looked on the world, and wisdom has become my armor against evil." Turning to Zal he said, "There's no need for such anger; speak as is fitting. First, you said no wise or perspicacious person was ever born of Turanian stock: I am the son of the great Seyavash, the scion of an invincible Kayanid king, the grandson of Kavus who was a wise, fortunate, and well-loved monarch. On my mother's side I am descended from Afrasyab, whose hatred deprived me of rest and food; his forebear was Feraydun and there is no shame in such an ancestry, for Iran's lion-like warriors fled to the sea in terror before Afrasyab. Then you said that Kavus built himself a flying chariot, and tried to go beyond what is fitting for a king: but you should know that ambition is not a fault in a king. Next I sought revenge for my father's death and won victory in all the world: I killed my enemies who had spread injustice throughout the land. My task in the world is complete; no trace remains of the evildoers against whom I fought. Whenever I think deeply about prosperity and enduring royal power I see the examples of Kavus and Jamshid before me; I fear that I'll forget my status as they did, that I'll become corrupt like Zahhak and Tur, whose evil sickened the world. I fear that when the thread of my days draws to an end I, like them, shall be headed for hell.

"For these five weeks in which I have prayed day and night, know that the great God has freed me from the sorrows of this dark earth. I am sated with my army, the crown, and the throne: I am unencumbered now, and ready to depart. You Zal, with all the experience of your advanced age, say that I have fallen into a demon's trap, that I am wandering far from the right road in darkness and sin: but I cannot see how I have done evil, or where you can find God's punishment in all this."

Zal Asks for Forgiveness

When Zal heard these words he turned aside in shame; a cry came from his lips and he addressed Khosrow:

> "Great king, my words were hasty and unwise,
> Wisdom is yours, and I apologize;
> If demons have deluded anyone
> I am that person—forgive what I have done.
> I've lived for countless years, and always shown
> Unswerving loyalty to Persia's throne,
> Till now I've never seen a monarch pray
> For heaven's holy guidance in this way,
> But Kay Khosrow is now my sapient guide,
> And may I stay forever at his side.
> Throughout Iran all virtuous men will grieve
> To learn the king we've served now longs to leave,
> How can we hope for this? But what he chooses
> No loyal subject of the king refuses."

When Khosrow heard Zal's words he accepted his apology, knowing that all he said came only from his love for him: he took Zal by the hand and sat him next to himself on the throne. Then he said: "Go now with Rostam, Tus, Gudarz, Giv, and the rest of our nobility, and pitch tents and pavilions on the plain outside the city. Display our banners, assemble our troops and elephants there as if for a splendid celebration." Rostam did as the king ordered: the nobles brought tents and pavilions out of storage and filled the valley from mountain side to mountain side with white, black, purple, and blue tents; flags of red, yellow, and purple fluttered there, and in the midst of all stood the Kaviani banner. Zal's tent, with its black flag, was pitched next to the king's and on its left was Rostam's tent, where the dignitaries he had brought from Kabol were gathered. In the foreground were the tents of Tus, Gudarz, Giv, Gorgin, Kherrad, and Shapur; immediately behind them those of Bizhan, Gastahom, and the other important chieftains.

Kay Khosrow Addresses the Persians

The king sat on his golden throne and took the ox-headed mace in his hand. On one side, like a great mammoth and a savage lion, were Zal and Rostam and on the other Tus, Gudarz, Giv, Roham, Shapur, and Gorgin. All stared at the king, waiting to hear what he would say. He addressed them in a loud voice: "My champions, favored by Fortune, each of you with sense and wisdom knows that both good and evil pass away: we too, and the world itself, are ephemeral. Why then do we suffer such pain and sorrow and grief? We build with our hands and what we build we leave to our enemies, while we ourselves must depart: but the ox of our sorrows is still not skinned, since rewards and punishments are with God. Fear God then, and do not rejoice in this dark earth, for this day passes from everyone, and time counts every breath we breathe. From Hushang to Kavus there have been kings possessed of *farr*, the crown, and the throne; nothing remains of them but their names. No one can compute the number of those who have gone before us. Many turned against God, and in their last days they feared the evil they had done. I am a slave like them, and though I have striven and suffered I see that no one remains on this earth. Now that I have torn my heart and soul from this fleeting world, I have brought my grief and pain to an end. I have gained all I sought, and I have turned my face aside from the royal throne. I give to anyone I have offended whatever wealth he desires. I shall tell God, who knows all that is good, of the actions of those heroes who have helped me. I donate my possessions, my weapons, my treasuries, to the nobility of Iran. I have listed and hand over my cash and slaves and flocks, for I am setting out on a journey and have separated my heart from this earthly darkness. Rejoice now for a week, give yourself to pleasure and food and drink: wish me well, pray for my safe passage from this world, and that I may depart without suffering."

When the king finished speaking the heroes of Iran were bewildered and uncertain what to make of his words. One said, "This king is mad: wisdom and his heart are utter strangers to one another. Who knows what will become of him, or of the crown and throne?"

The plain and mountain slopes were filled with warriors; they formed groups and began to feast. The valley re-echoed with the sounds of flutes and singing and drunken shouts: the revels went on for a week, and no one gave a thought to pain or sorrow.

Kay Khosrow's Words to Gudarz

On the eighth day Kay Khosrow sat on his throne, but he wore neither the royal crown nor torque, and the royal mace was nowhere in evidence. Since he felt that the time for his departure was at hand he opened one of his treasuries and said to Gudarz: "Consider how the world passes, and take note of what is hidden as well as what is plain. There is a day for amassing treasure and a day for distributing it: look at our ruined frontier forts and bridges, at our crumbling reservoirs, destroyed by Afrasyab; look at our motherless children, at our widowed wives who sit alone and desolate, at our indigent old people, at those who harbor secret sorrows. Don't hold back the contents of our treasuries from those in need; distribute wealth to them, in fear of future bad fortune. And I have a treasury called 'Badavar' which is filled with jewels and diadems: use this for our ruined cities that have become lairs for leopards and tigers, for our smashed fire temples left without officiating priests, for those who are old and poor because they gave away their wealth when they were young, for our dried up wells left waterless for years. In the city of Sus there is another treasury built up by my grandfather; its name is 'Arus'; give its contents to Zal, Giv, and Rostam."

He then consigned the contents of his wardrobe to Rostam, together with his torques, royal jewels, corselet, and heavy maces. His flocks of horses he gave to Tus; his orchards and gardens to Gudarz; tired now of war, he gave his armor, in which he had endured so much, to brave Giv. To Fariborz, Kavus's son, he gave his castles, tents, pavilions, and stables, as well as his helmet and diadem. He gave to Bizhan a torque brighter than the planet Jupiter, and two famous rings set with rubies, with his name engraved on them, saying as he did so, "Take these in memory of me, and see that you sow only seeds of righteousness in this world."

The Persians Remonstrate with Kay Khosrow

The king said, "My life draws to an end, and I long for another dispensation. Ask from me what you will; the time has come for this assembly to disperse." All the nobles wept at the prospect of losing their sovereign lord, and said, "Who will inherit the king's crown?"

Zal, who had always been loyal to the Persian throne, kissed the ground and stood to speak: "Lord of the world, it is right that I express my desires openly. You know what Rostam has done for Iran; the pains he has taken, the labors he has undergone, the battles he has fought. When Kavus went to distant Mazanderan and was captured by demons, along with Gudarz and Tus, Rostam went there alone on a journey that pitted him against deserts, darkness, demons, a lion, a dragon, and a sorceress. He won through to the king in Mazanderan; he cut the White Demon in pieces and did the same to other demons there too, and he severed the head of Sanjeh, whose screams re-echoed to the heavens. Because of Kavus's enmity, he killed his son Sohrab, whose like the world had never seen, and wept for him for months and years. If I were to describe all the tales of his prowess I would never finish. If the king is tired of his crown and throne what will he leave to this loyal, lion-hearted warrior?"

Khosrow replied, "Who but God himself, the lord of justice and love, can know all that Rostam has done on my behalf, the struggles he has undertaken, the sorrows he has suffered? His valor is no secret, and no one has seen his equal in all the world."

He ordered that a scribe bring paper, musk, and ambergris, and a document was written, by Khosrow's command, conferring on Rostam, the mammoth-bodied warrior who was praised by all men, the lordship of Sistan. The document was affixed with the royal seal and Khosrow handed it to Rostam, saying, "May this land remain forever under Rostam's sovereignty." He then gave robes, gold, silver, and a goblet filled with jewels to the astrologers who had come to court with Zal.

Then Gudarz rose and addressed the king: "Victorious king, I have seen no occupant of the throne to equal you. From the time of Manuchehr to that of Kay Qobad, and throughout noble Kavus's reign, I stood ready and vigilant in our kings' service. I had seventy-eight sons and grandsons; eight are left to me and the others have perished. My son Giv lived as a fugitive in Turan for seven years; wild asses were his food, and he clothed himself in their skins. When the king reached Iran he saw all that Giv had endured on his behalf. And now that the lord of all the world is tired of the throne and crown, Giv hopes for a reward for his labors."

The king replied: "He did far more than this, and may he be blessed a thousand times! May God protect him, and may his enemies' hearts be lacerated with thorns! All I have is yours; I pray that you survive in health and glory!" He ordered that a charter be written on silk, conferring sovereignty of Qom and Esfahan, the cradle of champions, on Gudarz; a gold seal was attached to it, and Khosrow pronounced his benediction saying, "May God be pleased with Gudarz, and may his enemies' hearts be filled with confusion." To the Persian nobility he said, "My hope is that Giv will never tire of his noble deeds: know that he will be a remembrance of me in the world, the defender whom I leave to you. Obey him, and do not slight either his or his father's commands."

When Gudarz had taken his seat again, Tus rose and kissed the ground before Khosrow. He said: "Long live the king, and may evil never touch him! I alone of those here am descended from Feraydun, and I headed this clan until Kay Qobad came. I have led the Persians in battle, and have never relaxed my vigilance, not for a single day. In the mountains of Hamavan I endured the wounds my armor inflicted on my shirtless body; in the battle of revenge for Seyavash I kept watch every night; when Kavus was imprisoned in Mazanderan, Tus was imprisoned with him: I have never deserted our troops and no one has ever complained of my conduct. Now that the king, who knows all my abilities and faults, has grown tired of his crown and throne and prepares to leave this fleeting world, what orders does he give me? What authority does he leave me?"

Khosrow replied, "You have striven and suffered beyond measure; be lord of the Kaviani banner, commander of my armies, and the sovereign of Khorasan." This too was recorded before the nobles, written on a royal charter, and sealed with gold.

Kay Khosrow Confers the Crown on Lohrasp

When the king had dealt with his nobles' affairs, he sank back, exhausted and weak. One who had not been mentioned yet as a beneficiary of the king's bequests was Lohrasp, and Khosrow ordered Bizhan to bring this chieftain before him. As he entered, the king rose and opened his arms in welcome. Descending from the throne, he lifted the crown from his own head and gave it to Lohrasp saying, "I bestow on you sovereignty over the land of Iran: may this crown that is new to you bring you good fortune, and may all the world be as your slave. I hand over to you here the sovereignty and treasure which I have built up with such struggle and pain. Henceforth see that only justice issues from your mouth, since it is justice that will bring you victory and prosperity; if you would have your luck remain ever young and fresh, allow no demons access to your soul. Be wise, harm no one, and always guard your tongue." Then he turned to the Persians assembled there and said, "Rejoice in his throne and good fortune!"

The Persians were astonished by this turn of events, and bridled like angry lions; none could accept that they would have to call Lohrasp their king. Zal strode forward and said aloud what he felt in his heart: "My lord, is it right for you to dignify such dirt in this way? My curses on anyone who calls Lohrasp his king, no one here will submit to such injustice! I saw Lohrasp when he arrived in Iran; he was a wretch with one horse to his name. You sent him off to fight against the Alans, and gave him soldiers, a banner, and a sword belt. How many wellborn Persians has the king passed over for this man, whose family I've never set eyes on, whose ancestry's all unknown? No one has ever heard of such a man becoming a king."

As soon as Zal finished speaking a roar of agreement came from the courtiers there, and voices cried out, "We'll serve no longer! If Lohrasp is to be king he can count on us for neither his banquets nor his battles." When

Khosrow heard Zal's words he said to him, "Not so fast, and calm your rage: a man who speaks unjustly is more interested in smoke than fire. God does not approve of our doing evil, and the wicked will tremble before the revolutions of Fate. When God makes a man fortunate, deserving of sovereignty, an ornament to the throne, that man has wisdom then, as well as *farr*, dignity, and royal ancestry; he will be just and victorious, and his justice will bring him prosperity. As God is my witness, Lohrasp is possessed of these qualities. He is descended from the pure-souled Hushang, who was lord of all the world; he will cleanse the earth of evil magicians and establish the ways of God; the world will be renewed through his guidance, and his son will continue his legacy. Greet him as your king, and as you love me do not turn aside from my advice. Any man who ignores my words has destroyed whatever credit he may have built up fighting for me; he is ungrateful before God and his soul will be assailed from every side by terror."

When Zal had heard him out he touched the earth with his fingers and smeared black dirt on his lips. Loudly, he greeted Lohrasp as king, and said to Khosrow, "Live in happiness my lord, and may evil never touch you. Who but the king of victory and justice could have known that Lohrasp was of royal descent? I have sworn repentance for what I said, blackening my lips with dirt; may my sin be cancelled." The chieftains scattered jewels over Lohrasp, hailing him as king.

Kay Khosrow Bids Farewell

The great king said to his people, "The road I take now is the one you will take tomorrow: when I have left this wretched earth behind me I shall commend you to God." His eyelashes were wet with tears as he kissed each of them farewell: weeping openly, he embraced the heroes one by one. He said, "Would that I could take all of this company with me." Such a cry went up from the army that the sun lost its way in the heavens: women and little children wept for him in the streets and bazaars, and the houses were filled with groans and lamentation for the king's passing. The king said:

> "Glorious for your deeds, and glorious in descent,
> Rejoice in God's commands and be content.
> Now I prepare my soul for death; my name
> Shall live henceforth with undiminished fame,
> Sorush has come to guide me, and my heart
> Withdraws from life: I'm ready to depart."

He called for a horse, and as his soldiers lamented, he rode toward the royal apartments, his cypress-stature bent with age and weakness over the pommel. He had four women who were as beautiful as the sun, such that no man had ever seen except in dreams: he summoned them and told them what was in his heart. He said: "It is time for me to leave this fleeting world; I am tired of the earth's injustice, and you will never see me alive again. Keep your hearts free of pain and grief."

But the four fainted, and when they revived they wailed aloud for love and sorrow: they scored their cheeks and tore out their hair, they ripped their fine clothes and destroyed their jewelry, and cried out to him, "Take us with you from this hateful world, be our guide to the happiness you seek." The king answered, "The road I take now is the one you will take tomorrow: there Jamshid's sisters live, and great kings in their pomp and glory; my mother, Afrasyab's daughter, is there, who fled across the Oxus with me, and Tur's incomparable daughter Mah Afarid. The bed and pillow of them all is dust, and I do not know whether they dwell in hell or heaven. Don't try to deflect me from my journey; it will be easy enough to find me." He wept and called Lohrasp to him and said to him, "These are my womenfolk, the glory of my bedchamber: while you are king, grant them the same privileges and quarters they have always had. See that they are no cause of shame to you when God summons you to His presence: remember, you will see me there, next to Seyavash. Do nothing that will humiliate you when you stand before us in the other world." Lohrasp agreed to all he said, promising to maintain the king's women in respectable privacy.

Then the king bound on his sword belt and went out to address his men, to whom he said: "Have no pain or fear in your hearts because of me. Do not rush to embrace this world, for its depths are but darkness: live in justice and happiness, and think only well of me." Iran's chieftains bowed their heads to the ground and said that they would remember his advice as long as they lived. He told Lohrasp to take up residence in the palace, saying that his own days were now at an end. "Maintain the royal throne in glory, sow only seeds of righteousness in the world: when nothing threatens or troubles you, see that the crown and luxury and wealth do not corrupt your soul. Remember that your departure will not be delayed for long, and that the days of your life narrow towards their end. Seek justice, act with justice, free those who are just from evil."

Lohrasp wept and dismounted from his horse and kissed the ground. Kay Khosrow said to him, "Farewell, be the warp and woof of justice in this world."

Zal, Rostam, Gudarz, Giv, Bizhan, and Gastahom, together with Kavus's son Fariborz who made a seventh and Tus who made an eighth, accompanied by their separate bands of troops, went with Kay Khosrow as he made his way from the plain to the mountain foothills. There they rested for a week, moistening their dry lips, wailing and weeping at the king's decision:

no man could reconcile himself to such sorrow, and the priests said in secret that no one had ever heard of a king acting in this way.

When the sun rose over the mountain peaks, groups came from every direction, a hundred thousand Persian men and women, weeping before the king; all the mountain side was filled with the sounds of mourning, and the granite slopes re-echoed with their cries. They said: "Great king, what has filled your bright soul with such pain and confusion? If you are angry with the army, or if you're tired of the crown, tell us why, but do not quit the Persian throne, or hold the crown in contempt. Stay, and we shall be the dust beneath your horse's hooves, the slaves of your eternal flame. But where is your knowledge, your judgment, your wisdom? The angel Sorush never appeared to a king before, not even to Feraydun: we pray before God and in our fire-temples that God will grant our desire, and that the priests' hearts will look favorably on us."

The king was astonished at this outpouring and called his priests to him. He said, "What happens from now on is a blessing, and why should men weep at a blessing? Be grateful to God, be pure and Godfearing: do not grieve at my departure for we shall all be reunited soon enough." Then he turned to his chieftains and said, "Descend this mountain side without your king: the road ahead is long, hard, and waterless, without vegetation or shade. No one can traverse these slopes unless he has the divine *farr* to help him." Three of the heroes, Zal, Rostam, and Gudarz, heard him and obeyed: but Tus, Giv, Fariborz, Bizhan, and Gastahom did not turn back.

The group went forward for a day and into the night, weakened by the wilderness and lack of water. Then they came on a stream, where they refreshed themselves and rested. The king said to his followers, "We'll stay the night here and talk over the past: you won't see me for much longer now. When the shining sun unfurls its banner and turns the purple land a liquid gold, the time for me to part from you will have come. Then I shall meet Sorush: if my heart trembles at this last journey I shall tear its darkness from my side."

Kay Khosrow Disappears

When part of the night had passed, Khosrow bent over the stream and washed his head and body in its clear water, murmuring the words of the Zend Avesta as he did so. Then he addressed his companions:

> "Farewell forever. When the sun's first beams
> Appear, henceforth I'll come to you in dreams
> But you will never see me here again.
> Go back tomorrow to the Persian plain—

Even if musk should rain down far and wide
Don't linger on this lonely mountain side;
A wind will blow here soon, a wind to freeze
The mountain slopes and uproot stalwart trees,
From dark clouds snow will fall, you'll lose your way
Back to your Persian home if you delay."
Weary and saddened by his words they wept,
Uneasily, at last, the heroes slept:
And when the dawn's light touched their resting place
The king had gone, leaving no earthly trace.

They searched the desolate mountain slopes, but as they found no sign of him they returned to the stream like men insensible with grief, and in their hearts they bade a last farewell to the world's king.

Fariborz said, "I can't believe that Khosrow's words were wise: the earth is warm and soft, and the weather's clear; given what we've suffered I don't think it's reasonable for us to set off immediately. We should rest and eat, and after we've slept we can leave this stream and go back." They camped by the stream and went over what Khosrow had done, saying that no one had ever seen or heard of such a wonder (nor would he even if he remained in the world for a long time) as this departure of the king which they had witnessed. They lamented his good fortune and wisdom, his greatness and nobility; but they added that the wise would laugh at the notion that a man could go before God while he was still alive. Who knew what had befallen Khosrow, and what could they say when people refused to believe them? Giv said, "No hero has ever heard of a man who was his equal, not for manliness, generosity, wisdom, valor, appearance, stature, glory, or lineage: leading his troops in battle he was massive as a mammoth, and presiding crowned at his banquets he was radiant as the full moon."

Tus, Fariborz, Giv, Bizhan, and Gastahom Die in the Snow

They ate the provisions they had with them and soon fell asleep. But a wind sprang up and black clouds amassed; the air became as dark as a lion's maw, a blizzard began to blow, and the snow piled higher than the heroes' lances. One by one they were buried in the snow; for a while they struggled beneath its canopy, trying to clear a space to survive, but finally their strength gave out and their sweet souls sought release.

Rostam, Zal, and Gudarz had waited for three days further down the mountain side. As the fourth day dawned they said, "This has gone on too long, how long must we wait here on these stony slopes? If the king has

disappeared from the world, like a wind that blows through a group of heroes and is gone, what has happened to our chieftains? Didn't they follow Khosrow's advice?" They waited for a week on the mountain side, but when the week was over they despaired of seeing their companions again. They mourned for them, and Gudarz tore out his hair and scored his cheeks with his nails. He said: "No man has ever seen such evil as has come to me from the seed of Kavus: I had an army of sons and grandsons, ambitious and noble youths all of them, and all were slain in the wars of revenge for Seyavash, so that our tribe was broken and lost its luster. And now another has disappeared from my sight; who has seen such sorrows as I have endured?"

Zal counseled him at length: "To be wise is to accept God's justice: they may yet find a way through the snow and return. But we should not stay on this mountain side and lamentation will not help us. We can send footsoldiers out to look for some trace of them." Weeping, they made their way down the mountain side, each thinking of one or another of the lost heroes, of his son or relative or friend, and of the king who had been like a cypress overtopping all the orchard.

> So turns the world; her favors are soon passed,
> All whom she nourishes must die at last.
> One she will raise from earth to heights unknown,
> One she will cast down from a royal throne;
> But there's no cause to triumph or complain,
> Such is the way she turns, and turns again:
> Where are those heroes now, those champions, where?
> Drive out such mortal thoughts, that bring despair.

*L*ohrasp became king of Iran, as Khosrow had directed. He had two sons Goshtasp and Zarir, and while still a young man Goshtasp demanded that his father name him as heir to the throne. His father refused to do this, and Goshtasp left the court in high dudgeon and traveled to India. His brother Zarir was sent to fetch him home again, but no sooner was he back in Iran than he quarreled with his father and set off on his travels again, this time to Rum, where he lived in disguise. There he tried his hand at various occupations but his royal qualities rendered him unfit for all of them. He was seen by Katayun, the King of Rum's daughter and she fell in love with him. Reluctantly the king allowed his daughter to marry the stranger, who then ingratiated himself with the court by killing a wolf and a dragon. Once established as his father-in-law's favorite, he began to threaten Iran. When he finally returned to Iran accompanied by his Rumi bride Katayun, Lohrasp ceded him the throne and went into religious retirement at Balkh.

At this point Ferdowsi includes in his text an account, by the poet Daqiqi, of the coming of the prophet Zoroaster to Goshtasp's court, and the acceptance by the court of the new religion promulgated by him.

A new king, Arjasp, now reigned in Turan, and at the prompting of Zoroaster Goshtasp demanded tribute from him. In response Arjasp attacked Iran. Goshtasp's brother Zarir was killed in the ensuing war, and it was only the valor of Goshtasp's son, Esfandyar, that was able to drive the Turanian army back. Esfandyar is presented as ambitious, but also righteous, chivalrous, and an invincible warrior: he embraced the court's new faith of Zoroastrianism with great zeal, and propagated the faith by the sword. But his enemies at court made his father suspicious of his ambitions for the throne: Goshtasp believed the calumny and imprisoned Esfandyar.

Hearing of this Arjasp sent an army against Balkh: the city was sacked, the aged Lohrasp killed, and many Persian prisoners, including Esfandyar's sisters, were taken back to Turan. Goshtasp appealed for help to Rostam, but the now aged hero made his excuses and refused to have anything to do with the situation. Goshtasp himself led the counter attack and was defeated, barely escaping from the battlefield with his life. His counselor Jamasp advised him that only Esfandyar could save the situation: Esfandyar was released from prison and drove back the Turanian army.

Goshtasp then asked Esfandyar to travel deep into Turanian territory to rescue his sisters, who were being held in a fortress made of brass. Esfandyar's journey to the brass fortress involved him in a series of seven trials, which closely parallel the trials undergone by Rostam when he traveled to Mazanderan to rescue Kavus from captivity. When Esfandyar reached the fortress he rescued his sisters, using the same trick to penetrate its impregnable defenses (of disguising himself and his warriors as merchants) that Rostam had used early in his career against the castle on the White Mountain. During the rescue, Arjasp was killed, and Esfandyar then returned in triumph to Iran, fully expecting to be given royal honors by his father. But Goshtasp had one more task in store for him.

یداز و فرخ اسفندیار
مند گفتا د پیت پشت شاد
در کفتش اسفندیار
و نکه نایم نفر مان کبی

که جو نست شاه آن کبنی مدار
پرشش را بو سپید و نامه بد
جبهٔ منی مرا اندرس روزگار
برون سر ده هاشم سر کهدی

⇥ ROSTAM AND ESFANDYAR ⇤

I heard a story from a nightingale, repeating words come down to us from ancient times.

One night, drunk and dejected, Esfandyar came from his father's palace and went to see his mother Katayun, the daughter of the king of Rum. He embraced her, called for more wine, and said: "The king treats me badly; he told me that once I'd avenged the death of his father by killing king Arjasp, freed my sisters from captivity, cleansed the world of evildoers and promoted our new faith of Zoroastrianism, then he would hand over to me the throne and crown; I'd be king and leader of our armies. When the sun rises and he wakes up I'm going to remind him of his own words: he shouldn't keep from me what's rightfully mine. By God who guides the heavens, I swear that if I see any hesitation in his face I'll place the crown on my own head and distribute the country to its local lords; I'll be as strong and fierce as a lion, and make you queen of Iran."

His mother's heart was saddened at his words; her silk clothes pricked like thorns against her skin. She knew that the king was in no hurry to hand over his crown, throne, country, and royal authority to his son. She said: "Brave boy, don't be so angry with your fate. The army and treasury are yours already, don't over-reach yourself. What's finer in all the world than a young lion-like warrior, girded for war, standing ready to serve his father? When Goshtasp dies, his crown, throne, greatness, and splendor will all be yours."

Esfandyar replied: "It was a wise man who said a man should never tell his secrets to women, because as soon as he opens his mouth he finds his words on everyone's lips. And he also said a man shouldn't do what a woman tells him to, because none of them have any sense." His mother's face clouded with pain and shame, and she regretted having spoken to him.

Esfandyar went back to his father's palace and spent two days and nights there drinking, surrounded by musicians and his womenfolk. Goshtasp brooded on his son's ambitions for the crown and throne, and on the third day he summoned his councilor Jamasp, and had Esfandyar's horoscope cast. He asked whether the prince would have a long and happy life, reigning in safety and splendor, and whether he would die at another's hand or greet the angel Sorush from a peaceful deathbed.

When Jamasp consulted the astrological tables, frowns furrowed his forehead and his eyes filled with tears. He said: "Evil is mine, and my knowledge brings me only evil; would that I had died before your brother Zarir, and not seen his body weltering in blood and dust, or that my father had killed me and this evil fate had not been mine. Esfandyar subdues lions, he has cleared Iran of its enemies, he is fearless in war, he has driven your foes from the face of the earth, he tears the dragon's body in two. But will not sorrow come from this, and the taste of bitterness and grief?"

The king replied, "I trust you to tell me what you know, and not to deviate from wisdom's ways. If he is to die as Zarir did, my life will be a misery to me. You frowned at my question, but tell me what you see: at whose hand will he die, bringing me tears and sorrow?"

Jamasp said, "My lord, misfortune will not hold back because of me. He will die in Zabolestan, fighting with Zal's son, Rostam."

Then the king said, "Take seriously what I'm about to say: if I give him my treasury, the throne and sovereignty, and if he never travels to Zabolestan, will he be safe from the turnings of Fate, will fortunate stars watch over him?" But the astrologer replied, "The heaven's turnings cannot be evaded; neither strength nor valor will save you from the dragon's claws. What is fated will surely come to pass, and a wise man does not ask when." The king grew pensive, and his thoughts made his soul like a tangled thicket. He brooded on the turnings of Fate, and his speculations turned him towards evil.

At dawn the next day the king sat on his throne, and Esfandyar stood humbly before him, his arms crossed on his chest. The court was filled with famous warriors, and the priests stood ranged before the king. Then the mighty champion Esfandyar spoke, and suffering was evident in his voice. He said: "Great king, may you live forever, blessed by the divine *farr*. Justice and love emanate from you, and the crown and throne are made more splendid by you. Father, I am your slave, prompt to carry out all you desire. You know that in the wars of religion with Arjasp, who attacked us with his Chinese cavalry, I swore before God that I would destroy any idolater who threatened our faith, that I would slash his trunk in two with my dagger and feel no fear. And when Arjasp came I did not flee from the leopard's lair. But drinking at your banquet you believed Gorazm's slander, and had me hung with heavy chains and fettered in the fortress of Gonbadan, despised among strangers. You abandoned Balkh and traveled to Zavol, thinking all battles were banquets, and forgetting the sight of your father Lohrasp pierced by Arjasp's sword, lying prone in his blood. When your councilor Jamasp came and saw me worn away by captivity, he tried to persuade me to accept the throne and sovereignty. I answered that I would show my heavy chains to God on the Day of Judgment. He told me of the chieftains who'd been killed, of my imprisoned sisters, of our king fleeing before the Turkish hordes, and asked me if such things did not wring my heart. He said much more besides, and all his words were filled with sorrow and pain. Then I smashed my chains and ran to the king's court: I slaughtered his enemies and rejoiced the king's heart. If I were to describe my seven trials the account would never end. I severed Arjasp's head from his body and avenged the name of Lohrasp. I brought here their treasure, their crown, their throne, and their women and children. I did all you had commanded me, kept to all your orders, never swerved from your advice. You'd said that if you ever saw me alive again you would cherish me more than your own wellbeing; that you would bestow the crown and ivory throne on me, because I would be worthy of both. And now when our nobles ask me where my treasure and army are, I blush for shame. What excuse do you have now? What's the point of my life? What has all my suffering been for?"

The king answered his son: "There's no way forward but the truth. You have acted as you say, and may God favor you for it. I see no enemy in all the world, neither open nor secret, who does not shudder at the mention of your name: shudder I say, he gives up his soul there and then. No one in all the world is your equal, unless it be that foolish son of Zal. His valor lifts him above the skies, and he thinks of himself as no

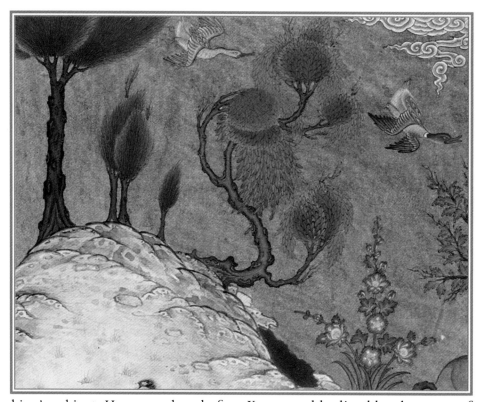

king's subject. He was a slave before Kavus, and he lived by the grace of Khosrow; but about me, Goshtasp, he says, 'His crown is new, mine is ancient; no man anywhere is my equal in battle, not in Rum nor Turan nor Iran.' Now, you must travel to Sistan and there use all your skill, all your ruses and devices. Draw your sword and your mace, bind Rostam in chains; do the same with Zavareh and Faramarz, and forbid them to ride in the saddle. I swear by the Judge of all the world, by Him who lights the sun and moon and stars, that when you do what I have commanded, you shall hear no more opposition from me. I shall hand over to you my treasury and crown, and I myself will seat you on the throne."

This was Esfandyar's response: "O noble and resourceful king, you are straying from the ancient ways; you should speak as is appropriate. Fight with the king of China, destroy the lords of the steppe, but what are you doing fighting against an old man whom Kavus called a conqueror of lions? From the time of Manuchehr and Kay Qobad all the kings of Iran have delighted in him, calling him Rakhsh's master, world-conqueror, lion-slayer, crown-bestower. He's not some young stripling making his way in the world; he is a great man, one who entered into a pact with Kay Khosrow. If such pacts are wrong then he shouldn't be seeking one with you, Goshtasp."

His father said: "My lion-hearted prince, you've heard that Kavus was led astray by the devil, that he attempted to fly into the skies on the wings

of eagles and fell wretchedly into the sea at Sari; that he brought a devil-born wife back from Hamaveran and gave her command of the royal harem; that Seyavash was destroyed by her wiles and the whole royal clan put in peril. When a man has broken his promise before God, it's wrong even to pass by his doorway. If you want the throne and crown, gather your troops and take the road for Sistan. When you arrive bind Rostam's arms, and lead him here. Watch that Zavareh, Faramarz, and Sam don't trick you: drag them all on foot to this court. And then no one, no matter how rich or illustrious he might be, will disobey my commands again."

The young prince answered: as he spoke he frowned,
"Enough! It isn't them you're circling round,
You're not pursuing Zal and Rostam—I,
Your son, am singled out by you to die;
Your jealous passion for your sovereignty
Has made you want to rid the world of me.
So be it! Keep your royal crown and throne,
Give me a corner to live in alone.
I'm one of many slaves, no more; my task
Is to perform whatever you may ask."

Goshtasp replied: "Don't be too impetuous, but if you're to achieve greatness don't hold back either. Choose experienced cavalry from our army; weapons, troops, and cash are all at your disposal, and any holding back will be because of your own suspicious mind. What would treasure, an army, the crown, and throne be to me without you?"

Esfandyar said, "An army will be of no use to me in this situation. If the time to die has come, a commander can't ward it off with troops." Troubled by thoughts of the crown, and by his father's words, he left the court and made his way to his own palace; there were sighs on his lips, and sadness filled his heart.

Katayun's Advice to Esfandyar

Weeping and in a turmoil of emotion, the beautiful Katayun came before her son, to whom she said: "You remind us of the ancient heroes, and I have heard from Bahman that you mean to leave our gardens and journey to the wastes of Zabolestan. You are to capture Zal's son, Rostam, the master of sword and mace. Listen to your mother's advice; don't be in a hurry either to suffer evil or commit it. Rostam is a horseman with a mammoth's strength, a river's force is nothing against him; he ripped out the guts of the White Demon, the sun is turned aside in its path by his sword. When he sought revenge for the death of Seyavash, and made war on Afrasyab, he turned the world to a sea of blood. Don't throw your life away for the sake of a crown; no king was ever born crowned. My curses on this throne and this crown, on all this slaughter and havoc and plundering. Your father's grown old, and you are young, strong, and capable; all the army looks to you, don't let this anger of yours put you in harm's way. There are other places in the world besides Sistan; there's no need to be so headstrong, so eager for combat. Don't make me the most wretched woman both here and in the world to come; pay attention to my words, they come from a mother's love."

Esfandyar replied: "Dear mother, listen to me: you know what Rostam is, you're always talking about his greatness. It would be wrong to kill him, and no good can come of the king's plan: there's no one in Iran who's finer or more noble than Rostam. All this is true, but don't break my heart, because if you do I shall tear it from my body. How can I ignore the king's orders, how can I refuse such a mission? If heaven wills it I shall die in Zabol, but if Rostam accepts my orders he'll hear no harsh words from me."

His mother said, "My mammoth warrior, your strength makes you careless of your soul, but you won't be strong enough to defeat Rostam. Don't leave here without warriors to help you, offering your life up to Rostam like this. If you're determined to go, this mission is the work of Ahriman; at least don't take your children to this hell, because the wise will not think well of you if you do," and as she spoke she wept bloody tears and tore at her hair.

Esfandyar replied, "It's wrong to keep youngsters away from battle. If a boy stays shut up with women he becomes weak and sullen; he should be present on the battle-field and learn what fighting means. I don't need to take an army with me: men from my own family and a few noblemen will suffice."

At cock-crow the next morning the din of drums rang out; Esfandyar mounted his horse and set off like the wind at the head of a band of warriors. They went forward until they came to a place where the road forked; one track led to the fortress of Gonbadan and the other toward Zabol. The camel that was in the lead lay down on the earth as if it never meant to rise again, and though its driver beat it with a stick it refused to budge, and the caravan halted. Esfandyar took this as a bad omen, and gave orders that the beast's head be severed, hoping to deflect the bad luck he foresaw. This was done, and although Esfandyar was alarmed he made light of it, saying:

"A noble warrior whose audacity
Lights up the world and brings him victory
Laughs at both good and evil, since he knows
Both come from God, whom no one can oppose."

Inwardly afraid of what lay ahead, he reached the River Hirmand, the border of Rostam's territory. A suitable place was selected, and the group pitched camp in the customary fashion. In Esfandyar's pavilion a throne was placed, and his warriors assembled before him. The prince called for wine and musicians, Pashutan sat opposite him, and as he drank and relaxed Esfandyar's face opened like a blossom in spring. He said to his companions: "I haven't carried out my father's orders; he told me to capture Rostam quickly, and not to hold back in humiliating him. I haven't done what he ordered me to, because this Rostam is a lion-hearted warrior, who has undergone many trials, whose mace has set the world in order, and in whose debt all Persians live whether they are princes or slaves. I must send him a messenger, someone who's wise and sensible, a horseman who has some dignity and presence, someone whom Rostam can't deceive. If he'll come to me and dispel this darkness in my soul, if he'll let me bind his arms and in so doing bind the evil that haunts me, and if he has no malevolence against me, I will treat him with nothing but kindness."

Pashutan said, "This is the right path; stick to it, and try to bring peace between men."

Esfandyar ordered his son Bahman to come before him, and said to him: "Saddle your black horse, and dress yourself in a robe of Chinese brocade; put a royal diadem studded with fine jewels on your head, so that whoever sees you will single you out as the most splendid of all warriors and know that you are of royal blood. Take with you ten reputable priests and five horses with golden bridles. Make your way to Rostam's palace, but do so at a leisurely pace. Greet him from me, be polite, flatter him with eloquent words, and then say to him: 'No one with any sense ignores a king's commands. A man must be grateful before God, who knows eternally what is good. If a man augments what is good and holds his heart back from evil, God will fulfill his desires and he will live happily in this fleeting world. If he abstains from evil he will find paradise in the other world; a wise man knows that in the end his bed will be the dark earth and his soul will fly up towards God. One who can distinguish between the good and evil of this world will be loyal to his king.

'Now we wish to reckon up what you have done, neither adding to nor diminishing your achievements. You've lived for many years and seen many kings come and go in the world, and if you follow the way of wisdom you know that it was not right for someone who has received so much in the way of wealth and glory from my family to have refused to visit Lohrasp's court. When he passed on sovereignty over the land of Iran to his son, Goshtasp, you paid no attention. You wrote no congratulatory letter to him, you ignored the duties of a subject, you didn't travel to his court to pay homage: you call no one king. Since the time of Hushang, Jamshid, and Feraydun, who wrested sovereignty from Zahhak, to the time of Kay Qobad, there never was such a king as Goshtasp, not for fighting or feasting or hunting. He has adopted the pure faith, and injustice and error have hidden themselves away: the way of God shines out like the sun, and the way of demons is destroyed. When Arjasp attacked with an innumerable army,

Goshtasp confronted him and made the battlefield a graveyard for his dead: great men will talk about this exploit until the end of the world. He breaks the back of every lion, and all the east and west are his: travel from Turan to China to Byzantium and you'll see that the world is like wax in his hands. The desert Arabs brandishing their lances send him tribute, because they have no heart or strength to fight against him. I tell you all this because the king is offended by your behavior. You haven't gone to his palace or seen his noble courtiers; instead, you've hidden yourself away in this remote province. But how can our leaders forget you, unless they have neither brains nor hearts remaining to them? You always strove for the good, and held yourself ready to do your kings' bidding. If your pains are reckoned up they exceed the treasure you've accumulated, but no king has ever accepted that his subject could act in this contemptuous way. Goshtasp has said to me that Rostam is so wealthy now that he sits drunk in Zavolestan and gives no thought to us. One day in his fury he swore an oath by the shining day and darkness of the night that no one would ever see you at his court unless it were in chains. Now, I have come from Iran for this purpose, and the king ordered me not to delay in carrying it out. Draw back now, and fear his anger. If you will go along with this and give up your contemptuous ways, I swear by the sun, by the spirit of Zarir, by my lion-like father's soul, that I will make the king take back his words, and that your glory will shine with splendor once again. Pashutan is my guide and witness that I have tried to fathom the king's purposes in this, and see no fault in him. My father is my king and I am his subject; I can never refuse his orders. Your whole clan—Zavareh, Faramarz, Zal, and all the rest of your tried and true chieftains—should hear my words and take my advice. This house must not be left a prey to Persian warriors and destroyed. When I take you bound before the king, and then go over your faults with him, I'll calm his anger and make him forget all thoughts of vengeance. I am a prince, and I give you my word that I will not let even the wind touch you.'"

Bahman Goes as a Messenger to Rostam

Bahman dressed himself in cloth of gold, placed a princely crown on his head, and set out from the encampment, his banner fluttering behind him. A proud young man, on a splendid horse, he made his way toward the River Hirmand, and as soon as the lookout saw him he shouted out to his companions in Zabolestan, "A fine warrior on a black horse is coming our way; his harness tinkles with golden bells, and he's followed by a group of mounted soldiers; he's already crossed the river with no difficulty."

As soon as he heard this Zal rode to the lookout post, his lariat coiled at his saddle and his mace at the ready. When he caught sight of Bahman he sighed and said, "This lordly young man with his royal clothes must be someone from Lohrasp's clan; may his coming here be auspicious for us." Pensively, his heart filled with foreboding, he rode back toward his castle. Radiating princely pride, Bahman approached; he did not recognize Zal, and raising his arm he called out, "My noble friend, where can I find great Rostam, the prop of our times? Esfandyar has camped by the river, and is looking for him."

Zal replied, "There's no need for such hurry, young man! Dismount, and call for wine, and calm yourself. Rostam is out hunting with Faramarz and a few friends; they'll be back soon enough. Rest here with your retinue, and drink a little wine."

But Bahman answered, "Esfandyar said nothing to us about wine and rest: find someone to guide us to the hunting grounds."

Zal said, "What's your name? Whose clan do you belong to, and what have you come here for? I think you're kin to Lohrasp, and descended from Goshtasp too."

Bahman said, "I am Bahman, son to invincible Esfandyar, lord of the world."

When he heard this Zal dismounted and made his obeisance before him. Bahman laughed and dismounted as well, and the two embraced and kissed. Zal urged him to stay, saying that his haste was unnecessary, but Bahman replied that Esfandyar's message could not be treated so lightly. And so Zal chose a warrior who knew the lie of the land and sent him with Bahman to where Rostam was hunting. He was an experienced man called Shirkhun, and after he had led him a fair distance he pointed out the way and went back, leaving Bahman to go on ahead.

Bahman urged his horse up a mountain slope, and when he reached the summit he gazed at the hunting grounds spread out below. He saw there a mighty warrior, a man massive as the cliff of Bisitun, who had uprooted a tree and was using it as a spit on which to roast a wild ass, which he handled as easily as if it weighed no more than an ant. In his other hand he held a goblet full of wine, and in front of him a young man was standing ready to serve him. Nearby, close to a stream and a clump of trees, Rakhsh stood cropping grass. Bahman said, "This is either Rostam, or the sun itself. No one has ever seen such a man in all the world, or heard of his like among the ancient heroes. I fear that Esfandyar will be no match for him, and will flinch from him in battle. I'll kill him here and now with a rock, and so break Zal's heart." He tore a granite boulder from the mountain side and sent it tumbling down the slope. Zavareh heard the rumble of its descent and saw it plunging toward them; he shouted out, "Rostam, a great rock is rolling down the mountain." Rostam made no move; he didn't even put down the wild ass he was roasting. As Zavareh hung back in alarm, Rostam

waited until the boulder was almost on him, and the dust it sent up had obscured the mountain above; then he kicked it contemptuously aside. Zavareh and Rostam's son Faramarz cheered, but Bahman was horrified at the exploit, and said, "If Esfandyar fights with such a warrior he'll be humiliated by him; it'll be better if he treats him politely and circumspectly. If Rostam gets the better of Esfandyar in combat he will be able to conquer all Iran." Bahman remounted his horse, and with his heart full of foreboding descended the mountain slope.

He told a priest of the wonder he had seen, and made his way by an easier path at the foot of the mountain toward Rostam. As he approached, Rostam turned to a companion and said, "Who is this? I think it's someone from Goshtasp's clan." Then he caught sight of Bahman's retinue waiting on the mountain side, and he grew suspicious. He and Zavareh, and the rest of the hunting party, went forward to greet their guest. Bahman quickly dismounted and greeted Rostam civilly. Rostam said, "You'll get nothing from me until you tell me who you are." Bahman replied, "I am Esfandyar's son, chief of the Persians; I am Bahman." Rostam immediately embraced him and apologized for his tardy welcome.

Together they made their way back to Rostam's camp and when Bahman had sat himself down he greeted Rostam formally, and conveyed to him the greetings of the king and his nobility. Then he went on: "Esfandyar has come here and pitched camp by the River Hirmand, as the king ordered him to. If you will hear me out, I bring you a message from him."

Rostam replied: "Prince, you've taken a great deal of trouble and traversed a great deal of ground; first we should eat, and then the world is at your disposal." A cloth was spread on the ground, and soft bread was placed on it; then Rostam set a roasted wild ass, its flesh still hot, before Bahman. He called for his brother Zavareh to sit with them, but not the rest of his companions. He had another wild ass brought, since it was his custom to eat a whole animal himself. He sprinkled it with salt, cut the meat, and set to. Bahman watched him, and ate a little of the wild ass's meat, but less than a hundredth of the amount Rostam consumed. Rostam laughed and said:

> "A prince who's so abstemious surely needs
> An army to assist him in his deeds:
> I've heard that in your father's battles you
> Fought with him: what exactly did you do?
> You eat so little you're too weak to wield
> A warrior's weapons on the battlefield."

Bahman replied:

> "A noble prince will neither talk at length
> Nor eat too much: he'd rather save his strength
> For battles than for banquets, since it's war
> That shows a warrior's worth, not who eats more."

Rostam laughed long and loud and said, "A fighting spirit won't stay hidden long!" He called for enough wine to sink a ship: filling a golden goblet, he toasted the memory of noble heroes, then handed another to Bahman and said, "Toast whoever you want to!" Seeing the proffered goblet Bahman hesitated, so Faramarz drank first, saying, "You're a princely child, we hope you enjoy the wine, and our drinking together." Bahman took the goblet and reluctantly drank a little; he was as astonished by Rostam's capacity for food and drink as he was by his massive body, arms, and shoulders. When they had finished their meal, the two heroes rode together for a while, side by side, and Bahman told Rostam the details of Esfandyar's message.

Rostam's Answer to Esfandyar

As he listened to Bahman's words, the old man grew pensive. He said, "I've heard your message through and I'm pleased to see you. Now, take my answer back to Esfandyar: 'Great, lion-hearted warrior, any man who is wise considers the realities of a situation. A man like you who's rich, brave, and successful in war, who has authority and a good name among other

chieftains, should not give his heart to malice and suspicion. You and I should act justly toward one another; we should fear God and not make evil welcome. Words that have no meaning are like a tree without leaves or scent, and if your heart's given over to greed and ambition, you will toil long and hard and see no profit for your pains. When a nobleman speaks he should weigh his words well and avoid idle talk. I've always been happy to hear you praised, to hear people say that no mother ever bore a son like you, that you surpass your ancestors in bravery, chivalry, and wisdom. Your name is known in India and Byzantium, and in the realms of wizards and witches; I praise God for your glory day and night and I have always longed to set eyes on you, to see for myself your splendor and graciousness. I welcome your arrival, and I ask that we sit together and drink to the king's health. I'll come to you alone, without my men, and listen to what the king has commanded. I'll bring you the charters past kings, from Kay Qobad to Kay Khosrow, have granted my family, and I'll make known to you the pains I've suffered, the difficulties I've endured, the good I've done for past princes, from ancient times up to the present day. If the right reward for all I have undergone is to be led in chains, would that I had never been born, or that once born I had soon died. Am I, who broke elephants' backs and flung their carcasses in the ocean, to come to court and publish all my secrets to the world, my arms tied, my feet hobbled in leather bonds? If it becomes known that I've committed any sin, may my head be severed from my body. May I never speak unseemly words, and you should keep yours for cursing devils; don't say these things that no one has ever said, and don't think your valor will enable you to catch the wind in a cage. No matter how great a man is, he can't pass through fire, or survive the seas if he can't swim, or dim the moon's light, or make a fox a lion's equal. Don't provoke me to a fight, because fighting with me will be no trivial matter: no man has ever seen fetters on my ankles, and no savage lion has ever made me give ground.

'Act as becomes a king; don't let yourself be guided by devils and demons. Be a man, drive anger and malice out of your heart, don't see the world through a young man's eyes. May God keep you happy and prosperous; cross the river, honor my house with your presence, don't refuse to see someone who offers you his allegiance. As I was Kay Qobad's subject, so I will serve you, willingly and cheerfully. Come to me without your armed companions, stay with me for two months; there's good hunting here, the waterways are full of fowl, and if you tire of this you can watch my swordsmen in combat with lions. When you want to return to the Persian court I'll load you with gifts from my treasury and travel side by side with you. I'll enter the king's presence and gently ask his pardon: when I've kissed his head and eyes and feet in sign of submission, I'll ask him why my feet should be shackled.' Now, remember everything I've said and repeat it to noble Esfandyar."

Bahman went back with his retinue of priests: Rostam remained in the roadway for a while, and called Zavareh and Faramarz to him. He said, "Go to Zal and tell him that Esfandyar has arrived, and that he's full of ambitious plans. Have a fine welcome prepared, something even more splendid than was customary in Kay Kavus's time: place a golden throne in the audience hall and have royal carpets spread before it. The king's son has come here and he's bent on war; tell Zal that this prince is a famous fighter and that he'd feel no fear confronted by a whole plain filled with lions. I'll go to him, and if he'll accept to be our guest we can hope for a good outcome; if I see that he's a well-disposed young man I'll give him a golden crown set with rubies, and I won't stint him jewels or fine cloth or weapons either. But if he turns me away and I come back here with no hope of a peaceful resolution, then you know that my looped lariat, which has caught wild elephants' heads in its coils, is always ready."

Zavareh said, "Give the matter no thought: a man who has no quarrel with someone doesn't go looking for a fight. I know of no stronger or more chivalrous warrior in all the world than Esfandyar. Wise men don't act in evil ways, and we've done him no harm." Zavareh made his way to Zal's court, and Rostam rode to the shore of the River Hirmand, fearful of the harm he foresaw. At the river's edge he tugged on the reins, halting his horse, and prayed to God.

Bahman Takes His Father Rostam's Message

When Bahman reached camp, his father was standing before the royal pavilion, waiting for him, and he called out "What did the hero tell you then?" Bahman went over all he'd heard. He began by giving Rostam's message and then he described Rostam himself. He told everything he'd seen, and much that he'd inferred, and ended by saying, "There's no one like Rostam anywhere. He has a lion's heart and a mammoth's body, he could snatch a sea monster from the waves. He's coming unarmed, with no corselet, helmet, mace, or lariat, to the banks of the Hirmand: he wants to see the king, and he has some private business I don't know about with you."

But Esfandyar angrily turned on Bahman and humiliated him before their companions saying,

> "No self-respecting warrior would ask
> Advice from women for a warrior's task,
> And no one who is soldierly or wise
> Would send a boy on such an enterprise.
> Just where have you seen champions, that you praise

This Rostam for his fine courageous ways?
He's like a mammoth in the wars you say—
D'you want my men to fight or run away!"

Then he said in an undertone to brave Pashutan, "This Rostam still acts like a young man, age hasn't broken him yet."

He gave orders that a black horse be saddled in gold, and then he led his men toward the bank of the Hirmand, his lariat coiled at his side.

Rostam Comes to Greet Esfandyar

Rakhsh neighed on one side of the river, and on the other the Persian prince's horse answered. Rostam urged Rakhsh from dry land into the water: when he had crossed he dismounted and greeted Esfandyar. He said: "I have asked God continually to guide you here as you have now come, in good health and accompanied by your army. Now, let us sit together and discuss things courteously and kindly. As God is my witness, wisdom will guide me in what I say; I will not try to snatch any advantage from our conversation, nor will I lie to you. If I had seen Seyavash himself I would not rejoice as I do now seeing you; indeed, you resemble no one so much as that noble and unfortunate prince. Happy is the king who has a son like you; happy are the people of Iran who see your throne and your good fortune: and woe to whoever fights against you, since dust will overwhelm both his throne and his luck. May all your enemies be filled with fear, may the hearts of those who are against you be cut in two, may you remain victorious forever, and may your dark nights be as bright as the days of spring!"

When he heard him Esfandyar too dismounted, embraced Rostam, and greeted him warmly and respectfully, saying "I thank God to see you cheerful and confident like this: you deserve all men's praise, and our heroes are like your slaves. Happy is the man who has a son like you, who sees the branch he has put forth bear fruit: happy is the man who has you as his support, since he need fear nothing from Fate's harshness. When I saw you I thought of Zarir, that lionlike warrior and tamer of horses."

Rostam replied, "I have one request, and if you grant it to me my desires are fulfilled: delight my soul by coming to my house. It is unworthy of you, but we can make do with what there is and so confirm our friendship."

Esfandyar answered, "You are like the heroes of old, and any man who has your reputation rejoices the land of Iran. It would be wrong to ignore your wishes, but I cannot turn aside from the king's orders. He gave me no permission to stay in Zavol with its chieftains. You should quickly do what the king has ordered; place the fetters on your own feet, because a king's fetters are no cause for shame. When I take you before him, bound like this, all the guilt will redound on him. I must bind you, but my soul is grieved by it, and I would rather serve you: I won't let you stay in chains beyond nightfall, and I won't let the least harm come to you. Believe me, the king will not injure you, and when I place the crown on my own head I will give the world into your safekeeping. This will not be a sin before God, and there is no shame in doing what a king demands; and when the blossoms and roses open, and you return to your Zavolestan, you'll find that I'll be generous, and load you down with gifts to beautify your land."

Rostam replied, "I have prayed God that I might see you and rejoice, and now I've heard what you have to say. We are two noble warriors, one old, one young, both wise and alert; but I fear the evil eye has struck, and that I'll never know sweet sleep again. Some demon has pushed in between us, ambition for a crown and glory has perverted your soul. It will be an eternal shame to me if a great chieftain like yourself refuses to come to my house and be my guest while he is in this country. If you can expel this hatred from your mind, and undo this demon's work, I'll agree to anything you wish, except to be chained: chains will bring shame, the ruin of my greatness, and an ugly aftermath. No one will ever see me in chains alive; my mind's made up and there's nothing more to be said."

Esfandyar answered: "The heroes of the past are met in you, all you have said is true, and perverse paths bring no man glory. But Pashutan knows the orders the king gave me when I set out: if I come now to your home, and stay there enjoying myself as your guest, and you then refuse to accept the king's orders, I shall burn in hell's flames when I pass to the other world. If you wish, we can drink together for a day and swear friendship to one another; who knows what tomorrow will bring or what will be said of this later?"

Rostam replied: "I must go and rid myself of these clothes. I've been hunting for a week, eating wild ass instead of lamb; call for me when you're seated with your people, ready to eat." He mounted Rakhsh and deep in thought galloped back to his castle. He saw his father's face and said, "I've visited this Esfandyar: I saw him mounted, tall as a cypress tree, wise and splendid, as if the great Feraydun himself had given him strength and knowledge. He exceeds the reports about him; the royal *farr* radiates from his face."

When Rostam rode away from the river Hirmand, Esfandyar was filled with foreboding. At that moment, Pashutan, who was his councilor, came into his tent, and Esfandyar addressed him:

> "We thought this would be easy, but we've found
> Our way's unsure, and over rocky ground;
> I shouldn't visit Rostam's home, and he
> For his part ought to stay away from me.
> If he neglects to come I won't complain
> Or summon him to sit with me again.
> If one of us should die in this affair
> The other will be vanquished by despair."

Pashutan said, "My lord, who has a brother to equal Esfandyar? When I saw that you two were not looking to fight with one another, my heart opened like the blossoms in springtime, both for Rostam and for Esfandyar. I look at what you're doing here and I see that some demon has blocked off wisdom's way forward. You're a religious and honorable man, one who obeys God and his father: hold back, don't give your soul over to violence; my brother, listen to what I'm telling you. I heard all Rostam said: he is a great man, your chains will never bind his feet and he will not lightly take your advice. The son of Zal will not walk into your trap so easily; I fear that this will be a long drawn out contest between two haughty warriors, and one with an ugly ending to it. You are a great man too, and wiser than the king; you're a better soldier and a finer man than he is. One of you wants rejoicing and reconciliation, and the other wants battles and vengeance. Consider for yourself, which of you is more praiseworthy?"

Esfandyar replied,

> "But if I turn away from what my king
> Commands there's no excuse that I can bring,
> I'll be reproached in this world, and I fear
> God's probing of my life when death draws near;
> For Rostam's sake I cannot throw away
> My life both here and after Judgment Day—
> There is no needle that can sew the eyes
> Of Faith tight shut, no matter how one tries."

Pashutan said, "I've given my advice, and it will benefit you physically and morally. I've said all I can; now, choose the right way, but remember that princes' hearts are not inclined to vengeance."

Esfandyar ordered his cooks to prepare supper, but he sent no one to summon Rostam. When the food had been eaten he lifted his winecup and began to boast of his past exploits, toasting the king occasionally as he did so. Rostam was in his castle all this while, waiting for Esfandyar's invitation. But as time passed and no one came, and then supper time was over and he was still staring at the empty road, fury took possession of his mind. He laughed and said to his brother, "Have the meal prepared and call our men to eat. So this is our famous hero's way of behaving, is it? See that you never forget his splendid manners!" Then he ordered that Rakhsh be saddled and richly caparisoned after the Chinese fashion, and said,

> "I'm going to tell this noble prince that he
> Has now deliberately insulted me."

Rostam and Esfandyar Meet for the Second Time

The mammoth warrior mounted Rakhsh, whose neigh resounded for two miles, and made his way quickly to the river's edge. The Persian troops there were astonished by his massive frame and martial bearing, and said to one another "He resembles no one but Esfandyar himself, and would be the victor in combat with an elephant. The king's unwise obsession with his throne has made him send a splendid hero to his death; as he grows older all the king thinks of is wealth and his royal authority."

Esfandyar welcomed him, and Rostam replied, "My fine young warrior, it seems you've developed new customs, new ways of behaving. Why am I unworthy to drink with you? Is this how you keep your promises? Now, take seriously what I tell you, and don't be so foolish as to get angry with an old man. You think you're greater than everyone else and you take pride in your chieftains: you consider me a lightweight, someone whose opinions don't matter. But know that the world knows I am Rostam, scion of the great Nariman; black demons bite their hands in horror at my approach, and I fling wizards into the pit of death. When chieftains see my armor and my Rakhsh like a raging lion they flee in terror; I have caught in my lariat's coils warriors like Kamus and the Khaqan of China, I have dragged them from their saddles and bound their feet. I am the keeper of Iran and its lion-like chieftains, the support of its warriors on every side. Don't slight my overtures to you, don't think of yourself as higher than the heavens. I'm seeking a pact with you, and I respect your royal *farr* and glory. I have no desire for a prince like you to die at my hands. I am descended from Sam, before whom lions fled from their lairs, and you are the son of a king. For a long time now I have been the world's first warrior, and I have never stooped to evil: I have cleared the world of my enemies, and I have suffered countless pains and sorrows. I thank God that in my old age I have met with a fine strong warrior willing to fight with a man of the pure faith, one whom all the world praises."

Esfandyar laughed, and said, "And all this anger is simply because no invitation came? The weather's so hot and it's such a long way that I didn't want to put you to the effort of coming back. I said to myself that I'd go to you at dawn tomorrow and offer my apologies: I'd be happy to see Zal and I'd spend time drinking with you both. But now that you've taken the trouble to leave your house and cross the plain to get here, calm yourself, sit down, take the winecup in your hand, and put aside your anger and irritation." And he moved over so that there was a place for Rostam to his left. But Rostam's response was, "That's no place for me, I'll sit where I wish to." Esfandyar ordered Bahman to vacate the space to the right, but Rostam retorted in fury, "Open your eyes and look at me: look at my greatness and at my noble ancestry, I'm of the seed of Sam, and if there's no place worthy of me in your company I still have my victories and fame." Then the prince ordered that a golden throne be brought and placed opposite his own: still enraged Rostam sat himself down on the throne, and toyed with a scented orange in his hand.

Esfandyar addressed Rostam, "You're a powerful and well-intentioned hero, but I've heard from priests, chieftains, and other wise men that Zal was nothing but demon-spawn, and can boast of no better lineage. They hid him from Sam for a long time, and the court was in an uproar because he was so ugly, with a black body and white hair and face; when Sam finally saw him he was in despair and gave orders that he be exposed on the seashore as a prey for the birds and fish. The Simorgh came down, flapping its wings, and seeing no signs of grandeur or glory in the child to deter him, he snatched him up and took him to his nest, but even though he was hungry

Zal's puny body didn't seem worth eating. So he flung him naked in a corner of the nest, where the child lived off scraps. Finally the Simorgh took pity on him, and after he'd subsisted on the Simorgh's leavings for a number of years he set off, naked as he was, for Sistan. Now because Sam had no other children, and was old and stupid as well, he welcomed him back. My great ancestors, who were noble and generous men, gave him wealth and position, and when many years had passed he grew to be a fine tall cypress of a man. And a branch of this same cypress is Rostam, who by his valor and splendid appearance and fine deeds outreached the heavens, until his ambition and excesses have procured a kingdom for him."

Rostam replied; "Calm yourself; why are you saying such offensive things? Your heart's filled with perversity and your soul's puffed up with demonic pride. Speak as becomes a royal personage; kings say nothing but the truth. The lord of the world knows that Sam's son Zal is a great, wise, and renowned man. And Sam was the son of Nariman, who was descended from Kariman, whose father was Hushang, the crowned king of all the earth. Haven't you heard of Sam's incomparable fame? There was a dragon in Tus, a monster that terrorized the beasts of the sea and the birds of the air; and then there was a wicked demon so huge that the sea of China reached only to its waist while its head towered into the sky and obscured the sun; it would snatch fish up from the ocean depths and store them beyond the sphere of the moon, and cook them by holding them against the sun; the turning heavens wept to see such a monster. These two hideous beings trembled before Sam's courage and his sword, and perished by his hand.

"My mother was the daughter of Mehrab, under whose rule India flourished, and who was descended, through five generations, from Zahhak, a monarch who lifted his head higher than all the kings of the world. Who has a more noble lineage than this? A wise man does not try to deny the truth. Any man who makes claims to heroism has to test himself against me. I hold my fiefdom by irreproachable treaty from Kavus, and it was renewed by the greatest of warrior-kings, Khosrow. I have traveled the world, and slain many unjust kings: when I crossed the Oxus Afrasyab fled from Turan to China; I fought for Kavus in Hamaveran and when I journeyed alone to Mazanderan, neither Arzhang, nor the white demon, nor Sanjeh, nor Ulad Ghandi hindered me. For that king's sake I killed my own son, and there never was such a strong, chivalrous, war-tried hero as Sohrab. It is more than six hundred years since I was born of Zal's seed: in all that time I have been the world's heroic champion, and my thoughts and deeds have always been one. I'm like the noble Feraydun, who crowned himself, and dragged Zahhak from the throne and laid him in the dust. And then Sam, whose wisdom and knowledge of magic are unmatched in the world, is my grandfather. Thirdly, when I have girded on my sword our kings have lived free from all anxieties: there's never been such pleasure at the court, or such security from evil's inroads. The world was as I willed it to be, ordered by my sword and mace.

> I've told you this so that you'll understand
> That though you govern with a princely hand,
> You're new to this world's ancient ways, in spite
> Of all your splendor and imperial might.
> You look out on the earth and all you see
> Is your own image and ability,
> But gazing at yourself you're unaware
> Of all the hidden dangers lurking there.
> I've talked enough; let's drink, and may the wine
> Dispel all your anxieties, and mine."

Hearing him, Esfandyar laughed, and his heart lightened. He said, "I've listened to the tale of your exploits and sufferings, now hear how I've distinguished myself. First, I have fought for the true faith, clearing the land of idol-worshippers, and no one's seen any warrior slaughter them in such numbers as I have, covering the ground with their corpses. I'm Goshtasp's child, and he was the child of Lohrasp, who was the child of Orandshah, a descendant of the Kayanid kings. My mother's the daughter of Caesar, who rules the Romans and is descended from Salm, the son of Feraydun, the king who established the ways of faith and fair-dealing, and without whose glory there would be little enough justice in the world, as no one can deny. You're a man who stood as a slave before my royal ancestors, you and your forebears too. I'm not saying this to cause dissension between us, but you received sovereignty as a gift from my family, even though you're now trying to kick over the traces. Wait now, and let me tell you how things are, and if there's one lie in what I say, show it to me.

"Since Goshtasp has been king my chivalry and good fortune have been at his service. I was the man who was praised for spreading the faith, even though I was then imprisoned because of Gorazm's slanders. Because I couldn't help him Lohrasp was defeated, and our land was overrun by enemies, until Jamasp came to release me from my chains. The blacksmiths tried to free me, but my impatient heart was the sword that finally broke my fetters: I roared at their delay, and it was my own strength that smashed the shackles binding me. Arjasp, our enemy, fled before me, and so did all his chieftains, and I harried their routed army like a savage lion. You've heard how lions and Ahriman beset me during my seven trials, how I entered the Brass Fortress by a trick, and destroyed everything there; how I sought revenge for our nobles' deaths, how I took war to Turan and China and suffered hardships and privations there more terrible than a leopard inflicts on a wild ass, or than the sailor's hook that torments a great fish's gullet. There was a dark castle high on a distant ridge, shunned for its evil reputation and filled with depraved idol-worshippers: I took that castle, smashed its images against the ground, and lit the sacred flame of Zoroaster in their place. I came home with my God-given victory, and not an enemy of ours survived; not a temple or an idol-worshipper remained.

> These battles that I fought, I fought alone,
> No man has shown the valor I have shown.
> But we have talked enough: if you agree,
> Take up your wine, and slake your thirst with me."

Rostam replied: "Our deeds will be our memorial in the world. Now, in fairness to me, listen to the tale of an old warrior's exploits. If I had not taken my heavy mace to Mazanderan where Kavus, Giv, Gudarz, and Tus were imprisoned, their hearing shattered by the din of wardrums, who would have disemboweled the White Demon? Who could have hoped to accomplish such a deed by his own strength? I took Kavus from his chains back to the throne, and Iran rejoiced to receive him. I cut off their wizards' heads, and left their bodies unburied and unlamented. And my only companions were my courage, my horse Rakhsh, and my world-conquering sword. And then when Kavus went to Hamaveran and was imprisoned, I led a Persian army there and killed their kings in war. King Kavus was a prisoner, heart sick and wretched, and Afrasyab was harrying Iran. I freed Kavus, Giv, Gudarz, and Tus, and brought them and our army back to Iran. Eager for fame, careless of my own ease, I went on ahead in the darkness of the night, and when Afrasyab saw my fluttering banner and heard Rakhsh neigh, he fled from Iran toward China; the world was filled with justice and my praises. If Kavus's blood had flowed then, how could he have sired Seyavash, who in turn fathered Kay Khosrow, who placed the crown on Lohrasp's head? My father is a great warrior, and he swallowed the dust of shame when he had to call your insignificant Lohrasp his king. Why do you boast of Goshtasp's crown and Lohrasp's throne?

> Who says, 'Go now, and shackle Rostam's hands?'
> The heavens themselves don't issue such commands.
> I've never seen, not since I was a child,
> A man as headstrong, obstinate, and wild
> As you: my courtesy is your excuse
> To treat me with contemptuous abuse!"

Esfandyar laughed with delight at his rage and grasped him firmly by the hand, saying: "Great, mammoth bodied warrior, you're just as I've heard you described: your arm's as massive as a lion's thigh, your chest and shoulders like a dragon's, your waist lean as a leopard's." As he spoke he squeezed Rostam's hand, and the old man laughed at the young man's efforts: lymph dripped from his finger nails, but he didn't wince at the pain. Then he in turn gripped Esfandyar's hand, and said, "My God-fearing prince, I congratulate king Goshtasp on having such a son as you, and your mother, whose glory is increased by bearing you." He spoke and, as his grip tightened, Esfandyar's cheeks turned crimson; bloody liquid spurted from beneath his nails, and the pain showed in his face. Nevertheless he laughed and said, "Enjoy your wine today, because tomorrow when we meet in combat you won't be thinking of pleasure. I'll saddle my black horse, put on my princely helmet, and unseat you with a lance; that'll put an end to your wrangling and rebellion. I'll bind your arms together and take you to the king. But I'll tell him that I've found no fault in you; I'll go before him as a suppliant, and clear up all this quarrel. I'll free you from sorrow and pain, and in their place you'll find treasure and kindness."

Rostam too laughed and said, "You'll tire of battle soon enough. Where have you ever seen real warriors fight, or felt the wind a mace makes as it whistles by you? If the heavens will that no love's lost between us, we'll drink down vengeance, not red wine; our fate will be ambush, the bow and lariat, the din of drums instead of the sound of lutes, and our farewells will be said with sword and mace. When we meet man to man on the battlefield tomorrow, you'll see which way the fight will go. I'll pluck you from your saddle, and bear you off to noble Zal. There I'll sit you on an ivory throne and place on your head a splendid crown that I had from Kay Qobad, and may his soul rejoice in heaven! I'll open our treasury's gates and lay our wealth before you: I'll give you troops, and raise your head up to the skies. Then, laughing and lighthearted, we'll make our way to the king: I'll crown you there, and that's how I'll show my loyalty to Goshtasp. Only then will I agree to serve him, as I served the Kayanid kings before. My heart will grow young again with joy, like a garden cleared of weeds: and when you're king and I'm your champion, a universal happiness will come."

Rostam Drinks with Esfandyar

Esfandyar answered: "Too much talk is pointless: our stomachs are empty, the day's half over, and we've said enough about battles. Bring whatever you have to our supper, and don't invite those who talk the whole time." When Rostam began to eat the others were astonished at his appetite; they sat opposite him watching him feast. Then Esfandyar gave orders that Rostam be served with red wine, saying "We'll see what he wants when the wine affects him, and he talks about King Kavus." A servant brought old wine in a goblet, and Rostam toasted Goshtasp and drank it off. The boy refilled it with a royal vintage, and Rostam said to him quietly, "There's no need to dilute it with water, it takes the edge off an old wine. Why do you put water in it?" Pashutan said to the serving boy, "Bring him a goblet filled with undiluted wine." Wine was brought, musicians were summoned, and the group watched in wonder as Rostam drank. When it was time for Rostam to return to Zal, Esfandyar said to him: "May you live happily and forever, may the food and wine you've consumed here nourish you, and may righteousness sustain your soul!"

Rostam replied: "Prince, may wisdom always be your guide! The wine I've drunk with you has nourished me, and my wise mind wants for nothing. If you can be intelligent enough, and man enough, to lay aside this desire for combat, come out of the desert to my home and take your ease as my guest: I'll do everything I promised, and I'll give you good advice. Rest for a while, turn aside from evil, be civil, and come back to your senses."

Esfandyar replied: "Don't sow seeds that will never grow. Tomorrow when I bind on my sword belt for combat you'll see what a warrior is. Stop praising yourself: get back to your palace and prepare yourself for the morning. A battle is as of little account to me as a drinking party. But my advice is that you don't try to fight with me: do what I say, accept the king's command that you be bound in chains, and when we go from Zabol to Goshtasp's court you'll see that I'll be even more chivalrous than I have promised. Don't try to cause me any more sorrow."

Then grief filled Rostam's heart, and in his sight
The world seemed like a wood bereft of light.
He thought: "Either I let him bind my hands,
And in so doing bow to his commands,
Or I must fight against him face to face
And bring on him destruction and disgrace.
No good can come of either course, and I
Shall be despised and cursed until I die:
His chains will be the symbol of my shame,
Goshtasp will kill me and destroy my fame—
The world will laugh at me, and men will say
'Rostam was hung with chains and led away,
A stripling conquered him.' And all I've done
Will be forgotten then by everyone.
But if we fight each other and he's slain
I cannot show my face at court again;
They'll say I left a fine young prince for dead
Because of one or two harsh words he'd said;
In death I'll be reviled, my name will be
A byword for disgrace and infamy.
And then if I'm to perish at his hand
My clan will lose Zabol, our native land—
One thing would still survive though, since my name
Would be remembered and not lose its fame."

Then he spoke to his haughty companion, saying: "Anxiety robs my skin of its color; you talk so much about chains and binding me, and everything you do alarms me. What the heavens will is sovereign over us, and who knows how they will turn? You're following a demon's advice, and refusing to listen to reason. You haven't lived many years in this world, and you don't know how deceptive and evil it is, my prince. You're a simple, straightforward man, and you know nothing about life: you should realize that evil men are trying to destroy you. Goshtasp will never tire of his crown and throne, and he will drive you throughout the world, make you face every danger, to keep you away from them. In his mind he searched the world, his intelligence hacking away like an axe, to find some hero who would not refuse to fight with you, so that such a man would destroy you, and the crown and throne would remain his. You blame my motives, but why don't you examine your own heart? Prince, don't act like some thoughtless youth, don't persist in this disastrous course. Be ashamed before God and before my face, don't betray yourself, and don't think that combat with me would be a game. If Fate has driven you and your men here, you will be destroyed by me: I shall leave an evil name behind me in the world, and may the same fate be Goshtasp's!"

Esfandyar replied: "Great Rostam, think of what a wise sage once said, 'A man in his dotage is a fool, no matter how wise or victorious or knowledgeable he's been.' You want to trick me and slip out of this, you want to convince people by your smooth talk, so that they'll say 'Rostam welcomed him warmly' and call you a wise benevolent man, while they'll say that I was unrighteous—I, who always act from righteous motives! You want them to say, 'The prince refused to listen to him, so that he had no choice but to fight. All his pleas were treated with contempt, and bitter words passed between them.' But I shall not swerve aside from the king's commands, not for the crown itself: all the good and evil of the world I find in him, and in him lie both heaven and hell. May what you've eaten here nourish you and confound your enemies: now, go home and tell Zal everything you have seen here. Prepare your armor for battle, and bandy no more words with me. Come back at dawn ready to fight, and don't draw this business out any further. Tomorrow on the battlefield you'll see the world grow dark before your eyes: you'll see what combat with a real warrior is."

Rostam replied: "If this is what you want I'll return your hospitality with Rakhsh's hooves, and my mace will be a medicine for your head. You've listened to your own court telling you that no one can match his sword against Esfandyar's; but tomorrow you'll see me grasping Rakhsh's reins, with my lance couched, and after that you'll never look to fight again."

The young man's lips broke into bewitching laughter, and he said: "For a fighting man you've let our conversation anger you too easily! Tomorrow you'll see how a man fights on the battlefield: I'm no mountain, and my horse beneath me's no mountain either, I'm one man like any other. If you run from me with your head still on your shoulders your mother will weep for your humiliation; and if you're killed I'll tie you to my saddle and bear you off to the king, so that no vassal of his will ever challenge him again."

Rostam Addresses Esfandyar's Tent

When Rostam left Esfandyar's pavilion he paused for a moment, and spoke to it:

> "O tent of hope, what glorious days you've known!
> Once you were shelter to great Jamshid's throne,
> In you Khosrow's and King Kavus's days
> Were passed in splendor, pageantry, and praise—
> Closed is that glorious gate that once you knew,
> A man unworthy of you reigns in you."

Esfandyar heard him, planted himself in front of Rostam, and said: "Why should you speak to our pavilion so intemperately? This Zabolestan of yours should be called 'Lout-estan,' because when a guest has eaten his fill here he starts loutishly insulting his host!" Then he too addressed the royal tent:

> "You sheltered Jamshid once, who erred and strayed,
> Who heard God's heavenly laws and disobeyed;
> Then came Kavus, whose blasphemous desires
> Sought to control the skies' celestial fires—
> Tumult and plunder, plots, perfidy, pain
> Filled all the land throughout his wretched reign,
> But now your walls encompass King Goshtasp
> Who rules with his wise councillor Jamasp;
> The prophet Zoroaster, who has brought
> Heaven's scriptures to us, shares his noble court,
> Good Pashutan is here, and so am I
> His prince, watched over by the turning sky,
> Protector of the good, scourge of the hoard
> Of evildoers, who bow before my sword."

When Rostam had left, Esfandyar turned to Pashutan and said, "There's no hiding such heroism: I've never seen such a horseman, and I don't know what will happen tomorrow on the battlefield. When he comes armored to battle he must be like a raging elephant; his stature's a marvel to gaze upon. Nevertheless, I fear that tomorrow he will face defeat. My heart aches for his kindness and glory, but I can't evade God's commands: tomorrow when he faces me in combat I'll turn his shining days to darkness."

Pashutan replied: "Listen to what I have to say. Brother, do not do this. I have said it before and I will say it again, because I will not wash my hands of what is right. Don't harry him like this; a free man will never willingly submit to another's tyranny. Sleep tonight and, when dawn comes, we'll go to his castle, without an escort, and there we'll be his guests and answer his every anxiety. Everything he has done in the world has been for the good, benefiting the nobility and the general populace alike. He won't refuse your orders, I can see that he'll be loyal to you. How long are you going to go on with all this rage and anger and malice? Drive them out of your heart!"

Esfandyar answered him: "Thorns have appeared among the roses then: a man of pure faith shouldn't talk as you're doing. You're the first councilor to Persia's king, the heart, eyes, and ears of its chieftains, and yet you think it right and wise to disobey the king like this? Then all my pains and struggles were pointless, and Zoroaster's faith's to be forgotten, because he

has said that hell will be the home of whoever turns aside from his king's command. How long are you going to tell me to disobey Goshtasp? You can say this, but how can I agree to it? If you're afraid for my life, I'll rid you of that fear today: no man ever died except at his appointed time, and a man whose reputation lives on never dies. Tomorrow you'll see how I'll fight against this fearsome warrior."

Pashutan said: "And for how long are you going to talk about fighting? Since you first took up arms, Eblis has had no control over your thoughts: but now you're opening your heart to demons, and refusing to hear good advice. How can I drive fear from my heart when I see that two great warriors, two lions in battle, are to face one another, and what will come of this is all unknown?"

The hero made no answer: his heart was filled with pain, and a sigh escaped his lips.

Rostam Returns to His Castle

By the time Rostam reached his castle he could see no remedy but warfare. Zavareh came out to greet him and saw his pallor, and that his heart was filled with darkness. Rostam said to him, "Prepare my Indian sword, my lance and helmet, my bow and the barding for Rakhsh: bring me my tiger skin, and my heavy mace." Zavareh had the steward bring what Rostam had asked for, and when Rostam saw his weapons and armor he heaved a cold sigh and said,

> "My armor, for a while you've been at peace,
> But now this indolence of yours must cease—
> A hard fight lies ahead, and I shall need
> All of the luck you bring me to succeed:
> Two warriors who have never known defeat
> Like two enraged and roaring lions will meet,
> And in that struggle on the battlefield
> Who knows what tricks he'll try to make me yield!"

Zal Advises Rostam

When Zal heard from Rostam what had happened, his aged mind was troubled. He said, "What are you telling me? You're filling my mind with darkness. Since first you sat in the saddle you've been a chivalrous and righteous warrior, proud to serve your kings and contemptuous of hardships. But I fear your days are drawing to an end, that your lucky stars are in decline, that the seed of Zal will be eradicated from this land, and our women and children hurled to the ground as slaves. If you're killed in combat by a young stripling like Esfandyar, Zabolestan will be laid waste and all our glory will be razed and cast into a pit. And if he's hurt in this encounter your good name will be destroyed: everyone will tell the tale of how you killed a young prince because of a few harsh words he'd said. Go to him, stand before him as his subject: and if you can't do that then leave, go and hide yourself in some corner where no one will hear of you. You can buy the world with treasure and trouble, but you can't cut Chinese silk with an axe. Give his retinue robes of honor, get back your independence with gifts. When he leaves the banks of the Hirmand, saddle Rakhsh and go with him: as you travel to the court swear fealty to him. And when Goshtasp sees you, there's no danger he'll harm you: it would be an act unworthy of a monarch."

Rostam replied: "Old man, don't take what I've said so lightly. I've fought for years and have experienced the world's good and evil. I encountered the demons of Mazanderan and the horsemen of Hamaveran, I fought against Kamus and the Emperor of China whose armies were so mighty the earth trembled beneath their horses' hooves. But if I now flee from Esfandyar there will be no castles or gardens for you in Zabolestan. I may be old, but when I put on my tiger skin for battle it makes no difference whether I face a hundred maddened elephants or a plain filled with warriors. I've done all that you're asking me to, I read the book of loyalty to him; he treats my words with contempt and ignores my wisdom and advice. If he could bring his head down from the heavens and welcome me in his heart, there's no wealth in my treasury, no weapon or armor, that I wouldn't give him. But he took no notice of all my talk and left me empty-handed.

"If we were to fight tomorrow, you could despair of his life. But I won't take my sharp sword in hand, I'll bear him off to a banquet: he'll see no mace or lance from me, and I won't oppose him man to man. I'll simply lift him from the saddle and acknowledge him as king in Goshtasp's place. I'll bring him here and seat him on an ivory throne, load him with presents, keep him as my guest for three days, and on the fourth when the sun's red ruby splits the darkness I'll set off with him for Goshtasp's court. When I enthrone him and crown him I'll stand before him as his loyal subject, concerned only for Esfandyar's commands. You remember how I acted with Qobad, and you know how it's my quarrelsome, passionate nature that's made my reputation in the world. And now you're telling me either to run off and hide, or to submit to his chains!"

Zal broke into laughter, shaking his head in wonder at his son's words. He said, "Don't say such things, even demons couldn't put up with such foolish talk. You chatter about what we did with Qobad, but he was living obscurely in the mountains then, he wasn't a great king with a throne, crown, treasure, and cash at his disposal. You're talking about Esfandyar, who counts the emperor of China among his subjects, and you say you'll lift him from the saddle and bear him off to Zal's palace! An old, experienced man doesn't talk like this. Don't court bad luck by setting yourself up as the Persian king's equal. You're the best of all our chieftains, but I've given you my advice, and may you follow it!"

Having spoken, he bent his forehead to the ground in prayer: "Just judge, I pray you to preserve us from an evil Fate." And so he prayed throughout the night, his tongue untiring until the sun rose above the mountains.

When day broke Rostam put on his mail and tigerskin, hitched his lariat to his saddle, and mounted Rakhsh. He summoned Zavareh and told him to have their army's ranks drawn up in the foothills. Zavareh saw that this was done, and Rostam couched his lance and rode out from the palace. His soldiers called out encouragement as he went forward, followed by Zavareh who was acting as his lieutenant. Privately Rostam said to him, "Somehow, I'll put paid to this evil devil's spawn, and get my soul back into the light again. But I fear I shall have to harm him, and I don't know what good can come out of all this. You stay with our troops, while I go to see what Fate has in store for me. If I find he's still the same hot-head, spoiling for a fight, let me face him alone, I don't want any of our warriors hurt in this. Victory favors the just."

He crossed the river and began to climb the opposite bank, and wonder at the world's ways filled his mind.

He faced Esfandyar and shouted, "Your enemy has come: prepare yourself."

When Esfandyar heard the old lion's words he laughed and shouted back, "I've been prepared since I woke." He gave orders that his armor, helmet, lance, and mace be brought, and when he was accoutered he had his black horse saddled and brought before him. Then, glorying in his strength and agility, he thrust his lance point into the ground and, like a leopard leaping on a wild ass and striking terror into its heart, he vaulted into the saddle. The soldiers were delighted, and roared their approval.

Esfandyar rode toward Rostam and when he saw his opponent had come alone, he turned to Pashutan and said, "I need no companions in this: he is alone, and I shall be too: we'll move off to higher ground."

Pashutan withdrew to where the Persian soldiers waited, and the two combatants went forward to battle, as grimly as if all pleasure had been driven from the world. When the old man and his young opponent faced each other, both their horses neighed violently, and the noise was as though the ground beneath them split open.

Rostam's voice was serious when he spoke: "Young man, you're fortune's favorite, and your heart's filled with the joys of youth; don't go forward with this, don't give yourself up to anger. For once, listen to wisdom's words. If you're set on bloodshed say so, and I'll have my Zaboli warriors come here, and you can send Persians against them, and the two groups can show their mettle. We'll watch from the sidelines, and your desire for blood and combat will be satisfied."

Esfandyar answered him: "How long are you going to go on with this pointless talk? You got up at dawn and summoned me to this hillside. Was that simply deception? Or is it that now you foresee your own defeat? What could a battle between your warriors and mine mean to me? God forbid I should agree to send my Persians into battle while I held back and crowned myself king. For a man of my faith, such an act would be contemptible. I lead my warriors into battle, and am the first to face the foe even if it is a leopard. If you need companions to fight with you summon them, but I shall never call on anyone's aid. God is my companion in battle, and Good Fortune smiles on me. You're looking for a fight, and I'm ready for one: let's face each other man to man, without our armies. And let's see whether Esfandyar's horse returns riderless to its stable, or Rostam's turns masterless toward his palace."

The Combat between Rostam and Esfandyar

They swore that no one would come to their aid while they fought. Again and again they rode against one another with couched lances; blood poured from their armor, and their lances' heads were shattered, so that the combatants were forced to draw their swords. Weaving and dodging to right and left, they attacked one another, and their horses' maneuvers flung them against one another with such violence that their swords too were shattered. They drew their maces then, and the blows they dealt resounded like a blacksmith's hammer striking steel. Their bodies wounded and exhausted, they fought like enraged lions until the handles of their maces splintered; then they leant forward and grasped each other by the belt, each struggling to throw the other, while their horses reared and pranced. But though they strained against one another, exerting all their strength and massive weight, neither warrior was shifted from his saddle. And so they separated, sick at heart, their mouths smeared with dust and blood, their armor and barding dented and pierced, their horses wearied by their struggle.

Zavareh and Nushazar Quarrel

When the combat had gone on for some time, Zavareh grew impatient at the delay and shouted to the Persian soldiers: "Where is Rostam? Why should we hang back on a day like this? You came to fight against Rostam, but you're never going to be able to bind his hands, and we won't sit here while a battle's going on." Then he began cursing his opponents, and Esfandyar's son Nushazar, who was a fiery ambitious youth, was enraged at the insults this provincial from Sistan was heaping upon them, and responded in kind. "Is it right for a noble warrior to make fun of a king's commands? Our leader Esfandyar gave us no orders to fight with dogs like you, and who would ignore or override his wishes? But if you want to challenge us, you'll see how real warriors can fight with swords and spears and maces."

In response, Zavareh gave the signal for Sistan's warcry to ring out, and for his men to attack: he himself rushed forward from the rear of his troops, and a tumultuous noise of fighting began. Countless Persians were slaughtered, and when Nushazar saw this he mounted his horse, grasped his Indian sword in his hand, and headed for the fray. Among the Sistani troops one of their best warriors was a wild tamer of horses, a man named Alvad, who was Rostam's spear bearer and always accompanied him into battle. Nushazar caught sight of him, wheeled towards him, and struck him a mighty blow with his sword: his head was severed and his body slid lifeless from its saddle into the dirt. Zavareh urged his horse forward and called out, "You've laid him low, but stand your ground and fight, because Alvad is not what I'd call a horseman." With that Zavareh flung his lance, which pierced Nushazar's chest, and a moment later the Persian warrior's head lay in the dirt.

Nushazar and Mehrnush Are Killed by Faramarz and Zavareh

When the great Nushazar was killed, good fortune deserted the Persian army. His brother, Mehrnush, saw Nushazar's death; at once weeping and enraged he urged his great horse forward to the fray, and the froth of fury stood on his lips. Faramarz stood before him like a massive maddened elephant, and attacked him with his Indian sword: a huge cry went up from both armies as the two noble fighters closed, the one a prince, the other a mighty champion. They fell on one another like enraged lions, but Mehrnush's eagerness for combat was not sufficient to prevail against Faramarz: thinking to sever his opponent's head with a sword blow, he brought his weapon down on his own horse's neck, and his mount sank to the ground beneath him. Once he was on foot Faramarz was able to overcome him, and his red blood stained the dust of the battlefield.

When Bahman saw his brother killed, and the dirt beneath him mired with his blood, he made his way to where Esfandyar had been in combat with Rostam, and said, "Lion-warrior, an army has come up from Sistan, and your two sons Nushazar and Mehrnush have been pitifully slain by them. While you're here in combat, two of our princes lie prone in the dust, and the sorrow and shame of this will live forever." Esfandyar's heart clouded with rage, sighs escaped his lips, and tears stood in his eyes: he turned to Rostam and said, "Devil's spawn, why have you forsaken the path of justice and good custom? Didn't you say that you would not bring your troops into this conflict? You don't deserve your fame: have you no shame before me, no fear of what God will demand of you on the Day of Judgment? Don't you know that no one praises a man who goes back on his word? Two of your Sistani troops have killed two of my sons, and your men are still wreaking havoc."

When Rostam heard this, sorrow seized him and he trembled like a bough in the wind. He swore by the soul and head of the king, by the sun and his sword and the battlefield, by the fire that Kavus had lit and through which Seyavash had passed unscathed, by the Kayanid throne and the Zend Avesta, by the soul and head of Esfandyar himself: "I did not give the orders for this attack, and I've no praise for whoever carried it out. I shall bind my own brother's hands if he has been responsible for this evil, and I shall bind my son Faramarz's arms too, and bring him here to you. If they are guilty,

kill them both in vengeance for your sons' split blood. But don't let your judgment be clouded by what has happened."

Esfandyar replied,

> To avenge a peacock's death, no king would take
> The worthless life of an ignoble snake:
> Look to your weapons now, you wretch, defend
> Yourself, your days on earth are at an end:
> I'll stake your thighs against your horse's hide,
> My arrows will transfix you to his side
> And you and he shall be like water when
> It's mixed with milk and can't be found again.
> From now on no base slave shall ever strive
> To spill a prince's blood: if you survive
> I'll bind your arms—without delay I'll bring
> You as my captive to our court and king,
> And if my arrows leave you here for dead
> Think of my sons, whose blood your warriors shed."

Rostam replied: "What good is all this talk, which only increases our shame? Turn toward God and trust in Him, who guides us to both good and evil ends."

Rostam and Esfandyar Renew the Battle

They turned then to their bows and poplar wood arrows; the sun turned pale and fire flashed from Esfandyar's armor where the arrow heads struck. He frowned with shame, since he was a man whose arrows no one escaped: he notched diamond headed shafts to his bow, bolts that pierced armor as if it were paper, and sorely wounded both Rostam and Rakhsh. Esfandyar wheeled round, circling Rostam, whose arrows had no effect, and who felt that he faced defeat. He said to himself, "This Esfandyar is invincible," and he knew that both he and Rakhsh were growing weaker. In desperation he dismounted and began to climb the mountain side, while Rakhsh returned home riderless and wounded. Blood poured from Rostam's body, and as his strength ebbed from him this great mountain of a man began to tremble and shake. Esfandyar laughed to see this, and called out:

> "Where is your mammoth strength, your warrior's pride?
> Have arrows pierced that iron mountain side?
> Where is your mace now and your martial might,
> That glorious strength with which you used to fight?

What are you running from, or did you hear
A lion's roar that filled your heart with fear?
Are you the man before whom demons wept?
Whose sword killed everything that flew or crept?
Why has the mammoth turned into a fox
That tries to hide among these mountain rocks?"

Zavareh saw Rakhsh in the distance, wounded, returning home: the world darkened before his eyes, and he cried aloud and hurried to the place where Rostam and Esfandyar had fought. He saw his brother there, covered in unstanched wounds, and said to him, "Get up, use my horse, and I shall buckle on my armor to avenge you." But Rostam replied, "Go, tell our father that the tribe of Sam has lost its power and glory, and that he must seek out some remedy. My wounds are more terrible than any disaster I've survived, but I know that, if I live through this night, tomorrow I shall be like a man reborn again. See that you look after Rakhsh, and even if I stay here for a long time I'll rejoin you eventually." Zavareh left his brother and went in search of Rakhsh.

Esfandyar waited a while, and then shouted: "How long are you going to stay up there: who do you think is going to come and guide you now? Throw your bow down, strip off your tiger skin, undo your sword belt. Submit, and let me bind your arms, and you'll never see any harm from me again. I'll take you, wounded as you are, to the king, and there I'll have all your sins forgiven. But if you want to continue fighting, make your will and appoint someone else to rule these marches. Ask pardon for your sins from God, since God forgives those who repent, and it would be right for Him to guide you from this fleeting world when you must leave it."

Rostam replied: "It's too late to go on fighting: who wages war in the dark? Go back to your encampment and spend the night there; I shall make my way to my palace and rest, and sleep awhile. I'll bind my wounds up, then I'll call the chieftains of my tribe to me, Zavareh, Faramarz, and Zal, and I'll set out to them whatever you command: we'll accept your guarantee of justice."

Esfandyar answered him: "Old man, you're infinitely clever, a great man, tempered by time, knowing many tricks and wiles and stratagems. I've seen your deceit, but even so I don't want to see your destruction. I'll give you quarter tonight, but don't be thinking up some new dishonest ploy. Stick to what you've agreed to, and don't bandy words with me any more!"

Rostam's only reply was: "Now I must seek help for my wounds."

Esfandyar watched him make his way back to his own territory.

Once Rostam had crossed the river he congratulated himself on his narrow escape and prayed: "O Lord of Justice, if I die from these wounds, who of our heroes will avenge me, and who has the courage and wisdom to take my place?"

Esfandyar saw him gain dry land and murmured to himself, "This is no man, this is a mammoth of unmatched might." In wonder he said, "O God of all desires, time and place are in your hands, and you have created him as you willed. He has crossed the river with ease, despite the terrible wounds he's suffered from my weapons."

As Esfandyar approached his encampment, he heard the noise of lamentation for Nushazar and Mehrnush. The royal tent was filled with dust, and his chieftains had rent their clothes: Esfandyar dismounted and, embracing the heads of his two dead sons, spoke quietly to them:

> "Brave warriors, whose bodies here lie dead,
> Who knows to what abode your souls have fled?"

Then he turned to Pashutan who knelt lamenting before him and said: "Don't weep for the dead any longer: I see no profit in such tears, and it is wrong to trouble one's soul in this way. Young and old, we are all destined for death, and may wisdom guide us when we depart."

They sent the two bodies in golden coffins, on teakwood litters, to the court, and Esfandyar sent with them a letter to his father: "The tree you planted has borne fruit. You launched this boat on the water: it was you that wanted Rostam as a slave, so now when you see the coffins of Nushazar and Mehrnush, do not lament overmuch. My own future is still uncertain, and I don't know what evil Fate has in store for me."

He sat on the throne, grieving for his sons, and then began to talk about Rostam. He said to Pashutan: "The lion has evaded the warrior's grasp. Today I saw Rostam, the massive height and strength of him, and I praised God, from whom come all hope and fear, that such a man existed. He has done such things in his time: he has fished in the Sea of China and drawn forth monsters, and on the plains he has trapped leopards. And I hurt him so severely that his blood turned the earth to mud; his body was a mass of arrow wounds but he made his way on foot up that mountain side, and then, still encumbered with his sword and armor, he hurried across the river. I know that as soon as he reaches his palace his soul will fly up to the heavens."

Rostam Consults with His Family

When Rostam reached the palace his kinsfolk clustered around him: Zavareh and Faramarz wept to see his wounds, and his mother Rudabeh tore at her hair and scored her cheeks in her grief. Zavareh removed his armor and tiger skin, and the leaders of the tribe gathered before him. Rostam asked that Rakhsh be brought to him, and that farriers be found to treat his wounds. Zal tore at his hair and pressed his aged face against Rostam's wounds, saying "Woe that I with my white hairs should ever see my noble son in this state!"

But Rostam said to him: "What use are tears, if heaven has decreed this? There is a harder task ahead of me, one that fills my soul with fear. I have never seen a warrior on the battlefield like this invincible Esfandyar, although I have traveled the world and have knowledge of what is plain and what is hidden. I lifted the White Demon by the waist and flung him against the ground like a willow branch. My arrows have pierced anvils and rendered shields futile, but no matter how many blows I rained on Esfandyar's armor my strength was useless against him. When leopards saw my mace they would hide themselves among the rocks, but it made no impression on his armor, or even so much as damaged the silk pennant on his helmet. But how much more can I plead with him and offer him friendship? He is stubborn in all he does and says, and wants only enmity from me. I thank God that night came on, and that our eyes grew dim in the darkness so that I was able to escape this dragon's claws. I don't know whether I'll be able to survive these wounds: I see nothing for it but to leave Rakhsh tomorrow, and seek out some obscure corner where Esfandyar will never hear of me, even if this means that he'll sack Zabolestan. He'll get tired of that eventually, although his nature rejoices in the evils of conquest."

Zal said to him: "My son, listen to me, and think carefully about what I'm going to say. There is one way out of all this world's troubles, and that is the way of death. But I know of a remedy, and you should seize on it. I shall summon the Simorgh, and if he will help us we may yet save our tribe and country. If not, then our land will be destroyed by this malevolent Esfandyar, who rejoices in the evil he does."

The Simorgh Appears Before Zal

They agreed to the plan. Zal filled three braziers with fire, and with three wise companions set out from the palace. They climbed to a high peak, and there the magician drew a feather from its brocade wrapping; fanning the flames in one of the braziers he burnt a portion of the feather in the fire. One watch of the night passed, and suddenly the air turned much darker. Zal peered into the night, and it seemed as if the fire and the Simorgh's flight were liquefying the air: then he caught sight of the Simorgh and the flames flared up. Fearful, with anguish in his heart, Zal sat and watched as the bird drew closer: next, he threw sandalwood on the braziers and went forward, making his obeisance to the Simorgh. Perfume rose up from the fires, and the sweat of fear shone on Zal's face. The Simorgh said to him:

> *"O king, explain to me what you desire*
> *That you have summoned me in smoke and fire."*

Zal answered: "May all the evils that have come to me from this base-born wretch light on my enemies! The lion-hearted Rostam lies grievously wounded, and my feet feel as though shackled by his sorrows. No man has ever seen such wounds and we despair of his life. And it seems that Rakhsh too will die from the arrow heads that torment him. Esfandyar came to our country, and the only gate he knocked at was the gate of war. He will not be content with taking our land and wealth and throne from us, he wants to uproot our family, to extirpate us from the face of the earth."

The Simorgh said:

> *"Great hero, put away all grief and fear,*
> *Bring Rakhsh and noble Rostam to me here."*

Zal sent one of his companions to Rostam who, together with Rakhsh, was brought up the mountain side. When Rostam reached the summit, the Simorgh saw him and said:

> *"O mammoth-bodied warrior, tell me who*
> *Has laid you low like this and wounded you.*
> *Why did you fight with Persia's prince, and face*
> *The fire of mortal combat and disgrace?"*

Zal said: "Now that you have vouchsafed us the sight of your pure face, tell me, if Rostam is not cured, where can my people go in all the world? Our tribe will be uprooted, and this is no time to be questioning him."

The bird examined Rostam's wounds, looking for how they could be healed. With his beak he sucked blood from the lesions, and drew out eight arrow heads. Then he pressed one of his feathers against the wounds, and immediately Rostam's spirits began to return. The Simorgh said: "Bind up your wounds and keep them safe from further injury for seven days: then soak one of my feathers in milk and place it on the scars to help them heal." He treated Rakhsh in the same manner, using his beak to draw six arrow heads from the horse's neck, and immediately Rakhsh neighed loudly, and Rostam laughed for joy. The Simorgh then turned to Rostam and said: "Why did you choose to fight against Esfandyar, who is famous for being invincible in battle?"

Rostam replied: "He talked incessantly of chains, despite all the advice I gave him. Death is easier for me than shame."

The Simorgh said: "To bow your head down to the ground before Esfandyar would be no shame: he is a prince and a fine warrior, he lives purely and possesses the divine *farr*. If you swear to me that you will renounce this war and not try to overcome Esfandyar, if you will speak humbly to him tomorrow and offer to submit to him (and if in fact his time has come, he will ignore your overtures of peace) then I will assist you, and raise your head to the sun's sphere."

Rostam was overjoyed to hear this, and was freed of the fear of killing Esfandyar. He said: "Even if heaven should rain swords on my head I shall keep faith with what you say to me."

The Simorgh said: "Out of my love for you, I shall tell you a secret from heaven: Fate will harry whoever spills Esfandyar's blood, he will live in sorrow, and his wealth will be taken from him; his life in this world will be one of suffering, and torment will be his after death. If you agree to what I say, and overcome your enmity, I shall show you wonders tonight and seal your lips against all evil words. Choose a glittering dagger, and mount Rakhsh."

Rostam prepared himself, mounted Rakhsh, and followed the Simorgh as it flew until they reached a seashore. The air turned dark from the Simorgh's shadow as it descended and came to rest on the beach. He showed Rostam a pathway that led over dry land, over which the air seemed impregnated with musk. He touched Rostam's forehead with one of his feathers, and indicated that they should follow the pathway. They reached a tamarisk tree rooted deep in the earth, its branches reaching into the sky, and the Simorgh alighted on one of the branches. He said to Rostam: "Choose the straightest branch you can find, one that tapers to a point: do not despise this piece of wood, for it holds Esfandyar's Fate. Temper it in fire, place an ancient arrow head at its tip, and fix feathers to the shaft. Now I have told you how to wound Esfandyar."

Rostam cut the tamarisk branch and returned to his castle, and as he came the Simorgh guided him, its talons clutching his helmet. The Simorgh said: "Now, when Esfandyar tries to fight with you, plead with him and try to guide him toward righteousness, and don't attempt to trick him in any way. Your sweet words might remind him of the ancient days, and of how you have fought and suffered throughout the world for Persia's cause. But if you speak fairly to him and he rejects your words, treating you with contempt, take this arrow, having steeped it in wine, and aim it for his eyes, as is the custom of those who worship the tamarisk. Fate will guide the arrow to his eyes, where his *farr* resides, and his death."

The Simorgh took its farewell of Zal, embracing him as if they were warp and weft of one cloth. Filled with hope and joy, Rostam lit the fire and watched the Simorgh fly serenely up into the air. Then he fitted the arrow head and feathers, as he had been instructed.

Rostam Kills Esfandyar

Dawn touched the mountain tops and dispersed the darkness of the night. Rostam put on his armor, prayed to the world's creator, and, eager for combat, made his way toward the Persian army. As he rode he called out exultantly: "Brave lion-heart, how long will you sleep? Rostam has saddled Rakhsh: rise from your sweet sleep and face Rostam's vengeance."

When Esfandyar heard his voice, all worldly weapons seemed useless to him. He said to Pashutan: "A lion cannot fight with a magician. I didn't think that Rostam would be able even to drag his armor and helmet back to his palace, and now he comes here riding Rakhsh, whose body yesterday was a mass of wounds. I have heard that Zal is a magician, that he stretches out his hands towards the sun, and that in his mantic fury he surpasses all other magicians: it would be unwise for me to face his son."

Pashutan said: "Why are you so hesitant today? Didn't you sleep through the night? What is it between you and Rostam, that you must both suffer so much in this business? I think your luck is abandoning you; all it does is lead you from one war to another."

Esfandyar dressed himself in his armor and went out to Rostam. When he saw his face he cried out: "May your name disappear from the surface of the earth! Aren't you the man who fled from me yesterday, shorn of heart, soul, courage, life itself? Have you forgotten then, you Sistani wretch, the power of my bow? It's only through the magic you've practiced that you're able to stand before me again: Zal's magic cured you, otherwise you'd be food for wild cats by now. But this time I shall fill you so full of arrows that all Zal's magic will be useless: I shall so batter your body that Zal shall never see you alive again."

Rostam replied: "Will you never tire of combat? I have not come to fight against you today, I have come humbly offering an honorable reconciliation. Fear God, and do not drive wisdom from your heart. Constantly you try to treat me unjustly, blinding yourself to wisdom's ways. By God Himself, by Zoroaster and the pure faith, by the sacred fire and the divine *farr*, by the sun and moon and the Zend Avesta, I swear to you that the road you are following is one of harm and evil. Forget the harsh words that have passed between us. I shall open to you my ancient treasuries, filled with marvels I have gathered over many years: I shall load my own horses with wealth and you can give them to your treasurer to drive before you. I shall ride with you, and if you so command me I shall come into the king's presence, and if the king then kills me or enslaves me I accept this as my due. Remember what an ancient sage once said, 'Never seek to have shame as your companion.' I am doing everything in my power to make you give up your thirst for combat."

Esfandyar said: "I'm not a fraud who looks one day for battle and the next day skulks in fear. Why do you talk so much about your wealth and possessions, washing your face with the waters of friendship? If you want to stay alive, submit your body to my chains."

Once more Rostam spoke: "Forget this injustice, prince. Don't sully my name and make your own soul contemptible; only evil will come of this struggle. I shall give you a thousand royal gems, along with torques and pearls and ear-rings. I shall give you a thousand sweet lipped boys to serve you day and night, and a thousand girls, all from Khallokhi whose women are famous for their charm, to make your court splendid with their beauty.

My lord, I shall open the treasuries of Sam and Zal before you and give you all they contain; I shall bring men from Kabolestan for you, fit companions for your feasting and fearless in war. And then I shall go before you like a servant, accompanying you to your vengeful king's court. But you, my prince, should drive vengeance from your heart, and keep devils from dwelling in your body. You are a king, one who fears God, and you have other ways of binding men to you than by chains; your chains will disgrace my name forever, how can such an evil be worthy of you?"

Esfandyar replied:

> *"How long will you tell me to turn away*
> *From God and from my king? To disobey*
> *My sovereign lord and king is to rebel*
> *Against God's justice and to merit hell.*
> *Accept my chains, or enmity and war—*
> *But bandy pointless words with me no more."*

When Rostam saw that his offers of friendship had no effect on Esfandyar, he notched the wine-soaked tamarisk arrow to his bow and lifted his eyes to the heavens, saying:

> *"Just Lord, who gives us knowledge, strength, and life,*
> *You know how I have sought to end this strife;*
> *Creator of the moon and Mercury*
> *You see my weakness and humility,*
> *And his unjust demands: I pray that you*
> *See nothing sinful in what I must do."*

Rostam hung back for a moment, and Esfandyar taunted him: "Well, famous Rostam, it seems your soul's grown tired of combat, now that you're faced with the arrows of Goshtasp, the lion heart and spear points of Lohrasp."

Then, as the Simorgh had ordered him, Rostam drew back his bow. Aiming at Esfandyar's eyes he released the arrow, and for the Persian prince the world was turned to darkness. The tall cypress swayed and bent, knowledge and glory fled from him; the God-fearing prince bowed his head and slumped forward, and his Chinese bow slipped from his hand. He grasped at his black horse's mane as his blood soaked into the earth beneath him.

Rostam addressed Esfandyar: "Your harshness has borne fruit. You were the man who said, 'I am invincible, I can bow the heavens down to the earth.' Yesterday I was wounded by eight arrows, and bore this silently: one arrow has removed you from combat and left you slumped over your horse. In another moment your head will be on the ground, and your mother will mourn for you."

Esfandyar lost consciousness and fell to the ground. Slowly he came to himself, and grasped the arrow: when he withdrew it, its head and feathers were soaked in blood. The news immediately reached Bahman that the royal glory was shrouded in darkness: he ran to Pashutan and said: "Our expedition here has ended in disaster: his mammoth body lies in the dirt, and the world is a dark pit to him."

They ran to him, and saw him lying soaked in his blood, a bloody arrow in his hand. Pashutan said: "Who of our great men can understand the world's ways? Only God who guides our souls and the heavens, and the planets in their courses, knows its truth. One like Esfandyar who fought for the pure faith, who cleared the world of the evils of idol-worship and never stretched out his hand to evil deeds, dies in the prime of youth, and his royal head lies in the dirt; while one who spreads strife in the world, who torments the souls of free men, lives for many years unharmed by Fate."

The young men cradled the fallen hero's head, wiping away the blood. With sorrow in his heart, his face smeared with blood, Pashutan lamented over him: "O Esfandyar, prince and world conqueror, who has toppled this mountain, who has trampled underfoot this raging lion? Who has torn out the elephant's tusks, who has held back the torrent of the Nile? Where have your heart and soul and courage fled, and your strength and fortune and faith? Where now are your weapons of war, where now is your sweet voice at our banquets? You cleansed the world of malevolence, you were fearless before lions and demons, and all your reward is to reign in the earth. My curses on the crown and throne: may they and your faithless father king Goshtasp be forgotten forever!"

Esfandyar said: "Do not torment yourself for me. This came to me from the crown and court: the killed body goes into the earth, and you should not distress yourself at my death. Where now are Feraydun, Hushang, and Jamshid? They came on the wind and were gone with a breath. My noble ancestors too departed and ceded their place to me: no one remains in this fleeting world. I have traveled the earth and known its wonders, both those that are clear and those that are hidden, trying to establish the ways of God, taking wisdom as my guide; and now that my words have gone forth and the hands of Ahriman are tied, Fate stretches out its lion claws for me. My hope is that I shall reap the reward of my efforts in Paradise. Zal's son did not kill me by chivalrous means. Look at this tamarisk wood grasped in my fist: it was this wood that ended my days, directed by the Simorgh and by that wily cheat Rostam. Zal, who knows all the world's sorcery, cast this spell."

Hearing his words, Rostam turned aside, his heart wrung with anguish. He said: "Some evil demon has brought this suffering to you. It's as he said; he acted honorably. Since I have been a warrior in the world I have seen no armed horseman like Esfandyar, and because in myself I was helpless against his bow and strength I sought for help rather than yield to him. It was his death that I notched to my bow, and released, since his time had come. If Fate had meant him to live, how could I have found the tamarisk? Man must leave this dark earth, and cannot prolong his life by so much as a breath beyond his appointed time. I was the means by which the tamarisk arrow struck him down."

Esfandyar said: "Now my life draws to an end. Come closer, don't leave me. My thoughts are different now from what they were. Listen to my advice, and what I ask of you concerning my son, who is the center of my life. Take him under your wing, show him the path to greatness."

Hearing his words, Rostam came weeping to his side, lamenting loudly, with tears of shame flowing from his eyes. News reached the palace: Zal came like the wind, and Zavareh and Faramarz approached, bewildered with sorrow. Zal addressed Rostam: "My son, I weep heart's blood for you, because I have heard from our priests and astrologers that whoever spills Esfandyar's blood will be harried by Fate: his life in this world will be harsh, and when he dies he will inherit torment."

Esfandyar's Last Words to Rostam

Esfandyar spoke to Rostam:

> "All that has happened happened as Fate willed.
> Not you, your arrow, or the Simorgh killed

Me here: Goshtasp's, my father's, enmity
Made you the means by which to murder me.
He ordered me to sack Sistan, to turn
It to a wilderness, to slay and burn,
To suffer war's travails, while he alone
Enjoyed the glory of his crown and throne.
I ask you to accept my son, to raise
Him in Sistan, to teach him manhood's ways:
He is a wise and willing youth: from you
He'll learn the skills of war, what he must do
At courtly banquets when the wine goes round,
How to negotiate or stand his ground,
Hunting, the game of polo—everything
That suits the education of a king.
As for Jamasp, may his accursed name
Perish, and may he waste away in shame!"

When Rostam had heard him out he stood and laid his hand on his chest and said: "If you die I swear to fulfill what you have said: I shall seat him on the ivory throne and place the royal crown upon his head myself. I shall stand before him as his servant, and call him my lord and king."

Esfandyar answered: "You are an old man, a champion of many wars, but, as God is my witness, and by the Faith that guides me, all this good that you have done for the world's kings will avail you nothing: your good name has turned to evil and the earth is filled with mourning for my death. This deed will bring sorrow to your soul, as God willed should happen." Then he addressed Pashutan: "I expect now nothing but my shroud. When I have left this fleeting world, lead our army back to Iran, and there tell my father that I say to him: 'As you have achieved what you desire, don't look for excuses. The world has turned out entirely as you wished, and all authority is yours now. With my just sword I spread righteousness in the world and no one dared oppose you, and when the true Faith had been established in Iran I was ready for greatness. Before our courtiers you praised me, and behind their backs you sent me to my death. You have gained what you sought; rejoice and put your anxieties to rest. Forget about death, let your palace be filled with celebration. The throne is yours; sorrow and a harsh fate are mine: the crown is yours; a coffin and a shroud are mine. But what have the wise said? "No arrow can defeat Death." Put no faith in your wealth and crown and court: I shall be watching for you when you come to that other place, and when you do we shall go together before the world's Judge to speak before him and to hear his verdict.' When you leave him go to my mother, and tell her that death has taken her brave ambitious son; that against death's arrow his helmet was like air, and that not even a mountain of steel could have withstood it. Tell her that she shall come soon after me, and that she should not grieve her soul for my sake, or unveil her face before the court, or look on my face in its shroud. To see me would make her weep, and no wise man would praise her grief. And bid my sisters and my wife an eternal farewell from me. Evil came to me from my father's crown; the key to his treasury was my life. Tell my womenfolk that I have sent you to the court to shame his dark soul." He paused, and caught his breath, and said, "It was Goshtasp, my father, who destroyed me," and at that moment his pure soul left his wounded body, which lay dead in the dust.

Rostam tore his clothes and in an agony of grief smeared dust upon his head. Weeping he said: "Great knight, son and grandson of a king, famed throughout the world, Goshtasp brought you to an evil end." When he had wept copiously he addressed the corpse again:

> *"To the high heavens your pure soul has flown,*
> *May your detractors reap what they have sown!"*

Zavareh said to him: "You should not accept this trust. An ancient saying says that, if you rear a lion cub, when it cuts its teeth and the instinct for hunting grows in it, the first person it will turn on is its keeper. Our two countries have an evil history: evil has come to Iran with the death of Esfandyar, and Bahman will bring evil to Zabolestan. Mark my words, when he becomes king he will seek vengeance for his father's death."

Rostam replied: "No one, good or evil, can deflect what the heavens will. I shall do what is wise and honorable: if he turns to evil, Fate will answer him. Don't provoke disaster by your prophecies."

Pashutan Takes Esfandyar's Corpse to the Court of Goshtasp

They made an iron coffin lined with Chinese silk, and wrapped him in a shroud of gold brocade. His chieftains lamented for him as his body was clothed and his turquoise crown placed upon his head. Then the coffin was closed, and the royal tree that had borne so much fruit was hidden from men's sight. The coffin was sealed with pitch and smeared with musk and sweet smelling oils.

Rostam brought forty camels caparisoned in Chinese brocade, one of which bore the coffin, while the rest formed columns to right and left of the army. All who were there scored their faces and plucked out their hair, calling out the prince's name as they did so. At the head of the army Pashutan led Esfandyar's black horse, which had had its mane and tail docked: the saddle on the horse's back was reversed, and Esfandyar's mace, armor, helmet, and spear hung from it. The army made its way back to Persia, but Bahman stayed weeping and mourning in Zabolestan.

Rostam took him to his palace, and looked after him there as if he were his own soul.

Goshtasp Learns that Esfandyar Has Been Killed

News reached Goshtasp that the young prince's head had been brought low in death. The king rent his clothes, and poured dust on his head and crown: the palace resounded with the noise of lamentation, and the world was filled with Esfandyar's name.

Goshtasp said: "O pure of Faith, our land and time will never see your like again! Since Manuchehr reigned there has been no warrior to equal you: your sword was always at the service of our Faith, and you maintained our chieftains in their glory."

But the Persian nobles were angered by his words, and washed their eyes of all sympathy for the king. With one voice they said: "Accursed king, to keep your throne and crown you sent Esfandyar to his death in Zabolestan: may the Kayanid crown shame your head, may the star of your good fortune falter in its course!"

When the news came to the women's quarters his mother and sisters, together with their daughters, went out to meet the returning army: their heads were unveiled, and they went barefoot in the dust, tearing their clothes as they walked. They saw the weeping Pashutan approach, and behind him Esfandyar's black horse, and the coffin. The women clung to Pashutan, weeping and wailing, begging him to open the coffin and let them see the slaughtered prince. Grief-stricken and hemmed in by the lamenting women who tore at their flesh in their anguish, Pashutan called to the army's blacksmiths to bring tools to open the coffin. The lid was lifted and a new wave of lamentation broke out as his mother and sisters saw the prince's face, and his black beard anointed with musk. The women fainted, and their black curls were clotted with blood. When they revived, they turned to Esfandyar's horse, caressing its neck and back: Katayun wept to think that this horse had carried her son when he was killed, and said, "What hero can you carry off to war now? Who can you deliver to the dragon's claws?" They clung to its shorn mane and heaped dust on its head, and all the while the soldiers' lamentations rose into the sky.

When Pashutan reached the king's audience hall he neither paused at the door, nor made his obeisance, nor came forward to the throne. He shouted out: "Most arrogant of men, the signs of your downfall are there for all to see. You have destroyed Iran and yourself with this deed: wisdom and the divine *farr* have deserted you, and God will repay you for what you have done. The back of your power is broken, and all you will hold in your grasp from now on is wind. For the sake of your throne you imbrued your son in blood, and may your eyes never see the throne or good fortune again! The world is filled with evil, and you will lose your throne forever: in this world you will be despised and in the world to come you will be judged." Then he turned to Jamasp and said: "And you, you worthless evil councilor, who knows no speech in all the world but lies, who turns all splendor to crooked deceit, who stirs up enmity between princes, setting one against another, all you know how to do is to teach men to desert virtue and cleave to evil. But as you have sown so shall you reap. With your talk you destroyed a great man, saying that Esfandyar's life was in the palm of Rostam's hand."

Pashutan paused, and then he told the king plainly what had passed between Rostam and Bahman. When he had heard him out the king regretted what he had done. The court was cleared and his daughters, Beh Afarid and Homay, came before their father, their cheeks scored and their hair torn out in their sorrow for their dead brother.

They said: "Great king, haven't you considered what Esfandyar's death means? He was the first to avenge Zarir's death, he led the attack against the Turks, it was he who stabilized your kingdom. Then on the words of some slanderer you imprisoned him, and immediately our army was defeated and our grandfather was killed. When Arjasp reached Balkh he struck terror into the land, and we who live veiled from men's eyes were driven naked from the palace into the common highway. Arjasp extinguished the sacred fire of Zoroaster and seized the kingdom. And then you saw what your son did: he utterly destroyed our enemies and brought us back safely from the Brass Fortress where we'd been imprisoned. He was the savior of our country and of your throne. And so you sent him to Sistan, filling him with specious talk so that he'd give up his life for the sake of your crown, and the world would lament his death. Neither the Simorgh nor Rostam nor Zal killed him: you killed him, and as you killed him you have no right to weep and complain. Shame on your white beard, that you killed your son for the sake of greed. Before you, there have been many kings worthy of the throne; none killed his own son or turned against his own family."

The king turned to Pashutan and said: "Bestir yourself, and pour water on these children's fiery rage." Pashutan led the women from the court, saying to Esfandyar's mother Katayun, "How long will you rage and grieve like this? He sleeps happily, and his bright soul rests from the strife and sorrow of this world. Why should you grieve for him, since he is now in heaven?"

Katayun took his wise advice, and accepted God's justice. For a year, in every house and in the palace, there was mourning throughout the country, and for many years men wept to think of the tamarisk arrow, and the Simorgh's trick, and Zal.

Meanwhile Bahman lived in Zabolestan, hunting, drinking, taking his ease in the country's gardens. Rostam taught this vengeful youth how to ride, to drink wine, and the customs of a royal court. He treated him more warmly than if he'd been his own son, and rejoiced in his company day and night. When he had fulfilled his promise, the door of Goshtasp's revenge was closed.

Rostam's Letter to King Goshtasp

Rostam wrote a sorrowful letter, setting out his kindness to the king's son. He began by invoking Zoroaster and then went on: "As God is my witness, and Pashutan can testify, I said many times to Esfandyar that he should lay aside all enmity and desire for war. I told him I would give him land and wealth, but he chose otherwise; Fate willed that he ignored my pleas, and who can oppose what the heavens bring about? His son Bahman has lived with me, and is more splendid in my eyes than shining Jupiter: I have taught him how to be a king, instructing him in the elements of wisdom. If the king will promise to forget the tamarisk arrow and accept my repentance, all I have is at his disposal—my body, soul, wealth, crown, my very flesh and bones are his."

When the letter arrived at Goshtasp's court his courtiers soon learned of it. Pashutan came and confirmed everything Rostam had said: he recalled Rostam's grief at having to face Esfandyar, and the way that he had counseled him. He spoke too of Rostam's wealth, and of the land he ruled over. Pashutan's remarks pleased the king and had a good effect. The king's heart warmed towards Rostam, and he put aside his sorrow. Immediately he wrote a magnanimous answer to Rostam's letter: "When the heavens will someone an injury, who has the wisdom to prevent this? Pashutan has told me of what you tried to do, and this has filled my heart with kindness towards you. Who can withstand the heavens' turning? A wise man does not linger on the past. You are as you have always been, and more than this: you are the lord of Hend and Qannuj, and whatever more you desire, be it a throne or authority or arms, ask for it from me." As his master had ordered him, Rostam's messenger quickly took back the king's answer.

Time passed, and Prince Bahman grew to be a man. He was wise, knowledgeable, authoritative, every inch a king. Jamasp, with his understanding of good and evil, knew that the kingdom would one day be Bahman's, and he said to Goshtasp: "My lord, you should consider Bahman's situation. He is mature in knowledge, and an honorable man. But he's lived in a foreign land for too long, and no one has ever read him a letter from you. A letter should be written to him, something as splendid as a tree in Paradise. Who have you but Bahman to cleanse the sorrow of Esfandyar's fate from your mind?"

Goshtasp was pleased by this suggestion and answered: "Write him a letter, and write one also to Rostam, saying: 'God be thanked, great champion, that I am pleased with you, and my mind is at rest. My grandson Bahman, who is dearer to me than our own soul and is wiser than my councilor Jamasp, has learned all kingly skills from you: now you should send him back to me.' To Bahman write: 'As soon as you read this letter stay in Zabol no longer: I have a great desire to see you. Put your affairs in order and come as quickly as you can.'"

When the letter was read to him, Rostam was pleased, and he prepared a parting gift for Bahman. He opened his treasury and brought out armor, shining daggers, barding for horses, bows, arrows, maces, Indian swords, camphor, musk, sandalwood, jewels, gold, silver, horses, uncut cloth, servants and young boys, gold belts and saddles, and two golden goblets filled with rubies. All these he handed over to Bahman.

Bahman Returns to King Goshtasp

Rostam came two stages of the road with the prince, and then sent him on his way to the king. When Goshtasp saw his grandson's face, tears covered his cheeks and he said: "You are another Esfandyar, you resemble no one but him." Bahman was intelligent and quick witted, and from then on he was called Ardeshir. He was a strong, fine warrior: wise, knowledgeable, and God-fearing. When he stood, his finger tips came to below his knees. In all things he was like his father, whether fighting or feasting or hunting. Goshtasp could not be separated from him, and made him his drinking companion. He would say:

> "Now, since my noble, warlike son has died,
> May Bahman live forever at my side."

ఈ THE DEATH OF ROSTAM ఈ

Zal had a female slave who was a musician and story teller. She gave birth to a son whose beauty eclipsed the moon's: in appearance he resembled Sam, and the whole family rejoiced at his birth. Astrologers and wise men from Kabol and Kashmir came with their astronomical charts to cast the boy's horoscope, and to see whether the heavens would smile on him. But when they had done so they looked at one another in alarm and dismay, and said to Zal: "You and your family have been favored by the stars, but when we searched the secrets of the heavens we saw that this boy's fortune is not an auspicious one. When this handsome lad reaches manhood and becomes a warrior he will destroy the seed of Sam and Nariman, he will break your family's power. Because of him Sistan will be filled with lamentation and the land of Iran will be thrown into confusion: he will bring bitter days to everyone, and few enough of you will survive his onslaught."

Zal was saddened by these words and turned to God in his anxiety: "Lord of the heavens, my refuge and support, my guide in all my actions, creator of the heavens and the stars: may we hope for good fortune, and may nothing but goodness and peace come to us." Then he named the boy Shaghad.

His mother kept him by her until he was weaned; he was a talkative, charming, and quick witted child. When his strength had begun to develop, Zal sent him to the king of Kabol. There he grew into a fine young man, cypress statured, a good horseman, and skillful with mace and lariat. The king of Kabol looked on him with favor, and considered him worthy of the throne: he bestowed his own daughter on him in marriage and provided her with a splendid dowry. Shaghad was the apple of his eye, and he thought nothing of the stars and the astrologers' predictions.

The chieftains of Persia and India told Rostam that every year the kingdom of Kabol was required to hand over as tribute the hide of a cow. But the king of Kabol was sure that, now his son-in-law was Rostam's brother, no one would be concerned about a cow skin worth a few coins.

But when the time came for the tribute to be paid it was demanded, and the people of Kabol took offense at this. Shaghad was disgusted by his brother's behavior, but he told no one, except the king to whom he said, in secret: "I am tired of the world's ways: my brother treats me with disrespect, he has no time for me. He's more like a stranger to me than an older brother, more like a fool than a wise man. You and I should work together to entrap him, and this will win us fame in the world." The two confabulated together, and in their own eyes they overtopped the moon: but listen to what the wise have said, "Whoever does evil will be repaid in kind."

All night, until the sun rose above the mountains, the two evaded sleep, plotting how to wipe Rostam's name from the world, and make Zal's eyes wet with tears of grief. Shaghad said to the king: "If we're going to turn our words into actions, I suggest you give a banquet with wine, musicians, and entertainers, and invite our chieftains. Whilst we're drinking wine, in front of all the courtiers and guests, speak coldly and slightingly to me. Then I'll go to my brother, and to my father, and curse the lord of Kabol for a low-born wretch, and complain about how he has treated me. Meanwhile, you should go to the plain where we hunt, and have pits dug there. Make them deep enough to swallow up both Rostam and Rakhsh, and in the base of the pits plant sharpened stakes, spears, javelins, swords, and so on. If you can dig a hundred pits rather than just five, so much the better. Get a hundred men together, dig the pits, and don't breathe a word even to the wind. Then cover over the pits' surface, and see that you mention what you've done to no one at all."

The king's good sense deserted him, and he gave orders for a banquet to be prepared, as this fool had suggested to him. He summoned the chieftains of his kingdom to a splendid feast and, when they had eaten, they settled to their wine, watching entertainers and listening to musicians. When his head was well-filled with royal wine, Shaghad suddenly sprang up and bragged to the king:

> "I am the first in any company—
> What noble chieftain can compare with me?
> Rostam's my brother, Zal's my father, can
> Such boasts be made by any other man?"

Then the king too sprang up and retorted:

> "This is your constant boast, but it's not true,
> The tribe of Sam has turned its back on you:
> Rostam is not your brother, when has he
> So much as mentioned your base name to me?
> You're a slave's son, not Zal's. And Rostam's mother
> Has never said that you're that hero's brother."

Shaghad was infuriated by his words, and with a few Kaboli warriors he immediately set out for Zabolestan, revolving thoughts of vengeance in his heart. He entered his noble father's court in a rage, and when Zal saw his son's stature and splendor he made much of him, questioned him closely, and sent him to Rostam.

Rostam was delighted to see him, thinking of him as a wise and pure hearted man, and greeted him warmly: "Sam is a lion, and his progeny produce only strong, courageous warriors. How is your life now in Kabol, and what do they say about Rostam there?"

Shaghad's answer was: "Don't mention the king of Kabol to me. He treated me well before, addressing me with respect, but now as soon as he drinks a little wine he becomes quarrelsome, thinking he's superior to everyone else: he humiliated me in front of his courtiers, and talked publicly about my low origins. Then he said, 'How long do we have to pay this tribute? Don't we have the strength to defy Sistan? Don't tell me, "But it's Rostam you're dealing with." He's no more of a man than I am, and no more nobly born either.' Then he said that I wasn't Zal's son; or that, if I was, Zal didn't care about me. I was ashamed to be spoken to like this in front of his chieftains, and when I left Kabol my cheeks were pale with fury."

Rostam was enraged, and said: "Such talk won't stay private for long. Don't bother yourself with his army: my curses on his army and on his crown too. I'll destroy him for these words of his, I'll make him and his whole tribe tremble for what he's said. I'll place you on his throne, and I'll drag his luck down into the dust."

He entertained Shaghad royally for a few days, putting a splendid residence at his disposal; then he picked his best warriors and ordered them to get ready to travel to Kabol. When the preparations for departure had been made, Shaghad came to Rostam and said, "Don't think of going to war against the king of Kabol. I'd only have to trace the letters of your name in water for everyone in Kabol to be sleepless with anxiety. Who would dare to stand against you in war, and if you set out who is going to wait for you to confront them? I think that by now the king must regret what he's done, that he's searching for some way to neutralize the effects of my departure, and that he'll send some of his chieftains here to apologize."

Rostam replied: "Here's what we should do: there's no need for me to lead my army against Kabol, Zavareh and about a hundred horsemen, together with a hundred infantry, should be sufficient."

The King of Kabol Prepares the Pits

As soon as the malignant Shaghad had left Kabol the king hurried off to his hunting grounds. He took sappers renowned for their ability from his army, and had them excavate pits at various places on the road that led through the area. At the bottom of each pit javelins, spears, and sharp swords were stuck into the ground. Then the pits were covered over with straw and brush so that neither men nor their mounts could see them.

When Rostam was ready to set out, Shaghad rode on ahead of him and told the king of Kabol that Rostam and his men were approaching, and that the king should go to meet them and apologize for what he had done. The king came out of the city, his tongue ready with glozing talk, his heart filled with poison and the longing for vengeance.

As soon as he saw Rostam he dismounted. He removed his Indian turban and placed his hands on his forehead: then he removed his boots, began to weep, and bowed his face down to the ground, asking pardon for what he had done to Shaghad, saying that if he had spoken intemperately it was because he was drunk, and that Rostam should forgive him. He came forward, barefoot, but his mind was filled with thoughts of vengeance.

Rostam forgave him, awarding him new honors, and told him to replace his turban and boots, and to remount his horse.

There was a green, delightful garden in Kabol, filled with streams and trees. Seats were set there, and the king ordered that a banquet be brought; then he called for wine and musicians to entertain his chieftains and courtiers. Whilst the festivities were in progress he turned to Rostam and said: "What would you say to a hunting expedition? I have a place near here which includes both open country and mountain landscape, and it's filled with game. There are mountain sheep, deer, and wild asses: a man with a good horse can run down any number of prey: it's a pleasure no one should miss."

His description of the landscape with its streams and wild asses filled Rostam with enthusiasm:

> For when a man's days reach their end, his mind
> And heart grow undiscerning, dim, and blind:
> The world has no desire that we should see
> The hidden secrets of our destiny.
> The crocodile, the lion, the elephant
> Are one with the mosquito and the ant
> Within the grip of Death: no beast or man
> Lives longer than his life's allotted span.

Rostam gave orders that Rakhsh be saddled, and that hunting hawks be made ready: he took up his bow, and rode out on the plain with Shaghad. Zavareh and a few of their retinue accompanied them. The group dispersed, some going toward solid ground, others to where the earth had been excavated; as Fate would have it, Zavareh and Rostam went to the area where the pits had been dug. But Rakhsh smelt the freshly dug earth: his muscles tensed and he reared up in fright, his hooves pawing at the ground. He went forward, placing his hooves with care, until he was between two of the pits. Rostam was irritated by his caution, and Fate blinded the hero's wisdom. He lightly touched Rakhsh with his whip, and the horse bounded forward, searching for firm ground. But his forelegs struck where one of the pits had been dug, and there was nowhere for him to find a hold. The base of the pit was lined with spears and sharp swords: courage was of no avail, and there was no means of escape. Rakhsh's flanks were lacerated by the weapons, and Rostam's legs and trunk were pierced by them: exerting all his strength, he pulled himself from their points, and raised his head above the pit's edge.

When in his agony he opened his eyes, he saw the malignant face of Shaghad before him. He knew then that Shaghad had tricked him, and that this evil was his doing. He said:

> "Ill-fated wretch, what you have done will leave
> Our land a desert where men curse and grieve:
> You will regret your evil, senseless rage;
> Tormented, you will never see old age."

Shaghad replied: "The turning heavens have dealt justly with you. How often you've boasted of the blood you've spilt, of your devastation of Iran, and of your battles. You won't be demanding tribute from Kabol any more, and no kings will tremble before you now. Your days are at an end, and you shall perish in the snare of Ahriman."

At that moment the king of Kabol reached them: he saw Rostam's open, bleeding wounds and said, "My lord, what has happened to you here in our hunting grounds? I shall hurry to bring doctors to heal your wounds, and to dry my tears of sympathy for your suffering."

Rostam replied: "Devious and lowborn wretch, the days when doctors could help me are over, and you need weep no tears for me. You too will not live long; no one passes to the heavens while still alive. I possess no more glory than Jamshid, who was hacked in two by Zahhak; and Gerui slit Seyavash's throat when his time had come. All the great kings of Iran, all those who were lions in battle, have departed, and we are left here like lions at the wayside. My son Faramarz will demand vengeance from you for my death." Then he turned to Shaghad and said: "Now that this evil has come to

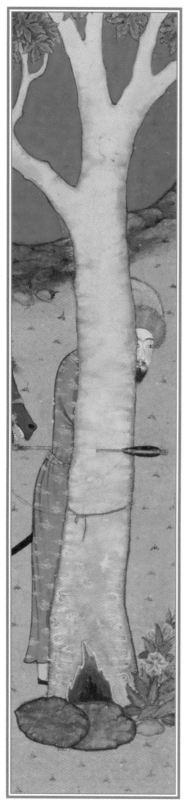

me, take my bow from its case: don't refuse me this last request. String my bow and put it in front of me, together with two arrows: a lion may come looking for prey, and if it sees me helpless here it will attack me; my bow will defend me then. And if no lion tears my flesh, my body will lie beneath the earth soon enough."

Shaghad came forward and took out the bow; he strung it, and pulled back the string to test it. Then he laughed and placed it in front of Rostam, filled with joy at the thought of his brother's death. With a mighty effort, Rostam picked up the bow, and notched an arrow to the string. His brother was filled with fear at the sight of the arrow, and to shield himself he went behind a huge, ancient plane tree, the trunk of which was hollow, although it still bore leaves.

Rostam watched him go, and then, summoning his last strength, he drew back the bowstring and released the arrow. The shaft pierced the tree and his brother, pinning them to one another, and the dying Rostam's heart rejoiced to see this. Shaghad cried out with the pain of his wound, but Rostam soon put him out of his misery. Then he said:

"Thanks be to God, to whom for all my days
I've offered worship and unceasing praise
That now, as night comes on, with my last breath,
Vengeance and power are mine before my death."

With these words his soul left his body, and those who stood nearby lamented and wept.

In another pit Zavareh too died, as did those who had ridden with Rostam, both his chieftains and their followers.

Zal Learns of Rostam's Death

But one of his retinue survived and, sometimes riding, sometimes on foot, made his way back to Zabolestan, where he said: "Our mammoth warrior is made one with the dust; Zavareh too, and all their men, are dead, and only I have escaped from the evil that befell them."

The noise of mourning was heard throughout Zabolestan, and execrations against Shaghad and the king of Kabol. Zal strewed his body with dust, and clawed at his face and chest in his grief.

> Then in his agony he cried aloud:
> "All I can bring you, Rostam, is your shroud;
> And Zavareh, that lion chief in war,
> That dragon in close combat, is no more:
> My curses on Shaghad, whose treachery
> Has ripped up by the roots our royal tree.
> Who would have thought a cunning fox could leave
> Our mammoth heroes dead, and me to grieve?
> Why could I not have died before them? Why
> Should I endure the world whilst they must die?
> What's life to me that I should breathe and live,
> What comfort can my throne or glory give?"

And he wept bitterly, lamenting Rostam's departed greatness. His lion courage and bravery, his chivalry and good council, his mighty weapons and valor in war—all were gone, now that he was one with the earth.

Then Zal cursed his son's enemies and summoned Faramarz: he sent him to make war on the king of Kabol, to retrieve the dead bodies from the pits, and to give the world there cause for lamentation.

But when Faramarz reached Kabol he found none of the nobility there: they had all fled from the town, weeping and terrified by the world-conqueror's death. He made his way to the hunting grounds, where the pits had been dug, and when he saw his father's face, and his body lying on the ground, soaked in blood, he roared like a lion in pain. He said: "Great warrior, who has done this evil to you? My curses on his boldness, and may dust cover his head in place of his crown! I swear by God and by your soul, by the dust of Nariman and Sam, that I shall not remove my armor until I have wreaked revenge upon this treacherous people for your death. I shall not leave one of those who were any part of this plot alive."

He removed his father's armor, and the clothes beneath it, and gently washed the blood from his body and beard. The company burnt ambergris and saffron, and with it sealed his wounds. Faramarz poured rosewater on his father's brow, and smeared camphor over the body. Then they wrapped him in brocade, over which they sprinkled rosewater, musk, and wine. Two great boards were necessary to carry his corpse, which seemed more like the trunk of a huge shade-giving tree, than the body of a man. A magnificent coffin was made of teak, with a design inlaid in ivory, and the nails were of gold: the joints were sealed with pitch that had been mixed with musk and ambergris.

Then Rakhsh's body was drawn up from the pit and washed, and draped in fine brocade: carpenters spent two days making a litter from heavy boards for the body, and this was loaded onto an elephant. From Kabol to Zabol the land was filled with lamentation. Men and women stood crowded at the wayside to see the procession, and the crowds passed the coffins of Rostam and Zavareh from hand to hand; so great was the number who did this that the burden seemed light as air. The journey took ten days and ten nights, and not once were the coffins set down. The world was filled with mourning for Rostam, and the plain seemed to seethe with sorrow; so great was the noise that no individual's voice could be heard within the roar of sound.

In a garden they built a great tomb whose roof reached to the clouds. Within, two golden daises were built, on which were laid the dead heroes: freemen and slaves came together and poured rosewater mixed with musk over the heroes' feet, and addressed Rostam:

> "Why is it grief and musk that we must bring
> And not the glory that attends a king?
> You have no need for sovereignty, no need
> For armor, weapons, or your warlike steed,
> Never again will your largesse reward
> Courtiers with gifts from your rich treasure hoard.
> Justice was yours, and truth, and chivalry,
> May joy be yours for all eternity."

Then they sealed the tomb and went on their way: so ended the lion hero who had lifted up his head in the world with such pride and valor.

Faramarz Marches on Kabol

When his father's obsequies were completed, Faramarz gathered an army on the plain and equipped it from Rostam's treasury. At dawn the tucket sounded, and was answered by the din of drums and Indian bells. The army set out for Kabol, the sun obscured by its dust.

News reached Kabol's king of their approach: he gathered his scattered army together and the ground became a mass of iron armor, while the air was darkened with dust. He marched his men out to confront Faramarz, and the sun and moon were dimmed. The armies met and the world was filled with the sounds of battle. A wind sprang up, and a dust cloud hid the earth and sky: but Faramarz at the head of his army never took his eyes from the enemy king. The din of drums rang out on each side, and Faramarz together with a small escort forced his way into the center of the Kaboli troops. There in the dusty darkness stirred up by the cavalry he closed in on the king and captured him. That great army scattered, and the warriors of Zabol fell on the retreating men like wolves: they ambushed them from every side, and pursued them as they fled. They killed so many Indian soldiers, so many warriors from Sind, that the dust of the battlefield was turned to mud with their gore: their hearts forgot their country and their homes, their wives and little children were left unprotected.

Kabol's king, his body covered in blood, was flung into a chest hoisted on an elephant's back. Faramarz led his men to the hunting grounds where the pits had been dug. Then the king was dragged forward, with his hands bound, together with forty members of his tribe. They trussed the king so tightly that his bones showed through his skin, and he was suspended upside down in one of the pits, his body covered in filth, his mouth filled with blood. Next Faramarz had a fire lit in which the forty members of the king's family were burnt; then he turned to where Shaghad was still pinned to the plane tree. Shaghad's body, the tree, and the surrounding countryside were consumed by flames, that flared up like a great mountain of fire. When he set out again for Zabol, he brought the ashes of Shaghad to give them to Zal.

Having killed those who had committed evil, Faramarz appointed a new king for Kabol, as the old king's family had been annihilated. He returned from Kabol still filled with fury and grief; the brilliance of his days had turned to darkness. All Zabolestan shared his grief, and there was no man who had not rent his clothes in mourning. All of Sistan lamented for a year, and all its inhabitants wore the black and dark blue clothes of mourning.

Rudabeh's Madness

One day Rudabeh said to Zal: "Weep for Rostam in bitterness of heart, for since the world has existed no one has ever seen a darker day than this." Zal turned on her and said, "Foolish woman, the pain of hunger is far worse than this sorrow." Rudabeh was offended and swore an oath, saying: "I shall neither eat nor sleep in the hopes that my soul will join Rostam, and see him in that blessed company."

In her heart she communicated with Rostam's soul, and for a week she kept herself from eating anything. Weakened by hunger, her eyes darkened, and her slender body became frail and feeble. Everywhere she went, her serving maids followed her, afraid that she would harm herself. By the week's end her reason had deserted her, and she was expected to die.

When the world was asleep she went into the palace kitchen garden, and there she saw a dead snake lying in the pool. She reached down and picked it up by the head, intending to eat it, but a serving girl snatched the snake from her hand, and the girl's companions led Rudabeh away to her apartments. They made her comfortable, and prepared food for her. She ate whatever they brought, until she was full, and then her servants laid her gently on her bed.

When she woke her reason had returned, and she said to Zal: "What you told me was wise: the sorrow of death is like a festival to someone who has neither eaten nor slept. He has gone, and we shall follow after him: we trust in the world creator's justice. Then she distributed her secret wealth to the poor, and prayed to God:

> "O Thou, who art above all name and place,
> Wash guilt and worldly sin from Rostam's face:
> Give him his place in Heaven: let him be shown
> The fruitful harvest of the seeds he's sown."

Bahman and Faramarz

Goshtasp's fortunes declined, and he summoned his councilor, Jamasp. He said to him: "My heart is seared with such sorrow for this business of Esfandyar that not one day of my life passes in pleasure: malignant stars have destroyed me. After me, Bahman will be king, and Pashutan will be his confidant. Keep faith with Bahman, and obey him: guide him in his duties, point by point, and he will add luster to the throne and crown."

He handed Bahman the keys to his treasury, and heaved a cold and bitter sigh. Then he said: "My work is over; the waters overtop my head. I have reigned for a hundred and twenty years, and I have seen no one else with my power in all the world. Strive to act justly, and if you do you will escape from sorrow. Keep wise men near you and treat them well, darken the world of those who wish you ill: act righteously, and you will avoid both deviousness and failure. I give you my throne, my diadem, and my wealth: I have experienced enough sorrow and grief." He spoke, and his days on the earth came to an end. They built a tomb for him of ebony and ivory, and his crown was suspended over the coffin.

When Bahman ascended his grandfather's throne he acted with decision and generosity, giving his army cash, and distributing land among them. He called a council of the wise, the noble, and those experienced in the ways of the world.

He said to them: "All of you, old and young, who have gracious souls, surely remember Esfandyar's life and the good and evil that Fate dealt him: and you recall what Rostam and that old wizard Zal did to him in the prime of his life. Openly and covertly Faramarz does nothing but plot vengeance against us. My head is filled with pain, my heart with blood, and my brain is empty of everything but thoughts of revenge: revenge for our two warriors Nushazar and Mehrnush, whose agonies caused such sorrow, and revenge for Esfandyar who had revived the fortunes of our nobility, who was slain in Zabolestan, for whose death the very beasts were maddened with grief, and the frescoed portraits in our palaces wept.

"Our ancestors, when they were brave young warriors, did not hide their valor in obscurity, but acted as the glorious king Feraydun did, who destroyed Zahhak in revenge for the blood of Jamshid. And Manuchehr brought an army from Amol and marched against Salm and the barbarous Tur, pursuing them to China in pursuit of vengeance for his grandfather's death. I too shall leave such a tale behind me. When Kay Khosrow escaped from Afrasyab's clutches he made the world like a lake of blood: my father demanded vengeance for Lohrasp, and piled the earth with a mountain of dead. And Faramarz, who exalts himself above the shining sun, went to Kabol pursuing vengeance for his father's blood, and razed the whole province to the ground: blood obscured all the land, and men rode their horses over the bodies of the dead. I, who ride out against raging lions, am more worthy than anyone to take revenge, since my vengeance will be for the peerless Esfandyar. Tell me how this matter appears to you; what answer can you give me? Try to give me wise advice."

When they heard Bahman's words everyone who wished him well said with one voice: "We are your slaves, our hearts are filled with goodwill towards you. You know more about what has happened in the past than we do, and you are more capable than any other warrior: do what you will in the world, and may you win praise and glory for your deeds. No one will refuse your orders, or break faith with you."

Hearing this answer Bahman became more intent on vengeance than ever, and prepared to invade Sistan. At daybreak the din of drums resounded, and the air was darkened by his armies' dust: a hundred thousand mounted warriors set out.

When he reached the banks of the River Hirmand he sent a messenger to Zal. He was to say on behalf of Bahman: "My days have been turned to bitterness because of what happened to Esfandyar, and to the two worthy princes Nushazar and Mehrnush. I will fill all the land of Sistan with blood, to slake my longing for vengeance."

The messenger arrived in Zabol and spoke as he had been instructed: Zal's heart was wrung with sorrow, and he said: "If the prince will consider what happened to Esfandyar, he will see that this was a fated event, and that I too suffered because of it. You were here, and saw all that happened, both the good and the evil, but from me you have only seen profit, and no loss. Rostam did not ignore your father's orders, and his fealty to him was heartfelt. But Esfandyar, who was a great king, in his last days became overbearing toward Rostam: even the lion in his thicket, and the savage dragon cannot escape the claws of Fate.

"And you have heard of Sam's chivalrous deeds, which he continued until Rostam, in his turn, drew his sharp sword from its scabbard. Rostam's heroism in battle was witnessed by your forebears, and he acted as your servant, your nurse, your guide in the ways of warfare. Day and night I weep and mourn for my dead son, my heart is filled with pain, my two cheeks have turned sallow with grief, and my lips are blue with my sufferings: my curses on the one who overthrew him, and on the man who guided him to do so. If you can consider the sorrow we now endure, and think well of us, if you can drive these thoughts of vengeance from your heart, and brighten our land with your mercy, I shall lay before you golden belts and golden bridles, and all my son's treasures and Sam's cash: you are our king, and our chieftains are your flock."

He gave the messenger a horse and money, and many other presents. But when the messenger reached Bahman and told him what he had seen and heard, the king refused to accept Zal's words, and flew into a rage. He entered the city with pain in his heart, and still revolving thoughts of vengeance. Zal and the nobility of Sistan rode out to welcome him: when he drew near to Bahman, Zal dismounted, made his obeisance before him, and said: "This is a time for forgiveness, to put aside suffering and the desire for vengeance. I, Zal, stand before you, wretched and supported by a staff: remember how good I was to you when you were young. Forgive the past and speak of it no more: seek honor, rather than revenge for those who have been killed."

But Bahman so despised Zal that his words enraged the king: without further ado he had Zal's legs shackled and, ignoring the protests of both councilor and treasurer, he gave orders for camels to be loaded with the goods in the castle. Cash, uncut gems, thrones and fine cloth, silver and golden vessels, golden crowns, earrings, and belts, Arab horses with bridles worked in gold, Indian swords in golden scabbards, slaves, bags of coins, musk, camphor—all the wealth that Rostam had accumulated with such effort, or received as presents from kings and chieftains, was collected and taken. Purses and crowns were distributed to Bahman's nobility, and Zabolestan was given over to plunder.

Faramarz Makes War on Bahman

Faramarz was in the marches of Bost when he heard this; outraged by the treatment meted out to his grandfather, he prepared to take his revenge. His chieftains gathered about him and he said: "Zavareh would often sigh and say to my father that Bahman would seek revenge for the death of Esfandyar, and that this threat should not be taken lightly. But, for all his experience of the world, my father wouldn't listen to him, and this is the reason that his territories are now laid waste. When his grandfather died Bahman ascended the throne, and raised his crown to the moon's sphere; now that he's king he's once again intent on revenge for Esfandyar, and for Mehrnush and Nus-hazar too. He wants to destroy us as vengeance for their deaths, and he's led here from Iran an army like a black cloud. He's arrested and bound in chains my revered grandfather, who was a shield to the Persians in their wars, and always held himself ready to serve them. What will happen to our people now, what disasters will close in from every side? My father has been slain, my grandfather languishes in chains, all our land has been given over to plunder, and I am half mad with the grief of all this: well, my noble warriors, what have you to say about our situation?"

They answered him: "O bright souled hero, whose leadership has been passed down from father to father, we are all your slaves, and live only for your orders."

When he heard this, Faramarz's heart was filled with longing for vengeance, his head with thoughts of how to save his family's honor: he put on his armor and led his army against Bahman, and as he marched he rehearsed in his mind Rostam's battles.

When the news reached Bahman he acted immediately: he had the baggage trains loaded up, and then led his army towards Ghur, where he stayed for two weeks. Faramarz pursued him, and his cavalry turned the world black with their dust. For his part Bahman drew up his battle lines, and the shining sun could no longer see the ground. The mountains rang with the squeal of trumpets and the clanging of Indian bells. The sky seemed to soak the world in pitch, arrows rained down from the clouds like dew, and the earth seemed to shudder with the din of battleaxe blows, the humming of released bowstrings. For three days and nights, by sunlight and moonlight, maces and arrows rained down and the sky was filled with clouds of dust. On the fourth day a wind sprang up, and it was as if day had turned to night: the wind blew against Faramarz and his troops, and king Bahman rejoiced to see this. His sword drawn, he charged forward, following the billowing dust clouds, and raised such a hue and cry it seemed that the Last Judgment had come. The men of Bost, the army from Zabol, the warriors of Kabol, all were slaughtered or fled, and not one of their chieftains remained. All turned tail and forgot their allegiance to Faramarz: all the battlefield was strewn with mountainous piles of bodies of men from both sides.

With a few remaining warriors, his body covered in sword wounds, Faramarz fought on, for he was a lion fighter, descended from a race of lions. Finally, the long arm of Bahman's might caught him, and he was dragged before the king. Bahman glared at him in fury, and denied him all mercy. While still alive, Faramarz's body was hoisted upside down on a gibbet; and Bahman gave orders that he be killed in a storm of arrows.

Bahman Frees Zal, and Returns to Iran

Pashutan was the king's trusted advisor, and he was very troubled by this execution. Humbly he stood before his royal master and said: "Lord of Justice and Righteousness, if you desired vengeance you have achieved it. You would do well to give no more orders for plunder, killing, and warfare, and you should not take pleasure in such tumult. Fear God, and show shame before us: look at the turnings of the heavens, how they raise one to greatness, and cast another down to wretchedness and grief. Did not your great father, who brought the world beneath his command, find his coffin in Sistan? Was not Rostam lured to the hunting grounds in Kabol, and there destroyed in a pit? While you live my noble lord you should not harass those of exalted birth. You should tremble that Sam's son Zal complains of his fetters, since his stars will advocate his cause before God who keeps us all. And think of Rostam, who protected the Persian throne, and who was prompt to undergo all hardships for Persia's sake: it is because of him that this crown has come down to you, not because of Goshtasp and Esfandyar. Consider, from the time of Kay Qobad to that of Kay Khosrow, it was because of his sword that the kings were able to reign. If you are wise you will free Zal from his chains, and turn your heart away from evil paths."

When the king heard Pashutan's advice, he regretted the pain he had caused, and his old longing for revenge. A cry went up from the royal pavilion: "My noble chieftains, prepare for our return to Iran and stop this rampage of plunder and killing." He gave orders that Zal's legs were to be freed from their fetters, and, as Pashutan suggested, he had a tomb built for the slain Faramarz. Zal was brought from the prison to his palace, and there his wife Rudabeh wept bitterly when she saw him, saying:

> "Alas for Rostam, for his noble race,
> Our hero lies in his last resting place,
> And when he lived, who could have guessed or known
> That Goshtasp would ascend the royal throne?
> His wealth is gone, his father's now a slave,

His noble son lies murdered in the grave.
May no one ever know such grief, or see
The fateful sorrows that have come to me!
My curses on them: may the earth be freed
From Bahman and his evil father's seed!"

News of her rage reached Bahman and Pashutan, and Pashutan grieved to hear of Rudabeh's pain: his cheeks turned sallow with grief and he said to Bahman, "O king, when the moon has passed her zenith tonight, as dawn comes on, lead your army away from here. This business has grown weighty and serious: I pray that those who wish you evil cannot harm your crown, and that all your days may be passed in joy and festivities. My lord, it would be better if you remained in Zal's palace no longer."

When the mountain tops turned red in the rising sun, the din of drums rang out from the court, and Bahman, who had looked for vengeance for so long, commanded that the army be drawn up in marching order. Drums, trumpets, and Indian bells sounded in the royal pavilion, and the army set out for home, as Pashutan had suggested. When they reached Iran Bahman rested at last, and sat himself on the imperial throne. He gave himself to the business of government, distributing money to the poor; and some were pleased with his reign, while others lived in grief and sorrow.

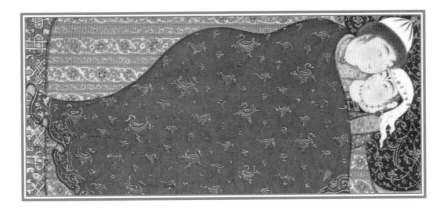

Bahman, now also referred to as Ardeshir, had a son called Sasan. He also had a beautiful daughter named Homai, with whom he fell in love, and he slept with her, "according to the custom called Pahlavi." When Homai was six months pregnant, Bahman became ill, and, realizing he was going to die, he resigned his throne to Homai and her heirs.

> But when Sasan heard this, in rage and shame,
> He fled to Nayshapour, forsook his fame,
> And inconspicuously lived out his life.
> A well-born local girl became his wife
> And she in time bore him a son, whom he
> Named Sasan too. Then, unexpectedly,
> The elder Sasan died. The son was wise
> But poverty obscured him from men's eyes
> And as a shepherd he was forced to keep
> The King of Nayshapour's rich flocks of sheep.

From this lowly shepherd would come the last of the great pre-Islamic dynasties of Iran, the Sasanians.

GLOSSARY OF NAMES AND THEIR PRONUNCIATION

The following is a list of the names which appear in the stories included in this volume, together with a brief description of who or what they designate.

Persian names are pronounced with a more even stress than is common in English, and to an English speaker's ear this often sounds as if the last syllable is being stressed. A slight extra stress on the last syllable of names will bring the reader closer to a Persian pronunciation.

Persian has two distinct sounds indicated in English by the letter "a." One is a long sound (as in "father") and this has been indicated here by the accent "ā" (e.g., Zāl). The other is a short sound (as in "cat") and this has been indicated by the standard "a" (e.g., Zav). The vowel given as "i" is a long vowel, like the second vowel in "police." The vowel given as "u" is also a long vowel, like the first vowel in "super." "Q" and "gh" are pronounced approximately as a guttural hard "g," far back in the throat. "Zh" is pronounced like the sound represented by the "s" in "pleasure." "Kh" is pronounced like the Scottish "ch" in "loch."

AFRĀSYĀB: a king of Turān, the brother of Aghriras and Garsivaz.

AGHRIRAS: the brother of Afrāsyāb and Garsivaz.

AHRIMAN: the evil god of the universe.

AKVĀN DIV: the name of a demon who tries to kill Rostam.

ALĀNS: a tribe living near the Caspian Sea.

ALVĀD: a warrior from Sistān.

ĀMOL: a town near the Caspian.

ANDARIMĀN: a warrior from Turān.

ARDESHIR: another name for Esfandyār's son, Bahman.

ARJĀSP: a king of Turān.

ARVAND: the name of a river.

ARZHANG: a demon of Māzanderān.

ASHKĀSH: a Persian warrior.

BĀDĀVAR: a royal treasury. The name means literally "windfall."

BAHMAN: Esfandyār's son, and Sāsān's and Homay's father. Also the name of an angel.

BAHRĀM: a warrior of Irān.

BALKH: a town in northern Afghānistān.

BALUCHISTAN: a province covering modern south eastern Irān and eastern Pakistan.

BĀRMĀN: two warriors of Turān go by this name; one is a son of Viseh and is killed by Qāren, the other accompanies Sohrāb on his expedition against Irān.

BARZIN: a warrior of Irān.

BEH ĀFARID: a daughter of Goshtasp, and sister to Esfandyar, Pashutan, and Homay.

BEHZĀD: the name of Seyavash's horse.

BISITUN: a mountain in south east Irān, about thirty miles from the city of Kermanshah. In medieval Persian verse the name is sometimes used simply to mean any large mountain.

BIZHAN: a Persian hero, the son of Giv.

BOKHĀRĀ: a city in Transoxiana.

BOST: an area to the east of Sistān; lying between Persia and India.

CHAJ: a city in Turkestan.

CHORASMIA: The area to the south of the Aral Sea.

DĀGHUI: this area, which must lie somewhere between Persia and Turān, has not been further identified.

DAMUR: a warrior of Turān.

EBLIS: the devil.

ERMĀN: Ermāni, an area to the north west of Irān, identified with present day Armenia.

ESFANDYĀR: a Persian prince: the son of Goshtāsp, and father of Bahman.

FARĀMARZ: Rostam's son.

FARHĀD: a warrior of Irān.

FARIBORZ: a Persian prince, the

son of Kay Kāvus.

FARIGIS: Afrāsyāb's daughter, and Seyavash's wife.

FARSHIDVARD: a warrior of Turān, and an associate of Piran.

FERAYDUN: a Persian king.

FORUD: Seyavash's son.

GARSHĀSP: a Persian king, Zav's son; the Persian army commander of the same name seems to be a different person and the father of Nariman is yet another bearer of the same name.

GARSIVAZ: a warrior of Turān, the brother of Afrāsyāb and Aghriras.

GAZHDAHAM: a warrior of Irān, the father of Gordāfarid.

GHUR: the area north of Kandahār, in Afghanistan.

GILĀN: a province to the south of the Caspian Sea.

GIV: a warrior of Irān, the son of Gudarz.

GOLBĀD: a warrior of Turān.

GOLSHAHR: the wife of Piran, Afrāsyāb's counselor.

GONBADĀN: a castle in Khorasan.

GORAZEH: a Persian nobleman.

GORĀZM: Afrāsyāb's son and Esfandyār's brother: he slanders Esfandyār out of jealousy.

GORGĀN: an area to the east of the Caspian.

GORGIN: a warrior of Irān.

GORGSARĀN: an unidentified area in Turān. There is a village of this name near Balkh, but this is too deep in Persian territory to be Bizhan's place of imprisonment. The word means "wolf-headed."

GORUI: a warrior of Turān.

GOSHTĀSP: a Persian king, the son of Lohrāsp.

GOSTAHAM: a warrior of Irān.

GOSTAHOM: a Persian nobleman.

GUDARZ: a warrior of Irān, the father of Giv, the son of Keshvād.

GURĀBĀD: an unidentified town or village near the border of Sistān and Irān. There are villages in modern Irān that have this name, but none of them are near Sistān.

HAMĀVAN: a mountain in Khorāsān.

HĀMĀVERĀN: the name of a country; its whereabouts are vague, but it is placed near the Barbary Coast (North Africa) and not far from Syria.

HEND: India.

HERĀT: a town in western Afghānistān.

HIRBAD: the keeper of king Kavus's harem.

HIRMAND: the river which marks the boundary of Rostam's territory. It is now called the Helmand, and flows through south western Afghanistan.

HOMĀ: a mythical bird, said to bestow sovereignty on whomever its shadow touches.

HOMĀY: a daughter of Goshtāsp, and sister to Esfandyār, Pashutan, and Beh Āfarid. Also, the name of Bahman's daughter.

HORMOZ: Ahura Mazda, the Good Principle of the universe.

HUSHANG: a Persian king, the grandson of Kayumars.

IRAJ: the youngest son of Feraydun.

JAHAN: a son of Afrāsyāb.

JĀMĀSP: King Goshtāsp's councilor.

JAMSHID: a Persian king.

JARAM: an area near Badakhshān.

JARIREH: Pirān's daughter; Forud's mother.

KĀBOL, KĀBOLESTĀN: eastern Afghānistān and its chief city.

KALĀT: the town in Turān where Forud and his mother live.

KAMUS: a western ally of Afrāsyāb, killed by Rostam.

KARIMĀN: an ancestor of Nariman, and therefore of the family of Zal and Rostam.

KATAYUN: A Byzantine princess who marries Goshtāsp; the mother of Esfandyār.

KAVARESTĀN: the area of Transoxiana.

KĀVIĀNI: an adjective from Kāveh, applied particularly to the banner made from Kāveh's leather apron.

KAY ĀRASH: a Persian prince, son of Kay Qobād.

KAY ĀRMIN: a Persian prince, son of Kay Qobād.

KAY KĀVUS: a Persian king, son of Kay Qobād.

KAY PASHIN: a Persian prince, son of Kay Qobād.

KAY QOBĀD: a Persian king.

KAYĀNID: the name of the Persian royal house.

KHALLOKHI: a town in Turkestan famous for its musk, and for the beauty of its inhabitants.

KHARRĀD: a Persian chieftain at Kay Khosrow's court.

KHAZAR: an area of Turkestān.

KHORASAN: A province including modern Khorasān, in north eastern Irān, but also the area to the north and south of the Oxus.

KHORDĀD: a Zoroastrian angel.

KHOSROW: Seyāvash's and Farigis's son. A Persian king.

KHOTAN: a province of Turān, ruled over by Pirān.

KUCH: the name of a tribe and of an area in south eastern Irān, near Kermān.

LAHĀK: Pirān's brother.

LOHRĀSP: a Persian warrior who is chosen by Khosrow to succeed him as king. The father of Goshtāsp.

MANIZHEH: a Princess of Turān. Afrasyāb's daughter.

MANUCHEHR: a Persian king, the grandson of Iraj.

MARVRUD: a town in Khorāsān, halfway between Balkh and Marv.

MAYAM: an indefinite area to the east and north of Irān.

MĀZANDERĀN: modern Māzanderān is the area to the south of the Caspian Sea. Various locations for Ferdowsi's Māzanderān have been suggested.

MEHRĀB: the king of Kābol, Rudābeh's father.

MEHREGĀN: a festival celebrating the autumnal equinox.

MEHRNUSH: one of Esfandyār's sons.

MILĀD: a warrior of Irān.

MORDĀD: a Zoroastrian angel.

NARIMĀN: the ancestor of Sām, Zāl, Rostam, and Farāmarz.

NASTIHAN: a warrior of Turān.

NOZAR: the son of Manuchehr, the king of Irān.

NUSHĀZAR: one of Esfandyār's sons.

ORANDSHĀH: an ancestor of Lohrāsp.

ORDIBEHESHT: a Zoroastrian angel.

PĀRS: a province in central southern Irān, and the homeland of the country's two most important pre-Islamic dynasties, the Achaemenids and the Sasanians.

PASHANG: two men bear this name; one is a king of Turān, and the father of Afrāsyāb, the other is a Persian, the nephew of Feraydun and the father of Manuchehr.

PASHUTAN: Goshtasp's son, and Esfandyār's brother.

PILSOM: Pirān's brother.

PIRĀN: a nobleman of Turān: counselor to Afrāsyāb.

PULĀD: a warrior of Irān.

QAJQAR: a town in Turān.

QANNUJ: a town in northern India.

QARĀ KHĀN: an advisor to Afrāsyāb.

QOBĀD: two men bear this name; one is a Persian warrior, the other a Persian king.

QOM: a city in central Irān.

RAKHSH: Rostam's horse.

RAY: a town south of modern Tehran.

RIVNIZ: a warrior of Irān, married to Tus's daughter.

ROHAM: a warrior of Irān.

ROSTAM: the preeminent hero of the epic; the son of Zāl and Rudābeh and father of Sohrāb.

RUDĀBEH: a princess of Kābol; Zāl's wife and Rostam's mother.

RUM: the West.

RUMI: of the West.

SALM: Feraydun's eldest son.

SANJEH: a demon of Māzanderān.

SARUCH: a plain near Kermān, in south eastern Irān.

SEND: approximately modern Pakistan; the sea adjacent to it.

SEPAHRAM: a warrior chieftain of Turān.

SEPANDARMEZ: a Zoroastrian angel.

SEPANJĀB: an area in Turkestan.

SEPED: an unidentified mountain in Turān.

SEYĀVASH: son of Kay Kāvus and father of Kay Khosrow and Forud.

SEYĀVASHGERD: the city Seyavash founds in Turān.

SHABRANG: Bizhan's horse (the name means "Color of Night").

SHAGHĀD: Rostam's brother.

SHAHRIVAR: a Zoroastrian angel.

SHĀPUR: a warrior of Irān.

SHAVRAN: a Persian warrior, the father of Zangeh.

SHIDEH: a son of Afrasyāb.

SHIDUSH: a Persian warrior.

SHIRKHUN: a warrior from Sistān.

SIMORGH: the fabulous bird which rears Zāl.

SIND: north western India.

SINDOKHT: the wife of Mehrāb and the mother of Rudābeh.

SISTĀN: the ancestral homeland of Sām, Zāl, and Rostam; also called Zābol, Zābolestān, Zāvol, Zāvolestān, and Nimruz.

SOGHDIA: Transoxiana generally, and in particular the area around Samarkand.

SOHRĀB: the son of Rostam.

SORUSH: an angel.

SUDĀBEH: the daughter of the king of Hāmāverān.

SUS: Susa, in south western Irān.

TAHMURES: a Persian king, the son of Hushang known as the Binder of Demons.

TALIMĀN: a warrior of Irān.

TĀLQĀN: a town in Transoxiana.

TERMEZ: a town in Transoxiana.

TOCHVAR: a warrior of Turān; advisor to Forud.

TUR: Feraydun's second son.

TURĀN: the country to the north of the Oxus.

TUS: a Persian prince, the son of Nozar.

UKHAST: a warrior of Turān.

ULĀD: a landowner and warrior of Māzanderān.

VISEH: a warrior of Turān.

ZĀBOL: a city in Zābolestān, the homeland of Sām, Zāl, and Rostam and another name for Rostam's province of Sistān.

ZAHHĀK: a demon-king brought down by Kāveh and Feraydun.

ZĀL: also called Zāl-e Zar and Zāl-Dastān, Sām's son, the father of Rostam.

ZANGEH: a Persian warrior.

ZARASP: a Persian warrior, the son of Tus.

ZARIR: a Persian prince, son of King Goshtāsp.

ZAV: a Persian king.

ZAVĀREH: a warrior of Irān, the brother of Rostam.

ZĀVOL/ZĀVOLESTĀN: another name for Sistān, the homeland of Sām, Zāl, and Rostam.

ZEND AVESTA: The Zoroastrian sacred text. Ferdowsi often, anachronistically, refers to it before the advent of Zoroastrianism.

CREDITS AND ACKNOWLEDGMENTS

The Publishers would like to thank Abolala Soudavar for generously allowing the use of miniatures from his private collection and for sharing his knowledge of other images available in collections around the world. Special thanks are also due to Prince Sadruddin Aga Khan for generously allowing us to use images from his collection. We would also like to thank, William Robinson at Christie's, Deana Cross and Sandra Wiskari at the Metropolitan Museum, and Mohammad Isa Waley at the British Library.

We would also like to thank George Constable for his astute editorial suggestions and Rostam Batmanglij for silhouetting the flowers for the chapter headings.

GUIDE TO THE ILLUSTRATIONS

The following fifteen pages catalog the *Shahnameh* illustrations used in the book and provide sources and credits. The list is organized in order of the painting's first appearance in the text and by manuscript and collection, beginning with those images that come from the Shah Tahmasb *Shahnameh* manuscript and then going on to images from other collections and manuscripts. Where details have been used to illustrate the text, the appropriate page numbers have been provided. Information such as the name of the painter and the date of the painting have been given wherever available. In some cases, painters are identified simply by a letter (e.g., "Painter A"). These designations refer to specific painters whose works have been identified but whose names remain unknown. The references to "r" and "v" indicate whether the original paintings were on the right (recto) or left (verso) side of the manuscript.

Seyavash Accused by Sudabeh
Painted by Abd al-Vahab c. 1520-30 / folio 163v
Courtesy of The Metropolitan Museum of Art, gift of Arthur A.
Houghton, Jr. (1970.301.23). Detail on page: 14

Sudabeh's Second Accusation.
Painted by Qasem, son of Ali c. 1520-30 / folio 164v
Courtesy of The Metropolitan Museum of Art, gift of Arthur A.
Houghton, Jr. (1970.301.24). Details on pages: 22, 25

Seyavash Accused by Sudabeh
Painted by painter c folio 166r
Courtesy of private collection
Detail on page: 27

Seyavash and Rostam Capture Balkh
Painted by painter A / folio 168v
Courtesy of private collection
Detail on page: 31

Seyavash Receives Gifts from Afrasyab
Painted by painter A c. 1520-30 / folio 171r
Courtesy of private collection
Detail on page: 37

Afrasyab Embraces Seyavash
Painted by painter D c. 1520-30 / folio 179r
Courtesy of private collection
Details on pages: 47, 82

Seyavsh Plays Polo
Painted by by Qasem son of Ali c. 1520-30 / folio 180v
Courtesy of The Metropolitan Museum of Art, gift of Arthur A.
Houghton, Jr. (1970.301.26). Details on pages: 6, 41, 51

Seyavash Hits the Target
Painted by painter B c. 1520-30 / folio 181v
Courtesy of private collection
Details on pages: 52, 53

Seyavash and Farigis Are Married
Painted by Qasem son of Ali, c. 1520-30 / folio 163v
Courtesy of The Metropolitan Museum of Art, gift of Arthur A.
Houghton, Jr. (1970.301.28). Details on pages: 57, 58, 59

Piran Visits Seyavashgerd
Painted by painter B, c. 1520-30 / folio 188v
Courtesy of private collection
Detail on page: 62

Garzivaz Visits Seyavashgerd
Painted by painter B, c. 1520-30 / folio 189v
Courtesy of private collection
Detail on page: 219

Seyavash's Prowess
Painted by painter A, c. 1520-30 / folio 190v
Courtesy of private collection
Detail on pages: 66-67, 69

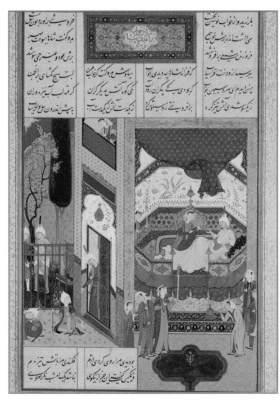

Seyavash Recounts His Nightmare to Farigis
Painted by Qadimi, c. 1520-30 / folio 195r
Courtesy of The Metropolitan Museum of Art, gift of Arthur A.
Houghton, Jr. (1970.301.29).Details on pages: 72, 77

Piran Takes Khosrow to Afrasyab
Painted by painter B c. 1520-30 / folio 201r
Courtesy of private collection
Details on pages: 71, 87

Rostam Blames Kay Kavus
Painted by painter A, c. 1520-30 / folio 202v
Courtesy of The Metropolitan Museum of Art, gift of Arthur A.
Houghton, Jr. (1970.301.30). Details on pages: 94, 223, 237

Rostam and Afrasyab Battle
Painted by painter A, c. 1520-30 / folio 206v
Courtesy of private collection
Details on pages: 250—251

Giv Discovers Kay Khosrow
Painted by Qadimi and Abdul Vahav c. 1520-30 / folio 210v
Courtesy of The Metropolitan Museum of Art, gift of Arthur A.
Houghton, Jr. (1970.301.32).

Kay Khosrow Rides Behzad
Painted by painter B, c. 1520-30 / folio 212r
Courtesy of The Metropolitan Museum of Art, gift of Arthur A.
Houghton, Jr. (1970.301.33). Details on pages: 220, 221

Piran Captured by Giv
Painted by painter B, c. 1520-30 / folio 214v
Courtesy of private collection
Details on pages: 88–89

Kay Khosrow, Farigis, and Giv Cross the River Jayhun
Painted by painter A c. 1520-30 / folio 216v
Courtesy of private collection
Details on pages: 92–93

Kay Khosrow Takes Bahman Castle
Painted by painter A, c. 1520-30 / folio 221r
Courtesy of private collection
Detail on page: 124

Kay Khosrow Celebrates His Accession
Painted by painter C, c. 1520-30 / folio 223r
Courtesy of private collection
Details on pages: 184, 186, 187, 194

Kay Khosrow Attacks Turan
Painted by painter A, c. 1520-30 / folio 226v
Courtesy of private collection
Details on pages: 96, 100, 101, 192

Forud Confronts The Iranians
Painted by painter A, c. 1520-30 / folio 229v
Courtesy of private collection
Details on pages: 99, 121, 183

Forud Humiliates the Iranians
Painted by painters D & F, c. 1520-30 / folio 232v
Courtesy of private collection
Details on pages: 103, 105, 107, 108, 111

Bizhan Forces Forud to flee
Painted by Aqa Mirak c. 1520-30 / folio 234r
Art and History Trust courtesy of the Arthur M. Sackler Museum,
Smithsonian Institution, Washington, D.C. Details on pages: 112–113

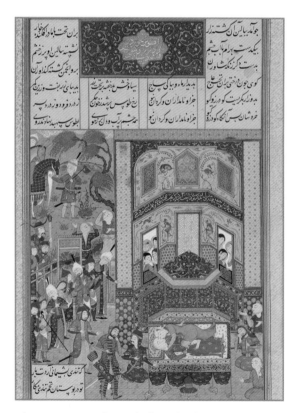

The Iranians Mourn the Death of Forud and Jarireh
Painted by Mirza Mohammad Qabahat, c. 1520-30 / folio 236r
Courtesy of The Metropolitan Museum of Art, gift of Arthur A.
Houghton, Jr. (1970.301.35). Details on pages: 114, 118

Iranian Camp Attacked at Night
Attributed to painter A, c. 1520-30 / folio 241r
Courtesy of The Metropolitan Museum of Art, gift of Arthur A.
Houghton, Jr. (1970.301.36). Details on pages: 122–123

Iranians Attack by Night
Attributed to painter A, c. 1520-30 / folio 257v
Courtesy of private collection
Details on pages: 180–181

Piran Hears Rostam's Terms for Peace
Attributed to painter C, c. 1520-30 / folio 274v
Courtesy of private collection
Details on pages: 232, 233

Rostam Destroys the Bidad Fortress
Attributed to painter D, c. 1520-30 / folio 286v
Courtesy of private collection
Details on pages: 245

Rostam Pursues the Akvan Div
Painted by Muzaffar Ali, c. 1520-30 / folio 294r
Art and History Trust courtesy of the Arthur M. Sackler Museum,
Smithsonian Institution, Washington, D.C. Detail on page: 131

Rostam Recovers Rakhsh (detail)
Attributed to Mirza Ali, c. 1520-30 / folio 295r
Courtesy of private collection
Details on pages: 128–129

Bizhan Receives Invitation from Manizheh's Nurse
Attributed to Abdul Vahab, c. 1520-30 / folio 300v
Courtesy of The Metropolitan Museum of Art, gift of Arthur A.
Houghton, Jr. (1970.301.42). Details on pages: 142, 145

Khosrow Fetes Rostam under the Jeweled-tree
Painted by Dust Mohammad, c. 1520-30 / folio 308v
Courtesy of private collection
Details on pages: 159, 160–161

Bizhan Kills Nastihan (detail)
Attributed to painter E, c. 1520-30 / folio 328r
Courtesy of private collection
Details on pages: 173, 174–175

Kay Khosrow Kills Afrasyab
Attributed to painter E, c. 1520-30 / folio 383v
Courtesy of private collection
Detail on page: 182

Jamasp Comes Before Afrasyab
Attributed to painter E, c. 1520-30 / folio 422r
Courtesy of private collection
Detail on page: 216

Esfanyar's Fourth Trial: He Slays the Sorceress
Attributed to Qasim son of Ali, c. 1520-30 / folio 435v
Courtesy of The Metropolitan Museum of Art, gift of Arthur A.
Houghton, Jr. (1970.301.3.52). Details on pages: 209, 214–215

Esfandyar's Sixth Trial: He Comes Through The Great Snow
Attributed to Abdul Vahab, c. 1520-30 / folio 438r
Courtesy of The Metropolitan Museum of Art, gift of Arthur A.
Houghton, Jr. (1970.301.53). Details on pages: 212–213

Esfandyar's Third Trial: He Slays the Dragon
Attributed to Qasim son of Ali, c. 1520-30 / folio 434v
Courtesy of The Metropolitan Museum of Art, gift of Arthur A.
Houghton, Jr. (1970.301.3.51). Detail on page: 211

Rostam Kills Esfandyar
Attributed to Qasem son of Ali, c. 1520-30 / folio 466r
Courtesy of The Metropolitan Museum of Art, gift of Arthur A.
Houghton, Jr. (1970.301.55). Detail on page: 263

Rostam Avenges His Own Impending Death
Attributed to Bashdan Qara, c. 1520-30 / folio 472r
Courtesy of The Metropolitan Museum of Art, gift of Arthur A.
Houghton, Jr. (1970.301.56). Details on pages: 276, 277

Seyavash at Afrasyab's Court
Painted by unknown artist in the Isfahan style 1630-40
By permission of The British Library (MSS. 1256 / folio 120v)
Detail on page: 49

The Fire Ordeal of Seyavash
Painted by Mu'in Mosavvar c. 1570 folio 92v
Courtesy of Collection Prince Sadruddin Aga Khan
Detail on page: 2

Murder of Seyavash
Painted by unknown artist in the Shiraz style 1630-40
By permission of the British Library (MSS. 3540 / folio 119v)
Detail on page: 81

The Iranians Ransack Forud's Castle
Painted by unknown artist in the Shiraz style 1630-40
By permission of the British Library (MSS. 3540 / folio 138v)
Detail on page: 117

The Akvan Div Hurls Rostam Into the Sea
Painted by unknown artist in the Isfahan/Safavid style 1628
By permission of the British Library (MSS. 27258/ folio 241r)
Detail on page: 127

Rostam Chasing Afrasyab's Shepard
Painted by unknown artist in the Shiraz style 1640-60
By permission of the British Library (MSS. 133 / folio 203r)
Detail on page: 133

Rostam Killing Afrasyab's Shepherd
Painted by unknown artist in the Shiraz style 1640-60
By permission of the British Library (MSS. 133 / folio 203v)
Detail on page: 134

Bizan Boar Hunting with Gorgin Watching
Painted by unknown artist in the Timurid style 1486
By permission of the British Library (MSS. 18188 / folio 172r)
Detail on page: 136

Piran Saves Bizhan
Painted by unknown artist in the Shiraz style 1630-40
By permission of the British Library (MSS. 3540 / folio 195v)
Detail on page: 149

Manizheh Meets Rostam
Painted by unknown artist in the Tabriz style 1536
By permission of the British Library (Add. 15531 / folio 198r)
Detail on page: 166

Rostam Rescues Bijan
Painted by unknown artist in the Shiraz style 1630-40
By permission of the British Library (MSS. 3540 / folio 138v)
Detail on page: 171

Rostam Rescues Bizhan
Painted by unknown artist c. 1444
Courtesy of the Collections of the Royal Asiatic Society, London
Detail on page: 169

Paladins in the Snow
Painted by unknown artist c. 1444
Courtesy of the Collections of the Royal Asiatic Society, London
Details on pages: 206–207

Rostam Kicks Aside Bahman's Boulder
Painted by unknown artist in the Timurid style 1486
By permission of the British Library (MSS. 18188 / folio 281r)
Details on pages: 226, 229

Simorgh Heals Rostam
Painted by unknown artist in Rajur near Hyderabad, 1719
By permission of the British Library (MSS. 18804 / folio 71r)
Detail on page: 257

Simorgh Heals Rakhsh
Painted by unknown artist in the Qazvin style 1590-95
By permission of the British Library (MSS. 27257 / folio 305v)
Detail on page: 258

Rostam Kills Esfandyar
Painted by unknown artist c. 1444
Courtesy of the Collections of the Royal Asiatic Society, London
Detail on page: 261